Praise for Chris Fabry

EVERY WAKING MOMENT

"Fabry crafts a character-driven tale of dignity and compassion for those who seem to have lost importance to society. This thought-provoking read challenges the prevailing cultural calculations of the value of a person's life."

PUBLISHERS WEEKLY

"Writing in his trademark lyrical style, Fabry spins a poignant tale."

BOOKLIST

"This is a heartbreaking but very hopeful story that left me with a satisfied sigh when I turned the last page."

NOVEL REVIEWS

BORDERS OF THE HEART

"A thoroughly enjoyable read. . . . Chris Fabry is a masterful storyteller."

CBA RETAILERS+RESOURCES

"In this edge-of-your-seat romantic suspense, all of the characters ring true. . . ."

"Ups the ante for fans of Fabry's high-charged, emotionally driven fiction by adding a strong suspense thread."

NOT IN THE HEART

"A story of hope, redemption, and sacrifice. . . . It's hard to imagine inspirational fiction done better than this."

"Christy Award–winning Fabry has written a nail-biter with plenty of twists and turns to keep readers riveted. Fans of Jerry B. Jenkins and Jodi Picoult might want to try this title."

"A fine piece of storytelling. . . . Down to its final pages, *Not in the Heart* is a gripping read. While the mystery at its core is compelling, it's Wiley's inner conflict that's truly engrossing."

"This absorbing novel should further boost Fabry's reputation as one of the most talented authors in Christian fiction."

ALMOST HEAVEN

"This mesmerizing tale . . . will surprise readers in the best possible way; plot twists unfold and unexpected character transformations occur throughout this tender story."

PUBLISHERS WEEKLY

"Fabry has a true gift for prose, and [*Almost Heaven*] is amazing. . . . You'll most definitely want to move this to the top of your 'to buy' list."

ROMANTIC TIMES, 4½-STAR TOP PICK REVIEW

"Fabry is a talented writer with a lifting flow to his words."

CROSSWALK.COM

JUNE BUG

"[*June Bug*] is a stunning success, and readers will find themselves responding with enthusiastic inner applause."

PUBLISHERS WEEKLY

"An involving novel with enough plot twists and dramatic tension to keep readers turning the pages."

BOOKLIST

"I haven't read anything so riveting and unforgettable since *Redeeming Love* by Francine Rivers. . . .

A remarkable love story, one that's filled with sacrifice, hope, and forgiveness!"

NOVEL REVIEWS

"Precise details of places and experiences immediately set you in the story, and the complex, likable characters give *June Bug* the enduring quality of a classic."

TITLETRAKK.COM

DOGWOOD

"[*Dogwood*] is difficult to put down, what with Fabry's surprising plot resolution and themes of forgiveness, sacrificial love, and suffering."

PUBLISHERS WEEKLY

"Ultimately a story of love and forgiveness, [*Dogwood*] should appeal to a wide audience."

CBA RETAILERS+RESOURCES

"Solidly literary fiction with deep, flawed characters and beautiful prose, *Dogwood* also contains a mystery within the story that adds tension and a deepening plot."

NOVEL REVIEWS

The Promise of Jesse Woods

THE
PROMISE
of
JESSE
WOODS

CHRIS FABRY

TYNDALE HOUSE PUBLISHERS, INC., CAROL STREAM, ILLINOIS

Visit Tyndale online at www.tyndale.com.

Visit Chris Fabry's website at www.chrisfabry.com.

TYNDALE and Tyndale's quill logo are registered trademarks of Tyndale House Publishers, Inc.

The Promise of Jesse Woods

Cover designed by Gearbox

Interior designed by Dean H. Renninger

Edited by Sarah Mason Rische

Scripture quotations are taken from the *Holy Bible*, King James Version.

The Promise of Jesse Woods is a work of fiction. Where real people, events, establishments, organizations, or locales appear, they are used fictitiously. All other elements of the novel are drawn from the author's imagination.

Library of Congress Cataloging-in-Publication Data

Names: Fabry, Chris, date, author.
Title: The promise of Jesse Woods / Chris Fabry.
Description: Carol Stream, Illinois : Tyndale House Publishers, Inc., [2016]
Identifiers: LCCN 2016005373 | ISBN 9781414387772 (softcover)
Subjects: LCSH: Life change events—Fiction. | Family secrets—Fiction. |
    Friendship—Fiction. | GSAFD: Christian fiction.
Classification: LCC PS3556.A26 P76 2016 | DDC 813/.54—dc23 LC record available at http://lccn.loc.gov/2016005373

Printed in the United States of America

22	21	20	19	18	17	16
7	6	5	4	3	2	1

In memory of Kristin Kent and Dantrell Davis

I was raised by my parents to believe that you had
a moral obligation to try to save the world.

ANNE LAMOTT

Chapter 1

The elevated train clacked outside my apartment, meandering on its predetermined path through Chicago. Beyond the tracks loomed the Cabrini-Green housing project, where Dantrelle Garrett lived. Dantrelle sat on my couch tossing a weathered baseball into my old glove, watching the final game of the NLCS between the Cubs and Padres.

"Who's that?" Dantrelle said, pointing at a picture on my bookshelf.

"My brother and me. That was a long time ago."

He studied the photo. "You're not from around here, are you?"

It was the first time in the three months since I'd met

Dantrelle that he had asked anything about my background. I took it as an invitation.

"I grew up in Pittsburgh, then moved to a little town in West Virginia."

"Where's that?"

"A long way from Cabrini," I said.

"Do you love you mama and daddy?"

"Sure."

"Then how come you don't have a picture of them?"

"I do, in an album somewhere."

"If you love somebody, they ought to be on top of the shelf."

I shrugged.

"How come you moved to Chicago?"

These were penetrating questions from an eight-year-old kid, but they grow up quickly in the projects. I told him about my schooling, how I had majored in theater and minored in counseling, but his eyes glazed.

"You want popcorn?" I said.

Dantrelle nodded and I pulled out my biggest pot and heated the oil. The smell of the popcorn and drizzled butter triggered a memory, but I pushed it aside and sat beside Dantrelle.

"When I was a kid, I loved the Pirates. The Pirates were my life. But we moved to this town where everybody rooted for the Reds. And the Pirates and Reds were rivals."

"Like the Cubs and the White Sox."

"Yeah, sort of. Except they were in the same league."

Dantrelle shoved a handful of popcorn in his mouth

and butter dripped from his chin. I handed him a napkin and he put it on his lap.

"You think the Cubs are going to win?" he said, ignoring my story.

It had been a phenomenal year to be a Cubs fan. Every game on channel 9. Harry Caray and Steve Stone and "Jump" by Van Halen. Sutcliffe and Sandberg and Cey.

"Yeah, I think they will. No way the Padres win three in a row."

It was disorienting to hear Don Drysdale, a lifelong Dodger, describe the game instead of Harry Caray. The Cubs had won the first two at home and lost the next two in San Diego.

In the bottom of the seventh, my phone rang and I almost let it go, thinking it might be my mother. But I picked up the cordless handset just as a ground ball rolled through Leon Durham's legs and into right field. Dantrelle cursed. The Padres evened the score at 3–3.

"Matt?" a voice said with a familiar twang.

"Who is this?" I said.

A chuckle on the other end. "A voice from your past."

"Dickie?" I said. Keith Moreland fired the ball to the infield, the Cubs' curse alive. "How are you?"

"Lookin' for a breakthrough," he said, and his words brought back every bittersweet thing from my youth. I had lost touch with Dickie. After high school I had ripped the rearview off my life.

"You're probably going to see a breakthrough sooner than the Cubs. You watching this game?"

"I was never into baseball."

I closed my eyes and saw the hills and Dickie's bike and trips to Blake's store.

Dickie Darrel Lee Hancock was the son of a white mother and an African American father. That would have been a hardship anywhere in 1972, but it was a knapsack full of rocks on his forced march through his childhood in Dogwood. Dickie lived with his mother in a garage apartment on the outskirts of town, and it always seemed he was outside looking in. I guess that's what drew the three of us together. We were all on the outside.

"How did you get my number?" I said.

"Called your parents, PB."

PB. I hadn't been called that in years and the sound of it warmed me.

"They said you don't have much contact with the past."

"That's not true," I lied.

"Took me a while to wrangle your number from them. I suspect they didn't want me to call because of the news."

I stood and touched Dantrelle's shoulder. "I'll be right back." I stepped out of the apartment into the hall and the door closed behind me. "What news is that?"

"Jesse's news."

Her name, and Dickie saying it, sent a shiver through me. I'd been waiting for this. I'd had a foreboding feeling for years. "Is she all right? Did something happen?"

"She's engaged, Matt. The wedding is Saturday."

"This Saturday?"

"Yeah. I just heard about it or I would have tracked you down sooner. My mama told me."

I walked down the hallway to a window that allowed a clear view of the el tracks and the specter of the housing project. From my building east was a thriving, churning city. A block west, past this Mason-Dixon Line, was another world. It reminded me of Dogwood.

"Who's she marrying?"

"What's that noise?" Dickie said, avoiding the question.

I paused, not hearing anything, then realized the train was passing. The open window let in not only the heavy autumn air but the clacking sound track of my life.

I told him about the train, then asked again, "So who's the lucky guy?"

"Earl Turley."

My stomach clenched. I couldn't speak.

"Yeah, I can't believe it either," Dickie said to my silence. "I know how you felt about her."

"Wow," I said. "I appreciate you telling me."

Dickie paused like there was more. "Matt, your dad is officiating."

His words felt like a dagger. "Well, we were never on the best of terms when it came to Jesse."

"I get that. I know how they felt about her too."

"Are you going to the wedding?" I said.

"Wasn't invited."

"You didn't answer the question."

"That's not the question, Matt. The question is, what are you going to do?"

"Do?" I said. "It's a little late in the game to do anything. Jesse has a mind of her own."

"Yeah, but you were the one she turned to when life got hard. Maybe it's not too late."

"If you're talking romance, Jesse never felt the same as I did."

"That's not true."

"What are you talking about?"

"You don't know everything about her. I know she confided in you, but there are some things . . . Look, it's none of my business. I thought I'd call and let you know."

"Wait, you know something. You remember something."

Dickie sighed. "I talked with her a couple of times. After you left for college. She told me things she regretted. Decisions she made. She made me promise to keep quiet about them. But she must've figured I would be the last person to tell you anything. I guess I'm breaking a promise even making this phone call."

"Which is something Jesse would never do," I said. Though there was one promise she was breaking by marrying Earl, and I couldn't shake that fact. Dickie was privy to many of the secrets between Jesse and me, but not all of them.

There is magical thinking a child develops when he believes the world revolves around him. He begins to think he has power to control life's events. I'd always blamed myself for the 1972 Pirates. If I hadn't left Pittsburgh, things would have turned out differently. A butterfly on the other side of the world flapping its wings. A child in a suburb praying for his team. I had grown out of that mindset by moving to Chicago and growing up, but something about the memory of Jesse and what she had done, what I had forced her to do, made me wonder if I could prevent another tragedy in her life.

Dickie broke the silence. "Do you ever think of what happened? Do you ever think of her?"

"Sometimes," I whispered, and the words began to flow. "Sometimes I smell woodsmoke or hear crickets at night and I'm back on the hill. It's all there, Dickie. All trapped inside like fireflies ready to rise."

"Riverfront?"

I smiled. "Yeah. We had fun, didn't we?"

"Remember the horse?" Dickie said.

"That was our first secret."

"What about Daisy?"

Daisy Grace. I could see her chubby face and a fistful of daisies held behind her, and the ramshackle house on the side of a hill that hung like a mole on the face of God.

"I remember it all, Dickie."

"Yeah, I do too."

"Especially the parts I try to forget."

He told me about his job and what he'd done after high school, but I couldn't hear his story for the memories he had stirred. I thanked him for calling.

"I'll say this, PB: I know it's been a long time and I don't know if you're seeing anybody, but I think you owe it to her to go back. You owe it to yourself."

"What about Earl?" I said. "You going to provide backup?"

"You're a bigger man than him, Matt. You've always been bigger than you thought you were."

His words stung my eyes. "Dickie, I'm sorry. I've never been able to tell you how sorry I am that—"

"You don't have to apologize. We were kids. I've thought about calling you and patching things up a hundred times. I was wrong to hold it against you in the first place."

"Thank you for saying that."

When I returned to the apartment, Dantrelle looked like he'd been gut-punched. The Cubs hadn't been to a World Series since 1945. Hadn't won since 1908. And with Goose Gossage throwing BBs, it wouldn't happen this year. Maybe if Jim Frey had relieved Sutcliffe, things would have turned out differently.

The old pain returned as I watched San Diego celebrate. Steve Garvey flashed his million-dollar smile and Gossage hopped around the field like a kid who had stolen candy from a general store. Bob Dernier and Jody Davis and Don Zimmer looked back in anguish. It was the end of a season and the only consolation was there would be next year.

"If they had played three in Chicago, we would have won," I said.

"Why didn't they?" Dantrelle said.

"Just the way it works. But the commissioner said if the Cubs had made the World Series, they'd have lost home-field advantage because they don't have lights."

"That's not fair."

"Yeah, well it was all about money. And life isn't fair. Especially when it comes to the Cubs."

As Dantrelle got his jacket, I took my old glove with faded words and held it to my face. The faint leather scent swirled warm, rich memories like fly balls in a summer sky. I returned the glove to a plastic bin in the apartment's only closet. Pictures lay scattered like dry leaves among the papers and playbills. The three of us, sweaty and smiling and spitting watermelon seeds.

"Who's that?" Dantrelle said, pointing at a Polaroid of Jesse sitting on a picnic table and holding a cat.

"A friend of mine from a long time ago." At the bottom of the box was a ticket. Reds vs. Pirates, July 1972.

I got out the yearbook and paged through until I found her. She stared at something beyond the camera. Her hair was too long and cut uneven and shadowed her eyes. The photo was a black-and-white, but I could see the emerald blue, her eyes like an ocean. Closing my eyes, I heard her laugh and her desperate cry for help in the year I discovered my heart.

People say you can't know love at such a young age. Maybe it wasn't love. But it was close. The longer I stared at Jesse's face, the more my heart broke for her and what had happened. I thought I had put all of that behind me, though. I had moved on with life, but one phone call had grabbed me by the throat.

"Can I watch some more TV while you look at this stuff?" Dantrelle said.

I apologized and put the bin back. "Dantrelle, I might have to take a trip. That would mean we couldn't meet this week."

His eyes looked hollow as he shrugged.

"Maybe I could ask Miss Kristin to help with your math."

He brightened. "I like Miss Kristin. You two going to get married?"

I tried to smile and shook my head. "I don't think that's going to happen."

"Why not?"

"That's a long story I'll tell another day."

A week earlier Kristin, a flaxen-haired beauty who attended a nearby Bible school and mentored young girls at Cabrini, had sat across the table from me at Houlihan's to splurge on an early dinner. I could tell there was something wrong before our salads arrived. As tears came, she said she cared deeply for me but that we couldn't go further.

"I think I just want to be friends," she said.

"What does that mean? That I'm not good enough for you?"

She shook her head. "No, you're a great guy. I see how much you care about the kids and how much you want things to change. But it feels like . . ."

"It feels like what?"

"Like you want to throw on a Superman cape and run to the rescue. I can't fix what's wrong at Cabrini. And neither can you. We can help some kids, maybe. We can make a difference. But it feels like you're doing all of this in your own power."

Her words stung because I could see Kristin and me together. I wondered who had gotten to her in her dorm and talked about me. Of course, whoever had pointed out the spiritual mismatch was right. She was a lot further down the road of faith. At times, it felt like I had taken an exit ramp miles earlier. So we agreed to part as friends and not let our relationship harm the work we were doing. It was all smiles and a polite hug while inside, the part of my heart that had come alive as I got to know her shattered.

I picked up the phone now and dialed her dorm. Someone answered and Kristin finally came to the phone.

"Hey, I have a favor to ask," I said, extending the antenna. "I need to take care of some stuff at home—but Dantrelle is counting on me this week. Do you think you could meet with him? I can't be back by Tuesday."

"Sure. I'm over there that afternoon anyway."

I gave Dantrelle a thumbs-up. "He just smiled at that news."

"He's with you?"

"We were watching the Cubs lose."

"Poor Cubs. So what's up? Is someone sick at home?"

"It's complicated. Maybe I'll have the chance to explain it someday." *If you give me another chance.*

"Well, tell Dantrelle to meet me at the ministry office."

"Thanks for doing that, Kristin."

I left a message with the coordinator at the counseling center, explaining as little as possible about the trip and leaving my parents' phone number in case someone needed to reach me. Then I walked Dantrelle home and up the urine-laced concrete stairs to his apartment. His mother came to the door, wild-eyed and unkempt. She grabbed him by the shoulder without speaking to me, and Dantrelle waved as he was hustled inside and the door shut.

I took the stairs two at a time and moved away from Cabrini, thinking of Jesse and her bad decision. If she said, "I do," that was it. She would. I had to do something to change her mind and keep her from throwing her life away. I had to help her see the truth. And though I didn't want to admit it, didn't want to open the door to even the possibility, something inside told me there might still be hope for us, even after all the years and distance.

I threw some clothes in a gym bag and set my alarm. Then I lay in bed, listening to the sounds of the city, knowing I wouldn't sleep. Dickie was right. I owed it to Jesse to make one more attempt. And before she walked the aisle that felt like a plank, I owed it to myself.

Well before midnight, I hopped in the car and headed toward the expressway, then south toward Indiana and beyond to my childhood home.

Chapter 2

JUNE 1972

My father was a Chevrolet man who believed buying anything other than an American-made car was a betrayal of
our founding fathers or, at the very least, Henry Ford. That
belief was sorely tested in the later 1970s with the oil crisis,
but he doggedly hung on to the Chevy Impala that we
drove from Pittsburgh to Dogwood, pulling a U-Haul. We
set out early, before sunup, just like we did for every vacation to "avoid traffic." We were going to a land where the
concept of traffic was two farmers on tractors passing each
other.

We'd hit I-70 by the time I awakened to Bill Withers's
pleading voice singing that he was right up the road and

it wouldn't be long till he needed a friend. I glanced at the scenery, and around the time homes disappeared and there was nothing but land, my father pushed in the eight-track. After a clunk, the strains of the "Blue Danube" waltz flowed. My parents were classical music aficionados. Though they had both been raised in the country, there was something about Mozart and Debussy and Strauss that spoke to them. I remember running into the house and hearing opera on Saturday afternoons while other homes moved and breathed to George Jones, the Statler Brothers, and the Oak Ridge Boys.

My father drove without the aid of a map, as if pulled by some unseen force to the place of his birth. My mother sat in the passenger seat, clearing her throat and pointing out homes she liked and features in yards that might be a nice touch to the parsonage. If my father's driving was an involuntary action, my mother's instructions filled in the gaps. She would comment on the dwindling gas gauge, the roadkill he should avoid, and a thousand reasons to speed up or slow down. She always preferred that he drive, but it felt like she controlled our speed and direction. Control was big with my mother.

The closer Dogwood came, the more I realized how much my life was about to change. I had visited through the years for a week in the summer. Going fishing with an uncle or hunting on my grandfather's property was an exotic once-a-year event. Now they would be my daily reality.

I can see myself, at thirteen, looking out the window

as we exited the interstate and wound our way through a neighboring town. We passed a stately bank building and a beauty salon, a feed store with two gas pumps, then farms and open land, a cemetery (there were several in the area and this was a point of contention among family members—where you were buried was almost as important as where you lived), and finally the sign that said, *Dogwood, Unincorporated.*

My father slowed and pointed. "That's the church up there."

"Calvin, take Matt over and show him," my mother said. "And watch out for that pothole."

Dutifully he drove off the paved road and up the gravel path. The church sat on a little knoll, a square white structure with a steeple. Behind it I saw a rusty basketball hoop nailed to a tree and a dirt patch for a court. At our house in Pittsburgh, we'd had a hoop over the garage and a flat patch of concrete.

"This is it," my father said. "This is where the Lord is calling us."

I didn't have questions or comments. Who was I to argue with the Lord's calling? At almost fourteen, you go with the tide. You eat what's in front of you. Life is a take-it-or-leave-it proposition.

"And that's the parsonage over there," he said, pointing.

A half-built house stood in the distance, and for some reason my father didn't take us there. We drove past the elementary school, and I was glad I didn't have to endure time in the run-down structure.

We drove through Dogwood, a town without a stoplight, and wound our way to the long road that led to my
grandmother's house. Unpaved and dusty—the window
down left grit in my teeth from passing cars. I could see
why John Denver would sing "Take Me Home, Country
Roads," but I wasn't sure I wanted to go.

My grandfather had died three years earlier, a few days
before Christmas. The phone rang late one night and my
father answered, his voice low and rumbling. I was reading
The Swiss Family Robinson in bed and heard him speak a
few words and then gently weep. My older brother, Ben,
home from college, leaned into the room, his hair hanging.
There was contention about the length of it.

"Pawpaw died," he whispered.

I nodded. "That's what I figured."

"You okay?" he said.

I nodded and kept reading.

We drove over the creek and up to the farm, past walnut
trees that lined the driveway. My mother said not to park
over the septic tank. My father stopped beneath a towering
hickory tree. There were two ponds above the house where
cattle used to roam and a decrepit barn that looked like it
wouldn't last the winter. Grandmother Plumley, known to
us as Mawmaw, toddled out of the house to welcome us
and hugged my parents. When she got to me, she squinted
through thick glasses that made her eyes look ten times bigger than they really were.

"And look at little Matt," she said, her breath stale with

morning coffee. She moved her mouth from side to side, adjusting her dentures. "You're just the fattest thing, aren't you?" She looked at my father. "He's getting wider than he is tall. Just a butterball."

My father forced a smile. My weight gain had been painful to him. I had heard him and my mother talking about how moving to Dogwood might help me exercise more, working on the farm and climbing the hills. I didn't understand the importance weight gain played for the people of Dogwood, but the longer I stayed, the more I'd realize it was like box scores for baseball. An extra ten pounds on a person was like counting walks or strikeouts. A person eating rhubarb pie might turn to a neighbor and say, "Have you seen how big Vestel is getting?" as if it were part news report, part prayer request. "If she keeps eating like that, we'll be able to fill her with helium and fly her over a golf tournament." The not-so-subtle message was that thin was preferred to fat. And I longed to be thin. I longed to run fast like my brother. But somewhere in my childhood, when my mother's depression caused her to turn to cooking and baking, I could not assuage my stomach's longings nor the longing to save her. The cakes and pies and casseroles beckoned like gastronomic sirens, and there was no one to lash me to the mast. So I lost myself in them as I lost myself in books until I became "Fat Matt." This was the only reason leaving Pittsburgh felt good.

My father was not one to criticize or cajole. He had the heart of a pastor, an encourager. He wanted to help my mother and me, just never figured out how. But once he

entered the kitchen while I was at the table eating brownies
my mother had baked with fistfuls of walnuts in every bite.
He glanced at me, then away, shaking his head. "Big as you
are and still shoveling it in." I stopped eating for a moment
until he exited, stage right, then took the brownie into
another room and read.

My humiliation always reached its apex when my
mother shopped for clothes at the start of the school year.
She would buy "husky" pants. But at the beginning of sixth
grade, even husky wouldn't fit. The pants were so tight
I couldn't get them buttoned. The woman in the clothing
department took out her measuring tape and leaned down,
wrapping it around my girth and pulling it tight.

"We'll have to go to men's," she said. "How old is he?"

She spoke as if I weren't there, as if I were an inanimate
object without feelings or emotion or appetite. As if my
weight prevented me from hearing.

The woman frowned at my mother's answer and said,
"Somebody needs to lay off the gravy."

The first thing Mawmaw said after greeting us and
observing my plumpness was to offer lunch. This was the
other constant in Dogwood. If people weren't commenting
about how thin or fat others were, they were offering food.
When you arrived and before you left. When company
came. Something's on TV? Let's eat. Everything that happened in the house began and ended at the kitchen table.

Mawmaw's kitchen featured bacon fat that hung as
heavy in the air as wet quilts on a clothesline. You could
hear eggs crackling in her iron skillet in the next county.

That day she fixed toasted ham and cheese sandwiches and I ate tentatively, watching to see if my father might object to me having more potato salad, which I loved. Mawmaw's potato salad was a concoction that could be fed intravenously and still enjoyed. Creamy and thick and good by itself or with saltines, it garnished all significant meals.

"Matt, why don't you get your bike out of the U-Haul and take a ride?" my mother said after lunch.

"That's a great idea," my father said.

I had no desire to explore the road that led past my grandmother's house—I had never been that way alone. But the appeal of getting out of the little house with the old-people smell and the creaky wooden floor and the conversation about my weight propelled me to the U-Haul. I tried opening it, but the metal handle was wedged tightly. I was round but short for my age and appeared younger than thirteen. I went back inside to ask my father's help.

"So you'll be staying here how long?" Mawmaw was saying as I stepped inside.

"Just until they get the parsonage finished," my mother said quickly.

"And what about Ben? Where is he?"

"He won't be coming with us," my mother said.

"Why not? Is he still going to college?"

"No," my father said.

"He's not with that girl, is he?"

"He's finding himself," my father said.

Silence followed. My brother's situation was a constant cause of concern. One of the unspoken prayer requests on

Wednesday nights that simply caused a raised hand. My grandmother's reference to Ben's girlfriend was unnerving to me because I knew very little about her.

"Is he still wearing his hair down on his shirt collar?" Mawmaw said.

"I suppose he is," my father said.

"Mmm-hmm."

You could tell a serious conversation was underway when my grandmother said *mmm-hmm*. It was her way of processing news she didn't like. The other thing she said was *well*—the sign she didn't agree with something someone had said but wasn't about to address it. Conflict was best avoided in the house of Plumley.

"Mmm-hmm," she repeated. "Well, we're all trying to do that, aren't we?"

My father seemed anxious to get outside, so he gladly opened the U-Haul when I asked. The contents had shifted and my bike was smushed into the back corner.

"When will the rest of the stuff get here?" I said.

"We're going to put that in storage until the new house is ready. There's not room here at the farm."

"How long before we move in?"

"It'll be a while. A month or two." There was a bit of apprehension in his voice. "It's going to be nice, Matt. This will be a new life for us. A fresh start." He got a far-off look in his eye. "I used to hunt and fish all over these hills when I was your age. Built a tree house. Your uncle Willy and I used to swing on grapevines and pretend we were

Tarzan. . . . Go on and get your bike out. Watch out for snakes on the road, though. It's that time of year."

He walked toward the barn and I struggled with the bike. I had asked for a ten-speed for Christmas and replaced the tiny seat with one more comfortable for my backside. The handlebars were wedged tightly under a box, and I pulled hard and heard a sickening crunch of glass. Something fell to the ground—my baseball glove. There's nothing in the world that could make me feel sadder than a lone baseball glove. I had written the names of all my favorite players on that glove. Clemente. Stargell. Sanguillen. Mazeroski. Zisk. This was the glove I had used to pitch with Ben, a highlight of summers past.

I put the glove safely into another box, closed the door without seeing what might have broken, and coasted down the driveway, past the walnut trees, and onto the little bridge over the creek. I paused at the end of the driveway and looked left and right, the road stretching out in both directions. I turned left, making the choice that would forever change me.

Chapter 3

Dogwood in June is a little like Eden. Corn rises from the earth's loamy soil and supplicates. Beans wrap around stalks and poles while melons stretch out along the ground in praise to the giver of everything seeded. Trees sprout leaves and reach heavenward in the heat and humidity, and the world feels like a greenhouse.

I didn't notice all this then. I was simply part of it, riding a bike on a gravel-strewn dirt road. In the middle, things were tamped down and smooth, but if you got to the side, your tires got lost in the cast-off rocks that flew with anyone traveling more than twenty miles an hour. Involuntarily, I began to sing the tune I had heard in the car. "'It won't be long till I'm gonna need somebody to lean on.'"

A low rumble sounded behind me and I pulled into the gravel. A pickup truck passed and all I could see was a weathered hand waving near the side mirror. This was something I learned quickly about hill people. They always acknowledged others making their way along the road of life. The simple gesture of throwing a hand up, noticing the image of God struggling along the path, was the least a person could give.

Dust settled and I learned not to look into the cloud with an open mouth or eyes. I spat the grit from my teeth, then followed the truck. It took a turn on a smaller path and I kept going, passing the few houses and trailers dotting the landscape. Nicer houses were farther back from the road, while those in trailers wanted closer access.

Dogs barked and stretched at chains. Chickens clucked, and along the road a meandering creek worked its way through the countryside like a wet scar. Rusty mailboxes hung to rotting wooden posts. Gnats buzzed about my head and gargantuan flies lit on my back and drew blood before I felt the sting. I would discover these were horseflies.

A little dog appeared on the front porch of a house set back from the road and gave a high-pitched bark. It looked like Toto in *The Wizard of Oz*. I couldn't resist whispering, "We're not in Pittsburgh anymore."

I rode past a weathered barn, up over a ridge, and then past a field that stretched out to my right, dotted with cows and a few horses. In the distance was a stately house sitting on a knoll overlooking the land. Behind it was a rocky hill. The grass had been eaten down to the dirt and there were burnt spots in the field. The road to the house was protected by a metal gate and signs that read, *Private Property. KEEP OUT.*

I kept pushing up the road, wondering how far I'd gone and how long it would take to get back and if anyone would miss me.

The road dipped and a bank of earth rose to my right. I heard a terrifying snort and slammed on my brakes. An animal towered over me, the sun silhouetting its head. I put up a hand and squinted.

"Hey, horse," I said, not knowing how to greet such an animal. I started to pedal again, but the thing snorted and shook its head. So I got off and put down the kickstand.

I tried to climb up the bank but slid down. I tried to make steps in the dirt, digging with my toes, but that didn't work either. The roots of an old tree were sticking out of the bank and I grabbed hold to pull myself up, but my weight and lack of balance or athletic ability sent me to the ground. Finally I walked several yards down the road where the bank dipped, climbed up, and walked the fence line. Whoever's property this was had pushed the fence to the very edge.

I grabbed a handful of grass, figuring I would present it as an offering, but when I reached the horse, a sickening sight made me draw back. He wasn't standing at the road-side looking down on me out of curiosity—he was stuck. A strand of barbed wire had come loose from the post nearby and lay on the ground in a tangled mess. Twisted and wound deeply into the animal's leg were sharp, rusted barbs. Blood ran down and covered the hoof, and to stand it had to keep the injured leg in the air.

"You're in trouble, aren't you, boy?" I said.

At my voice, the horse pulled back its head and put its bloody leg down, opening the wound until I saw meat and turned away. It nickered and quickly raised the leg again as a swarm of flies attacked. There was a strong smell about the animal that took my breath away.

"Okay, okay," I said. Talking to the horse seemed like a good thing. "I'm going to get help. You stay here."

I wanted to jump down to the road but thought better of it and ran the way I had come. I hopped on my bike, wondering if I should ask my father to help. I considered the house in the distance with its No Trespassing signs.

Across the road, tucked into a valley between two hills, sat a little house I hadn't noticed. Two tracks, with grass growing in the middle, served as a driveway. The mailbox was open and had no flag. On the side scrawled in black paint was *Woods*.

I rode on one track until I neared the house, then stepped off and put the kickstand down. I had never seen a house with such a dirty-brown color. It looked like roof shingles had been nailed to the sides. The foundation stood on stacked-up cinder blocks. A rusted-out car sat beside the house and in the front yard was a swing set, if you could call it that. It had sunk deeply in the mud and had only one swing that nearly touched the ground. There were old tires propped up against the other side of the house, and for a moment I thought it might be abandoned.

A mangy black dog flew out from underneath the house. Showing teeth and barking so hard that white flew from its mouth. I wanted to run but froze. The dog's ribs showed against its matted fur. I caught my breath when it reached the end of its chain, its leather collar cracking with age.

"Shut up, Carl!" someone yelled inside.

The dog turned and looked at the house, then back at me. He barked once more before another shout of "Carl!" sent him underneath the house with a whimper. It made me wonder who would name their dog Carl.

"Whatever you're sellin', we don't want none." It was a female voice. Young and breathy. A heavy West Virginia twang.

"I'm not selling anything," I said, my voice shaking.

"Get on out of here."

The harshness of her voice made me turn. Then I thought of the horse and the blood and held my ground.

"What do you want?" the girl yelled.

I struggled to find the words and took another step toward the house, keeping my eye on the dog panting underneath.

"I need help."

With some effort the front door creaked open and a girl pushed at the screen door, which had no screen or glass, just a metal frame. It clanged behind her and she jumped the cinder block steps.

She had dirty-blonde hair and was barefoot. Her cutoff

jeans were a little too big for her frame, but she had strung a piece of rope through the loops as a belt. The shorts were frayed white and her T-shirt had faded to a cream color that looked almost brown against her milky-white skin. When the dog stuck his head out from under the house and barked, she yelled, "Shut your yap," and Carl obeyed.

As she drew closer, I saw her lithe, wiry frame, thin legs and arms. She moved like a cat with no wasted motion. She crossed her arms in front of her and I noticed fingernails cut to the quick. Her cheeks were filled with freckles and when I caught sight of her blue eyes, I nearly forgot why I had walked up to the house. I had read about such beauty in books and about people so caught up with seeing someone that their heart skipped a beat, but I had never experienced the feeling until now.

"You're not from around here, are you?" she said.

She was a little taller than me, but not much, and two of her front teeth sat forward from the rest as if trying to get a better view.

"No."

"Where you from?"

"Pittsburgh."

Her mouth dropped open. "You the new preacher's kid?"

"Yeah," I said. I was sweating hard now and wiped my face with my sleeve.

She reached out a grimy hand. "Jesse Woods. Welcome to the neighborhood, what there is of it. You staying at your grandma's?"

I shook her rough hand and nodded.

"We don't go to your daddy's church, but I thank you for coming to invite us."

"I didn't come for that. I mean, you're more than invited. I'm here about the horse. Across the road."

Jesse looked hard at me like I'd cursed at her or called her mother a bad name. "At Blackwood's?"

"I don't know who owns it, it's just . . ." I pointed at the farm behind me.

She took a step closer and shook her head to clear the hair from her eyes, then pointed a bony finger at me. "There's one thing you've got to get straight . . . What's your name?"

"Matt Plumley."

"Matt. For Matthew?"

I nodded.

"You need to know that the man who owns that land will skin you alive if he finds you on his farm. Even near it. He's meaner than a copperhead and bites twice. You understand?"

"Who is it, Jesse?" a voice called from inside. Then came the coughing and wheezing of an older woman through the open window.

"It's our new neighbor, Mama. Preacher's kid."

"Tell him to get on home and go check on Daisy Grace. I don't hear her no more."

"I will, Mama," Jesse yelled. She turned back and lowered her voice. "Anyways, you stay away from that guy and his property. You hear?"

She walked past the rusted car to the back of the house
and I followed, looking first at Carl for permission.

"There's a horse caught in the fence," I said. "He's hurt
really bad."

Jesse kept walking, reaching a patch of weeds, and
I remembered what my father had said about snakes.

"Didn't you hear me?" she said. "If it's Blackwood's
horse, you best leave it alone."

"It's going to die if we don't do something."

She stopped and turned. "What are you talking about?"

I told her what I had seen and her face drew tight. "Is it
the little mare with the white patch on her face right here?"

I hadn't noticed anything about the horse other than its
bloody leg, but I took the open door and said, "I think so."

Jesse winced and bit at a nonexistent fingernail. "All
right, stay here."

She continued into the backyard, which looked more
like an unmown field. In a patch of wildflowers she yelled,
"Daisy Grace!" I heard giggling and Jesse ran, then bent
over, disappearing in the tall grass. She returned carrying a
girl over her shoulder who looked to be about three. The
child was also barefoot and held a fistful of daisies.

"Put me down!" she yelled, saying the word *down* in
two long syllables. "I want to give them to Mama."

"You can give them to her, but you need to stay inside,
all right? There's ticks everywhere, and you know what happens when you get bee stung."

"I don't care," Daisy Grace said.

"She swells up big as a pumpkin," Jesse said to me. Then

to her sister, "You're going to care after I get through with you. Now get inside. I have to go check on something."

Jesse opened the back door, which had no steps, and tossed the girl through to a linoleum floor. She closed the door and put a piece of wood against it. "That ought to keep her inside while I'm gone. She can't get the front door open yet."

I turned and hurried to my bike, surprised to see Jesse running beside me. She hopped onto the gravel road like it was a manicured lawn and padded next to me as I pedaled, actually pulling out in front of me to set a faster pace. Her feet were tough and her hair flew behind her.

I had noticed girls before. A late bloomer, I was scared to death of them, and being the son of a pastor, I felt like I had two strikes against me. But following Jesse and seeing the mix of femininity and strength stirred something.

I parked my bike at the bottom of the incline. Jesse ran up the bank with two steps, grabbed the tree root, and vaulted over the berm. I watched from below as she examined the horse.

"Poor thing," she said. "She must've been looking for something to eat on the other side of the fence and got tangled. And you're right, it's real bad."

"What should we do? Go to Mr. Blackwood?"

She frowned. "We got to get her free. Need some wire cutters. Big ones. Does your daddy have a pair?"

"I don't know. His tools aren't here yet, I don't think. We packed the necessities in the U-Haul but . . ."

"We don't have any." She snapped her fingers. "Dickie

does. We used them . . . Never mind what we used them for. Look, you ride over to his place and ask him for his big wire cutters."

"But—"

She saw my confusion. "You're new, that's right. You don't know where he lives."

"Why don't you go?" I said.

"Can I use your bike?"

"Sure. You don't have one?"

Jesse shook her head.

"Okay, take it and I'll stay here."

She looked at her house. "All right, but watch out for Daisy Grace. If she gets out, she'll come toward the road looking for me. You tell her to get back inside."

I nodded and she jumped on my bike and stood on the pedals barefoot, dust flying from my back tire, her leg muscles straining. The silence of the woods engulfed me and I wondered if I'd made a mistake. Maybe she'd just stolen my bike. Maybe I'd have to walk home. What if a snake bit me?

I noticed movement near Jesse's house and the little girl came to the road and leaned out. I ran toward her and waved. "You need to go back home," I yelled. "Your sister said."

When she heard me, she ran toward her house, still clutching her daisies, and Carl barked. So much for the girl not being able to get the front door open.

An eternity elapsed. I picked up some rocks and tossed them at empty beer bottles in the roadside dust. I talked to the horse. Finally I heard voices and tires and Jesse rounded the corner. Behind her was a dark-skinned kid with curly black hair.

Dickie Darrel Lee Hancock lived on the low end of the Dogwood totem pole. I came to understand that there was a pecking order of status and social standing even among the impoverished. The Woods family was the one everyone compared themselves with to make them feel better about their lot in life. A family could fall apart or experience a job loss, a diagnosis, a natural disaster—a flood of biblical proportions—and still say, "At least we don't have it as bad as the Woods."

Dickie Darrel Lee was not quite as low on the economic ladder, but he was socially as low as you could get. Because of his father's military service, Dickie's mom was, in effect, a single mother. Add his skin color and the fact that he was of mixed race and you had the perfect storm to create an outcast. That he and Jesse had found each other was not surprising.

Jesse rode my bike to the edge of the gravel, let it fall, and was up the bank in a flash. Dickie ran his into the ground across the road in some weeds.

"Hey," he said as he passed.

"How you doing?" I said stiffly.

"Lookin' for a breakthrough," Dickie said, then followed Jesse carrying the cutters.

I thought about trying to follow them, but the bank was too steep. When Dickie saw the horse's leg, he let out a string of curses.

Jesse glared. "I told you he's the preacher's kid."

Dickie looked back at me. "Sorry."

"It's okay," I said. "You know, I was thinking. Somebody might give us a reward for saving this horse's life."

"Blackwood won't do nothing but spit in your face and shoot the horse as quick as look at her."

Dickie nodded. "Yeah. He'll put her down, no question."

"Maybe you're wrong," I said. "My dad says you have to give people a chance to change."

Jesse grabbed for the cutters but Dickie held on. "Just wait. That wire is probably in so deep it's holding back the blood. You take it out and she'll bleed to death."

"Maybe I should go get Mr. Blackwood," I said.

Jesse ignored me and told Dickie, "If we do nothing, she'll bleed to death."

"They call that something, don't they?" Dickie said.

"A catch-22," I said. "It's from a book about World War II."

They both stared at me like I was something you'd have to clean out of a barn. Dickie looked back at the horse and said, "Maybe we should pray like those TV preachers. Do a healing service like Ernest Angley."

"My mama watched him once and said he smacked a man so hard he fell over."

"He's not smacking them. It's the Spirit—"

Jesse grabbed the cutters from him.

"What are you going to do?" I said.

"What's it look like I'm going to do? I'm cutting the wire."

Dickie tried to get the cutters back, but Jesse pushed him from the bank and he jumped, landing on his feet in the gravel.

"What'd you do that for?" Dickie yelled.

"We don't have time to argue," she said. "Y'all want to form a committee, go ahead."

"Let the record show I protested," Dickie said.

Jesse moved closer to the fence and out of our line of sight. Dickie and I backed up to see. The horse seemed to sense Jesse meant her no harm.

"I'm telling you, this is a mistake," Dickie said.

"Steady now," Jesse said, coaxing and soothing the horse as she moved the cutters near the injured leg. "You're gonna be all right."

Snip.

The sound echoed like a gunshot and the horse raised her head.

"It's okay," Jesse said gently. "One more cut and you're free."

She maneuvered the cutters to the other side and used both hands to clip the wire. Instead of running, the horse, not realizing she was free, allowed Jesse to push and twist the wire out of the wound. She was able to unwind it enough to grab it with the cutters. Then the horse reared and ran into the open field, the wire sticking out of her leg.

"Look at her go!" Jesse said, holding the cutters above her head in triumph.

Dickie ran up the bank and stood at the top, king of the hill. I headed for the easy way to join them.

"Hey," Dickie said. "Where you going?"

"I can't get up that way."

"Sure you can. Try it."

I took a run but slipped before I got a hand on the tree root.

"Do it again and just take two steps and hold out your hand."

I wanted to protest. I wanted to go the easy way. But something in Dickie's face made me try. It was the same encouragement my brother gave when he would throw a pop-up as high as he could and tell me to get under it and square up to catch it. But it usually hit the ground.

"Go," Jesse said to me, standing beside Dickie.

I ran through the gravel to the bank and took two steps on the incline. Dickie grabbed my hand and Jesse reached for the other and I stepped over the edge and stood, a feeling of victory and power shooting through me.

"Thanks," I said.

"That's one small step for man, one giant leap for the preacher's kid," Dickie said.

I laughed and caught my breath, looking down at where I'd come from. I could never have done that by myself.

"She looks free, don't she?" Jesse said, watching the horse.

"She's limping," Dickie said. "I still say we should have waited. I heard about a girl who fell on a pencil and it went right in her chest and when they pulled it out, she bled like a fire hydrant."

Whether it was his upbringing or his station in life,

Dickie took the glass half-empty to new levels. He knew people who had lost eyes and ears and just about every body part because of some regrettable mistake.

"Good thing that horse doesn't have access to a pencil sharpener," Jesse said. "What's that got to do with anything?"

"That wire could have been pinching an artery," Dickie said.

"Look," I said, pointing at the horse.

The mare had turned back toward us and swayed, her hurt leg in the air. She put the injured leg down and then tumbled to the ground, headfirst, and flopped to the side.

"Told you," Dickie said.

Jesse put a hand to her mouth. "Oh, the poor thing."

The horse lay motionless in the pasture and the three of us stared in horror.

"You think she's dead?" I said.

"She probably just passed out from gratitude," Dickie said.

"Well, at least we did something," I said. "And the last thing that horse ever saw was three kids trying to help her."

Jesse set her jaw and tears came to her eyes. "That's not good enough. We should have been able to save her."

A low rumble sounded behind us and I turned to see a red Ford F-100 with a white top coming up the road.

"OMB!" Jesse shouted.

The truck paused near the gate, then continued slowly toward us while I tried to figure out what *OMB* meant.

Except there was no *us* now. Jesse and Dickie had hit the dirt and hidden in the grass.

"Get on your bike and get out of here," Jesse whispered. "Hurry!"

I paused at the edge of the drop.

"Jump and slide down," Dickie said. "It's the fastest way."

I sat on the edge and tried to ease my way to the ground, but my weight and momentum propelled me and I landed on my stomach, air rushing from my lungs. "Ow, ow, ow," I said, trying to get my breath. By the time I got to my feet, I was staring at Old Man Blackwood through his open window.

"What's your problem, kid? Can't you read?"

I gasped for air.

"Speak up!"

"No, sir. I mean, yes, sir, I can read."

"Then what do you think 'No Trespassing' means?"

I didn't answer because the question was rhetorical and I didn't have air. The man had a rifle mounted in the back window of his cab. And if what Jesse had said was true, I had only seconds to live.

"What's your name, fatty?"

Over the rumble of the engine I heard Jesse whisper something. Blackwood couldn't see above the bank, couldn't see the broken fence or the little mare bleeding out. He couldn't see my new friends.

"Get outta here," Jesse hissed.

I ran to my bike and picked it up. Blackwood pulled the truck forward, blocking my exit.

"Whose kid are you?" Blackwood yelled. "Answer me!"

I pushed the bike into the road and jumped on it, riding past his open window. The man cleared his throat and spat, but I didn't stop or slow down.

"That's right! Get out of here, tub of lard. And don't let me catch you here again, you hear me?"

I pedaled fast, worried that Blackwood would follow me or run me over. I looked back once but didn't see Jesse or Dickie.

The death of the little mare was the first secret we promised we'd keep. It wouldn't be our last.

Chapter 4

I drove through the night, fueled by gas station coffee and cold Mountain Dew, the elixir of my childhood. I reached Dogwood Monday morning in time to see truckers and plant workers meeting by the interstate to share rides. There was now one stoplight in town, a sign of progress. I went past our high school and the church of my youth, a thousand questions about Jesse swirling. Could I save her from her grave mistake? Could I turn her heart a different direction before the wedding? It suddenly felt cliché, and a little desperate, me coming back.

I sat in my car, a six-year-old blue Toyota Corolla liftback, and stared at the plane outside the school, a WWII memorial featuring a real F-86 Sabre. It was under the left wing of that plane that I had asked Jesse to the prom. She had refused, saying, "I ain't prom material, Matt, and you know it."

"I don't know it, Jesse. You're the prettiest girl in school. You deserve to be queen."

"Can't make a silk purse out of a sow's ear," she said.

"If it's because you don't have money for a dress, I can help."

No matter how much I pleaded, the answer was no. And the sight of the plane brought back the old ache.

I passed the ghost of Blake's General Store, just a shell now. A half mile later I came to the Dogwood Food and Drug where Jesse worked. I knew this, as well as everyone who had died within a fifty-mile radius, from my mother. She clipped obituaries like coupons and sent them, but the names were just as hazy on the page as they were in my mind.

At my grandmother's house, which my parents had made their own after her death, I pulled halfway up the drive and sat overlooking the creek, water trickling underneath the bridge. The stately walnut trees were still there but the large hickory was a stump. Lightning had done its cruel work two summers before—my mother had sent a snapshot. The pine trees my father and I had planted as a project to replenish the deforested earth were huge. They had been about as big as my hand when we planted them and now they soared above me. Funny how much growth can happen in twelve years.

I was startled by a banging on the window and recognized Jasper Meadows, who lived across the road. He carried a shotgun and had a chaw of tobacco the size of a fist in his mouth. He was as weathered as his coveralls and as faded as the Cincinnati Reds hat that sat crooked on his head. I rolled down my window.

"What are you doing sittin' there?" he said around the chaw, an edge to his voice.

"Mr. Meadows? I didn't want to wake my parents."

He gave a crusty laugh. "You're Calvin's boy? The little one?"

"Matt."

He grinned, showing tobacco-stained teeth. "Well, I'll be. Matt Plumley. How's everything up in Chicago?" He said the name of the city with an "er" at the end.

"It was still there when I left," I said.

His eyes were milky in the middle and he cocked his head and pawed at the gravel. "Shame about them Cubs. I thought this might be their year."

"Yeah, me too."

"All right. Won't bother you. Just keeping an eye out on the groundhog that keeps getting in my muskmelons and I saw you sitting here and thought maybe you was up to no good."

"Not this morning," I said with a smile. "Are there a lot of people up to no good these days?"

"You'd be surprised. Don't know what the world is coming to." He took off his hat and scratched the side of his head with the bill. "Have you seen your mama lately?"

"No, sir. But I've talked with her."

"Well, she'll be happy to see you, I'm sure. All your family is good people. You ought to come around more often." He said it to me, but I could tell he meant it for his own children, who had flown and hadn't returned. "People are way too busy these days, if you ask me."

I wanted to ask him not to let anyone know I was home, but I figured Jasper would keep the news between him and the groundhog.

He waved a hand without turning around and kept walking.

I pulled up the driveway a few minutes later and parked over the septic tank. There was a garden above the house in full bloom, near the barn. My father's tools and mower were now in a shed below the house, but not much had changed since my childhood. I took a walk in the yard, the dew wet on the grass and clover.

The back clothesline was empty and the chinaberry tree by the walk had two lawn chairs near it. I pictured my parents here, talking, sharing news of the town and the church. I wondered how many times the conversation had turned to me at this spot.

The back door opened with a squeak and my mother appeared, wiping her hands on a dish towel. "Matt, is that you?"

I smiled and hugged her and she laughed and cried at the same time, clinging to my neck like a wisteria vine. "When did you get here?"

"A little bit ago."

"And why are you . . . ?" She pulled back and I could tell she had figured it out. My mother had an inner sense of everything from politics to which eligible single man belonged with which eligible single woman. She could overhear a conversation and precisely diagnose the relational problem. Call it horse sense or a sixth sense, she was always able to put two and two together.

"Matt, you're not going to mess things up, are you?"

I had prepared for that question, but I didn't know it would come so quickly. I used a tactic of my own to avoid it.

"Mom, I'm starving. You don't have anything for breakfast, do you?"

She knew I was playing her, but she joyfully led the way into the house and fried eggs and hash browns and bacon. She cut two English muffins and put them in the toaster.

"Where's Dad?" I said.

"You know what he does on Mondays. A man needs to get away from the world's troubles, Matthew. Every day has enough of its own."

She said my name as if using it would make me understand the deeper meaning, the Scriptural reference clear as the pain on her face.

In conversations with my mother, through college and beyond, she rarely asked about my classes or work. Most of our conversations centered on the town, the people, her physical problems, and whatever social or political crisis was going on in the world. It seemed easier to talk about these things.

She filled my plate and put it down, still steaming, as if handing me a serving of my childhood. The smell of cooked meat and eggs mingled with the memories and I took a deep breath. There was enough food on the plate to feed a small village, but this was my mother's way. A child of the Depression, she knew what it was like to be hungry and have next to nothing and still be better-off than most. She took any chance for abundance.

"Have you heard from Ben lately?" I said.

She nodded. "He called last week."

"Cindy and the kids?"

"They're fine. I always wanted to give my children wings so they could fly as far as possible but then fly back. And you've flown back to us, haven't you?" She patted my hand as I took a napkin from the stack in the center of the table.

"Let me bless the food," she said, bowing her head. She was losing hair around her crown.

I closed my eyes and bowed my head. In the house of my youth, prayer was not just for praise and petition, but also for teaching those in hearing distance.

"Lord, we thank you for a new day, a new week. Thank you for your blessings. We don't take them for granted. And thank you for bringing Matt. Bless him, Lord. Show him your love. Your grace. Give him wisdom about whatever he's trying to do here. Now bless this food to the nourishment of our bodies. In Jesus' name, amen."

"Amen," I said, spreading the napkin on a leg.

She spoke of the health of people at church and worked

her way around the neighborhood, hitting the highs and lows. When I asked about the Blackwood family, she got quiet, so I changed the subject.

"Did you see what happened to the Cubs?"

"Wasn't that something?" she said. "We didn't see the game because of the evening service, but your father was heartbroken for the team and the city."

"I used to think if I prayed hard enough and begged God enough, he'd help the Pirates win."

She smiled and shook her head. "You ate and drank to that team. And when they lost, it almost killed you." When I didn't speak, she added, "The Cubs will bounce back. You wait and see. Adversity is just an invitation to get better."

The words settled between us and I tried to think of something else to talk about, something to bring up that might keep her from prying. I didn't come up with anything before she said, "Matt, honey." Her voice lowered and turned sweet. "Sometimes I think the Lord wants us to move on and let go of what's behind. So that we can press on."

"Are you talking about the Cubs or me?"

She tipped her head back and laughed, but it felt obligatory. I had used humor in my youth to rescue my mother from her inner thoughts and demons. Music and food played the same role. Now I felt like I could push a little further. "Mom, you and Dad were called here. I always knew you felt that way. But I was thinking on the drive, what if it was God's will that I met Jesse? What if we were meant for each other?"

She winced as if she'd licked a cast-iron skillet. "Those

are old wounds. You have to move past them. And from what you've said about the work you're doing in Chicago with those kids, it sounds like you have."

I put my fork down after eating a few ounces of the two pounds in front of me. She picked up the plate and took it to the metal coffee can she kept outside the back door to feed the varmints, as she called them. My loss of appetite was a conscientious objection to our previous war with food.

I took the phone book from a shelf by the table and found Jesse's name. I jotted the number down on a scrap of paper and put it in my wallet as my mother returned from outside.

"You might get a call," I said. "I left your number in case anybody needs to get in touch."

"Shouldn't you go back? You don't want to jeopardize your job." The question hung as she turned resolutely toward the sink. My father had bought a dishwasher for her years earlier but I think she believed the Palmolive commercials with Madge, who said, "Relax, it's Palmolive."

As she scrubbed and cleaned, I looked around the house, not to escape domestic duties, but to create space. Sometimes you needed to walk into a different room for five minutes. I wandered to the piano and studied the hymnal, open to "Rescue the Perishing." I picked out the melody and read the words. The third verse caught my eye:

Down in the human heart, crushed by the tempter,
Feelings lie buried that grace can restore;

Touched by a loving heart, wakened by kindness,
Chords that were broken will vibrate once more.

I looked in the mirror and saw my mother's shadow near the hall. I stood and moved to the fireplace mantel, a shrine to Ben and me. In the pictures, I had a buzz cut that accentuated my ears and made me look like I could fly with a stiff breeze. Ben's hair was also painfully short. This was how they wanted to remember us, I assumed.

Departed loved ones were on an end table nearby. There was a photo of my grandfather and his wedding party, men dressed in turn-of-the-century wool. He was a hardworking man from the "old country" who hadn't known a word of English when he reached Ellis Island. He had become a coal miner, deep in the southern coalfields, but had moved his family to Dogwood when he discovered how hard life could be. Dogwood proved to be just as cruel but in different ways.

The front door opened and my father walked in smiling. He wore a long-sleeved shirt and dress pants, his wingtip shoes and signature wool fedora. In the crook of his arm was a worn, black Bible. So much for taking the day off, I thought.

"Matt? When did you get in?"

"Early this morning," I said, looking at my grandfather's picture and noticing the striking resemblance.

He took off his hat and looked at his watch. "Well, it's too hot to be Christmas. And it's not Mother's Day. What's the occasion?" He shook my hand.

I could write a book about my father's hands. They were rough and calloused from working on the farm as a boy. He gained more layers of calluses at the glass factory in Dogwood, and when he moved to Pittsburgh and got a job in the steel industry, he led with his hands. At some point the call from God pushed him from manual labor toward seminary, and he eventually returned to pastor the church he'd attended as a child.

"I think you know why I came back," I said.

"I'm not sure I do."

"When were you going to tell me? Were you going to let Mom send a clipping from the *Herald-Dispatch*?"

He shoved his hands into his pockets and looked at the thin, yellowish-brown carpet. How many people had traipsed through the living room and kitchen after a Sunday service? How many couples in crisis had sat on the old couch? As many struggles as my father had addressed here, he had spent little time with ours, or so it seemed to me.

"Well, the truth is, this came up quickly. Jesse and Earl asked if I would marry them, and I told them I wouldn't unless I could counsel them. To make sure theirs would be a Christian marriage."

"A Christian marriage? Dad, you know how Earl will treat her. And you've always known how I felt."

My mother walked in, wiping her hands on a drying towel like Lady Macbeth. She had a knack of interrupting significant conversations between my father and me. I could be close to some hidden revelation, about to uncover a nugget of truth, and she would appear, guiding us away from each other and back to our respective corners.

"I don't want you two to fight."

"We're not," I said, keeping my eyes on my father. "When were you going to tell me?"

"I really didn't think it was your business. What Jesse does with her life is her decision."

"You should see them together, Matt," my mother said. "If you could see how he cares and dotes on her . . ." She took a few steps closer, tears welling, and a hangdog look. "She's made a real nice girl. She works hard in the meat department at the Food and Drug. You know she didn't have a chance in the world. But she's become a fine Christian girl."

But she wasn't good enough for me or our family. That was what I wanted to say, but the look on my mother's face stopped me. I wondered what my parents would have said about Kristin and her decision that I wasn't the right guy for her because of the lack of depth to my faith.

Before I could respond, my mother held the towel to her face and gave the low moan of pain I remembered from my childhood. Back then it usually related to Ben. When my father preached about hell, it was always the weeping and gnashing of teeth that got me. That prospect for eternity made me want to run toward God. Abandon all hope, ye who enter my mother's grief.

She collected herself and looked up, a trace of a smile on her face. "Do you remember Gwen? Such a lovely girl. I saw her the other day at Eula's salon and she asked about you."

I held up a hand and turned to my father. When I was young, they'd played good cop/bad cop, mercy and justice. One was rugged, the other soft. One advanced, the other retreated. At times they switched roles, but mostly my mother was firm and my father soft. I rarely saw them march together in my teenage years. Instead it was a push-pull, teeter-totter parenting method that left me disoriented, wondering which to trust and who was really on my side. There was no debate, however, that my mother was commander in chief.

"Matt," my father said with a gentleness that surprised me, "you have a good heart. And I know you want to help. But you can't force someone to accept your love."

"Who said anything about love? I think she's making a mistake. I can't understand why you don't see that."

"She's not your responsibility, Matthew," my mother said.

"People make choices with their lives," my father added. "Some are good. Some aren't. And we all live with the fallout."

My mother waited to the count of ten. "Nothing good can come from this. Move on. Put the past behind. Press on toward the prize of the high calling—"

"What is it about the past that scares you?" I said, looking from his eyes to hers and back again. "I've spent a dozen years leaving the past, and here it is bubbling to the surface."

"Let's not go through this all again," my mother said, shaking her head.

Ticking like a time bomb in the corner of the room

was the grandfather clock my mother had received one Christmas. She'd always dreamed of owning one. It was a status symbol that countered her poverty-stricken childhood. The three of us were frozen and it felt like that first day when we'd arrived in Dogwood, the first dinner at my grandmother's house when I'd said I had made two friends. The air had gone out of the room when I said their names.

My grandmother had narrowed her gaze. "Don't hang around with that trash," she said.

My mother and father had stayed silent as we ate. I wanted to tell them about the dead horse and Old Man Blackwood, but the truth seemed better hidden.

Now my mother spoke over the clock's ticking and the memories that shouted. "Why don't you put your things in your bedroom? You've driven all night. You have to be tired." She looked at me and tried to smile. "That's what this is about. You're tired and you need rest."

"Take a shower and get some sleep," my father said. "We can talk more later."

I knew a shower couldn't wash the questions away, but I sighed and said, "It's been a long night."

"I'll get you a set of towels," my mother said, heading for the laundry room.

I opened the front door as the sun peeked over the edge of the hill and burned the dew. The air was fresh and crisp like October was supposed to be. I saw my gym bag in the passenger seat and went to retrieve it. As I opened the door, something inside told me not to sleep. I climbed behind the wheel and drove away, my father staring from the front window.

Chapter 5

JUNE 1972

Life is invigorating when you have friends, even if you
live far from civilization. I went to bed that first night to
the deafening sound of chirping crickets, falling asleep
almost as my head hit the pillow. A framed picture hung
by the door, still there from when my father was a child.
Pinocchio ran into the classroom late, and Jiminy Cricket
stood on the teacher's desk with arms folded, glaring. It was
the last thing I saw before sleep.

I awoke the next morning to sizzling bacon and my
grandmother humming "Channels Only" at the end of the
hall. She was in her nightgown, a long braid of hair down
her back swishing from side to side. My grandmother wore

clothing that made her look without shape or form. She was a head on top of a cylinder with varicose vein–laced ankles sticking out the bottom. She sang the words as she cracked the eggs into a metal bowl.

"How I praise Thee, precious Savior,
That Thy love laid hold of me;
Thou hast saved and cleansed and filled me
That I might Thy channel be.

Channels only, blessed Master,
But with all Thy wondrous pow'r
Flowing thro' us, Thou canst use us
Ev'ry day and ev'ry hour."

I walked into the kitchen, the linoleum creaking, and she turned and smiled. "How'd you sleep, Matty?"

"Like a rock."

"Your mama and daddy are at church. Getting ready for Sunday."

She told me what was planned as I ate the eggs and bacon and drank milk and orange juice and had a sweet roll. Either she was disregarding my parents' hopes about me losing weight or they hadn't discussed it with her.

"Do you know what the Pirates did last night?" I said.

"No, but the Reds won. I think they played the Mets." She handed me the sports page of the *Herald-Dispatch*, a paper she referred to as the *Herald-Disgrace* because of their treatment of Richard Nixon. My grandmother and parents were lifelong Republicans in a state that hadn't voted for one since Eisenhower. And Nixon was as close to a political saint as you could get in her book. She had a photo she'd clipped from a newspaper of Billy Graham and the president smiling next to each other. When Graham held a crusade at Pitt Stadium, my father had made sure to take us to hear Ethel Waters and Cliff Barrows.

I found the results of the previous night and saw that the Reds had indeed beaten the Mets 6–3, but the Pirates had played a double header in San Diego and won the first game. The second game wasn't listed. This would become the bane of my existence, this lack of connection with my old team. It felt unfair to be severed—even the local radio station rarely mentioned the Pirates.

When I was finished with breakfast, I took my plate to the sink, thanked Mawmaw, gave her a hug, and turned to leave.

She grabbed me and took my chubby cheeks in her hands. "Now, Matty, you listen. You're making a fresh start. One of the most important things is to carefully pick your friends. Some will take you down the garden path and others will lead to good."

"What's wrong with the garden path? Aren't gardens good?"

She thought a moment. "It's a saying. It means, pick good friends."

"I will, Mawmaw."

My bike wasn't in front of the house where I'd left it, and it wasn't anywhere around the house. I thought maybe my father had put it in the shed, but I checked and it wasn't there. Confounded, I walked down the driveway to the creek and spotted something moving in the grass beside the gravel. A turtle as big as my grandmother's skillet moved quickly toward the water, his pointy head out. The closer I got, the bigger the stink.

"Better not get close," Jesse said behind me.

I turned and there she was, her dirty-blonde hair hanging to her shoulders. She wore the same clothes as the day before and pedaled barefoot on the same bike—mine.

"That's a snapping turtle. He gets hold of you and he won't let go until lightning strikes."

"He smells like a sewer."

"They're bottom-feeders. They eat whatever's dead. My daddy used to love to cook him up a turtle. I can't stand them. You got a .22? We could shoot it."

"Why would you want to shoot it?"

"Because a turtle is a menace. I've seen ducks swimming on top of the water and all of a sudden they're gone. Snapping turtle got 'em."

"I thought they were bottom-feeders."

"Sometimes even bottom-feeders rise to the top."

"Let's leave him alone," I said.

Behind us a voice echoed against the hills, the words to the Jackson 5's "ABC." Dickie rolled into the driveway with a one-two-three and a do-re-mi.

"How's it goin', Dickie?" Jesse said, straight-faced.

"Lookin' for a breakthrough," Dickie said with all the

hope he could muster. He saw the turtle and winced. "You going to kill that thing?"

"He don't want us to," Jesse said, sticking a thumb out toward me.

Dickie stared at me like I had two heads. "Your mama and daddy will probably invite us for dinner if we do."

I was a bit more skeptical of my family's response to him and Jesse, but I kept that to myself.

"I don't want to kill it," I said.

Dickie shook his head.

"Have you heard anything about the horse?" I said. "Is it still in the field?"

"Still there," Jesse said. "Swolled up big as a water tank. Buzzards are at it."

"So Blackwood doesn't know yet?"

Jesse shrugged. "OMB will more than likely dig a hole with his tractor and bury it."

"So he won't know what happened," I said. "We're in the clear?"

"With Blackwood, you're never in the clear," Jesse said.

Dickie yawned. "Come on, Jesse, let's go over to Blake's."

She nodded and they were about to take off when I said, "But that's my bike."

"You can come, if you want," Dickie said. "We won't kill any turtles on the way since you care so much about them."

While I was trying to figure out how all three of us would ride to Blake's, wherever that was, Jesse climbed off the bike and leaned it toward me. "Get on." I threw a leg over and Jesse climbed up on the handlebars, her bottom fitting perfectly into the empty space between them.

"Drive on!" she said, pointing a finger toward the road like I was her chauffeur.

I had never ridden with anyone on the handlebars and I had to push the bike through the gravel to the road.

"You want me to pedal?" Jesse said. "You can ride up here."

"He won't fit," Dickie said, and though he was right, the observation hurt.

Once we got to the road, I gained balance and followed Dickie, leaning to one side so I could see. Jesse's hair blew back with the hot breeze and with each pedal of the bike she shifted from side to side. The sun was up and it felt like rain, the humidity high and the air thick. June bugs buzzed past us. I was sweating before we reached the first bend in the road.

"Watch the hole," Jesse said. "Go around it—"

Before I could react, we were in the middle of a rut, and when I hit the other side, she popped up on the handlebars and grabbed them to hang on. I slid to a stop.

"You trying to kill me?" she said, turning. Dickie laughed. I could swear I saw a little smile in Jesse's eyes.

Blake's was the only grocery in Dogwood in those days before the Food and Drug arrived. It was a two-story brick building with large windows in front and a glass door that jangled a bell when you walked inside. The building sat directly across from the elementary school and Jesse said she'd gotten in trouble in the first grade for crossing the road to the store.

A cooler filled with soda pop sat outside on the covered wooden porch. Inside was frigid, humming with freezers. The room smelled of red licorice and Pine-Sol. The floor was aged hardwood with strategically placed pieces of carpet and woven baskets to carry. You could find anything you wanted at Blake's, as long as what you wanted was something they carried. Bread and sliced ham and crackers and bologna. Macaroni and cheese and Hamburger Helper. Rice-A-Roni and PAL peanut butter. There was a hardware section with work gloves and various implements, but Jesse said everybody knew you could buy a shovel for half the price at Heck's just up the interstate.

A Labrador retriever lay by the front door and moved his bloodshot eyes each time it opened. He reminded me of *Old Yeller*, a film that had cured me of ever owning a dog. For months after seeing it I wouldn't go near any pet for fear of contracting rabies. Old Man Blake (Dickie and Jesse called any male they considered even slightly unfriendly "old man") stood behind the counter wearing suspenders and a bow tie. He had little hair on top, but he made good use of it, combing it over and back again to give an appearance of a wave. He wore round spectacles and when he spoke to you, he looked at an angle, using his peripheral vision. He scowled at Dickie and Jesse as they entered, then turned his eyes about a foot away from where I was standing.

"What do you kids think you're doing in here?" He

paused for an answer and I realized he was talking to me. "Who are you? I've never seen you before."

Jesse and Dickie headed for the candy section and grabbed two Zagnut bars each, stuffing them in their back pockets. I was horrified. I took a step to the right to try to get in the man's gaze, but he looked further away.

"My name's Matt," I said, a tremble in my voice.

"He's the new preacher's kid," Jesse said, returning to the front and facing the man, acting as sweet as angel food cake. "Plumley's his name."

"You're Calvin's boy?" Old Man Blake said.

I nodded as Dickie walked out the front, closely followed by Jesse, their backs hitting the door. Old Yeller actually lifted his head and sniffed.

"What are you doing with the likes of those two? You ought to know better."

"Yes, sir," I said, looking at the licorice in the glass jars behind him and a stack of oversize Little Debbie Oatmeal Creme Pies. My mouth watered. I had become so familiar with Little Debbie that I felt related. "My dad says the ground is level at the foot of the cross."

"I attend that church," the man said, leaning over and squinting at the door as glass clinked in the front cooler. "The ground may be level, but some people dig their own holes."

My father also said there was a high cost to low living, and I felt the weight of it right then. I fished in my pocket and found the five-dollar bill from the trip. "How much for four Zagnut bars and two pops?"

He stared at me, or maybe it was my shoulder, and hit the register. It dinged and the drawer popped out and he handed me the change.

"You're not having anything?" he said.

"I had a big breakfast."

Jesse rode with Dickie through town until we came to a wide place in the road. Jesse took a swig of her grape Nehi and Dickie drank his Orange Crush.

"I almost won a hundred dollars last night playing Let's Go to the Races," Dickie said.

"Playing the horses?" Jesse said. "That game is rigged."

I asked what they were talking about and Jesse explained that a grocery store a few miles away gave cards to customers with the number of a horse listed. If your horse won, you got money. You had to watch the TV show to know if you'd won.

"I swear, that number seven was leading until right at the end," Dickie protested. "Just veered off and ran into the fence."

"You might win a couple of dollars here and there, but they don't give hundred-dollar tickets away in this part of the country."

"How do you know that?" Dickie said.

"I just know it," she said.

"It could have happened. Number seven almost won."

I stood with them empty-handed. Finally Jesse said, "How come you didn't get you a drink?"

My mouth went dry. "Because it's stealing. You shouldn't do that."

"Old Man Blake is never gonna miss two pops and a couple of candy bars," Jesse said. "The Blakes are rich as Rockefellers."

"Always have been," Dickie said. "You're new. You'll figure it out."

"What if you owned that store?" I said. "What if it was your candy bars? How would you feel?"

Jesse pulled the Zagnuts from her back pocket and tossed one to me. "We didn't steal them. We just borrowed them."

"You stole them," I said. "But I made it good. You have to promise—"

"What do you mean you made it good?" Jesse said.

"My dad gave me some money for our trip. He said I could buy fireworks from Stuckey's. But we only found an Esso."

"So you paid for this?" Jesse said, an incredulous look on her face. "How did you know what we got?"

I gave her a look. "Even the dog saw you grab the Zagnuts and pop."

Jesse looked at Dickie as if she were impressed with my powers of observation.

"We have to take him to Heck's next time we go," Dickie said, smiling.

"Look, what you guys do is your business. Killing a turtle. Stealing from the store. I can't stop you. But when you're with me, I don't want you doing that. It's not right. And you'll get me in trouble."

Jesse stuffed the whole Zagnut in her mouth and chewed with relish. She wadded up the wrapper and tossed it away, and I thought of the Crying Indian in the TV commercial with a tear running down his cheek at the littering of his homeland.

Jesse shook the hair out of her face and ran her tongue across her teeth to the back of her mouth. "You think you're better than us, don't you?"

"I don't think that at all."

"You think because you come from a big city and your daddy is a preacher you can tell us what's right and wrong. And the reason you don't want us to do bad things is how it makes you look."

"No, I want to be your friend. But a friend doesn't let other people do stuff like that and not say anything."

"Is that so?" She looked away from me. "We got a man on a high horse, Dickie Darrel Lee. A high horse with ten speeds. And I think it's time we let him ride it alone."

She climbed up on Dickie's handlebars.

"Wait a minute," I said. "Come on." I tried to think of something else to say to quell the injured feelings.

Jesse shook her head.

"Where to?" Dickie said to her, beginning to pedal.

"Gotta get home and check on Daisy." She stuck out her hand and threw it forward like a football official signaling a first down. "Take me home, country roads!"

I watched the two ride away, then opened my Zagnut and found it ground to bits. It looked like it had been on Blake's shelf since the Kennedy administration. I ate most of it and let the crumbs fall, then stuffed the wrapper in my pocket. I had never felt so alone.

Chapter 6

After a dinner of pork chops, green beans, and sweet corn slathered in butter and as salty as Lot's wife, I got out my glove and threw a tennis ball against the house. My mother said I was giving Mawmaw a headache, so I moved to the barn, but there weren't two boards that were flat enough to get a grounder. The grass was tall around it and I was concerned about snakes. I had seen a grainy film on TV once of a woman from India who would climb up a mountain to a holy place, which was a little hole in a rock, and summon a king cobra. She danced and the cobra stood and swayed and she bent down and kissed the thing three times. I wouldn't have believed it if I hadn't seen it. But that vision of the snake danced in my own head on the farm, and I wondered when I would encounter one and what I would do.

I put the glove away and hopped on my bike, riding toward Jesse's. I could hear Daisy through an open window, crying and fussing, but I didn't see Jesse. I kept going up the road until I came to the scene of the crime, the pasture, and there in a lump was the horse in the same spot she had fallen. I felt just like the horse.

My father was on the front step when I returned, sitting in a lawn chair and smoking his pipe in the twilight. Whether it was the surgeon general's warning or his own inner sense of caring for "the temple of the Holy Spirit," my father had given up his Camels. But every evening after Walter Cronkite said, "And that's the way it is," my father would knock out the ashes against the bottom of his shoe and dip the pipe his father had given him in a tin of Borkum Riff and pack it tight. Sometimes he'd let me put the tobacco in and I'd hold the can up and smell the moist, sweet aroma. These are the smells of my childhood: fresh tobacco, cowhide leather, percolating coffee, sizzling bacon, and freshly mowed grass.

I sat on the porch and stared at my glove. Not only had I written every player's name from the 1971 season, it had an autograph I cherished. *To Matt, from Ben.* The glove had been given to me as a Christmas present. I could hold that glove to my face and take in the leather and see my brother through the webbing, tossing the ball.

"You go riding with your friends today?" my dad said.

"Yeah."

"You know what your grandmother says about friends."

I stood and took the position of my grandmother, with one hand on my hip and the other in the air, maintaining my balance. "'As a dog returneth to his vomit, so a fool returneth to his folly.'" I said it in the same pitch and twang as Mawmaw.

"No, that's not what I was thinking." My father stifled a grin. "Now, Matthew, you're going to have to keep those imitations just among us, you understand?"

"Yes, sir. But what does Mawmaw say about friends?"

He took a breath. "You can pick your friends and you can pick your nose, but you can't pick your friend's nose."

I tried not to smile, but my father could deliver a line like that and puff on his pipe and it was impossible not to laugh.

"Is there something wrong with my new friends?"

He dipped his head to one side and glanced at the field near the house. When he spoke without looking at me, he was trying to say something important. He'd do the same thing in the car, staring out the windshield. Somehow it was easier for him to speak truth looking away.

"Life is about making good choices, Matt. One after another. They pile up day after day. It's only when you look back that you can see what the choices led to. What you're able to stand on."

His words hung like smoke rings. He took another draw and leaned forward, his elbows on his knees. "You should invite them to the picnic Sunday."

"Who?"

"You know who."

"I haven't heard about a picnic."

"There's a potluck after the service—to welcome us. The whole community's invited."

I thought of Jesse and Dickie trying to fit in and seeing Old Man Blake. In a flash of unbound honesty, I said, "Dad, do we have to stay here?"

"No, the parsonage will be—"

"I don't mean at Mawmaw's. I mean here in Dogwood. I don't like it."

He crossed his legs and puffed a sweet plume in the air. "Matt, you know what we've decided. This is what we feel God wants. It won't be easy. And I know this is not at the top of your list of places to plant. The trick of life isn't getting everything you want. It's making the most of what you're given. You understand?"

It felt like an episode of *Andy Griffith* with me as Opie and him as Andy. "Yes, sir," I said. But I didn't understand. I got what he was saying, but I couldn't wrap my mind around this place and these people.

"Why don't you get the radio and we'll listen to a game," he said.

"We can't hear the Pirates. I've tried."

"We could listen to the Reds." My father had begrudgingly rooted for the Pirates, but his heart was with the Reds. It was the team he had grown up with, so I couldn't fault him.

I brought the transistor outside but couldn't find any play-by-play. The newscaster said the Reds had beaten Tom Seaver and the Mets for their ninth win in ten games and were headed to Montreal. He said nothing about the Pirates.

Fireflies rose from the earth like prayers. Locals called them lightning bugs. When we used to come here on vacation, we'd poke holes in mason jar lids and use the jars as lanterns. We'd put in grass to keep the bugs comfy, but they would be dead in a day or two. Living in Dogwood took all the fun out of lightning bugs.

"I miss Ben," I said.

"I do too." He puffed his pipe again and watched the smoke rise. "Life is changing. The whole world is spinning faster than I can keep up with. But we're going to be all right."

The next day my father took me to Heck's and bought a pitch-back net I set up in the front yard. No more throwing at the side of the house. If you hit the center of the target, the ball would fly right back, but more often than not I missed the center and the ball veered away or went through the springs and rolled to the barn.

That night he got out another glove and we pitched to each other, listening to Al Michaels and Joe Nuxhall. The Pirates were just getting underway in Los Angeles when the game ended, the Reds winning again.

"There's a place in Huntington where you can buy tickets to Cincinnati games," my father said.

"I'm not becoming a Reds fan," I said. "That's one thing I refuse to do."

"I thought you'd say that. But in July, about a month from now, the Pirates are coming to Riverfront. We could go for a couple of games. Stay overnight."

"Really? You mean it?"

"Maybe. We'll see."

"How long of a drive is it?"

"A little more than three hours."

My mind spun with the prospect of getting out of Dogwood. "When can we get the tickets?"

"I'll talk with your mother. But don't count on it."

I went to sleep that night with my glove on the night-stand, going around the field starting with Stargell at first and ending with Clemente in right. They had won the World Series the year before and I believed it was because of me. When the Pirates were up to bat, I held a bat and imitated each player's swing. When they were in the field, I grabbed my glove and bent and looked in for the sign like Dock Ellis or Steve Blass. When Gene Garber pitched, I threw submarine. When Bob Moose stood on the mound, I gave the high leg kick. It was my prayers for the team that had propelled them to the championship, and even at this distance it felt like I could make it happen again. Back-to-back World Series titles. The Pirates would become a baseball dynasty just like the Yankees, a team my father and I loathed.

Just as I drifted off, I thought of Jesse. I pictured her little house and her sister holding daisies. The snapping turtle and Jesse's bare feet and her thin behind in the crook of my handlebars. I wondered if I'd ever see her again.

Saturday morning came, and Mawmaw suggested I watch cartoons after breakfast. I didn't want to seem interested because cartoons were for little kids, but something about them brought comfort to me. Her house sat in a spot on the hill where you could get only two channels. I pretended to endure *Scooby-Doo* and *Underdog* reruns. Just as *The Jetsons* started, I heard a knock at the door.

I opened it to see Dickie. Jesse was at the end of the driveway pacing.

"Hey, how you doing?"

"Lookin' for a breakthrough," Dickie said. "You want to ride bikes? Jesse said there's a garage sale on Third Street. She's on the hunt."

Without thinking, I said, "Yeah." I ran to the living room and turned off the TV, yelling at my mom that I was going bike riding.

"Watch out for snakes," she yelled back.

I walked my bike down the driveway and waited for Dickie to speak. I had rehearsed an apology, but he wasn't talkative.

When we reached Jesse, she said, "Hey, Matt." She turned and hopped on my handlebars like nothing had happened. I wondered if I had imagined the whole thing.

I was becoming used to the temperature and climate, and Jesse's weight didn't add much struggle to the pedaling, just the turning of the handlebars around curves. I avoided the pothole from the previous ride and we made our way through town, taking a series of turns along a paved part of the road and through an alley by the volunteer fire department. Dickie pointed west and said his house was in that direction.

"Timing is everything," Jesse said. "If you get there too

soon, they won't take what you're offering. By this time of day they're itching for lunch and just want to get the driveway cleared."

Three houses in a row had tables on their driveways with rusted lawn mowers and tools on display. There was a kiddie pool Jesse thought Daisy would like, but she set her face toward the third house and a bike with two flat tires. It had a rusty basket on the front and a flat piece of metal above the back tire.

"I could strap a backseat here for Daisy and put groceries in the basket," Jesse whispered.

I looked for a price but didn't see one.

"Needs some work," Dickie said. "But I got a couple of tires at the house. A little oil for the chain. It's not a girl's bike."

"You think I care?" Jesse said.

The owner of the house approached, an older man in work boots and a white T-shirt that didn't quite cover his generous, hairy stomach. Later, Dickie would refer to him as Hairy Bellyfonte, though Jesse and I didn't understand the reference.

"It's a nice one, idn't it?" he said, putting his hand on the seat.

"It's rusty," Jesse said. "Does it work?"

"Works like a charm. Dust it off and put air in the tires and you're good to go. You can ride from here to Charleston and back."

I studied the cracked tires and wondered if it was even possible to push the thing home.

"How much you want for it?" Jesse said.

"It's worth a lot more, but I'll sell it to you for ten dollars."

Jesse's mouth dropped. "Ten?"

"That's highway robbery," Dickie said.

"It ain't neither," the man said, crossing his arms. "If you knew what I paid, you'd think different."

"I don't care what you paid for it," Jesse said. "I'm looking at what it's worth."

"A thing is worth what somebody will pay. And ten is the price. So that's what it's worth."

Jesse shook her head. "It ain't worth ten dollars."

The man put a hand to his stubbly cheek. "Then what are you willing to pay?"

"I got two dollars," Jesse said.

The man laughed. "Well, there's a big ditch between what you got and what I want." He stared at Dickie's hair, then back at Jesse. "You from back in the hollow?"

She nodded.

"I thought so. You're a Woods, ain't you?"

She raised her chin at him as if expecting a fight.

With a tenderness in his voice I didn't expect, he said, "I was at the tracks the day your daddy lost his arm."

I glanced at Jesse but she was inspecting the bike.

"How long ago did he run off?" the man said.

Jesse didn't look at him. "It's been a while."

"I expect it has been."

Jesse searched for words and came up with "You got a pump?"

"Excuse me?"

"You got something to pump up the tires?"

"Sure." He went to his shed and came back with a black pump. Jesse took it and started on the front tire, pumping the handle up and down until the tire inflated.

"What did they do with it?" Jesse said to the man.

"What did they do with what?"

"His arm. I always wondered. Did they take it to the hospital with him? Just load it into the ambulance?"

"There wasn't no ambulance. We tied the stump off with some sea grass off a bale of hay in the field across the tracks. Then we flagged down Shorty Childers, who was passing by, and loaded him onto Shorty's flatbed. He drove him to Cabell Huntington. I was surprised he didn't bleed out. It was bad."

Jesse unhooked the pump from the tire and a slow hissing came from several spots. She looked at the man, then moved to the back tire and pumped. "But what happened to the arm? The bottom half?"

He scratched his chin. "Come to think of it, we never picked it up that I know of. The train had stopped by then and it was somewhere underneath, I guess. Buzzards likely got it."

Jesse nodded and unhooked the pump. The front tire was flat again and the back tire was headed the same direction.

She handed back the pump. "Mister, I was taught that somebody's word is about all he has. If you can't count on a man's word, you can't count on nothing. Now you told me I could pump this thing up and ride it to Charleston. I wouldn't get to the feed store, and that's downhill and around the corner."

He looked surprised and a little apologetic. "Well, they were fine the last time I pumped them up. It appears I was wrong."

Jesse shook her head, waved a hand, and walked toward the street.

The man raised his voice. "Look, I'm sorry about your daddy running out. How's your mama 'n' 'em doin'?"

She stopped and without turning said, "They's all right."

His eyes looked sad and he ran his tongue around his yellowing teeth. "You had a sister, didn't you?"

"Her sister is Daisy Grace," Dickie said.

"No, I mean an older sister. What was her name?"

"Eva," Jesse said.

He thought a moment more and then put his hands on his hips like he had made a final decision about which door to take on *Let's Make a Deal*. "I'll tell you what, I'll let it go for five dollars."

"I told you, I only have two."

Dickie shrugged, pulling out empty pockets.

"I've got three left," I said.

Jesse looked at me, then pulled two crumpled dollar bills out and took mine. "Two and three make five. You got yourself a deal, mister."

Jesse pushed the squeaky bike down the road like she had given cash to the Red Sox for Babe Ruth. Dickie and I rode slowly beside her, coasting on the rutted road.

"I've had my eye on this since he put it out last year," she said.

"Good things come to those who wait," Dickie said.

She looked back at me. "I'll pay you back when my mama's check comes."

"You don't have to."

She stopped in the road, her hair falling over her face. When she shook it away, I noticed her lips, red as a beet, though she wore no lipstick. She studied my face like she was about to say something important.

"There ain't enough money in the world to buy friends, Matt."

"I'm not trying to buy a friend. I'm just trying to be nice."

"Reckon there's enough money in the world to rent a friend?" Dickie said.

Jesse frowned and pushed on, cutting through a farmer's field and crossing the creek, winding up at Dickie's house. It wasn't really a house, it was an apartment over a garage that Dickie's mother rented. She was at work at the warehouse across the railroad tracks, but Dickie grabbed the handle and opened the door and invited us into his shop. Dickie's father had collected tools and hubcaps and every imaginable castaway nut and bolt, and Dickie was a natural at fixing things. He pulled out a crescent wrench and a flathead screwdriver and went to work. Dickie seemed at home with dirty hands.

"I didn't know your dad got his arm cut off," I said, trying to make conversation.

"There's a lot of things you don't know," Jesse said.

She didn't seem to want to talk about that or her sister. I tried a different route as Dickie fussed and fumed over the tires.

"Say, we're having a picnic at church tomorrow. My dad said I should invite you."

"Picnic?" Jesse said.

"Right after church. People are bringing lots of food. It's kind of a celebration of my dad coming here."

Dickie looked up. "He said to invite us?"

I nodded.

"Do we have to come to the service, or can we just show up for the food?" Jesse said.

"That wouldn't be right," Dickie said. "The food is the reward for sitting through the service. Mama and me go to the Holiness church when she's not working her second job. I don't know if she's working tomorrow or not."

"What church do you go to?" I asked Jesse.

"We used to go to the little white one down yonder," she said, pointing.

"Don't believe her," Dickie said. "She attends Lazy Butt Baptist. Just sits at home Sunday mornings and watches TV preachers."

Jesse gave him a glare, then asked me, "Is your daddy one of them preachers that smacks people in the head and makes them fall over? 'Cause if he is, I'd come to see it. That'd be food and entertainment."

"He's not the smack-you-in-the-head type," I said.

"More reserved?" she said. "The people stay to their seats and don't hop around?"

I nodded.

Jesse frowned. "Well, I don't believe in God."

"Of course you do," Dickie said. "Don't believe her, Matt."

"Why not?" I said to her.

"Preacher at the white church said if you didn't get baptized, you'd split hell wide-open. And he didn't mean you had to believe in God or Jesus. That wasn't enough. If you didn't get dunked in the water, you didn't make it, even if you was sincere in being sorry for your sins and all that. Even if you're laid up in the hospital, if they don't get you into the water, you'll burn. I give up on it."

"Her cousins go there," Dickie said. "That's the real reason she don't believe in God."

"I won't be coming to your church picnic," Jesse said matter-of-factly.

"You don't have to believe in God to go to the picnic," Dickie said. "You just have to believe in fried chicken and potato salad. And flies."

Jesse almost smiled at that.

Chapter 7

I sat in the parking lot of the Dogwood Food and Drug
trying to figure out which car was Jesse's.

There wasn't a spot in town that didn't spark vivid
images. The gas station on the other side of the grocery,
for instance, had been an Esso. They had changed the sign
to Exxon, but the inside remained the same. Dickie had
found a copy of the *Green Book* behind a shelf when we
went inside for a pop. The smell of gasoline and oil hung
heavy as he leafed through it. Underneath the title were the
words *Negro Traveler's Guide, 1964.*

"Bet you never had to use one of these," he said.

Dogwood Food and Drug had eventually run Blake's

out of business. It was evidence of the slow economic encroachment. Dogwood Feed and Implement still stood on its original site, but most farmers drove farther east to a supply store. There was also fear that bigger churches would siphon off members of other congregations with revivals or special speakers. My father believed that faith was meant to be lived where you did. It wasn't a spectator sport. As a child, I'd agreed with him.

I closed my eyes and listened to the birds preparing for their flight south. A train whistled and rolled under the overpass. Tires on pavement lulled me and I drifted off, a trickle of sweat dropping from my underarm. A soft, leaf-laden breeze blew through both of my open windows and I felt a sense of contentment, wanting to bottle these sounds and feelings and smells.

A week after stealing from Blake's store, Jesse had turned to me as we rode by the railroad tracks. We were searching for signs of her father's missing arm. She spat in her hand and held it out.

I looked at it with disdain and horror. "What are you doing?"

"Go on and shake," she said.

Not understanding the native ways and not wanting to offend, I held out a tentative hand and Jesse grabbed it. "There, you satisfied?"

"I don't know what you're doing," I said, wiping my hand on my shorts.

"Dickie and I talked. You was right about Old Man

Blake. We promise not to do it again. Cross our hearts and hope to die."

"Dickie said that too?"

"He said he never liked stealing. He did it so I wouldn't feel alone."

That made me smile.

She stared a hole through me. "A promise is a promise. I give my word, you can bank on it. No more stealing from Blake's or anywhere else."

"Okay," I said, looking at my hand. "Thank you."

Jesse curled her top lip, something that always reminded me of Elvis, and poked me in the chest. "But don't go trying to change me. What you see is what you get."

So many memories flooded now, the good and bad flowing together in a torrent until I opened my door and walked into the Food and Drug like Odysseus returning from battle.

A cashier at the front didn't look up. You had to take the long route by the deli to get to the meat department. I had worked here as a bagger in high school. I knew every aisle, every rat in the back room, and where the "mystery item" was that went on sale each Tuesday.

"Matt Plumley?" someone said to my right.

I turned toward the canned goods and Gwen Bailey smiled at me.

Gwen had been a bright bulb in our class. She had excelled at Latin, biology, and physics and everyone saw her as most likely to become a medical doctor. Her family faithfully attended our church until they had a run-in with Blackwood. I shook her hand and her mother waved from the canned corn.

"What are you doing here?" Gwen said. "I heard you were in Chicago."

"I'm back for a visit."

Life has a way of circling. While I had looked at Jesse as an unrequited love, Gwen had looked at me the same. She had played Emily Webb in the production of *Our Town*, opposite my George Gibbs. Backstage in rehearsals she had invited me to her house to run lines. She was having trouble keeping her scenes straight, she said, and I obliged, showing up on the appointed evening at the appointed time.

Gwen's parents were out and I could tell she wanted to do more than practice the play. She wore loose terry-cloth shorts that crept up when she sat on the couch. She'd extended her bare feet and stretched them like a cat, touching my leg.

Gwen was not a homely girl. In fact, she was quite pretty. She had been on the plump side in junior high, like I had been in my early teens—all that studying and little interest in sports had given her a full figure. Now she smiled and again I saw the difference money and orthodontia can make.

"Do you ever think of our school days? All the fun we had?"

I could think of them, but Gwen's days had been pool parties and majorettes and pizza after football games.

Compared with Jesse, hers was an easy life with an intact family and a paved road with college at the end.

"Are you finished with school?" I said, changing the subject.

"I finish grad school in December."

"Something in the medical field, I suppose?"

"Anesthesiology," she said.

"Bless you," I said.

She laughed. "Oh, I miss that quick wit of yours. You were always so funny." She touched my shoulder. "One of these days I'm going to get up to Chicago and see you in a play."

I looked behind me at the meat counter, but there was no one there. "I haven't exactly broken into the big time. In fact, I'm mostly counseling young kids—"

"You were always such a success. Do you have a girl-friend up there?"

I winced but tried to hide it. "Still looking, I guess."

Someone pushed a cart past us and we moved closer to the stewed tomatoes.

"'Does anyone ever realize life while they live it . . . ?' Do you remember that from *Our Town*?"

I nodded.

"'Every, every minute?'"

I pulled the dialogue from memory. 'No. Saints and poets maybe . . . they do some.'" I said the line as a good-bye.

Gwen smiled sadly. "It's a shame about us. We would have been good together. Maybe we still can be."

I thought of some quick-witted joke about being married to an anesthesiologist, that you never had to worry about insomnia, but I held back. It was my quick wit that she loved.

"It was good seeing you again, Gwen."

She followed her mother toward checkout and I glanced behind me at the bloody meat counter. Gwen's life had been high heels and dance shoes and I couldn't help comparing her to Jesse's rough feet. Gwen waved from the front of the aisle and I turned to the back of the store.

The meat counter was empty but I noticed a fresh chicken on a wooden slab with a cleaver next to it. Dexter Crowley, a boy two years ahead of me in school, pushed a load of laundry detergent toward a far aisle and stopped.

"Matt Plumley," he said, sticking out a rough hand.

Dexter had the frame of a football player but not much coordination. He was all arms and gangling legs and a blank stare that felt like menace to opposing teams but was more Dexter trying to remember who he was supposed to block.

I shook his hand and he wiped his nose with his sleeve. "What are you doing here?"

"I'm back for a few days. Is Jesse working today?"

His mouth was open as he glanced at the counter. "Yeah, she was there a minute ago. She works all this week except for Saturday. Did you know she's getting married?"

"I heard."

"First time I heard it, I thought they was funnin' me. But she showed me the ring and said it was true. And Earl, he comes in here—why, there's Verle now."

Verle Turley was cut from the same cloth as his brother, and if there had been a sound track for his approach, it would have been a cross between the banjo from *Deliverance* and the strings in *Jaws*. He walked up to Dexter with a John Deere hat pulled low.

"Verle, you remember Matt Plumley, don't you? He was in those plays at school." He turned back to me. "You know, the one I remember was when you played that guy who sees the ghosts at Christmas. Remember that?"

I nodded as Verle gave me a slack-jawed stare. He crossed his arms and planted his logger boots. "I didn't know you was here." His voice was as flat as a skipping rock.

"I didn't know I had to file a report."

After an uncomfortable silence, Dexter threw back his head and laughed. He was slow but exuberant. "That's a good one, Matt."

"When I tell Earl you was in here, he's not going to be happy," Verle said.

"I doubt I'm as committed to his happiness as you are."

Verle drew a little closer, and judging from the bulge in his lower lip, he had only a couple of minutes before he needed to spit. "I'm watching you, Plumley."

"I see that," I said, matching his tone.

I turned and took one more look at the empty meat department. I didn't want to put her in the middle. Not now.

"Nice seeing you again, Dexter," I said, clapping his shoulder.

I went back to the car and drove through the parking lot to where Dumpsters lined the alley and the loading dock sat empty. I waited a few minutes, hoping she might appear behind the plastic liners over the door. When she didn't, I drove to my parents' house and slipped inside without notice. I closed the door to my room and fell into bed still dressed, burrowing my head into the pillow.

Chapter 8

The church picnic was not just the introduction of the new
pastor but a social affair rivaling a state dinner at the White
House. Instead of fine china and sterling, we had paper
plates and plastic forks. Instead of steak and lobster, we ate
freshly cut watermelon and coleslaw by the gallon along
with burgers and hot dogs. The weight of the potato salad
made the folding tables wobble.

The elders had canceled Sunday school that morning,
the only time that would happen in my days there, with
the exception of one major snowfall and a bitterly cold
day in 1978 when the downstairs pipes burst. My father
accompanied the elders to the platform and sat behind the

pulpit while my mother played the piano. The organist was a teenage boy not much older than me who tried valiantly to keep up.

On Sundays, all the Massey Ferguson and John Deere hats came off at the door, and the men who had strong leanings toward unions and political platforms politely put aside their differences and mingled, though it was interesting to walk through the parking lot and see the ratio of Nixon to McGovern bumper stickers. Older women wore dresses and hose and smelled of sickly sweet perfume. Their hair was usually up, while younger women wore theirs down, cascading to the shoulders of their modest dresses. Boys wore white T-shirts under their button-ups and there was a smattering of ties, but those boys usually stretched at their collars throughout the service. You could tell the haves and have-nots from pants and shoes. Well-fitting pants meant you were in the upper echelon. High-water pants meant it had been a while since you had enough money for new. Men who owned a pair of wing-tip oxfords were on one end of the economic scale, while at the other were those with freshly hosed work boots. Men smelled of tobacco, peppermint, and shoe polish.

"Matt, you're going to see people in church and school who don't have much," my mother had said that morning before we left the house. "Don't ever look down on anyone and never laugh at anybody's clothes. That's the cruelest thing you can do."

I could think of a few things more cruel, but her point was well-taken. I wondered if she was speaking from experience. She and my father had grown up in the Depression and I had heard stories about how hard things had been.

"Now I want you to look for Gwen Bailey," my mother said. "She's real smart. Loves to read, just like you. And she's real pretty."

The prospect of being set up made me sweat. I agreed I would look for her, but inside, I was hoping I wouldn't have to interact. I was always nervous around girls, another reason I liked Jesse. I could be myself around her.

"Is Mawmaw coming?"

"She doesn't feel comfortable in church with the medication she's on."

"You want me to keep her company?"

She pulled my tie tight. "Get in the car, Matt."

Red, spine-worn hymnals populated the pew back in front of me. I sat alone in the third row, feeling every eye of the congregation and tugging at my collar. My mother had insisted I have a haircut, so my father buzzed me the day before and stray hairs scratched. The church had not invested in air-conditioning, so the windows were open and the large ceiling fans were working overtime. They did little to quell the heat. As a heavy child, I was used to sweating even in winter. But sweating outside, riding your bike with the wind in your face, was different from sweating in your Sunday best.

The song leader, Gerald Grassley, was a middle-aged man with a mustache between a prominent nose and jutting chin. He had a car and lawn mower repair shop in Dogwood that gave free oil changes to widows. Though he tried to clean them, his fingernails were always a shade of black and he wore extra Brut to cover up the smell of ether and gasoline that seemed to leak through his pores.

Gerald's arm rose and fell the same way to any song he led, no matter the time signature. He had a nasal twang when he spoke and sang, like a younger Grandpa Jones, but his pitch wasn't bad and he seemed to enjoy song leading. His job was to get everybody started at the same place and everybody stopped when the song was over, but whatever happened in the middle was up to God and the congregation.

To his right were empty choir chairs in a loft section beside the pulpit. Those would be filled once my mother recruited eligible singers. Behind was the baptistery, a cutout section in the knotty pine walls that looked like an oversize window flanked by velvet curtains. There was a mural on the wall behind it painted by an art teacher from a nearby high school. It was a peaceful scene of trees and hills, and a stream flowed from top to bottom, ending in the baptismal waters. Something was off in the scale, though, because the trees in the foreground were smaller than those on the hills and the sparrow that sat on the limb of a sycamore looked the size of a crow. When you stared at it long enough, you got vertigo.

I peeked over my shoulder to see if Jesse and Dickie might have arrived, but every head turned toward me, including that of a girl with a pink ribbon in her hair and a dress suitable for Easter Sunday. That had to be Gwen.

I stared at the bulletin, scanning the names of church leaders. The order of service was printed on a mimeograph machine that made every *e* on the page look like an *o* with a faint, crooked line through it. The page had been printed crooked, so you had to hold it at an angle. After the words *Introduction of Now Pastor*, the name *Basil Blackwood* was printed.

Even with the uneven printing I recognized the man who owned the horse. My heart sank and I scooted down in the seat as he stepped to the pulpit.

"As you all know, we've gone and hired a new shepherd. Calvin Plumley grew up here, just down the road from me. He comes from a good family. A little mistaken in their politics, of course."

The congregation gave a reserved laugh.

"He has two children, one still in the nest," Mr. Blackwood said. "And his wife, Ramona, has graciously agreed to accompany us each week and get the choir started again. Anybody who wants to be in the choir, be here at five o'clock tonight before the evening service."

My mother stood at the piano and nodded, then lifted a hand toward me to stand. I was far down in the pew, trying to avoid the gaze of the man in the pulpit, but when my mother didn't relent, I stood. I lost my balance and grabbed the pew in front of me, nearly rocking it over. It banged with a terrific crack and I waved as I sat. The girl with the ribbon smiled.

Mr. Blackwood stared at me as if the abomination of desolation had just entered the Temple.

"We've made it clear the reason we're bringing in Plumley is to get us on track. We need the Word of God. What we have in this country is not the fear of the Lord, and that's what we sorely need. I'm hoping we'll hear messages about the great and terrible Day of the Lord. And the lake of fire God is preparing. And I'm expecting there to be some baptisms back there." Blackwood pointed a thumb behind him. "It's been a dry spell."

My stomach growled, half from hunger and half from nervousness for my father. I hadn't considered the people's expectations of him. He had preached in churches near Pittsburgh, but there's a difference between speaking once and walking out the door and having to live with those you're speaking to.

"Now we don't usually do this in the Lord's house, but before we hear him speak and commission him, I think it's appropriate to welcome our new pastor with a round of applause."

People clapped work-worn hands and my mother slipped into the pew beside me. I felt comforted by her presence. My father stood and put his Bible on the pulpit. I held my breath, hoping he would say something that disarmed Mr. Blackwood and appeased the skeptics.

He thanked them for giving him the opportunity and thanked God for leading us to Dogwood. "After all the things us Plumley boys got into as kids, I'm surprised you let me in the church, let alone called me as pastor."

There was polite laughter, though Mr. Blackwood frowned. My father's next words made me think the man might storm the pulpit and pull back their call.

"Now I'm all for preaching the Day of the Lord, the lake of fire, hell, eternal punishment, and the four horsemen of the Apocalypse. And a helping of weeping and gnashing of teeth, to boot. The truth is the truth. You don't hide that under a bushel. But I learned in seminary that if you preach the whole counsel of God's Word, you can never go wrong. So we're going one book at a time, verse by verse, and we're going to hit the Day of the Lord when it gets here. What I think you'll find is that there's more about the love and grace and mercy of God than there is hellfire and brimstone. Judgment is coming—God would have to apologize to Sodom and Gomorrah if he didn't judge us. But Jesus said that he would build his church and the gates of hell would not prevail against it. I believe that, and I want to be part of that. Do you?"

"Amen!" a few people said.

"So today, open to John, chapter one, verse one."

I associate the sound of flipping onionskin with every Sunday and Wednesday night of my youth.

"'In the beginning was the Word, and the Word was with God, and the Word was God.'"

My father preached well and seemed to hold the congregation's attention despite the few references to Greek words and Old Testament concepts. My mind turned toward the potato salad and Jesse. I looked at Mr. Blackwood, his jaw set as he listened, and wondered what had happened to the last pastor.

After the message, the elders rose and gathered around my father, put their hands on his shoulders, and prayed. The sound system, which was tinny and only came through one speaker, began to squeal as the man working the sound tried to pick up the prayers. When it was over, Mr. Blackwood dismissed the ladies to go to the kitchen. Several men left to get the coals going on the barbecues. My shirt was drenched by the end of the service and I couldn't wait to get my tie off.

My mother finished her postlude and scurried to the back while men congregated around my father, shaking hands and swapping stories. I heard someone say, "I remember when you and your brother went coon hunting on my daddy's property."

I did not see the man's approach or I might have run, but when I looked up, Mr. Blackwood leaned over the pew in front of me, his face inches from mine.

"I recognize you," he said, his voice emotionless. He said the word *recognize* without the *g—reckonize*. His eyes locked on me like lasers.

"Yes, sir," I said, a ball of sweat rolling down my neck.

"Am I going to have to speak to your daddy about you trespassing on my property?"

I wanted to tell him I was only trying to help his horse, but I said, "No, sir."

"Then we'll keep this between us. And don't let it happen again, you hear?"

"Yes, sir."

I quickly made my way out the back door into fresh air. Men gathered in the shade of a weeping willow. The women had set out covered dishes on folding tables. Somehow they had coordinated things so that there weren't too many bean casseroles or pasta salads. I saw a dish at the end, set off by itself, that looked a little disgusting and smelled like somebody had died. I later learned it was called ramps and that it was a delicacy in that neck of the woods. It was the only dish I never tried.

A circular table held desserts that looked like the bread of angels. Frosted pound cakes, walnut-filled brownies, cherry pies, apple pies, pecan and lemon meringue. I wanted to grab one of everything on the table, but as a heavy child you quickly learn that people judge how high you pile your plate. Instead, you pick opportunities to secretly indulge.

"Matt, honey, why don't you go see what the others are doing?" my mother said, gently prodding me away from the food.

Several boys were in a heated game of basketball at the sagging hoop on a dead walnut tree, and I wandered over, hands in my pockets. They would bounce the ball on the uneven ground and pick it up after every dribble. A wiry redheaded boy with a complexion that seemed too light, like Edgar Winter, made a shot and gave a teammate a high five.

"What did the Reds do last night?" someone said.

"Got rained out in Montreal."

They were bantering about their favorite team when a

big-boned girl came up beside me. She had the same red hair and light complexion as the boy playing basketball. She stared at me with abject fascination, then pulled at her dress, which could not hide her large frame or budding femininity. Her hair was short and she had the first signs of acne. Her upper lip didn't reach all the way to the lower one, so she had the countenance of a chipmunk.

"You the preacher's boy?" she said.

I introduced myself, holding out a hand. She took it daintily, like she wasn't sure how to respond, and dipped her head in a curtsy like I was royalty. "I'm Shur-uhl," she said. Later I learned that this was short for Shirley and her last name was Turley, and I immediately felt both sorrow for her and contempt for her parents. I also learned that Shirl's father, Burl, had been a leader in the church but had died several years earlier and that the Turleys and Blackwoods were cousins and stuck closer than worms in a can.

"I'm not going to be eatin' anything at the picnic," Shirl said.

I wasn't sure why she would offer such personal information, but I couldn't think of anything to say but "Why not?"

"Upset stomach. Mommy made me all the whipped cream I could eat last night. Once you get started, you can't stop."

I nodded.

"Earl?" Shirl shouted toward the gaggle. The redheaded kid picked up his dribble. "This here is the preacher's boy. You ought to let him play."

Earl walked toward me with the basketball tucked under his arm. When he spoke, it sounded like some country singer I had heard who whined his songs. "You gotta get somebody else if you want to play. Keep the sides even."

"He don't know nobody," Shirl said. "How's he gonna get somebody to play?"

"Wait till somebody shows up," Earl said.

"Fine," she said, spitting the word. "I'll be on their side, Matt. You be on Earl's."

"No girls!" a smaller redheaded boy said. It was the younger Turley, Verle, who hadn't scampered clear of the family rhyme scheme.

"That ain't fair," Shirl said. And there began a verbal back-and-forth I sensed might become an all-out war between the sexes.

Another boy pointed toward the road and yelled, "What are they doing here?" He said *they* like it was a curse word.

"It's the coon and that Woods girl," Verle said.

"He's only half-coon," Shirl said.

"Half is bad enough," Earl said. "Besides, he looks full-blooded to me."

At the first sight of my friends, I ran toward the road waving, elated. I was trying to influence those behind me toward a little diversity and acceptance. Jesse was on her bike and had something strapped to the back. As she got closer, I saw Daisy's legs dangling from a basket. Her legs bounced and she had a thumb in her mouth, her head bobbing.

"Dickie," I called, "come on, we need another player!"

Jesse was out of breath, pulling up the hill to the parking lot and scanning the grounds like an explorer fearing danger in the untouched wilderness. She stopped and put dilapidated flip-flops on the gravel. They looked like she had found them in someone's trash. Dickie looked skeptical of the gathering.

"Has the picnic started?" Jesse said.

"They're cooking the burgers and hot dogs now," I said. "Won't be long. Come on, I'll introduce you to my mom. And you can get a drink for Daisy."

"We don't allow coons around here," Earl said behind me.

"Shut your mouth, Turley," Jesse said. I could tell there was history here. History lessons came quick in Dogwood.

Shirl lumbered off. I wasn't sure if she was afraid of the turning tide or had heard someone open a tub of Dream Whip.

Earl stepped forward and glared at Jesse. "Come shut it yourself. And why don't you let the coon fight his own battles?"

"We don't have to play basketball," I said, my voice trembling. There had to be some way to defuse the situation. "Dickie, come on, let's just go over to the—"

"We don't allow skanks, either," another boy said, interrupting me. He had just walked up and was taller than the others and a little older, a deeper voice. Something in his face looked familiar.

I didn't understand the word *skank*, but I knew by the tone and Jesse's reaction that it was not a term of endearment. I had heard the word *coon* used for black people back in Pittsburgh, but my parents said only people of low intelligence and character used that term or the *n* word for "colored people." When I asked them why only people with black skin were considered "colored," they didn't have a good answer.

"Don't waste your energy on them, Jesse," Dickie said. "Let's get out of here."

"I'm not going nowhere," Jesse said, stepping off the bike and staring past the bigger boy to Earl.

"Nice bike, Jesse," Verle Turley said from a distance. "What dead coon did you steal it from?"

Jesse ignored him and motioned for me to come closer and grab the handlebars. "Hold this for me, Matt."

Earl took a step backward and grew paler, if that were possible. I wondered if he'd been through a tussle with Jesse before.

"Why don't you two get out of here," the bigger boy said. "Before you get yourself in a world of hurt."

"You tell them, Gentry," someone said.

I held up a hand. "I agree with Gentry. Let's calm down."

"Earl needs to be taught a lesson," Jesse said, her voice low and gravelly.

"And what lesson is that?" Earl said, seeming emboldened by Gentry's support.

"That you don't call people names if you're not ready to take responsibility for the name-callin'."

"Okay," Earl said, stepping forward. "Here you go, preacher boy. Hold this."

He threw the ball hard and I wasn't expecting it. Even if I had gotten my hands up, it would have done little good. The heavy, dusty ball hit me squarely in the nose and I fell back, closing my eyes and seeing stars. The bike fell, and I heard yelling. Daisy cried. I sat up. Ketchup on my tie and dress shirt. I touched my nose and pulled away a handful. It wasn't ketchup.

Dust flew, along with angry shouts and curses. I wanted to jump into the fray, but I was so stunned by the ball and the geyser that was my nose, all I could do was go to Daisy. Dickie had pulled her up and was dusting her off. He shouted over his shoulder for Jesse.

Gentry and Earl were in the middle and Jesse's bare feet stuck out from the pack, her flip-flops a memory. I heard screams of pain from the boys but Jesse wasn't talking, just grunting and struggling in the scrum.

Shirl returned with several adults, one of them Mr. Blackwood. When he pulled Gentry out of the heap, I saw the resemblance.

"She started it!" Gentry yelled to his dad. "I was just trying to help Earl not get killed."

"Jesse's just like her daddy!" another boy yelled.

Earl came up for air holding scratches on his face. Claw marks, more like it. Jesse was the last one up and her hair was dirty and her T-shirt torn. She still had a look of determination, like she had given more than she'd taken and wasn't finished.

"What happened here?" my dad said, running up.

My mother arrived with a bag of ice, somehow

anticipating that someone would need it, and put it to my nose. The women of the church were always the first to see trouble. Shirl had been the one to run for help. My mother brought ice.

"They started it, Preacher," Earl said.

"They came riding up here calling us names," Gentry said. "And taking the Lord's name in vain, too."

"That ain't true," Jesse said, spitting some blood in the dirt beside her and hugging Daisy. "We was invited."

"Who would invite the two of you?" Gentry said.

Jesse glanced at me, then back at Gentry. "Don't matter. A church is supposed to welcome people, no matter who they are."

"You all get out of here now," Mr. Blackwood said to the gathering. "Show's over."

Daisy cried and Jesse held her. I wanted to say something, wanted to speak up and tell what really happened, but battle lines had been drawn and I felt more comfortable in the demilitarized zone.

"As for you," Mr. Blackwood said to Jesse, "take your sister and the half-breed and don't come back."

My mother whispered in my ear, "Come on over to the kitchen and we'll wash you up. What in the world happened?"

Dickie got on his bike and Jesse tried to get Daisy into the metal basket, but it had bent when the bike fell and there wasn't room.

"I'm hungry," Daisy whined to Jesse. "You said we'd get something to eat."

"We'll get something when we get home," Jesse said, wiping blood from the corner of her mouth.

My mother went over to the bicycles and introduced herself. "You must be Jesse and Dickie. Matt told me about you."

They looked at me, then back at her.

"And this is Daisy Grace?" my mother said.

"Yes, ma'am," Jesse said. "She's three."

"Well, look at how pretty you are. Now y'all should stay for lunch. We have plenty."

Jesse looked at Gentry and Earl walking away and shook her head. "We ain't wanted here, ma'am."

"This is a celebration. Everybody in the community was invited."

"We just came to say hey to Matt," Dickie said. "Since we didn't come to the service, we shouldn't eat anything."

"Nonsense. You don't have to do anything to deserve a picnic."

"We have to be going," Jesse said, getting on her bike.

"I'm hungry," Daisy whined.

My mother turned and there was a pained look on her face. "Wait just a minute."

My father put his hand on my shoulder and got out his good white handkerchief and told me to hold it against my nose. "Keep your head back," he said. "And hold that ice right here." He didn't ask what happened.

My mother returned with three paper bags that hung with weight. "There's a hot dog and hamburger for each of you," she said. Her voice sounded polite and friendly, but there was a strain in it. "I wrapped them up. I would have put some potato salad in, but it would have gotten too messy." She leaned close to Daisy. "There's some dessert in there, too. And a cold can of pop."

"Thank you, ma'am," Jesse said.

"That's nice of you, Mrs. Plumley," Dickie said.

"You be careful with that hot dog with her," my mother said to Jesse. "It's easy to choke if she doesn't chew it good."

"I knew a guy that choked on a hot dog once," Dickie said, but he didn't finish the story.

Daisy opened her paper bag and looked inside like she was beholding the Holy of Holies.

"If y'all change your mind, you can come back and have some more, okay?"

"Yes, ma'am," Jesse said. "But we better be going."

Mr. Blackwood yelled in the distance and all the kids went running. My dad and mom walked toward the picnic hastily, as well, leaving me with my friends.

"Nice church you got here," Jesse said. "Some places only make visitors stand up."

Dickie smiled. "Does your daddy hold people under extra long when he baptizes them?"

"I'm sorry they said those things. I don't understand why they'd do that."

"You'll understand directly," Jesse said with a frown. "You okay?"

Her compassion moved me and I nodded, fighting off the tears. She was the one who had taken the punches and pulled hair and she was asking about me.

They started to pedal off and I called after them, "Hang on!" I sounded like Rudolph with the black nose shoved over my red one. "The burgers and hot dogs are going to get cold if you don't eat now."

"In this heat?" Jesse said. "They'll probably get warmer."

"Yeah, but if you went over on the front steps of the church, in the shade, we could eat together. We don't have to go to the picnic."

"I'm hungry," Daisy whined again. She opened her bag and stuck a grubby hand inside.

"Leave that alone," Jesse said. She looked back at me, then at the church. "I guess it wouldn't do no harm to just sit awhile. Then we'll head home."

I smiled, still pressing the handkerchief to my nose. I led the three to the concrete steps, and they put their bikes down and opened their bags and ate like they had missed several meals. Daisy struggled to open her can of root beer, so I took it from her and popped the top, and it bubbled up and ran down the side.

"You guys want anything else?" I said. "I can get some deviled eggs or a piece of chicken. Macaroni salad?"

"This is fine," Jesse said. "If she eats too much, she'll get sick." She took the last bite of hamburger and chewed it.

"What about some watermelon?" I said.

Dickie's eyes widened. "Yeah, I'll take some melon."

Before I could leave, Jesse said, "Your mama is real nice."

"Yeah," Dickie agreed. "If she'd start a church, I'd come Sundays and Wednesday nights."

"She plays the piano," I said, trying to think of something to say.

"She give lessons?" Jesse said.

"Not yet. I mean, she used to. Back in Pittsburgh."

"How much they cost?" Jesse said.

"I don't know. A few dollars a lesson, maybe?"

She scowled. "Do you play?"

"She was teaching me but I wanted somebody not related. She's been looking for someone—"

"What do we have here?" a voice said behind me. Gentry Blackwood came around the corner holding a watermelon rind. I glanced above him at a yellow jacket's nest that had been built in the eave of the roof. A few of them buzzed around the nest.

"Don't your mama know it's not good to feed strays?" Gentry said to me. "Feed 'em once and they'll keep coming back." He spat a black seed that landed near Dickie's foot. Daisy dug in her bag for her dessert and came out with a handful of brownie.

"If you feed a coon, he'll just dig around in your trash at night," Gentry said.

"What's your problem, Gentry?" Jesse said. "Why don't you mind your own business?"

"A coon and a skank at my dad's church is my business."

Jesse looked at me. "I thought *your* dad was the pastor."

"My dad runs this church and he already told you to leave," Gentry said. "So you best be getting out of here before we make you. And learn your lesson, Plumley. Don't go feedin' the strays. This is Dogwood trash."

Something inside took over. Though I was scared of Gentry, I was emboldened by new friends. I could never win a fistfight with him, but I could use words.

"I've been taught that people who call others names are the ones who have the worst arguments."

Gentry squinted at me like I was a cootie. "What did you say?"

"He didn't stutter," Jesse said.

"If you can't win an argument, you attack people with names. You call a person *coon* or *skank* or *trash*. That means the bully doesn't have the mental acuity to have real dialogue."

Gentry balled one hand into a fist, the other holding the rind.

"He said you don't have the brains to really fight," Dickie said. "All you got is . . ."

"Epithets," I said. "It's an adjective used for people, usually to put them down. But sometimes the epithets turn into nouns when people accept them."

Jesse squashed her paper bag. "You know what a noun is, don't you, Gentry? *Trash* is a noun, ain't it, Matt?"

"Absolutely. Person, place, or thing."

"You three are crazy," Gentry said, tossing the rind at Dickie. Dickie blocked it with his foot and let it fall harmlessly.

Gentry pointed a finger at me. "My daddy's going to hear about this. Which means your daddy is going to tan your hide."

"Is *tan* a verb?" Jesse said.

"It can be a verb or a noun," I said. "*Tan your hide* means to hit a person hard enough to change the color of their skin. But a farmer gets a tan in the summer, and that's a noun."

"You have to go easy on him, Matt," Jesse said. "He was held back so many times they gave him a permanent desk in second grade."

"Yeah," Dickie said. "He got out of the spelling bee on the word *cat*."

"Two years in a row," Jesse said.

"You think you're funny," Gentry said to Jesse. "You're not going to be laughing when my dad gets through with that sorry farm of yours."

"What's my farm got to do with the price of watermelon in China?" Jesse said, and Dickie and I both laughed.

Gentry walked away and I had a sick feeling mixed with a feeling of victory.

"You had enough?" Jesse said to Dickie.

"I'd like some watermelon, but I think we've overstayed our welcome. By about a half hour."

Daisy wanted to take her bag with her and Jesse didn't argue. I took the rind and the smashed bags of my friends and watched them ride away. When I turned from tossing the trash in a fifty-gallon drum, Mr. Blackwood and Gentry were both watching me.

Chapter 9

JUNE 1972

My father came into my room Sunday night after the picnic. My nose was swollen and my eyes puffy.

"Rough day at church today," he said.

"Yeah. There's some mean kids there."

"I noticed. I thought coming back here would take the ugliness away."

"Ugly happens all over, I guess."

He nodded. "Matt, about Jesse and Dickie."

I sensed something coming and sat up. There was a shadow behind him at the door. "What about them?"

"It's important to get off on the right foot. To choose your friends wisely. I'm not sure those two are the best."

"Did Old Man Blackwood say something to you?"

"Don't call him that. Basil is an elder and deserves our respect."

"Yes, sir."

"This has nothing to do with him. This is about you."

"I think I can be a good influence."

"Say again?"

"Jesse's not a Christian. At least, she says she's not. And Dickie is like . . . one of the least of these, you know?"

He squinted at me.

"You're always talking about serving the least of these."

"There's a difference between serving and following. You can lead people toward the truth or you can go over the cliff." He adjusted his glasses. "Mr. Blake told me what happened in his store."

This was one of the drawbacks of a small town. And I was quickly learning why they said a pastor's family lived in a fishbowl.

"They promised never to steal again," I said. "Jesse spit on it and crossed her heart and hoped to die. You can't get more repentant than that."

My father stifled a smile and sat on my bed. There were lines in his face, here in the darkness of my room, that I had never noticed. "Son, there are things you don't know about Jesse and her family. Things about their history."

"I don't care about history. I'm looking for friends and I found a couple of good ones."

My mother finally walked inside. "Matt, honey, we need to draw some lines. Set boundaries. You're not going to be spending the whole summer with those two traipsing all over the hills and stealing candy."

"I just told Dad they promised not to do that again."

"I won't have you spending your own money on bikes for the indigent population."

I stared at her, wondering how in the world she could have known about Jesse's bike. "She's going to pay me back as soon as her mother gets her check."

My dad studied the floor. My mom crossed her arms. Both were disappointed I was fighting. Finally she spoke.

"I'm glad you're adjusting. I know this is not easy, since we're not in the new house and living at your grandmother's is not ideal. But your father and I think it's better to structure your time so you don't have as much—"

"So I don't have free time to spend with Dickie and Jesse," I said. I grabbed my nose for sympathy.

"We've found a piano teacher," my father said.

"A piano teacher?" I said, incredulous. "A piano teacher is going to fix this?"

"You said you didn't want me to teach you and I understand that," my mother said, staring daggers. At night, when she got tired, the fangs came out. "And we agreed we would find you a different teacher."

"Mrs. McCormick has taught music for years," my father said. "She's glad to take you on."

A trickle ran down one nostril. I asked for something to catch the blood and my father brought a toilet paper roll from the bathroom. I unwrapped a few thin pieces and held the wad against my nose.

"Mom, it's summer. I'm supposed to have fun."

"Life's not all fun and games," she said quickly as if trying to comfort herself with the truth.

My dad turned to her. "This is a big adjustment. I think the piano lessons on Wednesdays and the church commitments will be enough structure, along with chores."

"And what about when his friends come knocking? You know they'll come, Cal. First thing in the morning. Late at night. Those kids are loose laundry."

"I can tell them not to come too early," I said. "They'll listen."

My mom shook her head.

"Why were you so nice to them, then?" I said. "Was that an act? Why did you give them food and tell them to come to the church picnic if you don't like them?"

"It's not that I don't like them. I feel sorry for them. I can only imagine what those girls have been through. It breaks my heart to see how they live. I know you don't understand but—"

"I do understand. You don't want me associating with a coon and a skank."

My mother's mouth dropped. "Matt Plumley."

"That's what the church kids called them. Are *those* the kids you want to influence me?"

"I will not have you talk that way," my mother said.

My father held up a hand. "That's enough. I see Matt's point. Sometimes Christians are hard to get along with. And I'm sorry you had to hear those ugly words." He rubbed his hands on his trousers, looking over at my baseball glove on the bed. I thought I could tell who he was thinking about.

"Let's just take this a day at a time," he said to my mother.

"Does that mean I can still be friends with them?"

He stood and glanced at my nightstand. I had been reading a dog-eared copy of *The Old Man and the Sea* that I found on a bookshelf in the living room. "It means you will get on your bike tomorrow and ride to the library. I want you to keep up on your reading. If Dickie and Jesse want to tag along, fine. And I want you reading something good."

"They can show me where it is," I said, a little hope in my voice.

He nodded and my mother touched my foot and slipped out of the room. My father tousled my hair and forced a smile. Then he leaned down. "I heard the Pirates beat the Dodgers. Won the series. Which is good for the Reds."

I couldn't hold back a smile. "Can we still see them when they come to Cincinnati?"

"We'll see."

"I don't like to read," Jesse said as we rode to the library the next day. "I never was no good at it."

"You *never were* good at it," I said.

"How would you know?" she said.

"He's correcting your grammar," Dickie said.

"He don't know my grammar. She died a long time ago."

Dickie laughed.

"Fine, I never were good at it."

Dickie laughed harder.

"Why do you want to go to the lie-berry?" Jesse said. "That's not what summers are for."

"Library," I said.

"You gonna correct everything I say? Fine, *library*. Satisfied?"

I smiled. "If you learn to read, you can do anything. Books will take you places you've never been. I was just reading Hemingway about an old man taken out to sea by a big fish. And there's baseball in it. He talks about the Yankees and DiMaggio."

"Who in the world is DiMaggio?" Jesse said.

"Does it talk about Jackie Robinson?" Dickie said.

"I don't think so, but I can find you another book that does."

"I'd rather go fishin' than to the *library*," Jesse said, accentuating the last word's correct pronunciation again. "At least you can eat if you catch something."

"Fine, we'll go fishing after we get some books."

One of the first things my mother had done after settling in was get library cards. I carried mine in my wallet as one of my means of identification. That and the NRA membership my uncle Willy had given me that came with a magazine I received each month.

The Dogwood library was a sorry little building with flooring much like Blake's store. I would have missed it entirely if Jesse and Dickie hadn't pointed it out. It was tucked in between the florist and the funeral home.

Dickie laughed when he noticed the first *r* was missing from the word painted on the front door. "Maybe that's why Jesse said it wrong."

Inside, the musty smell of old books and the quiet made something come alive in me. Ceiling fans blew knowledge and dust bunnies around the room. Just the aroma of those pages and the promise of words showed there was hope for even this tiny town.

"With this library card, we can go anywhere we want. On the sea with Moby Dick, to a deserted island with Robinson Crusoe—"

"Can it take us to Gilligan's island?" Jesse said.

The librarian behind the counter held an arthritic finger to her lips. "Shh. This is a library."

Jesse whispered to me, "It is? I thought it was the A&P."

Dickie chuckled and I turned red trying to hold in the laughter, but the more you try to hold something in, the harder it gets. I ducked into the stacks and some gas escaped with a noise that reverberated off the walls and I rushed to the bathroom. Jesse and Dickie never let me live that down. All they had to do was threaten to tell about making noise in the library to shut me up.

I returned to find them and the librarian in the fiction section. She was a thin, older woman whose earrings looked bigger than she was. Her hair was as white as flour and she wore a shawl that covered spindly arms. That she was cold in the heat and humidity of June made me feel sorry for her.

"I will not have you disturbing library patrons," she said, her voice deep and clipped. Her dentures clicked against her gums and her lower jaw jutted. She wore glasses secured to her head by a thin chain around her neck.

Jesse looked around and said politely, "We're the only ones here, ma'am."

"It doesn't matter," the woman whispered, narrowing her gaze. "You enter a library quietly, you stay quiet, and you leave quietly. This is a sacred place of learning. A library is a privilege, not a right."

"We're sorry, ma'am," Dickie said. "We only learned how to pronounce the name of the building this morning."

She glared at him, then turned to me. "I suggest you get what you need and leave. What were you looking for?"

"I'm looking for something good to read to my friends," I said.

"Read to us?" Jesse said.

"Can you recommend something?" I said to the librarian.

She scowled and looked at the stacks. She paused around the L/M section and turned back to me. "How old are you?"

"I'll be fourteen in a couple of weeks," I said.

"Your birthday's coming up?" Dickie said. "We'll have to have a party."

"We'll have to invite all the kids from church to play basketball and call people names," Jesse said. "We can play pin the tail on the preacher's kid."

The woman turned back to the shelf and pulled a book

down. "Have you ever read this?" She held out a copy of *To Kill a Mockingbird*.

"I seen the last part of that movie on TV," Jesse said. "The little girl dresses up like a ham, doesn't she?"

"I saw the movie too, but I've never read the book," I said.

The librarian looked at me, then at Dickie, weighing something in her gaze. "I think you're probably ready. Them, too."

She handed it to me and I opened the cover and saw the names of those who had checked it out before me. It was an original copy published in 1960.

"So we've got a hunting book now," Dickie said. "All we need is one about fishing and we're good."

"It's not a hunting book," I said. "It's fiction."

"What's it about?" Dickie said.

"It's about the South and a man who's accused of something . . ." I didn't want to give away too much. "You'll see."

I took the book to the front desk, where the librarian took out a card. I signed my name and handed it back, along with my library card. She stamped the book with the due date and did the same next to my name on the card before filing it in a drawer.

The woman looked at my friends. "Do you two have library cards?"

They shook their heads.

"Everyone should have one. This is a gateway to learning. Take advantage of this."

"Yes, ma'am," Jesse said.

"You got any books in here about the Mothman?" Dickie said. "Or UFOs?"

She nodded. "Come back after you finish that and I'll find some."

The three of us walked out with our treasure. Jesse let me put the book in her basket as we rode to Dickie's house and dug for worms by the shady side of the yard. They lifted rotting wood and flat rocks until we had enough. Dickie complained that we didn't have night crawlers and that we wouldn't catch any bass with small worms, and I had to admit I didn't know what a night crawler was.

"So you don't know everything?" Jesse said.

"There's a lot I don't know."

"Maybe you can check out *To Catch a Night Crawler* next week," Dickie said.

"I don't mind being read to, but I don't like to read," Jesse said. "Makes me nervous."

"How's that?"

"I remember in first grade reading about Dick and Jane and Spot and it never made no sense. They did a lot of running around but they never got anywhere. And then in second grade they put you in a reading group and you had to go around and read a paragraph and I always tripped on the words."

"The worst was the reading machine," Dickie said. "Remember when Mrs. Edwards got that thing out?"

"My lands, I wanted to throw up every day of second grade."

I asked what a reading machine was and the two were surprised I had never experienced it.

"It was like an overhead projector," Dickie said, "but it only showed a few words in the sentence and you had to keep up with it. It gauged how fast we could read, but it just made me dizzy."

"'Slow it down, Mrs. Edwards!'" Jesse said. "That's what everybody said, but she'd put the thing in high gear."

Jesse and Dickie felt about reading the way I felt about fishing. I had gone with my uncle Willy to the lake one vacation, but I didn't bait my own hook. Catching fish was nerve-racking because I was afraid the fish might bite me—and the smell turned my stomach.

We struck out for the reservoir and on our way passed a farmer pulling a wagon of what looked like black dirt. Jesse waved at the man like she knew him, but Dickie stopped.

"Hey, mister, whatcha got in the wagon?"

"Cow manure," the man said, spitting a brown stream at the other side of the road.

"What are you going to do with it?" Dickie said.

"Take it home and put it on my strawberries."

The man rode on and Dickie turned to me, the smell of the manure lingering. "I like whipped cream on mine. But to each his own."

Jesse slapped her leg and laughed hard and so did I.

When we reached the reservoir, I watched Jesse and Dickie in fascination as they baited their hooks and dropped their lines in the water. They each used a long, thin bamboo pole with nylon string tied to the end and a bobber in the middle of the line. They adjusted the bobbers and sat on the bank.

"You fishing or spectating?" Jesse said.

"I think I'll watch," I said, grabbing the book.

"No way. You have to fish."

"I think he's scared the worms will bite him," Dickie said.

Jesse stuck her hand in the Maxwell House can and pulled out a juicy worm. She stuck the hook into one end of the slimy creature and worked it up on the hook so that it was secure. The end of the worm wriggled.

"Looks tasty, don't it?" Jesse said.

"Not to me."

"You got to think like a fish. You're setting his dinner table. There. Now, you have to do the next worm."

I stared at the worm as she adjusted the bobber.

"You don't fish, you don't read to us. Got it?"

"Okay."

The three of us sat back in the worn grass on the side of the bank. Jesse placed her pole beside her and put her hands behind her head. "How many books you think they got in that library about the Mothman?"

"They got magazines about him, so I expect there would be lots of books," Dickie said.

"What are you guys talking about?" I said.

"You ain't never heard of the Mothman?" Jesse said. She shook her head and cursed under her breath. "They must not teach the fundamentals up there in Pittsburgh."

I pulled my line up and it was Dickie's turn to shake his head. "Don't be fiddling with it. Leave it alone. You only pick it up when you get a bite. Put dinner on the table and leave it."

"I know," I said, dropping the worm back in the water and watching the ripples from the bobber.

Jesse yawned. "The Mothman is a West Virginia phenomenon."

"Nice word," I said.

"But he's not just in West Virginia."

"He is too," Dickie said.

"Is not." Jesse turned to me. "You ever hear of the Silver Bridge collapse?"

I shook my head.

"It's the big bridge over the Ohio at Gallipolis. The kind with the cables on top of it."

"Suspension bridge," Dickie said.

"We've got three of those in Pittsburgh," I said.

Jesse rolled her eyes. "Here we go. We got one bridge and you have to have three of 'em."

"Tell the story," Dickie said.

"The other side of the bridge comes out in Point Pleasant, on the West Virginia side," Jesse said. "About a week or so before Christmas there was all these people driving on it when the whole thing fell. Something like a hundred people died."

"It wasn't that many," Dickie said.

"Well, how many was it?"

"Fortysome."

"I didn't know you was a historical expert on disasters," Jesse said.

"What's this got to do with the Mothman?" I said.

"I'm getting to that. So there was these kids out taking a ride at night and they seen this huge creature in the road. Eyes as big as saucers and red like blood. Glowing. It had a wingspan something like twenty feet wide. They hightailed it out of there and went racing back toward town, and they said they went as fast as a hundred miles an hour, and the thing flew right over top of them."

Jesse looked at Dickie to see if he would correct her. He threw a hand up. "Go on."

"That wasn't the only time they seen him. There was people all up and down the valley that did, and there was news reports about it and people interviewed on TV. And every one of them said he looked like a big moth."

"Creepy," I said. "Did he say anything?"

They both looked at me dumbfounded.

"He don't talk to people," Jesse said.

"Did anybody get attacked?" I said.

"That's the thing. Out of all the sightings, nobody said they got hurt. And then, one person saw him sitting on top of the Silver Bridge."

"I saw a picture of it in one of the UFO magazines at Blake's," Dickie said.

"Seriously?" I said. "What did it look like?"

"It was just a big blob on top of one of the points in the bridge. They blew it up to see better, but it was kind of fuzzy. But there was drawings of how people said he looked. Like a big man with wings that stretched out."

My bobber dipped in the water, but I was so enraptured with the story I let it go.

"It was a week later that the bridge collapsed and all them people died," Jesse said. "A hundred of them."

"Fortysome," Dickie corrected.

"Can you imagine what it must have been like? One minute you're sitting there in your car, a cold December day, people getting off work and going home or Christmas shopping. All of a sudden the bridge gives way and you're in the water and there ain't nothing you can do about it. And you're drowning."

It was a frightening thought and Jesse painted the scene in all its horror. She described some of the bodies pulled out, that some were children.

"You're getting a bite," Dickie said. "Jerk the pole."

I lifted the line out of the water and the tugging stopped.

"No, you gotta jerk it to set the hook," Jesse said, frowning. "Like this."

She showed me, whipping the pole back quickly. I tried to mimic her wrist motion. When I had it down, I lifted the line and saw most of my worm was gone.

"Bring it up so you can rebait it," Dickie said.

I pulled the line in and Jesse generously rebaited my hook. I tossed it back into the water. "I still don't get why the Mothman is so important."

"He was warning them," Jesse said. "Don't you see? He was telling them something bad was about to happen. Because as soon as the bridge collapsed, people around there never saw him again."

"You have to admit they were busy cleaning up the bridge and burying the dead," Dickie said.

Jesse ignored him. "And the same thing happened with the Marshall plane crash. I know this lady who lives down in Kenova—"

"This is not true," Dickie said.

"It is too. You can ask her."

"Ask her what?" I said.

"About the sighting a couple of days before the crash. There he was, up in the trees on the side of the hill where that plane came down. He was trying to warn people that something bad was coming."

I glanced at Dickie and he rolled his eyes.

"Same thing happened before President Kennedy got shot," Jesse said, her eyes wide.

"She's spinning one now," Dickie said.

"There's no spin to it. People over in Welch saw him before the president got shot by the school depository."

"If the Mothman was trying to warn about a shooting in Dallas, why would he show up in Welch?" Dickie said.

"I don't know. You'll have to ask him. I'm just reporting what I heard. And just before Farmington happened, he was seen too."

"What's Farmington?" I said.

"Coal mine," Dickie said. "It exploded and killed seventysome."

"You best pay attention when the Mothman shows up, is all I have to say," Jesse said.

"Hey, look at that!" Dickie yelled, and I just about

jumped out of my skin, looking back at the thick woods behind us.

"Not there, silly," Jesse said.

"I got one!" Dickie pulled the line out of the water and a long, silver fish with a big mouth was on the hook.

"That's too little to take home," Jesse said.

"It's a wide-mouth, though," Dickie said. "Maybe we'll catch his daddy."

I was still thinking about the Mothman and the prospect of riding my bike alone lost all allure. I was about to open the book when Jesse shrieked, "Set the hook, Matt!"

I jerked on the pole and immediately felt the weight on the other end of the line. The bamboo bent at the end.

"Don't pull it up too fast," Dickie said. "Flatten it out and get him up to the bank. It looks like a big one."

Dickie crept to the edge of the water. He had said this was a place where the reservoir was deepest and added that several people had fallen in and drowned in this very spot. I backed up, the fish weaving in the water, and Dickie navigated the biggest bass I would ever catch in my life onto the bank.

Jesse gasped. "Would you look how pretty he is?" She went down and held him up in both hands. "He's got to be at least five pounds."

Dickie pulled the hook from his mouth. I asked if I could be the one to let him go.

"What do you mean let him go?" Jesse said.

"We always let them go when I've fished."

The two looked at each other and then back at me.

"You can do what you want—he's your fish," Dickie said. "But I usually give anything I catch to Jesse."

"Daisy Grace loves her some fried fish," Jesse said, sizing up the catch.

"That's fine," I said. "I didn't think about you eating it."

Dickie got out a long piece of string with knots in it and put it through the fish's gills, then put the fish in the water and tied the string to a branch he stuck in the mud. We caught two more keepers that day, one catfish and one large bluegill, and a lot of other smaller fish. I couldn't help but feel like I had contributed in a small way to Jesse's family. Jesse covered the fish in her front basket with leaves and placed Harper Lee on top and we pedaled home.

When we got to the railroad tracks, Jesse stopped and looked both ways, sitting on the tracks. From my vantage point behind her, with her head turned, she looked like the prettiest thing I'd ever seen. Even with all the dirt and mountain toughness, I could see it. And I realized my fear of relating to girls disappeared around her. I wasn't nervous, probably because she was so much like Dickie and me. Her shirts were sweat-stained and her hair stuck up in the back where she'd slept.

She looked back, sitting on the tracks, her cute nose that gently turned up at the end glinting in the sunlight and her freckles giving extra color to her face.

"What's wrong?" I said.

"That's where it happened, right up there."

"What happened?"

"My daddy lost his arm. He was trying to jump a freight and fell underneath."

"Where was he going?" I said.

"Huntington, probably."

I tried to think of something to say. "It must have hurt."

"He was probably drunk."

On the way through town, the talk turned to Mothman again. Jesse said he was still wandering the woods and waiting, biding his time until the next big event. Dickie believed in Mothman but thought Jesse's version of the story was flawed. When Jesse brought up flying saucers, though, Dickie took the bait. He talked nonstop about pictures he'd seen in magazines and how the government had cataloged UFOs and that officials were hiding men from outer space who had crashed near Roswell, New Mexico.

"Can we talk about something else?" I said. "Maybe baseball?"

Jesse and Dickie smiled at each other and I knew I was the one who had taken the bait.

Chapter 10

I awoke to the muted sound of birds heralding Indian summer. Crickets and frogs brought back my childhood in full surround sound as I shook the sleep from me. I had fallen into bed without setting an alarm and slept the rest of the day and night. I wandered outside to the car early enough not to disturb my parents.

I rolled down the driveway in neutral, starting the car as I coasted onto the road. I had to have a clear plan of action but my brain was foggy. Returning to the Dogwood Food and Drug and catching Jesse before she went to work seemed best. I could have called or gone to her house, but I wasn't sure who I might encounter.

I wanted our conversation to be face-to-face and without interruption.

The store opened at seven, but I knew if Jesse worked the early shift, she would arrive before that. It was a little after six when I rolled into the Morning Dove to get gas and coffee. I paid inside and noticed a group of men gathered around coffee and pancakes and sausage biscuits served in Styrofoam containers.

"Is that Matt Plumley?" one of the men said from across the room.

"In the flesh," I said, smiling and trying to remember the man's name.

I approached and he stood, stretching out a big hand. "Jennings Caldwell," he said. "I remember when you were this high and this wide."

"It's good to see you, Mr. Caldwell."

He introduced me to the other men around the table, all retired—from the glass plant, Union Carbide, driving a bus, and Jennings was retired from the sheriff's department. He had attended our church before we arrived in Dogwood and then left for reasons unknown. I could, of course, imagine several reasons, all of which were tied to Basil Blackwood.

"How's your family?" Jennings said, taking his seat.

"Mom and Dad are good. Still busy with the church."

"How's Chicago? Treating you all right?"

I wondered how he knew where I had wound up, but small-town news travels. Before I could answer, the talk turned to the Cubs since Jennings had mentioned Chicago and that led to the Reds and their disappointing season and who they might trade for in the off-season.

"Baseball's not what it used to be," the retired glass-blower said. "When I was a kid, there was team loyalty. You played in one place and rooted for that team no matter what. Now, with free agency, it's all about the money. And you can root for the Cardinals or the Yankees from any-where in the country."

"The Yankees," Jennings said like he was cursing.

"It's always been about the money," the Carbide man said. "The only question is who's going to keep it." The man's words and tone reminded me of Dickie.

Jennings turned toward me. "What brings you back, Matt?"

"Just in for a visit." The look on his face gave me the impression he didn't believe me.

"That girl. Woods. You still keep in touch?"

"My parents do."

He shook his head. "She sure had a tough start, didn't she?"

I nodded. "The whole family had a tough time."

"You got that right. I got called over there a few times through the years."

"My dad mentioned your name at one point. The night that . . ." I didn't finish my sentence, and by the look on the man's face, I didn't have to.

"I got the call. When I pulled up, your daddy was talk-ing to her." He took a big swig of coffee. "I'll never forget how sad that girl looked up there."

A wave of guilt swept over me and I wished I hadn't set foot in the restaurant.

"What are you two talking about?" Bus Driver said.

Before Jennings could answer, I told them I had to get going. "It's nice seeing you again, Mr. Caldwell."

When I made it to the door, Jennings had launched into the story of that night. I didn't want to relive it, so I drove back to the grocery parking lot and drank my coffee, watching the clouds roll through the sky as it lightened from black to dark blue. Wind blew leaves that wouldn't give up their losing battle.

Twenty minutes later a car pulled up by the Dumpsters. I didn't recognize the man who got out, but a ring of keys pulled his belt low. He disappeared inside. Still hoping to see Jesse, I rehearsed my lines to a script that hadn't been written.

A Dodge Omni, a square car that didn't fit her personality, pulled into the lot and she rolled down the window. She stuck out a hand and opened the door using the outside handle, then rolled the window up again and slammed it without locking it.

She wore jeans and work shoes and a heavy cotton T-shirt with a pocket over the left breast. Her hair was cut short, just below her ears. She still had the same lithe build I remembered, like a dancer, and that same Jesse saunter, like she could conquer the world, even though she was going to grind beef or cut chicken all day.

I opened my door and she glanced back and stopped.

"Jesse," I said.

She squinted like she didn't believe what she was seeing. "Well, look what the cat drug in. Hey, PB." She crossed her arms and put one work boot in front of the other. "I heard you were in town."

"Who'd you hear that from?"

"People."

She stared at me with those blue eyes. I wanted to see her smile, to feel the warmth of being close, but she seemed like a chicken looking for a hawk. I had to admit I felt just as awkward and nervous.

"That's a creative way to get out of a car."

"Handle snapped last winter. I do what I gotta do, you know?" She bit her cheek. "So you heard the news?"

I nodded.

"Who told you?"

"Wasn't my parents, I can tell you that."

Her eyes had a deep sadness to them. "And you drove all the way down here for what?"

With a deadpan face, I said, "Jesse, you can't get married on the thirteenth. It's bad luck."

"Saturday the thirteenth is not bad. Besides, I don't believe in luck anymore."

"What do you believe in?"

"I believe you're going to get yourself into a bunch of trouble—and me, too—if you don't leave."

"Trouble never bothered you before. You thrived on it."

"Matt, don't do this."

"Do what?"

"What you're fixing to do."

"And what is that?"

She didn't answer, just looked at cracks in the asphalt and the grass poking through. "I saw you yesterday. In the store."

"Why didn't you come out and talk?"

"Because there's nothing to say."

"I think there's a lot to say. I have a lot of questions."

She shook her head. "No. Talking time is over. It was over a long while ago."

Her face had changed a little. There'd been a hardness to her eyes from the moment I had met her, but it seemed something in the intervening years had softened her. Her hair hung past her eyes like a shadow and she made no attempt to brush it away like she wanted to hide. But she was the same girl I had fallen in love with, the same girl who had cast a spell I wasn't sure I would ever escape.

"Do you ever think of me, Jesse?" I said, my voice soft, almost a whisper. I said it with affect, with the dramatic flair of a line I had practiced but never truly gotten right.

She turned her head like the question touched some open wound. "You need to leave me alone."

"I've thought of you a lot. And this choice you're making doesn't feel right to me."

She slung her purse over her shoulder—I could see a brown bag sticking out with her lunch in it—and shoved her hands in her back pockets. "I appreciate your concern."

"You're making a mistake."

She dipped her head and spoke without looking at me. "I'm grateful for everything you tried to do."

"You don't love him, Jesse."

She cocked her head. "How would you know who I love? You always thought you knew more. That you were better than me."

"I never thought that."

"You always thought because you knew big words and did well in school that you were on a high branch looking down."

I studied her face. Was the anger real or an act? "You know better than that. You and Dickie were my best friends."

She shook her head like a dog will shake water from its back and glanced toward the hills where we spent our childhood. "It's not safe, you being here. Go back and live your life. Make us proud."

"I don't want to make anybody proud. I want you to come to your senses. I'm not leaving until you do. I don't care if I have to sit in the baptistery and wait for you to walk down the aisle."

More shaking of the head. "Don't do this, Matt."

"You would."

"What?"

"If something was right to do, you'd do it. Like taking care of Daisy."

Just the mention of the name brought her eyes to mine. And there we were in the parking lot of Dogwood Food and Drug staring at each other and remembering, the salty and sweet of our past close enough to taste.

Another car pulled into the lot and we were no longer alone.

"I need to go. I'm sorry you came here for nothing."

She turned and walked past another employee, who looked back at me and tossed away a half-smoked cigarette. I got back in my car and started the engine. Nothing about this was going to be easy.

Chapter 11

JUNE–JULY 1972

June in West Virginia is a cruel month to subdue any child, but it is unusually cruel to subdue him with piano practice and lessons. I had seen the effect of my playing on my mother's depression. I was like David to King Saul, soothing the demons with my music. Under her tutelage, I had progressed and was ready for another level. I promised if she found a different teacher, I would apply myself to anything the G. Schirmer publishing company could come up with and practice on my grandmother's out-of-tune Baldwin. From Beethoven to Mozart I would learn the classics, though I was more interested in playing Elton John.

Enter stage right Mrs. Clara Ann McCormick. She

taught sixth grade at Dogwood Elementary and gave piano lessons to students of varying abilities. She was a short, stocky woman with hair much darker than her age and skin under her arms that nearly hung to the piano bench. She looked at the world through pin-size pupils and cat-eye glasses. Their edges turned up and had a fascinating silver design.

Mrs. McCormick talked and laughed with a raspy cackle like she had a perpetual frog in her throat, and she would clear it every few seconds, half in a cough and half in a clearing sound that made you think she needed an open window. It was unnerving to be in the middle of some complicated piece she was trying to teach and hear that "uh-hmm-hmm" sound. We settled on Wednesday afternoons and kept the weekly regimen into the school year. I was expected to practice an hour each day and be prepared for my lessons.

"These are the hands of a surgeon," she said the first time I met her. She held up my palms and studied them as if she were a psychic reading the rivers and tributaries of my life. I think she was just glad to have a student whose fingernails were somewhat trimmed and weren't black underneath.

My mother had dropped me at her home near the high school and we sat in the woman's living room, a sparsely decorated apartment on the second floor of a small, four-apartment building. She owned an upright Kimball that filled the room with a rich sound, but the keys were heavy and you had to really mean it when you played. I wondered about the apartments beside and beneath hers—I hoped they were occupied by older people with hearing problems.

Mrs. McCormick was not the warmest person on the planet. Her life was sketchy—a husband and children who were on the wall over the piano but never present. Why did she live alone? Where were her children? Music was her only connection with the world, it seemed. When she played, she got lost, closing her eyes as if some internal conductor were working her hands to bring forth the songs.

"Let's see what you can do," she said. "Play something."

I chose "The Spinning Song," one of my father's favorites because it was happy and jaunty. I played the piece, not flawlessly, but with only minor mistakes. Mrs. McCormick watched me and then put a simple song in front of me. I tried to play but struggled through. She removed it and crossed her arms.

"Matt, we need to come to an understanding. Your mother has hired me to teach you. But *you* have to want this. Why do you want to play?"

"I don't know."

"Not a good answer. Try again."

There were a thousand reasons to learn music. There were a thousand ways a life was enriched—that's what my mother had said. I could think of only one and it slipped out.

"It helps her," I said.

"It helps who?"

"My mother. My playing makes her feel better, I think."

"You've watched her play and mimicked her."

I nodded. "I've never seen any use in reading the notes if I can play them by hearing them."

She looked at me with a mixture of fascination and concern. Then she pulled a silver flask out of a suitcase-size purse and took a quick nip. "Well, I've never had a student like you. But if what your mother says is true about your acting ability, and how you can mimic others and remember dialogue, it only makes sense the good Lord made you this way for a reason."

"I don't understand," I said, hearing for the first time that my mother thought I had a talent for acting and remembering things.

"Helping your mother with whatever she's going through is laudable. I think she probably knows you don't read the notes. But I'm going to take on faith that you'll at some point come to the end of your ability to remember and repeat. One day you'll connect what your hands are doing and what's on the page. In other words, I'll teach your fingers and ears first and then your eyes. We'll go from your heart to your head rather than the other way around. Does that make sense?"

I nodded.

"At some point the music will have to be more for you than her. You can't learn and make it part of you when you're doing it only for someone else. This is about you, Matt."

I smiled, not really understanding, and stepped away from the piano while she played "Für Elise," a Beethoven piece about a girl he must have loved. I couldn't help but think of Jesse as she played the melody.

Music has a way of burrowing into your soul. As much as I wanted to play modern songs, old Ludwig did his work. The song was in A minor, and he had evidently gone through ups and downs in the relationship because one part was sad and the next was cheery, but it quickly turned again and sounded like his team had lost a doubleheader. Or maybe an arm on the train tracks. Or maybe Elise loved somebody else.

About two minutes in, the piece rose in intensity and Mrs. McCormick sat forward and focused her gaze on the page, her loose skin dangling and jiggling. The song, from its beginning to its flourishing end, was a story, the ebb and flow of life. I did not know if Beethoven had ever moved from Pittsburgh to Dogwood, or if his family had problems, but without any lyrics, he had captured my feelings about falling for an Appalachian girl.

"Now you try," she said.

We went through the first page that day and she taught me more about hand position and feeling the song than my mother ever communicated. Music, according to Mrs. McCormick, was not something performed as much as it was experienced. You didn't *play* a song, you breathed it and interpreted it, sifting and enhancing it through everything you saw and heard and loved. Despite the acrid, pungent aroma of her breath, the afternoon invigorated me.

"Practice, practice, practice," she said when my mother

arrived. She put the music book with "Für Elise" under my arm and winked.

There followed days of roaming the hills and riding bikes and fishing with Dickie and Jesse, though Jesse often broke away early. Her mother wasn't in the best of health and Jesse fetched groceries and medicine and bought packs of Pall Malls from a vending machine inside the only pool hall in town, which my parents strictly forbade me to enter.

"Only the lowest kinds of people go to a place like that," my mother said one day as we passed it. It looked dark inside and I imagined all sorts of illicit behavior, but Jesse and Dickie laughed when I revealed this.

"You preacher boys sure have it rough," Jesse said.

I heard my parents speaking in hushed tones early in the morning at the kitchen table. Ben was something we never talked about as a family. We talked freely of others' problems but never our own. But here they spoke of him and of his dropping out of school and, worse than that, taking up with a girlfriend who "wasn't good for him." He and Cindy were living together, and their travels had led to an even bigger source of family shame. There were also hints that things weren't going well at the church and that Old Man Blackwood was causing problems. Maybe it was the size of my ears, but I was always able to take in their conversations. When their words turned to me and they spoke of Jesse and Dickie, I heard sighs as if my friends were problems to solve. One morning they lowered their voices so far that I caught only bits and pieces.

"... should do it for him ...," my father said.

"... don't want to encourage ...," my mother said.

"But if we think of him ..."

I nearly crept into the hallway to hear but stayed in my bed until my grandmother called me to breakfast.

"How would you like to spend your birthday?" my mother said about a week before the big day as we drove to Huntington. She needed to pick up some sheet music from the Kenny Music Company.

"With Ben," I said. The look on her face made me regret saying it. "I don't know."

"You have no idea?"

I shook my head as she parallel parked on Third Avenue. As a child born in the summer, I was not accustomed to a fuss like my brethren who had birthdays during the school year. There were always cupcakes or popsicles celebrating classmates when I was in elementary school. As I entered junior high, there were parties at pizza parlors or the local pool. My birthday was always a muted family affair, but without Ben, it would be even less celebratory.

I browsed through the store, looking at music books and trying to come up with an answer. My mother bought several pieces of sheet music for her ensemble at church and we ate at Dwight's. I ordered a burger and fries and we talked.

Just as I took a big bite of coleslaw, a signature of the restaurant, my mother said, "What if we invited Dickie for the party?"

I stopped chewing. "Are you serious?"

"Matt, don't talk with your mouth full."

I swallowed. "Could Jesse come too?"

"I think Jesse might complicate things."

"Why?"

"It's just that . . ."

"Why do you hate her?"

"I don't hate her. I'm concerned about the kind of influence she's having."

"Then why are you saying Dickie is okay?"

She sipped some iced tea and sat back. "I thought it might mean something to you to have him."

"What about Dad?" I said.

"We can invite him, too." She smiled.

"No, I mean what does he say about it?"

"He's fine with Dickie."

"Could we ask him about Jesse?"

"Let's just make this a boys' birthday invite, okay?"

I finished my meal and we rode home, the conflict rising inside me about how to invite only one of my friends. We listened to Paul Harvey on the way. Every day at noon Mom heard his take on the news. She was tired of the normal war reporting and the country's unrest. She was tired of the constant negative coverage of the election and her beloved president. She would hit the Off switch on the TV each evening and say to Walter Cronkite, "No, that's the way you *say* it is."

Dickie immediately agreed to attend, but when he asked about Jesse, I told him it was a "boys only" party. He looked confused.

"This is not my idea, it's my parents'. They only want you."

He shook his head. "First time for everything."

"What do you mean?"

"Most people around here don't want me close to anything they're doing. But I got to say, it feels kind of mean not to let her come."

"Yeah," I said.

"And I don't want to go and try to keep it a secret. Even if it does cost me some cake."

"What if we tell her? What if we tell her to come by that day and when she shows up, we invite her inside? My parents will have to let her stay."

Dickie shrugged. "She's going to know she wasn't invited, though. You going to tell her the truth?"

"If we tell her my parents don't want her there, she'll never come. She'll boycott the whole thing. You know how she is."

"Yeah."

We thought about it, sitting there in Dickie's garage, flies swarming at a trash can in the corner. It seemed an impossible situation.

"Why don't you talk with your dad?" Dickie said.

I found my father alone at the church, studying. I knocked lightly on the door and he took off his glasses.

"I have a problem," I said.

He sat back. "All right."

I explained the whole thing in a long, rambling sentence that captured the situation as best I could.

"You're between a rock and a hard place."

"I just want Jesse to be there, Dad. And you're the only one who can convince Mom."

He scratched his chin and stared at the open Bible and his three-by-five cards. "Go ahead and invite her. I'll explain to your mother."

I didn't hesitate, didn't ask if he really meant it, just jumped up and ran to the door.

"Don't say anything to your mother between now and then, okay?"

I rode to Dickie's and gave him the good news. Then we rode to Jesse's house together.

"Do you have to wear something special?" she said after I told her she was invited.

"No, we're going to spit watermelon seeds and throw water balloons," I said. "Wear what you normally wear."

"Well, I got to bring a present, don't I?"

"No, that's the other thing. Nobody brings presents. Everything will be provided."

She looked relieved. "All right then. I guess I'll come."

On the appointed day, my mother drove to Huntington and bought a dozen Stewarts hot dogs. She got enough vanilla ice cream from Dairy Queen to feed the town. Jesse and Dickie were standing with me in the kitchen when she returned, and Daisy Grace was clinging to Jesse's leg like a tick. My grandmother looked like she wanted out of her own house.

My mother took one look at Jesse, then glanced at my father. She was clearly taken aback, but she covered well and collected herself. I guessed he hadn't told her of the plan and there were whispers in the pantry, so I took my friends to the backyard and we unwrapped our hot dogs from the paper napkins and ate.

Dickie and Jesse said it was the first time they'd ever had a Stewarts hot dog and they couldn't get over the sweetness of the root beer. We ate watermelon, spitting seeds from the top of the picnic table over the clothesline into the horseshoe pit. Dickie, it turned out, had the most air in his lungs and won the competition, though my father came in a respectable second. My uncle Willy and aunt Zenith made a cameo appearance and we took some pictures of all of us. We tossed horseshoes and played badminton. Closer to dark, after ice cream and sheet cake, my father handed me an envelope. Dickie and Jesse looked a little self-conscious that they didn't have presents.

"You've gone through a big change moving here," my dad said, "and I'm hoping this will help ease some of the pain."

I opened it quickly and pulled out eight tickets with the Cincinnati Reds logo on them. July 12 and 13, Reds vs. Pirates. I gave him a hug, then pulled back.

"Wait, why are there four tickets to each game?" I said.

My mother smiled, but it looked more like a grimace, and she nodded for my father to explain.

"There's one for you, one for me, and two for any friends you want to take along."

I stared at him, not comprehending. Then I looked at Dickie and Jesse. Their faces lit like Christmas trees. They looked like they had just won a thousand dollars on Let's Go to the Races.

"We'll go early Wednesday morning," my father said. "Gerald will handle the prayer meeting and Bible study. Thursday is an early game, so we'll come back late afternoon. I spoke with your mother, Dickie. She said it would be all right. Jesse, I haven't been able to reach your mother."

My mother's face showed a pain that looked almost like betrayal.

Jesse studied the ground and pulled Daisy close. "She's feeling poorly and we don't have a phone."

"We'll work it out," my father said. "I've made reservations at a hotel in Covington, Kentucky. We'll get two rooms—"

"Two?" my mother said.

"One for the women and one for the men—and then walk over the bridge to the game."

"You're staying in a real hotel?" Jesse said.

"Do you think your mom will let you?" I said.

"It might be a problem."

"We'll talk with her and explain," my father said. "It would mean a lot to Matt to have you two there watching the Reds get beat."

My mother quickly walked inside, apparently remembering something in the kitchen.

"Yeah, and you should bring your glove," I said, smiling. "My dad caught a foul ball once at a Pirates game. There are lots of pop-ups that come into the stands."

"You don't have to throw them back?" Jesse said. "That can't be true."

"It is, you'll see."

Later that night my mom came into my room while I was reading Harper Lee. Jem and Dill were trying to get Boo Radley to come out. Jesse and Dickie were not only slow readers, they were slow listeners. I had abandoned trying to read to them because they stopped me to ask questions so much and sometimes I didn't know the answers. So I read on without them.

"Were you surprised at your present?" my mother said.

I smiled. "Dad mentioned the game a few weeks ago, but I can't believe Jesse and Dickie are coming."

"Mm-hm. I can hardly believe it myself." She said it with a mix of irony and disdain.

"This is the best birthday ever," I said, trying to cheer her. I gave her a kiss but she walked out of the room looking weary.

Jesse returned early the next morning and knocked on our door. My grandmother peeked through the curtains and shook her head. "I told you, those Woods are like stray cats."

I walked outside and sat by her on the porch, where we watched Daisy Grace pull dandelions and blow on them in the yard. Jesse had a hangdog look.

"I can't go with you."

"Why not?"

She jerked her head toward Daisy. "Plus, I got chores."

"But it's just one night. Dickie and I can do your chores when we get back. And if your mom can't watch her, we could find somebody."

"There ain't nobody else to trust."

"Don't you have cousins who—?"

Her face flashed fire. "No way. It'll be a cold day in—" She caught herself. "It's just that Daisy can't be around them people."

It was ironic that Jesse's family felt the same about their cousins as my parents felt about Jesse.

"Maybe if we take Daisy Grace with us, I could go," Jesse said in a soft voice.

"You think?" That hadn't crossed my mind, and I wondered whether my mother would consider it. Our car had room for six, but it would be tight.

"Let me ask," I said.

I ran in the house and my grandmother complained about the noise. I found my mother in the backyard hanging laundry. She held clothespins in her mouth, working with unwieldy sheets, the dew from the clover staining her house shoes. I tried to explain the plan and cultivate sympathy for Jesse.

She held the sheet and pins, squinting into the sun just peeking over the hill. "What's going on with her mother? That doesn't make sense. That she would let that little girl tag along with us."

"She's not feeling well. Please, Mom? Daisy's not a problem." I said it convincingly, but I knew Daisy had a heart that was prone to wander. And if she caught sight of the pool, she would probably never want to leave the hotel.

My mother looked at me like I'd tried to play "Clair de Lune" with my feet. "Matt, I can barely handle the load I have. I can't take on Daisy Grace. And that Jesse's mother would suggest it . . ."

"I don't know that she suggested it. It's just an idea. There's got to be a way. Maybe Mawmaw . . ." The words escaped my lips before I realized their futility.

My mother frowned. "Let me call your father."

She went into the house and I walked to the front yard. Jesse was looking up at the hickory nut tree, where a squirrel flitted from limb to limb, swishing its tail. Daisy Grace was at the bottom of the walk going round and round the lamppost, her hand turning black from the fading paint.

"That party was fun," Jesse said. "That was my first one."

"Seriously?"

"Other than at school when they bring cupcakes. Daisy Grace loved those hot dogs and that root beer. She wasn't whining about being hungry when she went to bed. Full as a tick. Just went right to sleep like nobody's business."

I hadn't heard Daisy Grace say more than a handful of words since I'd met her, even when, in the last week, she'd accompanied us on all our bike rides and fishing.

My mother came out, shutting the screen door gently behind her. She smiled at Jesse and sat, watching Daisy Grace. "She's got a lot of energy, doesn't she?"

"Yes, ma'am. But she wears out real good when you give her enough leash to run." Jesse's hair was shining in the morning sun. She wore the same cutoff jeans every day and a T-shirt that was a size too big. Her feet were dark from walking barefoot, and she pulled at some clover by the porch as she spoke to my mother. "We was talking last night walking home and saying that you all have the nicest family."

"Why, thank you, Jesse," my mother said. "That's kind of you."

"Well, I wouldn't say it if it wasn't true. We sure appreciated the party and the food and the invitation to the ballgame."

"We were glad you could come. And about the game," my mother said, lowering her voice. "I don't think we can take Daisy with us. I'm really sorry."

"I understand, ma'am. She's a handful. Especially in a long car ride. One time we took her up to Charleston and I had to sit in the back with her and she squirmed and kicked the whole way. She slept coming home and I was glad of that. But she can wear a body out."

"That was the first birthday party Jesse's ever been to," I said, playing the sympathy card as if it were the Rook.

My mother ignored me. "Does your mama need help? I'm head of the women's group at church, and we're setting up a list of people who can provide meals. Would that be something she'd say yes to?"

"We don't go to your church, ma'am."

"I understand. We just want to bless people in the community who are . . . going through a rough patch."

"I appreciate your concern, Mrs. Plumley, I truly do," Jesse said, standing. "But we're fine."

She walked to the hickory nut tree and picked up her bike lying in the shade. My mother looked at me with concern.

"Daisy Grace, come on, we got to get home."

"Would you like some cake for your mom?" my mother said. "We've got plenty left over."

Daisy Grace skipped toward Jesse singing, "Cake" with every step.

"You hold on and I'll get you some," my mother said.

She disappeared into the house, the screen door banging twice behind her as the hydraulic hinge took over. Jesse lifted her sister onto the back of her bike.

"I wish you could come," I said. "Won't be the same with just Dickie and me."

"I reckon there'll be another chance down the road," she said, but I didn't believe her.

"There's a pool at the hotel. We were going to get there early and swim."

As soon as it was out of my mouth, I regretted saying it because Jesse's face fell.

"I don't have a bathing suit anyway," she said. "My mama took us to Rock Lake once. I ain't never seen so much water. There was these spray things at the front you had to go through. I think they wanted to hose us down before we jumped in. But I squealed going through that cold water."

From the sound of her voice, Rock Lake was a good memory.

My mother returned with a green Tupperware container

filled to the brim with cake, frosting oozing. She put it in the front basket of the bike.

"Oh, I almost forgot," Jesse said, digging a hand into her pocket. She pulled out three dollars and handed them to me. "Mama's check came. This is what I owe you for the bike."

"Oh, you don't have to do that, Jesse," my mother said before I could.

"No, ma'am, I do. I promised I'd pay him back. And if you can't keep a promise, what can you keep?"

My mother and I watched them ride away. Then she put an arm around my shoulder. I think she wanted to say something but couldn't.

Chapter 12

I suppose with every loss there is gain. The extra ticket
meant my mother could attend the game with us and that
we'd only need one hotel room. We pulled out early that
Wednesday morning and I looked up the road toward
Jesse's, wondering what she was doing and if her heart was
aching like mine. I wanted my mother to get to know her
and not judge her. I wanted to sit next to her and watch
her react to the game and see her swim in the pool.

When we pulled up to Dickie's place, he was sitting on
a ratty duffel bag as tall as he was. My father tossed it in the
trunk and Dickie jumped in.

"You planning on staying a few extra nights, Dickie?"
my dad said.

"No, sir, just want to be prepared."

"How are you, Dickie?" my mother said, filing her nails.

"Good." He smiled. "Lookin' for a breakthrough."

"Did you bring your swim trunks?" I said.

"My mom gave me a pair of my dad's. They're a little big, but I can tie them tight."

We started out in the crisp morning air, a fog lifting from the hills. When we hit the interstate, my dad glanced back. "So your father is in Vietnam?"

"Yes, sir. First Cav."

"I'll bet you're real proud of him," my mother said.

"Yes, ma'am. Keeping us safe from the Communists."

"Things seem to be winding down, from what I hear on the news," my father said. "Have you heard when he's coming home?"

"No, sir, but my mama and me have our fingers crossed. I mean, in a Christian sort of way."

My father looked in the rearview and I could see a crinkle of a smile on his face. My mother turned and gave him a look that I interpreted as a warning to change the topic of conversation.

"This has not been a popular war," my dad continued. "But I want you to know we appreciate your father's sacrifice and the sacrifice you and your mother are making."

"Thank you, sir."

The talk of Vietnam brought my brother to mind and as we settled in for the long ride, we played some games Ben and I would play on trips to the beach in the summer. We'd count the number of air conditioners we saw sticking out of houses and then try to find the alphabet on road signs and license plates.

"Sure wish Jesse could have come," I said kind of low to Dickie. "It would have been fun to go swimming and to the game."

He nodded. "Yeah, won't be as much fun. But it's probably for the best. Her mama's not well."

"What's wrong with her?"

Dickie shrugged. "Coughs a lot. My uncle had the black lung after working in the mines. She kind of sounds like that. Rattling when she breathes."

"I've never seen her. I've just heard her talking to Jesse and Daisy."

"I've only seen her a couple of times. Jesse don't like people going into her house."

"Why not?"

Dickie looked away. "I expect it's because of how it looks. Their furniture is the stuff other people toss out. Sometimes we pass trash by the road and Jesse'll say, 'Wonder if we could get that to my house.' They get by. And Mrs. Woods is real pretty."

"Really?"

"Yeah, there's not much to her, but you can tell she was beautiful once. My daddy taught me about the mother principle."

"The what?"

"The mother principle. He said if you get interested in a girl, look at her mother, 'cause that's what she'll look like in twenty years."

My mother and father had not turned on the radio or any of their music. They were looking straight ahead, but my mother's neck was red.

"I've thought about it and it works," Dickie said.

"Does it work with fathers?"

"I expect it would. If you was a girl interested in a guy and wondering how he would turn out, look at his daddy."

I looked at my father's receding hairline and the crow's-feet by his eyes and wondered if I would look like him in thirty years. And I wondered if sons are destined to become like their fathers in other ways.

Dickie picked up the black case that held my parents' eight-track collection. He unlatched the hook and studied the names of the artists, mostly classical music. He pulled out one and held it up. It was an essential collection of music by Wagner, including my favorite, "Ride of the Valkyries."

"Is this Porter?" Dickie said.

I tried not to laugh. "No, Wagner is a German composer," I said, pronouncing the *W* as a *V*. I handed the eight-track to my father. "You're thinking of Porter Wagoner."

"My mama likes 'Burning the Midnight Oil,'" Dickie said.

Dickie watched in fascination as the eight-track engaged with a clunk and the speakers filled the car with horns and strings. My father rolled his window down, stuck his hand out, and wove back and forth like we were flying. Dickie laughed and asked to hear the song again when it was over. My mother told my father to stop weaving, that she was getting carsick, but when he played it again, he repeated the maneuver. After Wagner, my dad put in the *1812 Overture*. Dickie didn't recognize it until a few minutes in just before the cannons sounded. He said he'd heard that on TV during a July Fourth celebration.

My mother put in her favorite, the "Blue Danube" waltz, and it felt like Dickie was getting his first taste of culture. He listened to the music enveloping us and smiled.

"It sounds like we're riding on the ocean, don't it?"

We exited the interstate and took the back way over a big hill, finally coming to some dirty streets with redbrick buildings and lots of stoplights. The Ohio River was nearby and across it the Queen City, Cincinnati. Older black men walked along the street and I couldn't help staring. This didn't look much different from some parts of downtown Pittsburgh. Dickie sat forward and I wondered what he was thinking but didn't ask.

Once we checked into the hotel, I grabbed the key and opened the door to our room and turned on the air conditioner full blast. This was always my job when we went to the beach. It rattled and blew the curtains. Dickie found a metal box with a coin slot mounted by the beds and asked what it was.

For your comfort and relaxation, the sign said, *Magic Fingers. Try it—you'll feel great.* There was a slot to put in a quarter that would vibrate the bed.

Dickie put a quarter in but nothing happened. He was about to put another one in when my parents suggested we go for a swim. Dickie dressed in the bathroom and I put on my trunks and kept my white T-shirt on. Dickie was in the water before the gate closed and I eased in. My father sat in a lounge chair and watched. There were three other families there with children. One girl was a little older than us and wore a skimpy bikini, and I tried not to stare.

"Why don't you take your shirt off?" Dickie said from the other side of the pool.

"I don't want to get burned," I lied.

"You guys are going to be hungry soon," my father said. "I'm going to get some food. No running, okay?"

We watched him leave and I tried again not to stare at the girl. Dickie found a beach ball and we batted it. I spiked it and the thing flew straight at the girl, landing by her with a splash.

"Sorry," I said.

She frowned and threw it in my general direction, then got out and toweled off, the water dripping from her bikini bottoms. I wondered what Jesse would look like in a bathing suit.

The girl left and I realized all of the people in the pool had gotten out.

"Looks like dinner's being served," I said.

"Nah, they got out because of me."

"Why would they do that?"

Dickie dipped his head as if anyone with half a brain could understand. "All those people were white. They got out because they think I'll dirty up the water."

"I'm still here."

He hit the beach ball to me and we swam, if you could call it that. We both tried to float but had to touch our feet on the bottom to get to the other side. We had a contest to see who could hold his breath the longest. Then Dickie found a life preserver that said, *For emergency use only* and sat in it with his hands behind his head, squinting into the sun.

"What if you could put on a pair of glasses and see everything?" he said.

"I saw glasses in a catalog that let you see through people's clothes," I said.

"I've seen those. I don't believe it. They don't cost enough to really work."

I hadn't thought of the cost, only the possibilities of X-ray glasses.

"I'm not talking about girls in their underwear or some-body's liver pumping out bile," Dickie said. "What if you could see all the way to a person's soul? What if you could see what makes that person who they really are? See all that happened in their life. The good and bad and every little thing that makes me different from you."

"What would you call them?"

"I don't know, but they'd be a gold mine."

"Soul glasses," I said.

"That could work. Too bad Jesse's not here—she would come up with a name. What do you think she'd say about them?"

I thought a minute. "Maybe she'd say that most people don't want to see inside a person's soul. They judge by what's on the outside. It's easier to look on the outside than to really look on the inside."

"That sounds like Jesse all right."

"There's a verse in the Bible that talks about that."

"Preacher boy in the pool," Dickie said and rolled off the life preserver and sank.

"No, seriously," I said when he bobbed to the surface. "Man looks on the outside but God looks at the heart."

"He won't need my glasses, then, will he?"

My father returned and called us in from the pool. I was ravenous and so was Dickie. We ate boiled ham and American cheese sandwiches on white bread with mustard. We put sour cream and onion potato chips on a paper plate and ate potato salad with plastic spoons, with powdered donuts for dessert, and no king was ever more satisfied. We didn't drink much pop at home, but my mother had iced some Dr Pepper and diet Faygo in a cooler. There was a talk show on TV and we watched and ate, sitting on the Magic Fingers bed that didn't work. When the news came on, my father said it was time to leave.

We walked the suspension bridge and I hesitated, remembering what had happened in Gallipolis. I looked up to see if maybe the Mothman was sitting there, but looking up made me unsteady. I didn't want Dickie to think I was scared, so I forged ahead, carrying my glove close. I couldn't help looking down through the steel grate at the murky water. The stadium sat in the distance like some giant flying saucer ready for takeoff. My father talked about going to games at Crosley Field, which was being torn down at the time, but I kept measuring my steps and thinking what I might do if the bridge collapsed.

We passed vendors selling peanuts as we neared the stadium and I smelled stale Hudepohl. Dickie stuck close to my mother as we passed men playing "When the Saints Go Marching In." Cigarette and cigar smoke filled the air.

A black man yelled, "Hey, Pirates," and pointed at my hat and smiled. "You guys gonna lose, little man! Big Red Machine gonna beat you tonight!"

I smiled and kept walking.

There is no feeling in the world like walking into a baseball stadium for the first time and seeing the green field, the white lines, the brown dirt at each base, and the colorful seats. I looked at Dickie when we got inside and saw his mouth drop.

We climbed to oxygen-deprived heights in the red seats. When the Reds came out of the dugout, Dickie said they looked like ants with numbers on their backs. My glove wasn't necessary after all, but I felt more comfortable holding it. I thought of Ben.

The Reds had won 5–0 the night before, so I was glad we didn't have tickets to that game. I looked to right field but Roberto Clemente wasn't there, and when the Pirates' lineup was announced, his name wasn't called. Mazeroski and Clemente were the two players left from the World Series champs in 1960. I told all of this to Dickie, but he was more interested in the popcorn my mother had bought.

I drank in the atmosphere and cheered in vain. We lost

6–3 and the Reds fans around us didn't hold back from rubbing it in as we walked home.

There were two double beds in the hotel room. My mom and dad slept in the one nearest the bathroom and I climbed into the other, exhausted. We watched the recap of the game on the news and it was surreal to see the action close up. Dickie said he was fine sleeping on the floor, that he could use his duffel bag as a mattress, but I told him, "You can sleep up here with the rest of us white people." He laughed at that.

My parents turned on Johnny Carson, but Dickie was gone as soon as his head hit the pillow. Even when my dad dropped one of the soda cans in the cooler, Dickie slept right through it, snoring loudly. I had a harder time going to sleep. There was something about being in enemy territory and watching my team lose that made me ache for Three Rivers. I went over the game, inning by inning, wondering if Clemente would be in the lineup the next day. Steve Blass was supposed to pitch, so that meant we were sure to win.

The next morning my mom and dad woke us and took us to a restaurant. Dickie poured as much syrup on his pancakes as Walter Cunningham at the Finch house, but I had the good sense not to ask what in the sam hill he was doing.

We checked out of the hotel and drove over the bridge and parked at Riverfront. My father complained about the price of everything. There was no Clemente in the lineup, but I thought we might be able to see him if we went closer to the field.

"You think we can get an autograph?" Dickie said.

We climbed down to the lower level, but the ushers turned us away when they saw our tickets. We only got close enough to see Richie Hebner's back.

Salvaging one game in the series wouldn't be great, but it would be a lot better than losing three in a row. The Pirates got ten hits in the game and Al Oliver went three for four, but Gary Nolan held us scoreless and the Reds eked out two runs off Blass. Another loss.

"We should get Jesse a souvenir," Dickie said as we passed a gift shop on the way out.

My mother frowned.

My father said, "Good idea, Dickie. What do you think she would like?"

Everything had *Cincinnati* printed on it, which turned my stomach. "Maybe one of those bobbleheads for Daisy," I said.

It was a bittersweet drive home. The time had gone so fast, and I didn't want it to end. About an hour from home Dickie, who must have felt the same way, devised a plan. He suggested we take the leftover ham and cheese from the cooler up the hill behind my grandmother's house and camp out that night. Dickie's father had left a real Army tent and Dickie knew how to set it up. We'd sleep under the stars, build a fire, and watch the sun come up.

My father looked at my mother. When she didn't object, he looked in the rearview and said, "If Dickie's mom says it's okay." It almost made the series sweep of the Pirates bearable.

Chapter 13

My father invited me to lunch, and because it would be
uninterrupted time without my mother, I agreed to meet
him at a restaurant after his hospital visits. In the meantime,
I started to write Jesse a letter three times and crumpled the
paper each time, knowing I needed to talk face-to-face.

I called work and checked in with the counseling center
to make sure they had gotten my message and that all my
appointments were covered. "Kristin is taking Dantrelle
this afternoon," I said.

"She mentioned that to me," Carl Sheets said. He
directed the center and was good-hearted, though a bit
scattered. We all worked for little pay, but there was a sense

that we were really making a difference in the community, the city, and individuals' lives.

"Do you have a better timetable of how long you'll need to be away?" Carl said.

"I'm trying to help a friend I met when I was a kid," I said. "She's getting married Saturday."

"I see. Well, we can cover for a few days, but I'd like you back as soon as possible. Do you think by the end of the week, or do you need to stay for the wedding?"

"End of the week is fine. I'll hash this out by then."

I met my father at a steak house off the interstate that overlooked the valley. The silverware was thin and the forks bent and the foil-wrapped potatoes were chewy, but the steak was edible if I doused it with enough A.1. sauce. The meal reminded me of dinners with Kristin and I shoved those thoughts away. One of the servers recognized my father and greeted him. He introduced me to her and we shook hands and exchanged pleasantries.

"Your daddy has helped a lot of people at his church. I hope you know that," she said.

I nodded and smiled. When she left, my father leaned closer.

"Years ago her mother dropped her off at the youth group. The girl was a mess. The whole family was. But something happened. God got hold of her heart and the mom noticed and she started coming. Now that whole family is changed. It's the power of the gospel you're looking at right over there."

"I'm surprised Blackwood allows teenagers in the church that aren't in his circle."

My dad speared a piece of steak and pointed it at me in thought. "You know, you should speak with the teenagers at church someday. Tell them what you do now." Even while he was speaking, he seemed to regret suggesting it.

"You didn't comment on Blackwood."

He wiped his face with a napkin from a dispenser on the table. "Every pastor has a thorn in the flesh. I have Basil Blackwood. He's my Diotrephes."

"Your who?"

"Third epistle of John. The man was a rabble-rouser. Had to have everything his own way and tossed people he didn't like out of the church."

"Did he promise a parsonage and renege on it?"

My father chewed his steak and took a sip of soda. "I've tried to look at Basil as God's way of keeping me humble. I've had to bite my tongue so many times I'm surprised I have one left."

"Maybe you shouldn't have bitten it. Maybe you should stand up to him."

"I think trying to get along with him and keeping peace is one way to show I'm taking God's Word seriously. As far as it depends on me, I will try to live with everybody. I know you don't agree with that—"

"I agree we should get along with people. But there's a time to take a stand. To grab a sling and some smooth stones."

He smiled at my Old Testament reference. "So I assume

you're going to talk with Jesse before you head back to Chicago?"

"That's my plan."

"Well, there's a bridal shower tonight. I doubt you're going to crash that party." When I didn't answer, he said, "Matt, if you don't mind my asking, where are you with the Lord?"

I put the steak knife down and stared at my plate. "I suppose I'm where I've been for a long time. And he doesn't seem to have moved much either."

He tried to smile, seemingly unable to come up with a follow-up. We finished our meal and walked toward the parking lot.

"You know what I think?" he said, a hand on my shoulder. "God is at work. Even though we're imperfect, he still uses us. And he's using you, Son."

By Tuesday evening every relative and church member within thirty miles had heard of my return. My mother said Uncle Willy had asked to see me and I told her I would stop by his house before I left.

I took a walk after dinner on the hill where Dickie, Jesse, and I had roamed. The old fire pit was still there with rocks circling it in a tangle of growth. I kicked at a tent peg driven too deep. It felt like a lifetime ago.

I looked out over the little town and wondered where Jesse was and what kind of presents she was opening. If there was anyone on the planet who deserved a bridal shower, it was her.

I heard the rumble of an engine through the trees and

made my way down. A red pickup sat near the lamp at the end of the walk and someone stood next to it, speaking to my father.

I could have waited but something told me I should face this trouble. As I passed what was left of my grandfather's barn, I heard the nasal whine of Earl Turley.

"And you know better than I do what he's up to, Pastor," Earl said, jabbing a finger in my father's face. "I'm a peaceful man. But he was at the store to see her. I'm not leaving till I have a word with him."

"Earl, I told you, he left a bit ago. I don't know where he went, but I do know—"

"Dad," I yelled from the barn. "I got this."

My father's shoulders slumped as if he had hoped I would stay away. Earl stepped back, his hands on his hips, sizing me up. He no longer suffered from a lack of height or muscle, but he had the same red hair and light complexion. He wore a buttoned work shirt with his name over the pocket and steel-toed shoes, and I guessed he worked on cars by the grease on his hands.

"Why are you getting into our business this close to the wedding?" Earl said, holding his head back like a snake ready to strike.

I reached out a hand but he just looked at it. The memory of the picnic came back to me and my nose throbbed with phantom pain.

"Why don't we go inside and talk?" my father said. "Earl, my wife made some apple pie for dessert. Would you—?"

"I ain't hungry. And if you'll excuse us, Pastor, I think this is something the two of us need to work out."

My father glanced at me as if asking permission to leave. "Earl's right."

My father walked away and closed the screen door quietly behind him. I moved toward Earl's truck, leaning against the bed, noticing the shotgun mounted on the inside of the cab window. A squirrel tail hung limp from the radio antenna.

"First of all, I didn't come back to make trouble."

"Your intentions don't matter. You're making trouble. That's the point."

"There's history between Jesse and me."

"And that history is over," Earl said. "The page is turned. She don't want nothing to do with you. She told me that. You think I didn't ask her?"

I cocked my head.

"Everybody knowed you was sweet on Jesse. The way you and Dickie hung around her." Earl looked down. He didn't seem as menacing. "She told me she had feelings when you two was kids. She felt sorry for you."

"She felt *sorry* for me?"

"You was fat and had big ears and didn't have no friends. And you were a preacher's son. So you had two strikes. And you were a Pirates fan."

"That was the third strike."

"That was a wild pitch," Earl said, grinning. It wasn't a bad dig, I had to admit.

"You was nice to her," Earl continued. "You was one of

the only people who showed kindness. I thank you for that. I know she appreciated your family."

"I was a lot nicer than you," I said, my voice edgy.

He pawed at the gravel with one foot. "I won't argue with that. I ain't proud of a lot of things I said and did. To her and others. I've turned over a new leaf, though."

"That's a big leaf to lift by yourself."

"I didn't lift it on my own." Earl looked up at me. "I love that girl. I love everything about her. And I want to give her a different life than the one she's had. She never got dealt a full hand and the cards she did have were twos and threes. Nobody should go through what she did."

"You've got no argument from me there."

"But you coming back, when her future is right there in front of her, when we've got all these plans—that ain't fair. Not for her. Not for me."

"How did you two get over your . . . differences? There was history between you, and none of it was good."

"That ain't none of your business. But I'll tell you anyway. And you should know that your daddy is the one who brought us together."

That revelation sent my stomach churning. "And how did that happen?"

"I always thought church was something you did, like paying union dues. My daddy treated it the same as Blackwood—a country club you joined for all the privileges. After he died, Blackwood stepped up and helped us out. He became like my own daddy. So I followed his lead.

Somewhere along the line, I took a hard look in the mirror. I saw the man I'd become."

If this had been a play, I would have easily been able to deliver the next line. In a dramatic production, you feed off the emotion of the other actors, take their intensity and volley it. You use the onstage chemistry, love or hate or indifference. I felt something genuine coming from Earl, but before I could respond with something snappy, he continued.

"Your daddy was preaching one Sunday about forgiveness. About coming to God all dressed and cleaned up when down inside things are dirty. He asked if there was anything hanging over us with somebody else. I was sitting there looking at the words in red and I remembered her. Her face just jumped right out at me. And I thought, *Poodle dog and apple butter—what is this?* I couldn't get Jesse out of my head. The names I'd called her. How ugly I had been. And to that colored boy, too."

I studied Earl's face, watching for some slip in the performance. That he still referred to Dickie as "that colored boy" let me know that his racism hadn't been washed in the blood.

"After what happened to her," Earl continued, "you know the church helped her out. And Blackwood didn't like it. So I went along with him and Gentry. There was ugly things said. Matt, I didn't go back to her to do anything but apologize. And I didn't really do it for her. I was doing it for me. To get the bad feelings out, you understand. So I went to the store . . . She was putting out meat in the case and there was blood all over her white apron." He paused at the memory. "I said, 'Jesse, I'm real sorry for the things I've said. Names I called you.' I just let it fly right there in the store. At first she turned away. She can be stubborn and bullheaded—you know that. But when I told her it was the Lord who convicted me, she turned around. I said, 'The Lord has done a work in my heart. And I'm trying to make amends for things I've done.' I told her she was at the top of the list of people I knew I'd hurt."

I glanced at the house and saw my mother at the window. She turned and the curtain fluttered.

"Are you sure you don't want some pie?" I said.

He shook his head and crossed his arms.

"What did Jesse say to you?"

The memory made Earl smile. "She told me to stick my amends where the sun don't shine. Jesse don't hold back. But when I didn't cuss at her or yell, I think she saw I meant it. And finally she said she'd consider forgiving me. That's what started the whole thing. We sat together in church. One thing led to another."

It was clear there had been a change in Earl, and it struck me that all my conversations with Jesse growing up hadn't yielded fruit, but this apology from an old enemy had. And it felt like I was looking from the outside in again on more than one level.

"You ever talk to Dickie?" I said. "You ever tell him you're sorry?"

"I ain't got to everybody I've hurt. And the truth is, the tally ain't all in yet. There's a long line waiting."

His story sounded convincing. Poignant, even. Part of me wanted to get in my car and head north. But there was something still there, a paper cut in my heart that kept rubbing the wrong way and opening at vulnerable moments.

"I saw Jesse this morning. Did she tell you?"

His back went rigid and he set his jaw. "I ain't talked with her today."

"I got there early and waited in the parking lot. I wanted to hear it from her. If marrying you is what she wants, I'll leave and never come back."

"You told her that?"

"I didn't get the chance."

"Then I'll answer you. She's choosing me. And the only thing you're doing is stirring up memories." He shook his head like he had bitten down on a hot pepper. "Let sleeping dogs lie, Matt. Because if you don't, them dogs will bite. And they bite hard."

I searched for something to say, something that felt genuine. "Jesse made me a promise. And you know she keeps her word. I think it was her way of breaking the family curse and being different than her father."

Earl curled his bottom lip under his overbite and blew air in a sigh. He stared at a spot on the hill like he was searching for a site for a deer stand. "She promised you something this morning?"

"No, it was a long time ago."

"Then forget it."

When I didn't respond, he took a step closer. "Look, I know what kind of family I'm from. I don't want to wind up like my daddy or Blackwood. I'm trying to turn things around."

When he didn't say anything more, I leaned in. "About the basketball at the picnic. Was that on purpose?"

"I didn't mean to bloody your schnoz, if that's what you mean. But that's another thing I'm sorry about."

"Then it's good I came back. You can get that off your tally."

Earl took a breath and lowered his voice. "I don't wish you ill, Matt. But there's something you ought to know. Not everybody around here has seen the light. Blackwood is spending a lot on the wedding ceremony."

"He hated Jesse. He hated her family. Why would he be for this?"

"He thinks he can finally buy her property and get her out of the hollow."

"Did he put you up to this? To get her land?"

He clenched his teeth. "I told you—I love that girl. I don't want nobody hurting her. And people won't be happy if you mess things up."

"So I'm not invited to the wedding?"

He ignored the question, which was meant to be ignored.

"If Jesse can convince me this is what she wants, I won't stand in your way. I might throw rice a little harder at you. But there's still something not right and I don't know what it is."

He bit his cheek and narrowed his gaze. "I'm going to tell you something nobody knows. I'm telling you because

I believe you care about her. I really believe that. And I think you'll keep this between us."

The look on his face concerned me, and the tumblers in my mind spun. Was Jesse addicted to something? Did she have a life-threatening illness?

"Jesse's pregnant," Earl said.

The basketball to the nose was nothing. This was a sledgehammer to my heart. I felt pale, like the blood had gushed from some wound.

Earl put a hand on my shoulder. "Now you know why it's important to leave. Do it for her. Just go on and get out of here."

He went to the other side of the truck and got in and drove away.

Chapter 14

Dickie and I took a load up the hill at dusk, and he set up the tent. I cleared the fire pit and arranged the rocks, then gathered firewood. Crickets sang as we made a final trip for sleeping bags and food. Frogs charummed and croaked in the creek and ponds. The whole world came alive after the sun slipped below the hills. We found Ben's sleeping bag in storage, on a high shelf in my grandmother's garage. Just pulling it out and smelling it brought memories, and I wished Ben were there. He would have loved Jesse and Dickie. I harbored the dream that he would walk up the driveway one day, just like Dickie felt about his father.

My father came from a meeting at church and climbed

the hill carrying a flashlight. He helped us get the fire started and brought out two potatoes wrapped in tinfoil that we put at the bottom of the fire. We assured him we would be all right.

"No staying up all night," he said.

"Yes, sir," I said.

He looked at Dickie. "That's a fine tent. I can tell you've set it up a time or two."

Dickie smiled. "Yes, sir. Mostly in the backyard when the landlord says it's okay."

My father smiled and looked out over the twinkling lights of the community below. It reminded me of the verse that said Jesus looked at the people with compassion. There was something about Dogwood that felt white unto harvest, at least to my dad.

Watching him walk down the hill, the light flashing on the path in front of him, was exciting and lonely. It was my first night away from them since moving to Dogwood. Part of me felt sad. What would happen when I went to college? I'd never had these thoughts but they came in waves as we popped the tops on sodas and ate the rest of the ham and cheese and chips.

Dickie began singing the words of "In the Year 2525" and making comments about life twenty, thirty, and a thousand years in the future. He spoke of UFOs and pointed out constellations. He was a big fan of *Star Trek* and had seen every episode that ran for the three seasons it was aired. He believed within ten years we would all have communicators.

"What do you mean?"

"You know, a way to talk to each other."

"Like a phone?" I said, not having watched much *Star Trek*. "How are you going to get a wire long enough to go to the store?"

"You won't have wires with it. You don't have a wire on the radio and you can hear people talking, right?"

"So everybody's going to have their own radio station?"

"It's not like that. And it won't just be a phone. You'll take your blood pressure, your temperature. You'll push a button and order a pizza. Call your family anywhere in the world."

"Sounds like the Jetsons." It was too wild to believe but Dickie could see it like he could see the fire in front of us.

My mother had put marshmallows in the cooler, unbeknownst to us, and we cut branches with Dickie's pocketknife and sharpened them and roasted the marshmallows over the fire until they bubbled. Dickie held one in too long and burned it. When we'd eaten plenty, we burnt the rest, seeing what kind of glop they would make on the firewood.

It was just before midnight when we crawled into our sleeping bags. It was too hot in the tent, so I pulled my sleeping bag outside by the fire and stared at the stars.

"Hey, we didn't eat the potatoes," I said to Dickie.

"We'll have them for breakfast," he said, yawning. "Now if Mothman comes, you wake me up."

All the Mothman and UFO talk revved my imagination. The flickering fire made the field and tree line swim.

Soon, Dickie was gone and the light snoring became a gale force wind. My mother conjectured that Dickie had a broken nose that hadn't been repaired.

At the edge of the fire, mosquitoes and gnats were chased away by the heat. Fireflies swirled from the earth, but as the night wore on, their numbers dwindled. I watched the sky, hands behind my head, and wondered if there was life on a distant planet. I wondered if Ben was looking at the same sky. Did he miss us? Would he ever come home?

Something moved along the tree line and I sat up. There was something down there. Maybe a deer. It looked too big to be an opossum or raccoon. I peered into the darkness, wondering if it could be a wildcat. The fire would keep it away, I reassured myself. Someone said a bear had pillaged trash cans the previous summer. I also knew from *Old Yeller* that animals with hydrophobia acted irrationally. My father had told me about a man from his childhood who had been bitten by a rabid dog and said it was a horrible death. He'd never filled in the details but my imagination ran wild.

Something white came up the hill. My heart beat wildly. Was it a ghost?

"Dickie, I think there's something coming," I said in a loud whisper.

Nothing but snoring from the tent.

"Dickie, you'd better get out here," I said, full-voiced now.

And then I heard someone chuckle. Up the hill, into the

firelight, barefoot through the tall grass came Jesse Woods, her hair lifting in the night breeze.

I gave a sigh. "I thought you were the Mothman."

She put a hand on her hip. "You sure know how to compliment a girl."

"I didn't mean it like that," I said.

She waved a hand and stood over the fire, then sat at the end of my sleeping bag. I wished we hadn't burned all the marshmallows because I wanted to offer her one. A can of Faygo was all we had, and she opened it.

"What in the world is that noise?" she said.

"Hurricane Dickie. You should have heard him in the hotel."

"It sounds like a chain saw with the croup."

I laughed. "How did you know we were up here?"

"I didn't. I saw the fire from the road yonder. I figured it was probably you and your dad. How'd the birthday trip go?"

"Wait. You ride your bike at midnight?"

"Sometimes, when I can't sleep. It gets so hot in the house in the summer, even with the fan going and opening all the windows and taking off . . . Well, it's hot no matter what you do. Sometimes I climb up on the roof to find a breeze."

I told her about the trip, the games, what we saw and ate and how the Pirates lost. I tried to hold back on some of the fun we had so she wouldn't feel bad.

"We got Daisy something in the gift shop," I said. I described the bobblehead and a peaceful look came over her.

"She'll like that. And I bet Dickie had fun." She picked up the transistor radio and flicked it on. At night, the AM band pulled in stations from around the country and it felt like the world came and settled down right next to me. Voices from Chicago and New York and St. Louis. Jesse stopped at a twangy guitar song from a station in Texas. A country singer laughed and sang, "When you're hot, you're hot. When you're not, you're not." Jesse wiggled and held up her hands and bit her lip as she moved to the music. I couldn't help but stare at her shape and the easy way she moved. She caught me looking at her and smiled, shaking her hips in exaggerated movement.

When the song ended, she turned off the radio and put it down, staring at the stars. "Sure is pretty, ain't it?"

I agreed. "Do you really think there's a Mothman? I know you guys are trying to scare me, but the pictures Dickie describes sound real."

"I ain't never seen him, so I can't give you an eyewitness report. And I think Dickie wants there to be a Mothman. You know, something out there trying to help. Those people up in Gallipolis saw something. There was too many who seen him."

"And what about the Martians the government is hiding? The ones who landed in New Mexico. Are those real?"

"Some things in this world you can't explain. Like the Loch Ness monster. Bigfoot. God. They're all the same. They keep us guessing and trying to figure out what we'll never explain."

"You think God and Bigfoot are in the same category?"

She grabbed a handful of grass and pulled it, tossing it in the air. "I ain't saying this to offend you, PB. It's just that—"

"PB?" I said.

"Preacher Boy."

I smiled.

"I don't know if there's a God," she continued, looking straight up. "Maybe he's hiding behind some star. And if he is there, I don't know that he cares much."

"I think he does."

"You think he does because your daddy's a preacher. You've got skin in the game."

"That has something to do with it. But I believe God is there because it's true. Whether my dad is a preacher or a coal miner doesn't matter."

She picked up a stick and broke it and threw the pieces into the fire. "It would be easier if there wasn't a God."

"How do you figure that?"

"All the pain and suffering in the world would make a lot more sense. Some people are rich. Others have nothing. Kids in Africa starve to death because they was born on the wrong continent. If there ain't no God and we're here by chance, trouble just comes to you. But if there is a God, it means you got to explain things that can't be explained."

I hadn't considered the suffering masses as much as I had considered the Pirates' losing streak. Leave it to Jesse to help me see life globally.

"I've heard that we compare God with our fathers," I said. "We make him out to be what we've experienced."

Jesse shook her head. "If that's the case, I sure don't want nothing to do with him."

We listened to the fire crackle and I remembered the potatoes. I offered her one and she dug it out of the ashes with a crooked stick Dickie had whittled. She tried to unwrap the potato but dropped it when steam came out.

"I wish your mom would have let you come with us," I said.

"Yeah. It was probably for the best. Did you swim?"

I nodded. "They had a nice pool. All the white people got out when Dickie got in, though."

"Figures. Dickie's just looking for a break, you know? Hoping his dad comes back in one piece. That's one of the reasons he wanted to go to your church."

"Really?"

"Yeah, the day of the picnic. We talked about coming early to the service. He said he wanted to get his daddy on the prayer list."

"You don't have to go to our church in order to get us to pray."

"Well, he seemed to think you did."

I told her I would pray for Dickie's father every night until he returned.

"That's nice of you. He'll appreciate that."

"Why didn't you come to the service?"

She tried to pick up the potato but dropped it again. "For the same reason we didn't stay. I swear, Matt, them church people are meaner than snakes."

"We can all be meaner than snakes."

We listened to the noise coming from the tent. Instead of talking about what was on my mind, I made a joke about Dickie getting married someday and what his wife would endure.

"Maybe he'll marry a woman with a hearing aid and she can take it out every night," Jesse said.

I laughed and the silence between us unnerved me. The thought of Dickie's father and his war service brought the conversation in the car to mind—the one my mother had tried to quell. The secret about my family felt like a weight holding me underwater.

"Jesse, can I tell you something? Something nobody around here knows?"

She shrugged. "Sure."

"It's hard because pastors and their kids are supposed to be perfect . . . It's like living in a fishbowl. It feels like everybody looks at you."

"What's the big secret?"

"My brother got drafted. He was supposed to go to Vietnam. But he didn't."

"I thought if you were drafted, you had to go."

"I know. But he didn't."

"Where is he? Hiding in your grandmother's pump house?"

"He went to Canada. He and a friend went to somebody's house up there."

"A friend?"

"His girlfriend."

"Whoa. I'll bet your mama and daddy don't like that much."

"I don't know which is worse: living with a girl my parents don't like or running to Canada to avoid the Army. I feel real bad about it because of Dickie's dad . . ."

I could see the tumblers going in her head. "He's a draft dodger?"

"If you knew him, you'd like him. He's nice. I think he didn't wanted to kill people."

"He didn't want to die is what he didn't want."

"Maybe so."

She stared at me, but it seemed like she was looking through me. "People run from their problems all the time. I understand him being scared. But when your country calls, it seems chicken to hightail it."

"You think it's okay to love somebody who makes a bad choice?"

"The way I look at it, you ain't got no choice who you love. You either do or you don't. And you don't control what other people do. You can't help that your brother ran off." She grabbed some more grass and tossed it at me. Then she pointed a finger. "But I'll tell you one thing. You'd better not tell Dickie. He gets worked up about stuff like that. There's a lot of folks who didn't want to go or send their kids but they did. There was a boy down the next hollow who got drafted a few years ago. He was coming home, riding in a Jeep somewhere over there, when some sniper shot him from the trees. I think that's what

Dickie is afraid of. His daddy will be ready to come home and something will happen."

"My parents don't talk about Ben. It's like he's dead. He always remembered my birthday, but I didn't hear anything from him this year."

Jesse frowned. "You and birthdays. Don't nobody remember mine and I'm not the worse for the wear."

"When is it?"

She picked up the potato gingerly and tore it in two, steam rising again. She blew on it and took a bite. "It don't matter."

I didn't press her. "Sometimes I look at his stuff, the books he left. This sleeping bag. His ball glove. I wonder if things will ever be the same."

"Probably not. But just because they're not the same don't mean you can't live." She took another bite and said she wished she had some cow butter and salt. When she finished the potato, she wadded the foil and threw it in the fire. "You better hope Blackwood never finds out. He'll use that against your daddy."

"Use it for what?"

"I don't know. To get what he wants. That man has so many people in his back pocket, it's a wonder he can walk straight. Nobody stands up to him. He's had his eye on our property for years."

I recalled Gentry Blackwood saying something about that at the picnic. "Why would Old Man Blackwood want your place? He owns most of the county, doesn't he?"

"Some people are never satisfied. Always got to have

a little more. Always got to have what somebody else has." She stared at the fire and I wondered what was going through her mind. The light flickered in her eyes. "I think he want us out of the way. He thinks our family is trash."

"You're not."

She looked at me, then at the fire again. It seemed she was trying to decide something. Finally she lay down beside me on the sleeping bag with her back to the fire, one arm crooked under her head. Her hair hung in her face and she gave me a stare that was unnerving because I couldn't stop staring back. I thought about the girl in the swimming pool in the bikini.

"I won't say nothing to nobody about your brother."

"Thanks," I said, swallowing hard. I had never been this close to Jesse or any other girl. I could smell the potato on her breath. "I appreciate that."

She looked down and opened her mouth, running her tongue along her lips.

"Jesse, what's wrong? You didn't come out here to watch the stars and eat a potato."

"I reckon I don't know why I came out here," she said, sitting up.

"No, don't go," I said, touching her arm.

She lay down, on her back this time. Watching her was a transcendent experience. She blinked her long eyelashes, her eyes roaming. Finally she whispered to the sky, "Can you keep one of my secrets?"

"Sure."

"This is something you can't tell nobody on God's green earth."

"I thought you didn't believe in God."

She cocked her head. "Don't get smart. This is serious."

"Okay, I won't tell anybody."

She rolled onto her side and looked me in the face. "This is a cross-your-heart-and-hope-to-die kind of deal. Swear on a stack of Bibles. I got to know if I can trust you."

I held up a hand like I was swearing in a courtroom. "I solemnly swear I won't tell anybody what Jesse Woods is about to say. So help me God."

She put her hand on my arm and something came over her face I'd never seen. There were tears welling in her eyes.

"My mama died," she said.

Chapter 15

"Don't joke about stuff like that," I said. Jesse didn't respond and I sat up. "Your mother's really dead? When? What happened?"

She put a hand on my chest and pushed me down. "Shhh. Be quiet and listen, okay?"

I watched her face, a thousand questions forming. Before she could speak, I said, "I heard her talk to you. The first day I came to your house."

She nodded. "She was okay then but she got worse. She'd been sickly before, but every time she bounced back. This time her cough got deeper and she couldn't catch her breath."

I tried to wrap my head around her words. What would I have done if my mother had died? I wouldn't be holding it together like Jesse and I wouldn't have kept it a secret. I also wouldn't have been as alone as she was.

"Why didn't she go to the hospital?"

"I wish she had. I wish I would have called somebody."

"My dad would have given her a ride. Or my mom."

"I know. Your family is good people. I wanted to get to a phone but Mama said no. She said people who go to the hospital die quicker."

"That's not true."

"Well, it's what she believed. I doubt they could have done much for her, as far gone as she was. Maybe they could have helped her breathe. I don't know. It was bad, Matt. There at the end it was awful." She crumbled and put her hands over her face. This was another thing about Jesse—she rarely smiled or cried. Most of the time her face was like those pictures you see of people living in the dust bowl, stoic and hard.

I couldn't think of anything to say except for "I'm so sorry, Jesse."

She wiped her nose on her sleeve and stared at the sleeping bag, another tear running down her cheek. "We live and we die. Simple as that. It happened to my sister. Remember the day I bought the bike—the man talked about my sister?"

I nodded. It had been a question I wanted to ask but couldn't.

"Her name was Eva. They think she got it at the pool."

"Got what?"

"The polio. Daddy was still around. And they had her in the hospital in this big iron case. It took about every cent we had to treat her. Then they brought her home. She would smile with these stubby teeth. Daisy Grace looks like her. I don't remember Eva, but I have pictures."

"What happened?"

"She just slipped away. She's buried out at the cemetery at the back of the road. I go talk to her sometimes. That's one reason I wanted a bike, so I could go back there. It's a long walk. Now I got more kin to talk with under the ground than above it. Ain't that something?"

I was interested in Eva and Jesse's mother and where her father might be. I was interested in everything about her, but I couldn't process the information.

"When did it happen—with your mom?"

"You can't tell nobody, Matt," she said with urgency.

"I'm not going to," I said, then wondered how I would ever keep that secret.

"A couple weeks ago. Before your birthday."

"That's why you brought Daisy Grace to the party."

She nodded. "That's why I've had to take her every-where. I can't leave her. She wanders."

"Who's with her now?"

"She's sleeping. When she finally nods off, she sleeps so hard thunder don't wake her. Kind of like Dickie with-out the log sawing. It's really the only time I get to myself. I haven't gotten much sleep since Mama passed. I see her walking through the woods. I hear her talking to me."

"Your mother?" The thought gave me a shiver.

"You think that's normal? You think the tiredness plays with your mind so you think you see her? Or do you think maybe there are ghosts? You know, dead people walking through the woods?"

I looked at the tree line and wondered what I'd do if I saw Jesse's mother. The prospect frightened me more than the Mothman. "I don't think people become ghosts, Jesse. Maybe you should talk with somebody."

"What do you think I'm doing?"

"I mean a grown-up. Somebody you can trust, like a pastor. Do they have a counselor at the school?"

"I done told you, I can't tell nobody."

"Why not?"

"You got to believe me. Here's what'll happen. I tell somebody and first thing they'll do is go to the authorities. Next thing you know, the law comes and takes Daisy Grace. She'll get put in with relatives. And I ain't having that."

"If you don't want your family to help, there's someone at church who can."

"You seen how church people treated Dickie and me." She shook her head. "And if the government gets involved, they'll split us up. I've seen it happen."

I looked away and took a deep breath. I was not as adept at the spiritual life as my parents, but I lifted a prayer for wisdom, asking God to give me words.

"I been wondering how I'm going to do school," Jesse said, "with Daisy Grace not even in kindygarten. If she was in school, I could probably work it out, but I'm up a creek."

"You can't drop out and stay home," I said.

"That's not the worst idea. But the truant officer would come knocking. I can't have that."

I sat up again but this time she couldn't push me down. "Jesse, you have to tell. You need help. There are programs, there's government assistance—"

"I don't need no help." She set her jaw. "I promised Mama I would care for Daisy. And when I make a promise, I keep it. She's staying with me."

I saw her resolve and decided to go a different direction. Then another thought crept in. A thought so morbid it surprised me.

"Jesse, if your mother is still in the house after two weeks—"

"You think I'm stupid? I didn't just fall off the turnip truck. I know you can't keep a body around like that."

I decided to ignore the turnip truck reference and asked with equal amounts of horror and fascination, "What did you do?"

"Mama died of a night. She was coughing a lot and I tried to get Daisy to bed, but she put up a fuss. She wanted to sit with Mama and I told her no, that Mama was sick and she could sit with her in the morning." Jesse stopped for a minute and looked away. "I wish I'd have let her say good-bye. Just let her sit there. She wasn't hurting nobody."

"You didn't know what was going to happen."

She nodded and wiped at another tear. "I got Daisy
to bed and Mama went into this spell where she couldn't
catch her breath, big gobs of blood coming up. I would
have run to the Blackwoods'—that's how bad it was. But
she grabbed hold of me and looked me right in the eyes.
'You got to promise me you'll take care of her. You got to
promise you won't let them take her.' I told her they'd never
get Daisy Grace. That seemed to calm her.

"She told me she loved me and then her eyes got kind of
glassy. And then it was over. She just laid back, staring up
at the ceiling, and I heard the rattle. I felt for a pulse and
pumped on her chest like they do on *Emergency!* trying to
get her to breathe, but there wasn't no bringing her back."

"What did you do then?"

"I just set there. I held her hand and told her we would
be okay. Told her I loved her. Promised her I wouldn't let
them get Daisy Grace. And that Old Man Blackwood
wouldn't get the farm. She was afraid of that, too. After my
daddy left, she signed the deed over to me. Had it notarized
and everything. And I been looking, but I can't find it.

"I probably said all that stuff more for myself than her.
I want to believe I can do everything I promised." She rolled
onto her back and looked at the stars. "Then I closed her
eyes. I seen them do that on TV. Put coins on her eyelids.
And then I cleaned her up as best I could. It was a mess, I'll
tell you that. I always asked Mama if we could get carpet
and I was glad right then we never did. Of course you can't
get blood out of the couch, but I wiped it down and put a
pillow over it and told Daisy somebody spilled Kool-Aid."

I had never seen Jesse's mother or the inside of their house, but I imagined the couch and Jesse with a wet washcloth, on her hands and knees scrubbing, her dead mother there, her sister sleeping in a back room.

"I knowed I couldn't call the funeral home. They'd report it. You have to promise me, now that you know. You can't tell nobody, Matt. That would be the biggest hurt you could ever give me."

"I don't want to hurt you, Jesse. I want to help. And I won't tell. But at some point somebody is going to find out."

"No, they're not. I got it figured. I just need help."

I stared at the moon. The secret about my brother was the biggest problem in my life and it weighed terribly. Jesse's problem felt like a thousand pounds and she was asking me to get on the other end and lift. I realized she was agreeing. She couldn't do this alone, and she had brought me into the struggle.

"I knew if I was going to keep my promise to Mama, I had to act quick," she continued. "I lit the lantern and found the shovel out back and went into the field. The ground was soft from the runoff of the rain and I started digging. It took most of the night to get down far enough so the critters wouldn't come along and dig her up. I couldn't let that happen. I hit rock a few feet down and that slowed me. But I used that later to put on top of her to protect her."

I nodded, unable to do more.

"I wrapped her in her favorite quilt. Mama, she loved

that old quilt because she said it came from the old country. Her own mama had used it and the smell of it reminded her of home. It's funny what a smell like that can do, just take you back to something better."

I think it was then, with Jesse telling her story, that I moved from pity to something deeper. I'd been attracted to her from the moment we met, drawn by her cocksure attitude, her quick wit, her toughness of skin and spirit, and the way she accepted me. Drawn by those blue eyes and the shape of her and the way she moved. There was something primal about the way she processed her life. I couldn't help being pulled into her orbit, like the moon clinging by gravity to the Earth. Part of me wanted to be Jesse. Part of me knew I never would.

There are some people who take. They sap energy and make life about them. Other people leave you richer. They come at empty times and fill. Even in the loss, Jesse was giving, though I wasn't sure what.

"Eva's death nearly killed Mama," Jesse said. "I don't think she ever got over it. I was little, but I remember the life going out of her. I wonder if she might have met up with Eva."

"So you do believe in heaven?"

She frowned at me. "Mama believed like you do, about God and all. That Jesus was waiting to welcome her. I guess, if she's right, she's an angel looking down on us right now. You think so?"

I knew enough about what the Bible said regarding heaven to know people don't become angels. My father had

discussed this with us after my grandfather died and someone said we had another angel looking down. But there are
times for correcting a person's theology and times for listening, and I didn't think Jesse needed a lesson right then.

I looked up at the moon hanging above us. "It sounds
like she's in God's presence. And that's a real comfort."

"Yeah. If there's a heaven, Mama's there. If God don't
accept her, he won't accept none of us."

I also hesitated to correct Jesse's view of salvation.
I wanted to say you don't earn your way to heaven, but
lying by her pool of pain wasn't the place.

"She did everything she could to give us a good life after
my daddy ran away."

"Are you angry he wasn't there to help?"

"Angry enough to spit. But if he'd been there, he'd have
probably been drunk. So I'm glad he's gone."

"Why did he run away?"

"You'd have to ask him."

"Maybe he was still upset about Eva dying."

She put her hands behind her head. "That ain't no
excuse. If you got a wife and two little kids to take care of,
you don't run off."

"What happened to him?"

"I don't rightly know. He probably got killed somewhere
in a card game or drank too much and fell onto the train
tracks again. I asked Mama once why she married a man who
never cared about her and she said he wasn't always like that. I
don't believe it. I think people are the way they are and there's
no changing them, as much as you want to believe they can."

"What about Daisy? How is she taking your mom's death?"

"She don't know."

I closed my eyes, trying not to react too strongly.

"I couldn't tell her. It would have broken her little heart. And she'd up and blab about it to everybody. I told her Mama went away for a spell and we have to get along without her. I told her to keep picking daisies until Mama gets back and we'll put them in the jar by the front window so she can have them. I've been picking out the dead ones and throwing them away. And Daisy Grace just stands at the window lookin' out. It's pitiful. She's called to me, 'Here she comes!' It just breaks your heart."

Jesse shook the emotion away and put her head on my shoulder, moving closer, and I let her, my body tingling from her touch, her reliance on me.

I gave my handkerchief to her. It was something my mother said, that a gentleman always has a handkerchief, and I had carried it out of obligation for so long but never used it. Right then, under the stars on that hill behind my grandmother's house, I gave thanks to the God of a persistent mother who had insisted on me being a gentleman.

Jesse blew her nose and put her head down in the crook of my arm, her tears falling on my T-shirt, and I felt grown-up, like the story she had told had called up strength I didn't know I possessed.

"Why me?" I said.

"Why you, what?"

"Why did you choose to tell me and not somebody else?"

"Why not you?"

"You don't know me like you know Dickie. And there has to be some girl you could tell."

"People in this town compare themselves with my family to make themselves feel better. I can't talk to nobody here."

"Do you compare yourself to another family to make you feel better?"

"It's a useless exercise. Some people look like they don't have anything, but the truth is, they're richer than folks who seem to have everything."

"Not rich in stuff, though."

"Right. Rich in the heart. People would feel sorry for me if they found out about my mama and they would bring food for a while. Then everybody goes on their way. But Daisy and I will always have each other. And we'll remember our mama's love. Some folks don't have that."

"But why me?"

"I don't know. I reckon it was something I could tell about you." She sat up and looked at the tree line while she talked. "Here you was, riding alone, coming from a far-off city, and you were the one to see that horse. Most people would have rode right by. She was probably stuck there a day or so before we got to her. But you crawled up there. And it was scary to come to my house, not knowing anybody and Carl barking. You didn't run. I made my decision about what kind of feller you was right then. You're the kind who won't let anything stop you from doing good."

Her words felt like water to a dying man in the desert.

"Okay, let's think this through," I said when she was quiet. "Somebody's going to come looking for your mama. A relative. A bill collector. It's bound to happen. She doesn't show up for some appointment and people will ask questions."

"I got that figured. She gets her Social Security check each month and I cash it over at the bank. They let me do that. So I keep paying bills. We own the property, so we don't have no rent or whatever you call it."

"Mortgage."

"Right. Mama says all we have to do is keep up with the taxes. Now I don't know how I'm going to do that, but they don't come due till next summer."

"What about school? What if a teacher wants to talk to your mom about something?"

She cursed. "Mama never went to them parent-teacher things. They'd probably faint if she showed up. I'll just say she's sick. Half the kids' parents don't come to those meetings."

"And what about when Daisy Grace starts school? You going to handle all that?"

"I ain't figured it all out yet. I'm going to take it a step at a time. And the first step is me going to school in the fall."

"I still don't understand why you won't take help. There's a verse in the Bible that says the truth will set you free."

"The truth will get your sister taken away is what it'll do. Sometimes you got to work your way around the truth."

"But what would be so bad about you and Daisy going to live with a relative you trusted?"

"If my mama had any living kin, we'd go. But she don't. The only people I got is my daddy's side. It'll be a cold day in hell when I let them take Daisy."

"Why?"

"First of all, if Blackwood finds out my mama passed, he'll get the land. He's tried all kinds of tricks and she fought him tooth and nail. Second of all, they'll take Daisy over to the Branches. We used to go there when I was younger. And my cousins are boys who . . . do things to you. There ain't no little girl safe at that place. Do you understand?"

I swallowed hard and nodded, trying to take in what she had just revealed.

"I can fend for myself but Daisy can't. She's not strong enough. I got to figure out a way to stay at my house."

"But what if there was a way to keep Daisy safe *and* keep you two together?"

She stood so fast it took my breath away. "If you're gonna sit there and argue me about something I know, then you ain't helpin'."

"Sit down," I said, holding up my hands for calm. "This is just like the horse. You've got barbed wire wrapped around your leg and we're trying to figure a way out without somebody bleeding to death."

I regretted using that analogy after what she'd gone through with her mother, but the words calmed her and she sat.

I took a deep breath. "Okay. You can get by the rest of

the summer. I can help. But when school starts, it's a new ballgame. We have to have an adult."

"I told you—"

"Just listen. We have to pool resources. We bring Dickie in, for instance."

"No, Dickie can't keep a secret. Plus, if you and I can keep it from Dickie, we can keep it from anybody."

I thought about it for a moment and something percolated deep inside. Something scary to think and say, but I did. "What do I get out of the deal?"

She furrowed her brow. "What do you mean?"

"You haggled with the guy over the bike. I'm haggling with you over this."

"Are you serious?"

"Look, if I'm going to put my neck on the line, if I have to keep this from my parents and everybody who would want to know about it and to help, I want to know what's in it for me."

Jesse's face fell. "I never thought you'd stoop that low."

"It's not stooping. It's just the way things work. You do something for me, I do something for you."

"What do you want?"

I wasn't prepared for the question, partly because I had been taught that *wanting* was forbidden. I couldn't express my desire to stay in Pittsburgh because that was selfish. I couldn't even want my brother back or talk about him because of all that had happened. I had lived beating down the feeling of *wanting* anything. But Jesse's question opened a door and soon an impetuous thought waltzed through my mind. It was meant to be funny, and coming on the heels of her admission, it was sophomoric. But when you've just turned fourteen, you tend to blurt whatever comes to mind, whether it makes sense or not.

"Marry me," I said.

She shook her head like a dog with a tick in its ear. "Say what?"

"Not now. Just promise that someday you'll marry me."

A look came over her face like she had just seen the Mothman and her mother playing Rook on a tree stump. "Wouldn't that be something?" she said. "Somebody on my side of the tracks marrying somebody on your side."

"What do you say?"

She shook her head again like it was so far out of the realm of possibility she couldn't consider it. Then she set her jaw. "All right, then. I'll marry you someday."

"You gotta promise," I said.

She dipped her head with a frown. "Tell you what, Matt. You keep my secret and help me with Daisy Grace, let her keep picking daisies and bringing them home, and one of these days I'll say, 'I do.'"

"Cross your heart and hope to die," I said.

"Stop it."

"No. If you want my help, you have to do it."

She thought a moment, frowned again, then raised her hand and with fingers crossed swished them across her chest. "There. Satisfied?"

I spit in my hand and held it out. She shook with me, stood, and dusted off her shorts.

"You're disturbed, you know that?" she said.

"Yeah, but a promise is a promise, Jesse. I'll see you tomorrow and we'll plan. School will start before you know it."

"Come to the house," she said.

She walked down the hill into the darkness. I spent the rest of the night wishing that instead of spitting in my hand I had kissed her.

Chapter 16

I awoke from a fitful sleep to find sunlight streaming into the room. The small window was positioned high on the wall, like a prison window that was there only to let in light.

The news about Jesse's pregnancy made the puzzle pieces fit, at least in my head. No wonder she felt like she had to marry Earl. If she was finally on the inside of the church instead of looking in from the outside, she'd have to keep up appearances. She'd have to do the dutiful thing and commit to Earl for the rest of her life. In my mind, that was no way to start a lifelong relationship—out of obligation.

It was too late to catch Jesse before her shift at the store, so I crossed off a task on my mental to-do list and drove to Uncle Willy's house, marveling at how the neighborhood had changed and how much it hadn't. His home was across the street from the Holiness Church of Christ in God our Savior, which, having known some of the attendees, was more holy sounding than it actually was. The building had morphed and someone had constructed a steep wheelchair ramp to its front door. Uncle Willy had been a longtime elder. He had given only tacit approval to my father's ecclesial return to Dogwood, and it struck me how hard it must have been for my father to return as a spiritual leader to the town of his youth.

My uncle grew the largest watermelons and pumpkins in the region and won blue ribbons at the county fair, though there was talk among several Primitive Baptists (who also raised pumpkins and watermelons) that his special fertilizer should be investigated. I never asked my uncle about his growth concoction, but I would not be surprised to discover that his chemistry background had something to do with it. He had worked for forty years in research at Union Carbide and had recently retired.

He opened the screen door and wandered onto the porch, exercising his sixth sense about people driving up or walking onto his property. He was taller than my father and lanky, and his arms hung to his sides like drapes covering unopened windows. It was said he could eat any amount of food and not gain an ounce, and judging from the many times he had come to our house on a whim and received a piece of pie or cake, I believed it. He had the metabolism of a ground squirrel and teeth to match.

"How are you doing there, Matt? I was hoping you'd come by. Come on up and sit awhile."

He spoke with his teeth together, so you had to concentrate to translate his words. I had been in conversations with him in my teen years when he was out the door and home before I deciphered what he had actually said.

I sat in the metal lawn chair on the porch, the Indian summer humidity enveloping us, and he crossed his impossibly thin legs and rocked, the rusty chair squeaking with his mosquito-like weight.

"How much you weigh now, Matt?"

This was the central question of Uncle Willy's life. His preoccupation was so legendary I wondered if he kept a diary as part of a government program. He didn't follow baseball, football, or golf. He rarely hunted or fished. He was a spectator of other people's weight and seemed to have an encyclopedic knowledge of the ebb and flow of the community. To be honest, it was a pastime that kept him busy, for there were more than a few people who struggled.

"I actually haven't been weighing myself lately."

"Is that right?" he said, almost unintelligibly and with a certain amount of incredulity. *Is that right?* was a statement more than it was a question in Uncle Willy's vernacular.

He smiled and I could see my father in his eyes. There were hints of the family tree in the size of his ears, the way he held his mouth when he searched for an answer, and the wispy hair that barely covered his bald spot. He had eyes like armor-piercing bullets.

"Saw that pretty little girl you used to run around with is getting married. What was her name?"

I didn't want to answer because he knew her name and probably her dress size. He probably knew Jesse didn't weigh 120 soaking wet. But to be respectful I said, "Jesse?"

"That's her. Works over at the Food and Drug in the meat department. She's a Woods, isn't she?"

"Yes, she is."

"Used to know her father. Shame about the family. Some people go through more than their share. Seems to have come out all right, though."

"Yeah, I guess she did."

"What don't kill you makes you stronger."

"Unless it just makes you scared," I said.

"Heard she's marrying one of the Turleys."

"That's what I hear."

"What in the world has gotten into her? Why would she want to hook up with that bunch?"

"Maybe she loves him," I said, playing Turley's advocate.

"You think?" He leaned forward and studied a gopher hole near the porch. "The Turleys kind of went squirrelly, if you ask me. Hog wild. They bought guns and ammo back when the Iranians took hostages. I heard they dug a bunker and stocked it with food and water and a little mountain dew, if you know what I mean. Some of them left your daddy's church."

"Where did they go?"

"Up to the valley. Nazarene church, I think. Might have been with the Holy Rollers."

That my uncle referred to another church as "Holy Roller" seemed like the pot calling the kettle black. His church was known to get animated, though they didn't allow musical instruments. All of their singing was a cappella, but the running up and down the aisles filled in the musical gaps.

"You were sweet on her, weren't you, Matt?" he said, smiling and squinting, the lines in his cheeks like odd-numbered interstates running north and south. Perhaps it was his theology or some stray gene from the family DNA that disencumbered him from genial propriety, but Uncle Willy asked the questions nobody would ask but everyone was thinking.

"One fifty-five," I said.

"Excuse me?"

"Last time I stepped on the scale I was 155."

"Is that right? How tall are you? About five-eleven?"

"Close to it."

"You've grown up and thinned out, haven't you?" When I didn't respond, he said, "Boy, you ought to see Buck and Imogene." He pointed a crooked finger three houses and a cornfield away. "She's bigger than a Winnebago. They came this close to taking the front window out to get Buck to the hospital for his hernia surgery."

"Is that right?" I said, glad that he was onto someone else's weight. Glad that he was onto anything else.

"Whole family just puffed up like blowfish. Thyroid

problems, they say, though I have my doubts." He rubbed his wrinkled hands. "Talk around town is you're not too happy about Jesse. You've come back here to kindly change her mind."

"Is that what you hear or what you think?"

"Maybe a little of both," he said. "I remember the three of you riding up and down the road. Peas in a pod. What was the colored boy's name?"

"Dickie Darrel Lee."

"His mother still lives in town, I think. See her every now and then. She thinned out a little over the years."

My mind wandered as we sat, silently listening to the wind move my aunt Zenith's chimes that hung under the eaves. Uncle Willy had once come to our house after I had bought a used minibike. My father had paid half. I rode it to the barn, showing him what it would do, and it must have looked like so much fun that my uncle asked for a turn.

"You sure you know how to ride that thing?" my father, the younger brother, asked innocently.

He received a look of disdain before my uncle mounted the bike like an older child will try to fit on a tricycle, his knees sticking out. He was not as coordinated as he thought and not as adept with the concept of the accelerator and brake, which I showed him before he sped away. The trip up to the barn was uneventful. The return trip was horrifying. He gained natural momentum coming down the hill but instead of pulling on the brake, he increased the gas and the engine revved. Instead of a gentle halt, he sped up, his hair flying. He looked terrified as he put out his feet to stop. Ten feet past my father and me, he did the only thing he could do and ran the minibike into the ground. The smell of gasoline and exhaust overtook us and we ran to him, my uncle tumbling head over heels toward the hickory nut tree. The metal clamp securing the handlebars snapped. My father helped him up and inspected him, looking for broken bones.

"It kindly got away from me" was all Uncle Willy said. My father said he complained of a bad back for years afterward.

"He should have known better than to get on that thing," my mother said at dinner that night. "And you should have known better than to let him."

My uncle took the bike to a friend who owned an arc welder and mended the broken plate, but the bike was never the same. You had to point the handlebars in a slightly different direction than straight. I wound up selling it to a kid up the hollow who rode past every day wearing goggles and a football helmet.

I was rolling these memories around as my uncle went inside and called his wife with a shout. Aunt Zenith was also fascinated with people's weight but was more of a minor league observer, perhaps because of her own struggles. She appeared in the doorway bent with age and shuffling slightly quicker than her arthritic poodle beside her. Her hair was curly and gray but she had lost a lot of it. She carried a fistful of pictures and I rose to meet her. When she gave me a kiss on the cheek, I caught a whiff of dill pickles on her breath.

Aunt Zenith was not the most comely of women, but she was kind and loved her family. There was always room at her table.

"Look at you, Matt," she said. "Look at what a handsome man you've made. My goodness, look at you."

She sat in the metal chair, and it was like watching a crane positioning something from a great height. The chair bent backward and sprang forward and she wobbled a good two minutes, proving some theory of Einstein I had forgotten from school.

"I found these this morning," she said, holding out the pictures.

A vivid memory from when I visited Dogwood as a child was sitting on Aunt Zenith's couch and going through mounds of black-and-white pictures. She would point at faces and name each person. I had no recollection of them, but later my father would tell me it was polite to simply allow her to show the pictures. She was sharing her life and memories.

"But I don't know those people."

"You don't have to," my father said. "Pretend you're interested. It's about caring for your aunt Zenith."

"She does that because that's the way she shows love," my mother added. "Putting those pictures in front of you is like me putting a piece of pie in front of Uncle Willy."

I would much rather have had pie, of course, but this made sense. Each time we visited, I found the most comfortable spot in the room to sit, knowing a photo avalanche was coming.

Once, I held up a picture frame from the pile and asked

who the people were. They didn't look remotely related to our family.

"I don't recall who that is," Zenith said.

Uncle Willy was brought into the discussion and he was mystified. It wasn't until I opened the frame and saw the thin paper the picture was printed on that I solved the mystery. The picture had come with the frame and gotten mixed in with the family heirlooms. They had adopted the family as their own.

Aunt Zenith held out the photographs and I took them. Some were Polaroid shots I had taken the first summer we moved to Dogwood.

"Where did you get these?"

"You gave them to us a long time ago," Zenith said, cackling, her double chin moving like a turkey wattle.

One photo showed a family gathering that included Zenith and Uncle Willy at our house—my birthday party.

I picked up one of the Polaroids and held it out to my uncle. "Remember this camera? I got this because of you."

"Is that right?" Uncle Willy said.

"You gave me money for my birthday. Remember? I bought the Polaroid."

"As I recollect, I counted it as a tax write-off because you wanted to use it for a charitable cause."

"DOORS," I said. "Dogwood Outerspace Observation and Research Society."

He nodded.

"What were you all doing with that camera?" Zenith said, scratching her head.

"Dickie and Jesse were into UFOs and the Mothman and other unexplainable things. We started cataloging all the dead cows and dismembered cats we found. They convinced me to buy a Polaroid so we could take pictures of flying objects."

"Did you ever see any?" Uncle Willy said.

"I took a few blurry shots of something in the sky, but DOORS closed almost as soon as it started."

I studied the birthday party photo. My father had taken it with the family camera. My mother, Willy and Zenith, my grandmother and I stood in the shade of the hickory nut tree. In the background were Jesse, Dickie, and Daisy Grace.

"You can keep those if you want," Aunt Zenith said.

Uncle Willy pulled a black-and-white photo from his shirt pocket and it was clear that, even before I arrived, he had planned to show it to me. "You recognize these two?"

A man and a woman stood side by side along a split-rail fence. The man had his arm around the woman's shoulder. I recognized the man from his impish grin, but I couldn't place the woman.

"That's Wendell and Ada Woods," Aunt Zenith said. "They used to come over here and play dominoes."

"You knew them?" I said, looking at the faces more closely. I recalled Dickie's dictum about a young lady becoming her mother later in life. Jesse had the same slim figure and hair as her mother, but I had never seen her smile this way. There was something free and engaging about it. The photo of her father's smile brought up different emotions.

"They came over every now and then," my aunt said.

"I never met Jesse's mom face-to-face," I said.

"She was an uncommonly thin woman," Uncle Willy said.

Again I stared at the batch of Polaroids I held, the muted colors and blurry faces bringing back painful memories I couldn't quell.

"Take those with you," Aunt Zenith said to me. Then to Uncle Willy, "Go get him a poke."

Uncle Willy went into the house and came back with a paper bag, and I dropped the pictures inside. I leaned down and received a good-bye kiss from Aunt Zenith, her face a little scratchy. Uncle Willy walked me to my car, pointing out his zucchini patch.

"You always grew the biggest pumpkins," I said.

"Got out of the pumpkin business," he said through clenched teeth. "Everything good has to come to an end."

I nodded and shook his hand. He held on, blue eyes piercing mine.

"I expect your mom and dad were surprised to see you back, Matt. Especially with the wedding. Don't suppose they told you about it."

"No, they didn't."

"Well, I understand that. They're trying to help."

"How does marrying Earl help Jesse?"

"How does you coming back here help her?" he said. "Seems to me you're complicating things. Unless there's something you want."

"I want the best for her. Nobody looked out for her."

"So you're riding in to rescue the damsel who doesn't know she's in distress."

It was the first time I'd realized my uncle could focus on anything but weight, and his words hung heavy on me. Then he smiled and the way he held his mouth reminded me of my father.

"When we were kids, your daddy was always the one who climbed the tree to rescue the cat. Maybe it's in your DNA. But sometimes the cat's there because it wants to be. And it's a long way down from the top limb."

I waited until my parents left for church, then drove up the hollow to Jesse's place, but there was no car in the driveway. The little house she and Daisy had lived in had been torn down but a trailer sat on a slab of concrete. It wasn't a brick house, but getting indoor plumbing was a huge leap. People in the community had pulled together for Jesse and Daisy. Even people from the church. There was no light on inside the trailer. I knocked on the door but no one answered. I went to the church parking lot and watched people park and file inside, the scent of mildewed carpet and the sound of the heater firing up swirling in my memory. My mother had said Jesse worked with the youth on Wednesday nights, and as long as I could avoid Earl and his relatives, I figured I could snag a few minutes with her.

Younger children were taken to the steel building in the back, clad in gray shirts with medals and patches sewn onto them. I noticed an older woman get out of her car and rec-ognized Mrs. Talmage. She was the go-to person for anyone with an ailment or medical problem because of her nursing background. Her husband had died recently—my mother had informed me. It was a car accident or a heart attack or maybe both. I hadn't paid attention to the description of the events or the obituary she had sent. As Mrs. Talmage passed two men smoking on the front steps of the church, she stopped and said something, wagging a finger.

Several teenagers noisily took the steps two at a time and laughed and pushed each other. When Basil Blackwood pulled up in the same red truck I remembered, the sight of him caused those outside to scurry. He leaned forward as he walked as if there were some unseen tether propelling him. His imposing figure and our history caused my heart to race.

It's always in situations like these that you think of the things you'd say if you ever had the chance. And I had a few words for Blackwood I'm sure my father wouldn't want me to say.

Earl drove up and let Jesse out near the front. She had on an Awana leader's shirt and hurried toward the metal building. I wondered if she'd have to give up the shirt once people found out she was pregnant. And then I wondered if all of that were true.

Earl parked and followed her inside. I watched the door close and drove away.

Chapter 17

JULY 1972

As soon as Dickie went home the day after the campout, I
raced to Jesse's house. The closeness I had felt drew me like
a magnet. She opened the front door and waved me inside.

The first thing I noticed was the strong scent of mil-
dew. Then I saw their couch, a tattered, green-and-black
plaid with a throw pillow at one end. Above the couch
was a crooked picture of Jesus with a staff and a lamb.
There was nothing else on the walls except cobwebs. On
the other side of the room on a kitchen chair was a black-
and-white TV with two broken rabbit ears. The channel
knob was yellowed and the tube had a child's handprints
all over it.

The linoleum floor had bubbles and ridges. Each room had a different color, and at the edges the linoleum pulled up so it was easy to trip going from one room to another. Dishes were stacked in the kitchen sink next to a bucket of water. The refrigerator was short and rounded like an old Buick. I had seen a similar one in my grandmother's basement, unplugged, the handle removed. Dickie told horror stories about children playing hide-and-seek and suffocating inside refrigerators.

"I've been thinking about what you said last night," I said. "I think you need a phone."

Jesse shook her head. "A phone costs money we don't have. And they won't install one without a grown-up's signature."

"Well, we need a way to communicate. Like if you're in trouble and need help, some way you can tell me."

"Why wouldn't I just ride over to your house?"

"Because my parents will ask questions."

"Maybe a birdcall," she said. "I can do a mean bobwhite outside your window." She made the sound and it was frighteningly similar to the bird.

"We need to be able to talk whenever we have to."

Jesse snapped her fingers. "Dickie's got a CB. He talks to truckers up and down the interstate."

She put Daisy Grace in the basket and we rode to Dickie's house. He showed us his setup, a small CB hooked to an antenna on the side of the garage.

"How much do those cost?" I said.

"You can get a cheap one at Heck's for $20."

I was pretty sure I had enough birthday money to cover the expense. I knew Jesse couldn't afford it.

"What about the antenna?" Jesse said.

"Depends on how far you want to talk. What do you want it for?"

"I got to be able to communicate with the outside world," Jesse said, repeating the line I made her memorize.

"How much of the outside world?" Dickie said.

"Just Dogwood," I said.

"You two want to talk to each other?"

"Or talk to you," Jesse said. "If I need somebody to make a phone call, it'll save me a trip on the bike."

Dickie dug around in the corner of the garage and blew dust from a black box with a microphone. "The channel knob is broke on this. It stays on 17. But it still worked last time I checked."

"Where'd you get it?"

He looked sheepish and finally admitted he had found it in someone's trash.

"I could use some birthday money and see if my parents would take me to Heck's," I said. "What else would Jesse need to get it to work?"

"Just an antenna and coax." He thought a minute. "There's an old boy down the street who put up a Moon-raker—it's this big antenna on a tower that turns. He helped me set this up. I think he's got a little antenna he doesn't use anymore."

It took some finagling, and Dickie had to promise to mow the man's yard the rest of the summer, which Jesse said she would do, but the man gave us an antenna and the metal pole it was mounted on, plus the coax, a thick cord from the antenna to the CB that looked like a blacksnake. Dickie and I carried the antenna to Jesse's house and it felt like we were setting up the transcontinental railway. Each step brought us closer to breaking the communication barrier.

"We can run the wire out my bedroom window," Jesse said when we reached her house. She put up a rickety wooden ladder and pointed. "The antenna could go right there."

Dickie nearly turned white when he looked up. "Don't you dare put that ladder there. See that electric wire? I don't know who installed that, but that wire's hot. You put the antenna there and the thing will splatter every time you key the mike. And if we slip and the antenna touches it, they'll be burying all three of us."

Jesse's mouth dropped open. "I climb up there all the time and I've never gotten shocked."

"You put your hand on that and you'll see what I'm talking about."

"Where should we put it, then?" I said.

"At the front, right there. You could run the coax in the living room window. That way you can talk on it without waking Daisy Grace."

"She sleeps about as hard as you do, Dickie," Jesse said.

He squinted at us but didn't ask how she knew that.

Dickie marked a spot on the ground and dug with a posthole digger into the soft earth. Jesse and I leaned the metal pole up to the house and sank it deep in the hole, and Dickie packed it down with rocks and dirt. He said it should have cement but Jesse didn't have any.

"How are we going to keep it from falling over?" I said.

"Just hold it while I look for something."

He disappeared behind the house and Jesse looked at me. "You think this is really going to work?"

"You doubting Dickie's ability?"

She smiled. Her hands were next to mine. And I could see the blue-green ocean in her eyes. "I'm doubting our ability to dig a hole deep enough to keep this thing from blowing down in the wind."

Dickie returned with a flattened Maxwell House coffee can, four nails, and a hammer and climbed up the ladder. He put the can around the pole and drove nails in on either side. He pulled on it hard and smiled. "That ain't going nowhere."

The antenna stuck up above the roof. I backed up for a better view.

"Looks right pretty, don't it?" Jesse said.

Dickie climbed down and wiggled the pole again, seeming proud of his work. He fed the coax through the window and Jesse went inside and screwed the connector into the CB, but all we could hear was static. He showed us how to work the squelch knob to cut down the noise.

"Not many people on channel 17, but that's good if we just want to talk to each other," Dickie said. "You two need to come up with handles while I ride home and test it out."

"What do you mean, handles?" Jesse said.

"A name. What to call yourself so nobody knows who you are."

"Why wouldn't I want anybody to know?" Jesse said.

"It's got to do with the FCC. You wouldn't understand it. But everybody has a handle. Classy Chassis. Tin Bender. Electric Man. That kind of thing."

"What's your handle?" I said.

"Listen to the radio. You'll see."

Dickie rode Jesse's bike back to his house. She and I waited in the living room, watching the little lights flash on the CB. Every now and then we heard fuzzy voices that Dickie later said were from truckers passing along the interstate. Their voices bled over from channel 19.

"Breaker, breaker 1-7," Dickie said, his voice higher pitched but clear. "This is the Breakthrough Kid. You copy?"

I handed the microphone to Jesse but she shook her head. I keyed the mic. "I hear you, Dick—I mean, I got you, Breakthrough Kid."

Dickie laughed. "Who am I talking to?"

"This is the Dogwood Pirate," I said.

Jesse's mouth was wide-open. "It really works."

"Nice to meet you, Dogwood Pirate," Dickie said. "Now hand the mic to the little lady."

I handed Jesse the mic but she shook her head again.

"Come on, you're going to have to talk for him to hear you. This is a CB, not a TV."

Jesse frowned and picked up the mic like it was a dead mouse. She finally keyed it and said, "Hey, Breakthrough Kid."

"There you are—and who am I talking to?"

She shrugged. "I don't know."

"If you don't make up a name for yourself, I'm going to do it for you," Dickie said.

She thought a minute, then held the mic up and keyed it. "Call me Wildflower."

"Now that's the best handle I think I've ever heard. Fits you perfect, Wildflower."

It took some cajoling to get my mother to sign on to the idea of a CB in my room. But all the cajoling in the world wouldn't get my grandmother to agree to an antenna by her house, even if we did use a clamp instead of a coffee can. She said the CB was for low-class people.

Two days later, after considerable hounding, I convinced my father to take me to Heck's, where we looked over the inventory. There were base units that went in people's houses and mobile units for the car. I picked the cheapest one that plugged into the wall and asked the man behind the counter about an antenna.

"If you're talking with people short-range, you can get one of these," he said. He pulled out a small coil from the glass case. "Plugs right in the back. You'll want a bigger one soon, but this will get you started."

I connected everything when we got home and flipped the channels, listening to a few faint voices. I switched to channel 17 and keyed the mic.

"Break 1-7, for Wildflower."

My father sat on the bed and listened.

The needle on the meter flew from left to right and I heard a tiny voice say, "Daisy. I'm Daisy. . . ." She held the mic on and I heard Jesse in the background. "Turn loose of it. You can't hear if you don't let go of it."

The needle fell and my father laughed and left the room.

"Daisy, this is Dogwood Pirate. Is Wildflower there?"

"I'm here, Pirate. Looks like we're in business."

"Is the Breakthrough Kid on?"

I waited but didn't hear anything. Then Jesse said something to Dickie and we determined my antenna wasn't strong enough to pull in his signal. Dickie could hear me but I couldn't hear him.

"Breakthrough Kid says he'll work on your setup, Pirate."

"10-4," I said, beginning to learn the vocabulary of our new experiment.

Later that night, after all was quiet in our house and Daisy had gone to bed at Jesse's, I turned the sound down as far as it would go and put a pillow over my head to muffle my voice. The lights were out in my room and all I saw was the soft glow of the CB.

"This is the next best thing to a phone line," Jesse said.

"The antenna holding up over there?"

"Yeah. The wind wiggles the top but it's secure like Breakthrough said."

I pictured her in her living room, on the couch, holding the microphone and maybe in a nightgown. Then

I thought better of it because Jesse wore the same clothes every day, so she probably slept in her T-shirt and shorts too.

"What do you think is gonna become of us, Pirate?"

I took a deep breath, listening to the sounds of crickets and frogs through the open window. "I don't know, Wildflower, but I think something good's going to come from all of this."

She said something but was yawning while she spoke and I laughed and so did she.

"Daisy wore me out today. I'm going to bed. Talk to you tomorrow, Pirate."

We began an easy back-and-forth, Jesse and me. Because I couldn't hear Dickie, Jesse relayed his messages to me, acting as a repeater. Then late at night when I was reading, I'd hear her familiar *click click* of the microphone and I'd answer with two clicks.

"You okay?" I said one of those nights.

"Yeah, just a little lonely. I was up on the roof tonight, looking at the stars."

"You've got to be careful going up there with that live wire."

"I put the ladder a long ways from it. You can see stuff and there's a breeze up there. It helps me clear my mind."

I had never considered climbing on my grandmother's roof for any reason, but Jesse was a free spirit.

"Won't be long till you'll need to get a bigger antenna," Jesse said.

"Why's that?"

"Because you're moving to the parsonage, right?"

This was a constant topic of conversation around our dinner table. "There's a holdup on it. I don't think we'll be moving anytime soon."

"Good. I mean, good for me."

I smiled. "My mom is headed to the Kroger's tomorrow. You need anything?"

"No. Thank you, though."

There was silence a moment before Jesse spoke again.

"What's it like to play the piano?"

"It's okay, I guess. I don't really know how to explain it. You ever thought of playing an instrument?"

"I play the radio, that's about it. But I thought about the harmonica when I was younger. They had this thing at school in the second grade where if you brought fifty cents in, you could get a harmonica and take lessons, but my mama said we couldn't afford it. My music career went out the window before I got to third grade."

She meant it to be funny, but I thought it was sad. And it made me appreciate my piano lessons more knowing Jesse wanted to take them but would never be able to.

"I wish I could hear you when you talk," I said to Dickie at his house the next day.

"You should just hang a mobile antenna on the laundry pole," Dickie said.

"I suggested that and my grandmother said she doesn't want to get struck by lightning."

Dickie laughed. "When you move to your new house, you can put one up."

Dickie and I were poring over a magazine he'd found. It showed the cadavers of Martians discovered in the New Mexico desert, and Dickie said this was the kind of photograph he was hoping we could take with my new Polaroid. A car pulled up outside the garage and two uniformed men got out, put their berets on, and walked toward us. One man was white, the other black.

Dickie kept the magazine open on his lap as he studied their faces, not saying a word, as if he knew why they were there. I wasn't sure, but I immediately thought of my promise to Jesse about praying for Dickie's father. With all that had happened after Jesse's mother's death, I hadn't kept my side of the bargain.

"We're looking for Mrs. Leena Hancock," the white officer said.

"She ain't here, sir," Dickie said.

"Could you tell us where she is?" the black officer said.

Dickie's eyes danced between both of them. "Whatever it is, you can tell me."

"I'm sorry, son," the white officer said. "We need to talk with your mother." He walked up the steps behind us and knocked on the door.

"I told you, she ain't here," Dickie said over his shoulder. Then to the black officer he said, "Don't you believe me?"

When no one answered the door, the two officers retreated to their car. Dickie stood and followed them. "If this is about my dad, you can tell me."

The men didn't speak. They just got in their car and drove to the dead end and turned around. Before they returned, Dickie shouted, "Come on, Matt."

He jumped on his bike and I followed. I'd never seen him ride so fast. His legs pumped and his shirt flapped in the wind and he left me so far behind I could barely see the turns he made through town.

I finally caught up with him on the dirt alley that led past the volunteer fire department. "Why are you in such a hurry?"

"I need to go to the warehouse. That's where they're headed."

"How do you know?"

He slowed and wiped his face with his sleeve. "I just got to be there. You don't have to come."

He only slowed again when he crossed the main street in town and rode past the post office, the flag flying high and proud. We crossed the train tracks and wound through an industrial area, where there were big trucks and a long warehouse.

"There they go!" Dickie said, pointing at the parking lot.

In the distance I saw the men walking toward the building in lockstep. Dickie reached the warehouse entrance first and let his bike fall near the front door. I coasted up and stopped, wishing Jesse were with us. She would know what to do.

When Dickie opened the front door, I heard wailing. I've never been able to get the pain of that voice out of my mind. It reached to the bone. The door closed and muffled the sound, but I could still hear it through the glass.

A man in a blue work shirt with the name *Williams* on it walked up beside me. "What's going on?"

"Two Army guys just went inside looking for Mrs. Hancock," I said.

The man muttered a curse. When the door opened, the two men came out on either side of Dickie's mother, holding her up. Dickie followed them to their car. The man beside me took off his hat as they passed and put it over his heart. When Dickie walked by, the man said, "I'm sorry about your dad, son."

Dickie looked up in a daze. "Thank you." Then he turned to me. "Could you take care of my bike?"

One of the officers came back and put the bike in the trunk of Dickie's mother's car and they all drove away.

It was one of the longest bike rides I ever took alone. I rode to Jesse's place and found her in the backyard with Daisy and explained what happened.

Jesse shook her head. "It don't make sense, does it, PB? A good kid like Dickie losing his daddy?"

I had been to funerals for older people, but never for a friend's father. Dickie had told me stories of his dad and what he was like. He was not an easy man to live with, to hear Dickie tell it. He expected a lot, expected chores to be done correctly. But Dickie always spoke admiringly about him, as if he knew he was hard for a reason.

"I used to think my dad was mean," Dickie said one day

after the funeral. "But that's just how he was brought up. And he wanted me to learn."

Several people from the military got up to talk about Dickie's father, telling of things he had done in Vietnam and how he had saved lives. None of it made us feel any better. There was a closed casket with an eight-by-ten picture on top and flowers all over the church and people crying.

A full military team with rifles and a twenty-one-gun salute met us at the cemetery. Mr. Hancock could have been buried at Arlington in Virginia, but Dickie said his mother wanted him in Dogwood, where she could visit him.

Jesse didn't come to the church, but it wasn't because she didn't care. She had no place to take Daisy Grace and no nice clothes. I sat with my mother and father and didn't cry, but when we got to the cemetery, I saw Jesse in the shade of an oak tree with her little sister by her clutching a handful of daisies. I couldn't hold back the tears then or when they handed the folded flag to Dickie's mother.

Chapter 18

Jesse said we should leave Dickie alone for a while, but
I thought that was cruel—that he needed friends. So the
next day I went to Blake's and bought candy and soda
and took it to his house. It was overcast and he was in the
garage looking through an old trunk of his father's stuff,
pulling out letters and pictures.

"Funny how a life winds up just stuff in a box," Dickie
said. He wasn't crying or anything but he wasn't himself.

"Your dad was more than his stuff," I said. "More than
those medals the Army gave him."

"Maybe." He found a UFO magazine and flipped
through it. "Let's go do something else."

We rode our bikes to my house and climbed the hill. The gray sky was perfect for looking for UFOs. It was hot, and everyone knows UFOs hover when it's hot and Bigfoot comes out.

Dickie and I walked under low-hanging clouds on the hill as if this were the exact spot aliens would congregate. The fire siren sounded in the valley and Ford trucks raced down the dirt road, sending up a plume of dust. Dickie cursed as a thin line of smoke rose from the west end of town.

"What's wrong?" I said.

"I might have left the stove on. My mama said to make sure I turned it off, but now I can't remember. I better go check."

I thought about going with him, but I was sure his house was fine, and Jesse's place was just over the hill. She and I were in full preparation mode, trying to come up with a way to care for Daisy Grace after school started, and we could use the time to plan.

"I'll see you later," I said, watching as he ran down the hill.

I took the back route through the property that connected with my grandmother's land. It was a tangled path, and other than fences, there was no clear direction that would get you to the road. My father knew the trails as well as anyone, and I usually followed him when we came here—but we hadn't taken any long walks over the summer.

I remembered a briar patch and skirted that, making my way deeper into the woods. Winded, I leaned against a dead tree and realized I was lost. If I went the right direction, I could retreat to our house or reach the road, but I could also go in the opposite direction and walk for miles. I looked for the sun, but the clouds were thick. My breath came in short bursts and I noticed a high-pitched whine that seemed to get louder as I walked to the other side of the dead tree. I froze, staring at the biggest hornets' nest I had ever seen. It was huge at the top and tapered to a point at the end.

Like a line drive off the bat of some kid too big for Little League, a hornet flew straight at me and stuck its stinger between my eyes. I yelped and if my camera hadn't come with a nylon strap, I would have left it there. I've thought many times how the day would have turned out differently if I had dropped that camera.

I turned and flew down the hill, which, I learned, was not faster than a hornet can fly. I swatted wildly to fend them off, running from the path into virgin territory. My brother had told me years earlier about the Native Americans who had found this area rich for hunting—and he had the arrowheads to prove it.

Two stings on the neck later, I fell and rolled down the hill, scratching my face and arms and coming to rest on a creek bank. I didn't see bones protruding, so I brushed myself off and hurried past the trickling water.

Something moved in the underbrush and I thought of all the menacing animals—copperheads and bears—not to mention the unexplainable. My camera dangled in front of me and I cradled it, thinking my flash might fend off a threat, like my mother said Jimmy Stewart did in *Rear Window*. When I heard a car pass a hundred yards away and smelled the dust from the road, it was the happiest moment of my hiking life.

I stepped onto the rutted road as welts rose on my arms from the stings. But I was alive. I had survived the onslaught of the biggest hornets' nest in history, and I couldn't wait to tell my friends.

I exited the woods about a half mile from Jesse's house, so I headed that way, scratching and trying to pull stingers from my forehead and neck, which made the pain worse. Clouds roiled, releasing the first spitting of rain.

There were two entrances to the Blackwood farm. One gate accessed the lower fields and led to the barn. The upper entrance led straight to the brick house on the hill, and this was what I was passing when I saw someone walking through the field by the house. I stepped toward the gate, next to the mailbox, and stood on the berm of the road.

The Blackwood driveway was empty. An aged Massey Ferguson tractor sat by the barn along with equipment for cutting, tilling, and raking. I glanced at the field and realized it wasn't one person but two, one leading the other.

Raindrops kissed the earth in big, splotchy drops and I ducked through the fence, ignoring the No Trespassing signs. In spite of all the stories of Blackwood, I figured someone in that house would have pity on me and rescue me from the oncoming flood.

I ran waving up the graveled drive. Then I noticed

the second person had long, blonde hair, and before the
rain intensified, I recognized Jesse being pulled by Gentry
Blackwood.

I ran for the house, my feet crunching gravel, and put
my camera under my shirt to protect it from the rain. My
biggest concern now was Jesse. Gentry dragged her through
the back door just as I came to the house, and lightning
struck on the hill behind me with thunder crashing instantly.
I ducked under the eave of the house to get dry and heard
screaming inside. I couldn't imagine what was happening—
and then I could. And the prospect made me sick.

What should I do? If I tried to stop him, Gentry would
pummel me. I couldn't just stand there.

But I did.

I listened to Jesse scream and closed my eyes and wished
I were somewhere else. I wished I'd never come to Dogwood.

I wiped the rain and sweat from my face and noticed
a paint-blotched stepladder on the ground. I put it under
a window and climbed. I was near the top when I got my
head over the ledge and peered into the room. There was
a bed directly under the window. Gentry struggled to hold
Jesse down. I took one more rung of the ladder and it
shifted, but I held on to the ledge.

Gentry had ripped Jesse's shirt and her bra was
exposed—I didn't even know she wore one. He grabbed at
her shorts. I noticed marks of some sort on Jesse's stomach.
Jesse kicked and clawed and screamed, squirming back on
the bed, but Gentry was stronger. He pinned her legs with
his body and held her arms, yelling for her to lie still.

There are moments in life when the world slows or stops altogether, and I swear if I had turned around right then, I would have been able to count the billions of raindrops one by one. I smelled the fresh ozone and water and dirt, heaven and earth mixing together, and wished I were bigger and stronger and had more courage.

Unable to think of anything else to do, I lifted my camera and held it up to the window. I clicked the shutter and the flash blazed. The Polaroid whirred as the photo spat from it. I grabbed the picture and looked into the room and met the eyes of Jesse's attacker.

Gentry threw Jesse's legs away and gritted his teeth. "I'm going to kill you!"

He ran to the bedroom door, but I scrambled off the ladder and shoved the picture in my pocket. I sprinted past the front door, hoping Gentry would come out the back. When I reached the end of the house, a door slammed in the back and I had my chance. I raced for the barn.

The rain was coming in a torrent and lightning flashed, thunder cracking. I knew if Gentry caught me, my life was over. I made it to the barn and looked through the uneven boards at the downpour and the fog that hung between.

I climbed into a loft over the feeding trough and hid behind some hay bales in the back. Water blew through the cracks between the aged lumber, and mud daubers buzzed overhead. I didn't want another hornet sting, but I promised myself if I got stung a thousand times, I wouldn't make a sound.

The rain on the barn's tin roof was deafening. My

breathing settled. A month earlier I wouldn't have been able to climb and move that quickly. I couldn't even climb up on the edge of the road without help. Now I was running the hills and falling into creeks and getting stung with the best of them.

Grabbing the photo from my pocket, I pulled the back off, revealing the picture. You had to wait the right amount of time to let the photo finish, but I could only guess. The color was off—it was a greenish blue and the flash in the window had made the image ultrabright, but I clearly saw Jesse on the bed and Gentry over her. I had evidence. I knew that picture was important and that I had to get it into the hands of the right person before the wrong person got it.

Just then the wrong person walked into the barn. "Plumley! I know you're in here!"

There were probably a thousand hiding places in the barn. The question was, could I remain still enough to keep him from noticing me until Jesse got away? The noise subsided a little, in the usual ebb and flow of a mountain rain, and I saw someone running across the field. It was Jesse, her hair wet and clinging. She held her ripped shirt in front of her and I whispered, "Run, Jesse."

The cows lowed underneath me and the ladder sagged under Gentry's weight. I sat still, my heart picking up speed.

"I swear I'll kill you, Plumley."

I didn't doubt him. When I heard the ladder creak again, I prepared for a pitchfork in the heart. This was how

I would die. Gentry would kill me and bury me in a shallow grave, and my parents would never find me. Water and sweat trickled into my eyes. I wanted to wipe it away but was too scared to move, too scared to breathe.

The rain slowed to a pitter-pat on the roof, and a shaft of sunlight beamed through the cracks in the wall. I glanced through the slat nearest me and saw Gentry running toward his house, yelling and crisscrossing the soggy path.

I stuffed the picture in my pocket and ran for the ladder, then the road. With each three or four steps I looked back. I didn't stop at Jesse's house but galloped on, drawn to something more important. Someone I had to see.

I let my bike fall at the front steps of the church and took them two at a time to the front door. It was locked. My father's car was in the parking lot, so I was sure he was here. I checked the back entrance and found it unlocked, then ran up the right side of the sanctuary past the organ. The office was there and had access to the sanctuary, the baptistery, and the downstairs Sunday school rooms and basement. You could basically get anywhere in the church from there. The only downside was there were no windows in the room.

I burst through the door and my father looked up from his desk. He had the phone to his ear and his mouth was agape. An open mouth and slack jaw were signs of unintelligence, he always told me, but there he was. The bookshelves behind him were made of the same pine that fashioned the church walls. They were filled with commentaries and biographies. He had several versions of the Bible, his favorite being the New American Standard, but he rarely used it anymore because Old Man Blackwood said the King James was the only inspired version.

"He just got here," my father said. "All right, I'll call and let you know."

He put the phone down and I broke into a sweeping, breathless explanation of what had happened. It was clearly too much for him because he held up a hand.

"Matt, slow down. Do you mind telling me why Basil Blackwood and his son were at our house just now asking where you were?"

"I know exactly why they were there. Let me show you."

Before I could pull out the photo, he ducked into the little bathroom next to the baptistery and got a towel. "Dry yourself, you're dripping all over." He closed his Bible. "Your mother is beside herself. Did you go onto the Blackwood property?"

"Yes, but—"

"I've told you we need to respect other people's property. That place is filled with No Trespassing signs. What would possess you to go there?"

I pulled the towel around me to stanch the dripping, my clothes still wet from the rain and sweat. I had been proud of how fast I had ridden to the church—and that I hadn't stopped to say anything to my mother. I just took the camera from around my neck and put it in the shed and rode. I knew this was something men had to solve.

I told my father about going alone into the woods. A dipped head meant this was forbidden.

"I thought I remembered the way, but I got turned around and then there was this hornets' nest . . ." The more I revealed, the worse it became and I decided to forgo the part about falling and rolling and the downpour.

He cut me off. "You could have been snakebit. Struck by lightning. And no one would have known."

"I'm sorry. But listen." I made going onto the Blackwood property sound responsible. My father's face softened.

"I didn't mean to trespass, but I wanted to get out of the rain and lightning. I wanted somebody to call and have you or Mom come get me."

"You shouldn't have been up there with that storm brewing."

"Gentry was holding Jesse by the arm and dragging her through the field. I waved but they didn't see me. And then I realized she was trying to get away. He got her into his house."

"What did you do?"

"I ran under the eave. Jesse was screaming and Gentry was yelling for her to be quiet."

I paused there. Things of a sexual nature had been forbidden territory between us, though I had heard my parents discuss having "the talk" with me and that my father needed to do it. I had heard and seen enough on the bus to junior high to curl my mother's hair, but still nothing from him.

My father ran a hand over his mouth, his eyes looking at something not in the room. "Go on."

"I wanted to help but I was scared. Gentry can tear kids like me apart. I climbed up a ladder and took a picture. The flash stopped him."

"You did what?"

I reached in my pocket and pulled out the Polaroid photo and handed it to him. He looked at it and winced.

"He tore her shirt, Dad. She was scratching and clawing, but he was strong. If I hadn't done something . . ."

"He saw you?" he said.

I nodded and told him about running to the barn, then the feeling when I saw Jesse escape. "I got on my bike and came here."

He put the picture on his desk, facedown, and laid a hand on my shoulder. I could tell he wanted to say something, and I wanted him to, but a rumbling noise outside stopped him.

"Are you expecting somebody?" I said.

He shook his head and I saw a mixture of fear and resignation. Keys jangled and the front door opened and footsteps lumbered through the sanctuary. It was like waiting for two of the four horsemen of the Apocalypse. I moved behind my dad's desk and stuffed the picture in my pocket.

The office door flew open and Basil and Gentry Blackwood burst inside.

"Can I help you, Basil?" my father said.

"Is that him?" the man said to his son.

"Yeah, that's him," Gentry said.

Old Man Blackwood's eyes were fiery red and his neck veins raised like an overpumped bike tire. "Paul says a pastor 'ruleth well his own house, having his children in subjection with all gravity.'"

"I know the passage, Basil."

"'For if a man know not how to rule his own house, how shall he take care of the church of God?'"

"Indeed," my father said.

"You need to control your children," Blackwood said. "A man's property is sacred. Your son violated my property."

"Basil, I was just talking to Matt about what happened. He was looking for shelter from the—"

Gentry pointed a finger and interrupted. "He was spying on me and getting into my business."

"You were hurting Jesse," I said, my voice sounding like a mouse squeaking.

My father turned and gave me a look that told me to keep quiet.

"You defendin' that trash you hang out with?" Blackwood said to me. He said *trash* but seemed like he wanted to use a different word. "We've talked about this, Calvin. You're to be above reproach. You're raising a son who's a snare of the devil. Just like the other one."

My father looked pained at the reference to Ben but shook it off. "Now, Basil, let's be fair—"

"Get the camera from him," Gentry said.

Blackwood turned to his son. "You don't tell me what to do."

My father held up both hands and his voice was soft and low. "Why don't we calm down. We can work this out. This is probably all a misunderstanding. In fact, I'm—"

"It's not a misunderstanding," I said. I was a roaring mouse now. "Gentry was hurting Jesse. He had her in his room. He ripped her shirt."

"You lyin' sack of—"

"Shut up!" Blackwood thundered. He pointed a finger at me. "You know what bearing false witness against somebody means?"

"Yeah, it means lying. And I'm not lying. He had Jesse on his bed and she was screaming. It was me taking the picture that stopped him."

Blackwood looked back at his son before asking me, "Where's this picture?"

My father glanced at his desk, then at me.

"I'm not giving it to him," I said.

"You give it to me now," Blackwood said.

"Matt, let me have it," my father said.

He reminded me of Gregory Peck in the film version of *To Kill a Mockingbird*. His voice was just as deep and clipped when he spoke. He didn't sound like everyone else in Dogwood—his twang had lessened. But as he held out his hand, I took a step backward toward his bookshelf. I put a hand on a red copy of *Strong's Exhaustive Concordance* to steady myself.

"Just let him see what you're saying is true," my father said.

I searched my father's eyes for something I could trust. I wanted him to stand up to Blackwood. To order him out of his office, out of the church. I wanted him to be Atticus and stand against injustice and stick up for Jesse.

"Matt, show him the picture."

I reached in my pocket. My father handed the photo to Blackwood, who grabbed it and studied it closely. "Trash is growing up."

He tore the picture in two, flicked a cigarette lighter, and burned it in front of us, dropping it in the metal trash can. It smoked and my father tossed a cup of water inside.

Blackwood stepped toward me and leaned down. His breath was as smoky as the burning Polaroid. "You're never going to talk about this, you understand?"

I looked at my father, then at the floor.

"You answer me, son," Blackwood said. "You're never going to talk about this with anybody. And if you do, I'm going to talk about that brother of yours."

"Basil, that's not necessary," my father said weakly.

"And you're going to stay away from our property. You hear?"

I looked at my father, teeth clenched, tears welling. I was overcome by the man's venom and my father's impotence. I wanted to yell that I was going to call the sheriff. I wanted to say they would be sorry they hurt Jesse. But my trembling chin made me hold back.

"He understands," my father said.

Blackwood stood straight. "He'd better. And you better too, Calvin. That parsonage could run into more snags. You don't want to be living with your mama when winter comes."

Gentry smiled at me like he had won a gold medal at the Olympics. All the evidence of his wrongdoing was gone. All the evidence but Jesse and me.

Blackwood looked back as he was leaving. "Listen, boy. Don't worry about that trash. Pretty soon that family will be gone and the hollow will be better for it. We'll all be better off."

I looked at the smoldering ruins of my photo, then at my father. "I'll never forgive you for this," I said through tears. I ran past the Blackwoods and out of the sanctuary.

"Matt!" my father yelled.

I grabbed my bike and took off toward the road, tears streaming. When the truck passed me, Gentry made a face and rubbed his eyes, mouthing, "Poor baby."

I rode to Dickie's and was glad it wasn't burning. A smoke smell hung in the area. Dickie came outside and sat on the front steps eating a bag of Fritos.

"It was the Thompson place," he said. "Those kids like to play with matches when their parents aren't around. They were in a closet and things got out of hand."

"Are they okay?"

"Nobody died. I figure they learned a valuable lesson that'll last about a week. What are you up to?"

"Nothing," I said. I wanted to tell Dickie all about it. I wanted somebody else to know what had happened. But the more I thought, the more I knew this would have to be another secret Jesse and I would share.

That night I lay in bed with the microphone, giving two clicks every few minutes. My father came in and sat on the bed, but I turned my face to the wall. I wanted him to apologize or do something to explain his inaction. Instead he stood and walked out of the room.

I fell asleep waiting for the return clicks that never came. I dreamed I was running from a bear in the woods that growled and bared its fangs. The bear looked like Gentry Blackwood.

The next day I rode to Jesse's house. Daisy Grace was in the backyard picking flowers and Jesse was at the front window pulling dead ones from the Ball jar. Carl had gotten used to me and only barked a couple of times when I rode up, then retreated under the house. I wondered how Jesse managed to feed herself, Daisy, and the dog on the little they received in her mother's check.

Jesse opened the door, wearing the shirt from the day before, hand-sewn, and invited me inside. She must have felt self-conscious about her home, like a pretty woman with bad teeth will put a hand over her face when she smiles, but the walls were breaking down between us.

"I came to see if you were okay," I said.

She looked out the back window at Daisy Grace. "Why wouldn't I be?"

"I tried to reach you last night on the CB."

"I got tired early."

I pulled out one of the unmatched chairs at the kitchen table and sat. The table wobbled to one side and I figured it was probably because the floor was crooked.

"Is that the first time he's done something like that?"

She turned and pulled herself up onto the counter by

the sink, her dirty bare feet swinging. "What are you talking about?"

"Gentry."

The name took her aback and she looked out the window again. "I can take care of myself. I don't need your help."

"But you need my help with Daisy."

"That's different."

I took a deep breath. "There were marks on your stomach. Did Gentry do that?"

She squinted at me, not understanding. Then she lifted up her shirt. "You mean these?" She had a tight abdomen and I could see her ribs and a lot of her bra. She had bruises on her arms and a scratch on her neck, but it was the marks on her stomach that troubled me most. "These are my birthmarks."

They weren't birthmarks, but I turned my head and decided not to argue. "Pull your shirt down, please?"

"You're blushing, aren't you?" She sang, "Matt is blushing."

"Are you going to pretend yesterday didn't happen? Because I can't. I saw what he was trying to do."

She pulled her shirt down. "Yesterday happened. But what doesn't kill you makes you stronger. That's what my mama always said."

"What doesn't kill you will evidently leave a scar."

"I reckon you're right about that."

She stared at me and I didn't look away. I wanted to tell her what had happened in my father's office, but I couldn't.

A wailing sound wafted through the window and Jesse was off the counter and out the back door in a flash. She returned with Daisy Grace holding her arm.

"Quick, cut me an onion," Jesse said, pointing toward the corner. I grabbed a butcher knife and an onion, wondering what had happened. I cut the onion in two and Jesse took one slick, wet half and put it directly on Daisy's arm. "There, that'll draw out the poison. Just hold it there."

"What happened?" I said.

"Bee sting. There's a bunch at the outhouse."

I remembered the welts on my neck and face and thought I could have used a few onions.

"Run to our room and get a washcloth," Jesse said.

Nothing could have prepared me for the sadness of Jesse's bedroom. There was water damage to the windowsill. A small crib mattress lay on the floor in the corner. A tangled mess of a sheet covered it. Jesse's bed was a stained twin mattress without a box spring. It was on a slab of plywood with bricks underneath. A bare lightbulb hung from the ceiling with a piece of string swinging low.

There was a rickety dresser that had once held a mirror. On top of the dresser were scattered pictures, one frame showing a smiling woman I thought must have been Jesse's mother.

I found a pile of unfolded washcloths in the corner and returned to the kitchen. Jesse dunked the cloth in the water and put it in the freezer.

"I want Mama," Daisy whimpered.

"Mama ain't here. You got me."

Jesse waited a little, then took the cloth from the freezer and told Daisy to hold it to her arm. Gradually the girl calmed. Her arm swelled, but Jesse's quick action seemed to make a difference.

"You want to watch TV?" Jesse said to her.

Daisy put her head down and ran toward the living room. There was a loud click and a static sound.

"I've been brainstorming what we could do while you're at school," I said.

"I been thinking too. I'm just going to drop out."

"No. You said the truant officer will show up."

The channel knob turned and I heard the sound effects of Huckleberry Hound.

"I'll hide, just like when the Jehovah's Witnesses come."

"I think there's a better way."

"What way is that?"

"I saw a sign yesterday at a house in town that said, 'Child care.' I wrote down the number and the address."

Jesse stared at the scrap of paper I held out. "How much do they charge?"

"I don't know, but it's worth asking, don't you think?"

She nodded and bit her lip. "I can't leave her with just anybody."

Daisy giggled in the living room and turned up the sound.

"Turn that down," Jesse yelled.

"Then y'all be quiet!" Daisy said.

Jesse smiled and shook her head. I could tell she was rolling the idea over in her mind.

"Maybe you could call that lady and find out. I'd have to get her there early, before the bus runs, but then I could get on at the Second Street stop by the gas station. And then get off there in the afternoon and pick her up."

I nodded. It sounded plausible but exhausting. I had never considered how much my parents did until I thought of Jesse becoming a full-time mother.

"I'll call when I get home, but you need to keep the CB on so we can talk."

She rubbed her hands. "I'm worried somebody could listen, Matt. Like Blackwood." Jesse scrunched up her face. "How did you know about Gentry?"

"I was there. I saw through the window. Didn't you see me?"

"I saw lightning flash but didn't hear no thunder. And then Gentry was up and cussing and running for the door."

She didn't know I had taken a picture, and I wasn't about to tell her. "He saw me in the window and followed. But I hid. I was so happy you got away."

"We was out of meat. And Daisy broke the last eggs we had. I let her watch the TV while I went over to their pond, thinking there was nobody home. Then Gentry came along."

The cartoon sounds gave way to the familiar theme of *Gilligan's Island*.

"So you saw the trouble I was in and you tried to help," she said.

I nodded. "Jesse, how does this end? Are you going to be Daisy's mom the rest of your life?"

"Somebody has to be." She looked out the window at a car passing, the dust leaving a brown coating on the leaves. "I need her to get stronger so she can fend for herself. Maybe till she gets our age."

"That's a long time to keep a secret."

"You're right. But it's not too long to keep a promise."

Chapter 19

Dickie and Jesse and I planned an end-of-summer bike ride on Labor Day. We were riding to the end of the road no matter what the weather, and Daisy rode in Jesse's back basket. I don't know how Jesse pedaled up those hills with the added weight, but she did.

"You think he'll be able to do it?" Dickie said as we walked our bikes up the biggest hill. They were a little ahead of me and I hurried to catch up.

"Who will do what?" I said, intruding on their conversation.

"Jerry Lewis," Jesse said. "You think he'll be able to stay awake until the end of the telethon?"

"He always does," I said.

"Yeah, and then he sings that song at the end and cries every time," Jesse said, throwing back her head and singing, "'I did it my way!'" She had a surprisingly good voice.

"Do you think that crying is real or fake?" Dickie said.

"It's not 'My Way,'" I said. "It's 'You'll Never Walk Alone.' It's from *Carousel*."

Dickie ignored my correction. "I think he cries because he's exhausted and wants to go to sleep but people expect him to sing."

Jesse looked straight ahead as she walked. "I think it's because he sees all those sick kids and wants to help. I'd cry too."

The road went for miles. I had never ridden my bike to the end. My father had told me about families who had lived in the hills for generations, only coming to town when necessary. There were a few nice houses on the ridge, but most looked similar to Jesse's, old and ramshackle.

Dickie had gone to Blake's store before the trip and bought four Three Musketeers bars and distributed them. (He swore he didn't steal.) Daisy held on to hers until it was a gooey mess inside the wrapper. Dickie carried his in his shirt pocket, and as he traveled a little fast on a downhill slope, the bar popped out and landed in front of me. My front tire hit it right on the *M* and Dickie slammed on his brakes and circled.

He picked up the candy bar and looked like he wanted to curse but held back. "This is a bad omen. A tire track in the middle of a candy bar is an awful way to start a new school year."

"Just eat around it," Jesse said, winking at me. "That'll make it good luck."

At the end of the road was a house Dickie swore was haunted, and from the bend in the road where we could finally see it, I felt he was right. It hung on the horizon through the trees. Jesse whispered that ghosts had been seen at the windows. Daisy whimpered and I took a picture with my Polaroid. Shutters hung at odd angles and barely covered shattered windowpanes. Vines grew on the side of the house, and briars and brush surrounded it. The place gave me the creeps in the middle of the day and I could only imagine what it looked like at night. The house in *Psycho* had nothing on this one, though I hadn't seen the movie, just a picture of it in one of Dickie's magazines. Daisy whined that she didn't want to go any farther but she didn't have a choice.

We rode past the house and up a little hill where the road ended at the cemetery and parked our bikes by an iron gate. We ate our lunches and Daisy smeared the candy bar all over her face while we stared at the crumbling tombstones. She wandered off into the cemetery, chasing a butterfly.

"If the road ends here," I said, "where does that go?" I pointed to another gate that looked like it was to keep cows in. A two-lane path led into the woods.

"My dad said it goes all the way to Gobbler's Knob," Dickie said.

Jesse cocked her head. "That road don't go to no Gobbler's Knob."

"Does too. They closed it to keep people from taking the shortcut."

"Shortcut, my eye," Jesse said.

"What's Gobbler's Knob?" I said.

Dickie pointed. "It's over that way—hard to get to."

"I got kin on Gobbler's Knob," Jesse said.

"That road will take you to them," Dickie said. "Otherwise you got to get on the interstate, take the next exit up, and wind back around. Roads are closed anytime it rains hard. We drove it once and I got carsick. Hung my head out the window and—"

"Please," I said, my stomach turning. "I'm eating."

"Sorry, I forgot you're squeamish," Dickie said.

"I never knowed you could get there this way," Jesse said, studying the gate.

"Is it your mama's kin or your daddy's?" Dickie said, obviously knowing the difference it made.

Jesse frowned. "My daddy's. I never knowed them as well as his other relatives. I don't think they liked him very much. They stayed on their side of the mountain and we stayed on ours."

I thought about Jesse's family, her house, and Carl underneath it. When there was a lull, I said, "Why do you keep your dog on a chain?"

Jesse took a bite of a pickle and pimento spread sandwich I had packed. "Blackwood."

"He chained him up?"

"Might as well have. Carl would wander over there and chase cows and chickens. Eat the food put out for Blackwood's dogs. Mama chained him up because Old Man Blackwood said he'd shoot him if he caught him again. Been that way since I can remember."

"That's sad," Dickie said. "That's like chaining the wind. Dogs are supposed to be able to run free."

The conversation stayed on Old Man Blackwood for a while. When Gentry came up, Jesse bristled and changed the subject. She asked Dickie how his mother was doing since the funeral and he said she was better.

"She don't talk much," Dickie said. "Sometimes I catch her crying and I try to cheer her up. When anything comes on the news about the war, she shuts it off. I'll tell you this, though. If my number ever gets called, I'll go." He looked at me. "What about you?"

"What *about* me?"

"If you were drafted, would you go to war?"

I glanced at Jesse, then at my sandwich. "Sure. I guess."

"Can you imagine Matt with a gun?" Jesse said.

"I can imagine him with a Polaroid around his neck taking pictures. You could become a famous war photographer." Dickie paused. "I wonder what would happen if the Mothman's draft number ever got called."

"One day they'll draft women," Jesse said.

"No way," I said.

"Don't you think we deserve equal rights?"

"Women don't belong on the battlefield," Dickie said.

"And where do they belong? In the kitchen?" Jesse said.

Dickie winked at me, knowing he was pushing her buttons. "It's okay for women to be nurses and cook food and stuff, but they shouldn't be carrying grenades and shooting at people."

"And why not? I can shoot just as well as you can, and I can carry—Daisy, get back here!"

"See. You'd be out in some rice paddy, looking for a land mine or a trip wire, and some little kid would come along and you'd yell at them to watch out and you'd get blown up."

"I can do anything you two can do and probably better. There's no reason I can't fight in a war."

"You're already fighting one with Blackwood," Dickie said. "I'd concentrate on winning that before you ship out."

"My dad's fighting a war with Blackwood too," I said.

"How's that?" Dickie said.

"My dad likes to do expository preaching. And Blackwood—"

Jesse scrunched her face and interrupted. "Suppository preaching?"

Dickie laughed. "I've heard messages like that. Ones that make you go find the bathroom till they're over."

"*Expository* means you preach the Bible verse by verse. You explain what the words say instead of jumping around and doing one topic this week and another topic the next."

"And Blackwood's got his underwear in a bunch over that?" Jesse said.

I wadded the wax paper I'd wrapped our sandwiches

in and stuffed it in the paper bag. "He wants my dad to preach more about the dangers of rock music and talk about prophecy and how the world's going to end."

"How does your daddy think it'll end?" Jesse said. "Is somebody gonna set off a nuclear bomb and make it explode?"

I shrugged, unable to think of an answer before Dickie spoke.

"There's a preacher on the radio that says the Beatles are trying to hypnotize us and turn us all into Communists. I was listening to 'Hey Jude' the other day and I had the urge to move to Cuba, so there might be something to it."

"Blackwood said they might hire a preacher who will speak about that kind of stuff to come in and have a revival," I said.

"I told you from the get-go about him," Jesse said, frowning.

"I got a question for the preacher boy," Dickie said. "My mama's got this one Bible—some of the words are in red and the rest of them are in black. Why is that?"

"The words in red are things that Jesus said," Jesse said. "Everybody knows that."

Dickie nodded. "That's what I thought. But what does that mean? Are those words more important than the rest?"

"No," I said. "It just means those are things Jesus said."

"Well, when the teachers write red stuff on my papers, it's more important. If those words aren't more important, why call attention to them?"

"Dickie, you ought to buy stock in the Paper Mate

company," Jesse said. "With all the red pens teachers go through, you'd be rich."

I had never thought of the red words of Jesus quite like this, and I put it on a growing list of questions my friends had posed. Was the antichrist alive? Where did the dinosaurs go? If God made only two people, how did all the rest of us get here? But the list was not just theological in nature. It was also practical, the biggest question being when we might be moving into the parsonage that was being prepared. That led me to wonder when my father might grow a backbone.

"What's the difference between Protestants and Catholics?" Jesse said. "I've always wondered that."

"I got that one," Dickie said. "Catholics get to wear robes and swing incense and Protestants wear normal clothes. I think we're partly jealous."

"You're Protestant, right?" Jesse said.

I nodded. "But how do you know about Catholics? There aren't any Catholic churches around here."

"I seen them on TV at Christmas," she said. "Some big church and a guy with a big hat talking funny."

"That's the pope," Dickie said. "The better question is, what's the difference between a Baptist and a Pentecostal?"

I waited, wondering what might come out of Dickie's mouth. Since he was of the Pentecostal persuasion, I figured he might have something snarky to say about Baptists.

"What's the answer?" Jesse said.

"They both got their dos and don'ts. But a Baptist sings out of a hymnal and ends Sunday services at high noon.

A Baptist believes in the Holy Spirit, but only if he keeps quiet. They don't yell or jump around, they just sit there and soak and try not to fall asleep."

"And what about Pentecostals?" Jesse said.

"They do pretty much anything they want. You can holler or get all excited and they don't call you down for it. The way I look at it, going to a Baptist church is like riding a school bus where they're trying to get you from one place to another while keeping you quiet. And going to a Pentecostal church is like going on the same trip, only they make it more of a parade."

Jesse jumped up and ran to Daisy, who was lying back on a tombstone with her arms and legs spread wide. Dickie and I followed.

"You can't do that," Jesse said. "You got to show respect for the dead."

"Where's Eva?" Daisy said.

"She's over there."

Jesse pulled her sister down and they walked hand in hand to a stone on a flat patch of ground. The grave had settled over the years and was sunken rather than showing a bump.

"Is that your sister who got polio?" Dickie said softly.

Jesse nodded, staring at the words on the stone that had worn and faded. She opened her mouth to say something, then closed it.

"I want Mama," Daisy Grace whined. "When's Mama coming back?"

"I didn't know your mama was gone," Dickie said.

"She went on a trip," Daisy said.

"She did?" Dickie looked at Jesse. "To where?"

Jesse put her hand on the stone. "She's with some relatives."

"Is she feeling any better?" Dickie said.

"I reckon she's feeling a lot better."

I looked at my watch. "Hadn't we better start back? We're going to miss Jerry crying."

"Yeah, I'll pack the stuff," Dickie said. "But when's your mama coming back?"

Jesse looked at Daisy Grace, running toward the road. "Not soon enough."

Dickie left, and Jesse squatted down among the graves. "Why does he let things like that happen? Why do little kids get polio? Why do little kids lose their mother?"

"I don't know."

"I mean, if there's a God, of course, and he's supposed to love us, why does he allow it all? If it's to make us stronger, I don't want to be stronger."

It was another question for the list. My father had talked about God allowing bad things to happen for the greater good. He preached about Lazarus and how Jesus waited in another town until his friend died so he could raise him from the dead. Romans 8:28 was quoted like an old story in the family—all you needed was the first few words and everybody finished it. "We know that all things work together . . ." But the verse didn't help Jesse.

"If God knows everything that's going to happen and

it's all going to be bad, why did he make this old world in the first place?"

"My dad says if you ever doubt God's love, you should look at the cross."

"What's that supposed to mean? If I doubt God's love when my mama is spitting up blood on the linoleum, it's supposed to help that Jesus was up there bleeding? That's not much of a comfort to me."

"I'm not explaining it well. Bad things happen so that good can come out of it."

"You mean like Grissom and Chaffee and White?"

I didn't get the reference.

"Dickie can tell you. He's got a magazine with pictures. Three astronauts that burned up on the launching pad. So we went to the moon. Was it worth it to sacrifice those men? Is that how it works? God gives somebody heartache and trouble and somebody else gets to go to the moon and back?"

She stood, leaving a handful of wildflowers on top of her sister's grave. "I don't get it, Matt. I'm not seeing it. Tomorrow I'm going to take that little girl to a stranger's house and leave her. Why would he take our mama?"

The next day I was at the end of my grandmother's driveway early, waiting for the bus and hoping to see Jesse and Daisy pass, a sick feeling in my stomach. My mother had taken me to school for a tour of the classrooms, but the smell of the hallways and the imposing high ceilings still gave me a feeling of dread.

My father walked to the end of the driveway. He had been distant since the incident with Gentry Blackwood and though I still held it against him, I kept remembering the death of Dickie's father, and that softened me a little. I didn't want to keep my promise never to forgive him, but I didn't see a way around it, or a way toward him. He retrieved the newspaper and opened to the sports page. "Your Pirates did well yesterday. Won a doubleheader against Philadelphia. That's eight in a row. They might win a hundred this year."

"Going back to the World Series," I said. The Pirates had played the Reds again in late July and only won one of three. But they were almost twenty games over .500 and a sure bet for the postseason.

"Not if the Reds can help it. They split with the Dodgers."

"Wish we could see a doubleheader," I said.

He looked back at the paper. Mark Spitz had won his seventh gold medal at the Olympics in Munich. My father lingered a little, then finally put a big hand on my shoulder.

"I know going to a new school is not easy."

"It helps that I have a couple of friends."

He nodded, but I could tell his heart wasn't in it. He looked like he wanted to say something, wanted to give some encouragement, but finally he nodded again and patted me. "You have a good day."

I kept looking up the road, expecting to see Jesse's bike. My eye fell on the brick structure by the drive, something my grandfather had begun years earlier to hold the mail-box. He'd never finished it and it sat as a monument of sorts. I spotted a rock perched on it with an envelope underneath. I opened it and found a scrap of paper with pencil scrawl that read, *PB, save me a seat. And watch out for Blackwood.*

I stuffed the paper in my pocket, smiling. No matter what happened at school, Jesse was my friend.

The bus rumbled by and turned around somewhere up the hollow, and when it appeared again, there were already ten kids inside. I sat as far away from Gentry as I could. The bus wound along the country road and up another hollow and finally plunged toward Dogwood.

To everyone who passed in the aisle, I put a hand down and said, "It's saved." I hoped Dickie would be able to sit on my right and Jesse to my left. A boy with a fresh haircut who looked like he had no business anywhere near a junior high looked at me with such terror that I let him sit by the window. I knew Dickie would understand.

"Thanks," the kid said, his eyes darting around the bus. His clothes smelled faintly of smoke. "I'm Alan Thompson. What's your name?"

I told him and he nodded, then turned to watch the passing scenery.

My strategy of saving a seat for Jesse worked until we reached Brookwood Estates and a nicely dressed group got on. A smiling girl with short, dark hair bounded down the aisle. I recognized Gwen Bailey from church. She had introduced herself to me and sat by me on the first day of

Sunday school. Before I could tell her the seat was saved, she plopped her generous figure down and laid her notebooks on her lap.

"Morning, Matt."

"Hi," I said nervously, trying to figure out how to tell her she needed to move. She was dressed immaculately and her perfume was like some exotic island, all coconut and pineapple. "Um, I was going to save this for—"

"If you need any help your first day, I'd be glad to show you around. Shadow you to your classes. It's hard being the new kid at the start of school. If you come in the middle of the year, everybody knows you're new. But if you start in the fall, you get lost in the shuffle."

"Thanks," I said.

The bus rumbled ahead, the brakes squeaking as we stopped in town. I was about to ask if she could move when I saw Jesse at the back of the line of kids waiting across from the gas station. She had her head down and held on to a grocery bag.

"Your dad's sermon was really good Sunday. I got a lot out of it," Gwen said. "We're not the type of people who have roast pastor for lunch—you know, people who criticize everything. Not that the church is perfect."

"You're the new pastor's kid?" Alan said.

I nodded and watched Jesse board, looking for me. Finally she spotted me and her face tore at my heart. As she passed, I mouthed, "I'm sorry." I could only imagine what the morning had been like as she dropped Daisy at day care.

"What you got in the bag, Woods?" Gentry said. "Horse turd sandwich for lunch?"

Jesse didn't respond, just moved to the back and stood until the driver barked at her.

"Yeah, sit down, Woods," Gentry said.

"You'll learn quickly about our social order," Gwen said, leaning close and lowering her voice. "Choose your friends wisely and avoid the miscreants."

I had to give Gwen credit for her exemplary vocabulary, but the way she categorized Jesse turned my stomach. I glanced down at the notebooks on her lap and fear gripped me. "Are we supposed to bring notebooks?"

"I contacted my teachers ahead of time and found out what to bring. You don't have to worry. They'll pass out textbooks today and get everybody's name. It's low-key, other than gym."

My heart sank. "Does everybody dress for gym?"

"You can sit out the first day if you forgot your stuff."

I wondered if that was what Jesse was carrying in the bag. I looked back but couldn't see her.

Dickie got on at the last stop. I raised my head to him and he waved.

"How's it going, Dickie?" I yelled.

"Lookin' for a breakthrough," he said, then miraculously found a seat in front.

"I thought people like him are supposed to sit in the back of the bus," Gentry yelled. Others laughed and Gwen shook her head.

"Obviously affirmative action has not reached the hills.

The key to getting along here, Matt, is not to be different. You pay a price if you are."

"But being smart is different, isn't it?"

"You have to choose how you're going to be different. Some things are worth the slings and arrows."

We arrived at school and I was drawn by the tide of students. As I exited the bus, Gwen took me by the arm to introduce me to her friends. I mildly protested, turning to look for Jesse, but somehow I missed her. We had fifteen minutes before classes began, and Gwen pointed to the cafeteria in the lowest level of the school.

"They serve breakfast to the poor kids every morning," she said.

"Show me."

She took me there and I scanned the tables but didn't see Jesse. After meeting a few of Gwen's friends, I broke away, passing the gymnasium. Jesse walked through the doors, her hair dripping wet. She wore second-hand jeans and the same stitched shirt.

"Hey," I said.

"You make new friends?" she said, deadpan and moving toward the lockers.

"I'm sorry about the bus. There was nothing I could do."

"Didn't you get my note?"

"I did. I tried to save you a seat."

"I understand if you don't want to associate with me."

"Stop it," I said, grabbing her arm. She pulled away quickly, but I locked eyes with her. "This is not about me associating with anybody. You think I'm ashamed of you?"

She clenched her teeth, brow furrowed.

"What's wrong?"

Her chin quivered. "I just needed to tell somebody about this morning. It was awful. Daisy about scratched me to death when I left."

"She'll get used to it, don't you think?"

Jesse looked at the floor. "That's the story of our lives. We just get used to things."

"Why is your hair wet?"

"No reason," she said.

Then I put it together. Jesse had no running water. She used the school shower to get presentable.

"Did you get breakfast this morning?" I said.

"I'm all right."

I put a hand on her shoulder and she felt like nothing but skin and bones. "One day at a time, okay? You're going to make it." I paused. "No. We're going to make it."

Chapter 20

I knew when I woke up that this was the day I would talk
with Jesse again. I needed to fish or cut bait, as my father
often said when I was a kid. How I would fish was the
question.

I pulled out the pictures Uncle Willy had given me, and
that produced a desire for more remnants of my childhood.
In the back of my closet I found more pictures and newspaper clippings.

I'm convinced everyone has a pivotal year in their lives,
a year when things coalesce in a way that leaves you forever changed. For me, that year was 1972, and not just
because of the move to Dogwood. It was the last year

pitchers batted for themselves in the American League. The beginning of the baseball season was mired in strike talk. At the Olympics, eleven Israeli athletes were killed by terrorists, ushering in new fears in a world filled to the brim. World events swirled, lining up for big changes we could not anticipate. The Vietnam War was winding down, but there were flare-ups. People in West Virginia said the problem in Vietnam wasn't that we were at war, but that we weren't being allowed to win. President Richard Nixon went to China that year, but there was also a break-in at the Watergate Hotel. The seeds of an impeached president and the malaise of later years were sown in 1972, but I could not see any of this because that was the year I fell in love with Jesse Woods.

It was also the year I fell more deeply in love with drama, for it was the year I met Mr. Kerry Lambert. I had expected Dogwood to be culturally backward but Mr. Lambert was a ray of light. He saw something in me in our language arts class that he called forth over the next few years and I threw myself into every play and musical he produced.

This morning, the news of Jesse's pregnancy, if it was true, still hung over me, and I felt I needed someone else's wisdom before I approached her again. I drove to Mr. Lambert's neighborhood. The leaves were turning on the hillside and there was a fresh chill in the air. We'd had cast parties at his house and stayed by his pool until the wee hours. His wife had been one of the kindest people I have ever known. Mr. Lambert was a Christian, but my parents considered him just barely one since he was in what they considered a liberal denomination. Mr. Lambert always listened to their objections to the plays he chose, and it was a personal victory when we performed *The Sound of Music* in my junior year. My father had enthusiastically encouraged the congregation to see it because of its "story of faith in the crucible."

Mr. Lambert had sensed the friction between my father and me over drama and faith. My father's was a retreating religious system that had deemed Hollywood and Broadway as "of the devil." But there were glimpses of a cease-fire between us.

"I don't know why your dad wouldn't want to use that creative mind of yours," he said to me one day. It was a seed well-planted because a few weeks later, as my father was working his way through Colossians, I wandered into his office one day after school.

"I was reading ahead to chapter 3 for this week and had an idea about how you can illustrate the message," I said.

He put down his pen and leaned back in his wooden swivel chair. "I'm listening."

"It talks about putting away anger, wrath, malice. It's almost like Paul has attended our church."

He smiled wryly.

"The passage says to put off the old self and put on the new, right?"

He nodded. "What are you thinking?"

I explained my idea of illustrating the message with tattered clothes with symbolic words pinned to them—*anger, malice*, *lying*, etc. "And then, beside the pulpit you could have a coat tree. A shirt that says *compassion*, a tie that has *humility* on it. And you take off the tattered stuff and put on the new ones."

My father did not go for theatrics in the pulpit, but this idea struck him differently. "I like that. But I could never preach and do all of that at the same time."

I said I understood and turned to leave.

"What if you did?" he said. "What if we put up the coat tree and you wander up with the tattered clothes. As I speak, you take off the old and put on the new?"

It was the first glimmer of hope that my father could embrace my gift, and the vision was given by Mr. Lambert.

I rang the doorbell and an older version of my teacher appeared. His shoulders were stooped and he had the telltale hair loss of a cancer patient. But there was still fire in his voice as he bellowed, "Matt Plumley! Cynthia, look who's here."

He ushered me in like I was a conquering king and we sat at his kitchen table, he and his wife listening to my story over coffee. I told them where I had been, the truth about my work in Chicago, that I had abandoned my acting plans to go full-time helping struggling inner-city kids.

"But you're still auditioning, right?" Mr. Lambert said, cocking his head to one side.

"When I see an open audition, I try out, but I've had little or no success."

"If I were still teaching, I would have you tell your story. Kids need to hear it's possible to follow your dream—and that dreams can change."

"I'm not sure I'm the poster boy for that. But I wanted to thank you for seeing something in me and giving me confidence."

"It shows your character that you want to honor that. You were more than a good student. You helped others spread their wings. They fed on your example, your energy. And you're still doing that. I'm very proud of you."

His words were like water on parched ground and I drank them in. We talked more about his illness, the changes to the town and the encroachment of the outside world. I wanted to tell him about Jesse, but I couldn't find the right entrance to the subject. When he yawned, I thanked him again for all he had done and he walked me to my car, his steps growing more painful in his Dearfoams.

"You didn't come all the way here to thank me, though, did you?"

"Sure I did. Mostly. I also wanted some advice."

"About what?"

"I don't want to trouble you. I can see you're . . ."

He lowered his gaze and smirked.

"Okay," I said. "I came back because a girl I knew—"

"Knew?"

"A girl I fell in love with is about to make a big mistake. She's getting married. And I'm not sure whether to walk away or do something."

"You've been away a long time, Matt. Why did you wait?"

"Because I didn't know how strongly I felt, I guess. And I feel guilty for something that happened. That made her reject me."

"Guilty about what?"

"It's a long story. But I was responsible for someone's death twelve years ago."

"That's a huge weight to carry. Have you talked with her?"

I nodded. "She's made up her mind. But the guy she's marrying . . . could be a problem."

"Could be?"

"The jury's still out."

He put a hand over his mouth and studied me. "Are you sure this situation with the girl is really why you came back?"

Mr. Lambert was a teacher kids went to in high school about relationships. He talked a number of lonely hearts down from the ledge during his tenure. But his words clanged against my heart.

"Yeah, I got the call and got in the car and drove through the night. Why else would I be here?"

"I'm just not sure it's all about her."

"What do you mean?"

"Let me say this." He waved a hand. "I could be totally off base. Maybe it's the chemo talking. Chalk it up to that if this is out of left field. 'A fragment of an underdone potato,' right? But it sounds to me like you've come to a crossroads. I think you've come back to rescue someone. I don't doubt that. The only question is, *who?*"

"The girl," I said.

He looked away and pursed his lips in thought. "Have you considered that your trip might be less about romance and more about what's going on inside you? At the soul level?" He tapped my chest with three fingers. "Focus on what's going on in there. You'll make a good decision."

His words echoed as I drove and thought of Jesse. I had only two days to change her mind and rescue her from a difficult life. I wanted one more conversation with her, one more shot at the truth. But Mr. Lambert had said it really wasn't about her. I was confused and quickly drove home to gather my thoughts.

"Matt, someone from Chicago called," my mother said as I walked in the house. "It sounded urgent."

She handed me a slip of paper and I recognized the number. My mother had written *Kristen* beside it, spelling it with an *e* instead of an *i*. I went to the back bedroom and dialed from the extension.

"Matt, I'm sorry to bother you. I thought you would want to know."

"Want to know what?"

"It's Dantrelle. He came by and I met with him Tuesday. But he didn't show up yesterday."

"Did he seem upset that I wasn't there?"

"No, he was fine. I helped him with his homework, and he told me he would see me Wednesday."

My mind raced. "His home situation is awful."

"I know. And there was a shooting yesterday morning. At Cabrini. There were several children caught in the cross fire between some rival gangs."

I sat up. "Was he there? Could he have been hurt?"

"He's not been identified in the *Trib* or *Sun-Times*. And we—"

"Did you check the hospitals? Cook County? Rush?"

"We did, but we haven't found him. It's just strange that he didn't show. I thought maybe you would have contacts. . . ."

"He's talked about relatives at the Robert Taylor Homes. I wonder if he could have gone there. Maybe his mother sent him."

"Do you have a name?"

I racked my brain but couldn't remember. "Sometimes I walk to school with his little group in the morning. Those kids don't have a chance, Kristin."

"We'll keep looking. I knew you'd want to hear. I know how much you care."

"Thank you."

"I've been praying nonstop."

She said it like she meant it. She said it like prayer would make a difference. "Keep it up," I said.

"Is everything okay with you?" Kristin said.

Her tone showed she really cared. But the words she had spoken at the restaurant came flooding back. *Just friends.*

"Yeah, I'm fine. Just some old wounds opening from when I was a kid." I didn't say more, not wanting to explain. I wanted to scream or throw the phone. I wanted to drive back to Chicago and find Dantrelle and track down the shooter. I wanted to protect little kids who were just walking to school. But I felt powerless.

"I need to be there," I said. "I should come back."

"I understand," Kristin said. "But there's little you could do even if you were here."

"Yeah. Look, I'll head that way soon. I have one more thing to do here. We're going to find him."

She paused. "I'll call if we hear anything."

"Thanks, it means a lot."

I hung up and stared at the phone, then returned to the kitchen and told my mother the news. "I need to head back."

There were tears in her eyes when she hugged me. "I'm so sorry, Matt. I'll call the prayer chain right now and put Dantrelle's name on it. And I'll call your father. Can you stay for dinner? I'll make your favorites."

My favorites meant I would gain an extra five pounds before I left and I made a mental note to contain my portion sizes.

"I need to run an errand. Be back in a bit."

I drove to Burdette's Greenhouse and asked for daisies. On a card I wrote, *Meet me tonight, Wildflower. Top of the hill.* I put the card in an envelope, drove to the Food and Drug, and went straight to the meat department. I rang the bell but no one came. I left the flowers and note with the manager at the front. "Make sure Jesse gets this."

At home, I walked up the hill, remembering a summer filled with adventure and imagination and anything but boredom. I gathered firewood and cleared out the pit and prepared for one more conversation.

My father prayed a long, sonorous prayer for Dantrelle before we ate, asking God to protect him. He prayed

I would be able to give hope to the family and community and for "traveling mercies." Once he said, "Amen," I opened my eyes to the potato and macaroni salad, my mother's signature chicken and rice dish, along with green beans and a salad.

I ate chicken that literally fell off the bone and thought of Dantrelle. He had been to my apartment several times and was amazed at the food I prepared.

My mother interrupted my thoughts with "That Kristin sounded very polite. Is she pretty?"

"She is. But I don't think she's interested."

"Well, if she went to the trouble to call, maybe she is. Don't count her out. I don't know what kind of list you have for your future spouse, but you shouldn't be too picky."

My father said, "I think it's good to be choosy. It worked for me."

"Calvin," my mother said, demurring. "I'm just saying indecision is your enemy. If you see what you want, get in the game."

"It's funny," I said. "That was part of why I came back."

Her face fell and she hovered over her plate as if it were the Last Supper.

"I saw Mr. Lambert today," I said, changing the subject.

"How's he doing?" my mother said. "I heard he was having chemo."

"He looks older, but he's okay, considering."

"He was such a kind man to you, wasn't he?"

"He gave you wings when I couldn't," my father said.

I stared at him. "What do you mean?"

He put down his fork. "I didn't understand you, Matt. We weren't on the same wavelength. I can see that now. He was able to reach a part of you I couldn't. I'll always be grateful."

It was as close to an apology or admission of guilt as I had ever heard, and I decided then if I ever became a parent, I wouldn't hold back on this kind of conversation.

"Thanks for saying that."

He nodded. "So you're headed back in the morning, early?"

"Yes. I was wondering if we still have a sleeping bag."

"What for?" my mother said.

"I'm going to camp on the hill tonight."

"Matt, it's supposed to be cold."

"If we have one, it's in the basement," my father said.

"But you won't be rested for the drive," she said.

"I'll be fine, Mom."

"Let me check and see—"

"No, I'll get it after we do the dishes," I said.

"You're doing the dishes?" she said. "Do I need to get my hearing checked?"

After we'd washed and dried everything, I went to the basement and found Ben's sleeping bag on a dusty shelf in the storage area. There were shoe boxes of baseball cards that brought back memories. Canned beans and vegetables sat in a lonely line.

In the corner was an old medicine chest with a mirror.

I had spent hours here reading and pilfering through scrapbooks and pictures. I spotted a box marked *Pastor Plumley* and opened it. Inside were books my father didn't have room for in his office, but I was surprised to see a stack of journals among them. The entries in the first one were short and to the point. Seminary life didn't allow much latitude for personal reflection, evidently. But later, after my father became a pastor, the entries were longer and more detailed. I felt guilty reading his words, but it was like peering into my own history, just looking over a different shoulder.

I found a journal for 1972 and skimmed my father's reflections of our first summer in Dogwood. *Still praying for Ben. O Lord, let your word not return void. Also for Matt to adjust.*

I never knew my father kept such accounts. Turned to the date of the trip to Cincinnati, I found, *Reds beat the Pirates two straight. Matt and Dickie had a good time. Fun trip. Ramona upset about me inviting Jesse, but things worked out for the best. Unsure how to move forward to keep Jesse and Matt apart. Lord, give me wisdom.*

I stared at the words. That my father had been concerned about keeping Jesse and me apart surprised me, especially since he was the one who had invited her to the game. I wondered what he had recorded about the events of that fall. I flipped forward, but the date I was looking for had been skipped for some reason. I closed the diary and returned it to the box.

My mother was waiting with hot cherry pie and ice

cream. We ate and my father handed me a flashlight and a few twenty-dollar bills.

"If I don't see you in the morning, it's been great having you back. I'm proud of you, Matt."

"For what?"

"I don't know. For following your own path. I respect that."

I smiled and shook his hand, and he brought me in for a hug. The two of them watched as I walked past the barn and up the path to the hill.

Chapter 21

I fell into a rhythm of school, homework, church, and
piano practice, and the carefree nature of summer ended.
Jesse had her plate full with Daisy Grace and school.
I helped as much as I could but she seemed exhausted by
the weekends. Dickie threw himself into whatever was
in front of him—school and sports, but when we were
together, he was either looking for flying saucers and the
Mothman or following the exploits of Evel Knievel, riding
his bike up embankments and thinking up jumps.

"It's all about the speed," he said one day as we rode
through town. "It doesn't matter what you put under him,

a tank full of rattlesnakes or a line of cars—if you've got the speed and the right incline, you can jump anything."

Jesse rode with Daisy in the back, the girl's chubby cheeks jiggling with each pothole. With all the pain she'd been through trying to keep her big secret, riding with Dickie felt like a respite. But Dickie was going through his own changes, and we could see subtle differences in his moods. He would get quiet suddenly or get angry at something Jesse called "piddly." Things boiled over on us that day.

"People who have to jump things are trying to prove something to somebody," Jesse said.

"How you figure that?" Dickie said, an edge to his voice. "He gets paid a lot. I'd rather jump school buses once a month than go to work every day and sell insurance or work at the glass factory."

"There's going to come a day when he gets killed and everybody's going to be sad—"

"He'll never be killed. He'll always make those jumps because he plans it."

"People don't watch to see if he makes it. They watch because he might not."

"Exactly. And he's got the broken bones to prove it. That guy has courage."

"It don't take courage to jump a motorcycle over stuff when they're paying you. Courage is something different."

Dickie put on his brakes and swung his bike around. "So you don't think Evel has courage?"

"I think he's a daredevil who doesn't want to make a living like the rest of us."

"He's a showman," I said. "He takes chances in front of others like the guy who sticks his head in a lion's mouth at the circus. But his risks are calculated. He knows how fast he has to go to hit the jump and land on the other side. It's math and physics. The only question is whether he can pull it off."

Dickie looked at me like I had two heads. "So you two think there's nothing to it? Why don't we make a jump and see if it's so all-fired easy?"

"I didn't say it was easy," I said. "I just said it was calculated—"

"Fine," Jesse said. "What do you want us to jump? The reservoir?"

Dickie cursed. "You two couldn't jump a mud puddle."

Jesse stood her ground. "Come on. Whatever you jump, I'll jump."

"On that thing?" Dickie said. "It's too heavy."

"It's like Matt says: it's just speed and physical."

"Physics," I corrected.

"Whatever. Pick something. I'll jump it."

Dickie thought a moment, then snapped his fingers. "I got it. The creek in front of Matt's house. There's a wide place just down from the curve in the road. I can set up a ramp right now."

"You're on," Jesse said.

"That's crazy," I said. "You two are going to break your necks."

Dickie took us to his house and rummaged through the garage. He came up with a wide plank of wood that was long enough for a ramp. He carried it under his arm and rode to my house, and we searched the barn. Dickie found two cinder blocks and chose the spot where the creek was widest. There was a telephone pole nearby, and as Dickie began to construct the ramp, I had a sinking feeling he might crash into it.

"I think you ought to start with something smaller," I said. "You know, just to get in the rhythm."

Dickie shook his head in disgust, but I could tell he was becoming intimidated by the jump. The bank here was higher than on the other side and fell at least ten feet because of the last flood. He pulled the wood and cinder blocks further up the creek where it wasn't as wide and both sides were level. Daisy sat in the grass and watched, eating a bag of chips.

Jesse added some rocks from the creek underneath the plank because she said the wood would sag when the bike hit it.

Dickie went first and started on the road, then came through the field and hit a muddy patch that slowed him. He put on his brakes and slid to the edge of the creek.

"It's harder than it looks," he said.

Jesse rolled her eyes. "Get off and let me try."

"No, just watch."

He pedaled farther up the road and entered the field at a different spot, his hair blowing. Instead of slowing, he picked up speed and hit the ramp squarely. When the tires left the ramp, the wood flew up and followed him, splashing in the shallow water. Dickie didn't elevate much, but his momentum carried him across the chasm and he landed in the tall grass on the other side.

Daisy clapped and I whooped.

"Now you go, Matty!" Daisy said.

I laughed nervously. "I don't think I want to be Evel Knievel today."

Jesse wasn't as impressed. "Pull it back yonder. This part of the creek is for babies."

I picked up a cinder block and a rock or two and Dickie brought the rest. Jesse put Daisy in the bike and pushed her past the telephone pole. The basket always seemed to subdue the girl and allowed us to continue.

"Now you stay there and watch," Jesse said to Daisy Grace, sitting her in the shade of a scrub oak.

There wasn't much water in the creek, but we had seen snakes chasing minnows. The more troubling aspect of the jump was landing. The ground was hard and rock-filled. The bank on our side was higher, so the rider had to get altitude and let gravity work. At least that's what Jesse figured.

"How fast you think you need to go to get across?" I said.

"Fast as I can," Jesse said, pushing her bike up the hill.

"Don't take that one, Jesse," Dickie said. "If you crash it, you won't be able to ride with Daisy to the store."

"Take mine," I said. It was in much better shape and could go a lot faster than her heavy bike.

"You two are worrywarts," she said. She pushed her bike out of the way and came back for mine, but when she reached for it, I held on.

"I got a bad feeling about this."

"Grow a spine, Plumley," Jesse said and her words cut to the quick.

She took my bike and ran up the hill to the road. She would get speed coasting down the hill, but I wasn't sure it would be enough. Once she moved out of sight, Daisy stood and craned her neck. Then we heard the tires on the dirt and furious pedaling. Jesse appeared at the edge of the road, gravel and dust flying, and raced down the hill at an incredible speed. She was focused like a laser on the jump, pumping and leaning forward.

My heart pounded. I couldn't watch her kill herself, so I moved into her path and waved my arms.

"Stop!"

She was concentrating so hard she didn't see me at first, and she got spooked. The bike wobbled and she applied the brake, the front one, flipping the bike over. Jesse fell hard, the bike careening over the embankment and into the creek. She landed dangerously close to the phone pole, Daisy laughing.

Jesse bounced up, holding a bloody spot on her elbow and cursing. "You trying to kill me?"

"I was trying to stop you from killing yourself," I yelled.

She jerked away, her face contorted. Dickie climbed down the embankment and got the bike.

"I swear, Matt, you're just like your brother," she said.

Her words stunned me. I turned away, not knowing how to respond.

After climbing up the bank, Dickie handed the bike to

me. The handlebars were crooked. "If we take it back to my place, I can fix it." He looked at Jesse. "How is Matt like his brother?"

She had grabbed Daisy and put her in the basket. "He's chicken. Go on and tell him, Matt." Her face was red and she was limping. "Tell him where your brother is and why he's there."

"Jesse," I said, pleading with her to stop. "Don't leave. Look, I'm sorry."

"I would have made it if you hadn't got in my way," she said, wincing as she pushed her bike.

"Where's your brother?" Dickie said.

I watched her climb on the bike and pedal away, Daisy licking salt from her fingers. I thought Jesse might yell, "Draft dodger," but she kept her promise and didn't reveal any more about my brother. As she made it to the road, I thought I heard her crying, but I wasn't sure.

"I was trying to help," I yelled.

When I turned around, Dickie was staring at me. "Where's your brother?"

"Look, I don't know where my brother is. I haven't talked to him in a long time."

"Don't lie to me, Plumley. Where is he?"

I knew I needed to tell Dickie the truth, but that didn't make it any easier. I explained that he was supposed to go in the military but decided to move to Canada. I left out the part where he moved there with his girlfriend.

"He got drafted?" Dickie said.

"I guess."

"And he didn't go?"

I shrugged. "Dickie, I'm not my brother. He didn't ask my opinion about what he should do."

"And if he had, what would you have told him?"

"I don't know, Dickie. What's your problem?"

Dickie clenched his fists and the veins in his neck stood out. "My problem is, my dad went to fight for our country. Laid down his life. He went because they asked. Your brother ran. That's my problem."

I wanted to say something to appease him, but nothing came to mind.

"Jesse was right. You're just like him. You're yellow, Plumley."

It was painful to watch Jesse get off the bus each day and then pass our house on her bike as she rode home. Sometimes Daisy would ride in back of her holding a shopping bag. I stayed upset at her for about a day and then the old feelings crept in and I spoke to her on the bus. She held up a hand and moved to the back even though there was an open seat beside me.

Dickie stopped talking to Jesse on the CB because of me, and Jesse didn't respond to my clicks of the microphone. Two days later I brought some leftovers and snacks to her house as a peace offering.

"One day your mama's going to notice and she's going to drag the truth from you about me."

A few days later my mother did notice a missing box of Little Debbie cakes, so I decided to be more discreet.

The strange thing was, nobody saw Jesse's plight. Dickie hadn't, the lady who watched Daisy every day hadn't, and for everyone up and down the road it seemed common that Jesse took care of her sister.

Every so often she would ask me to make a phone call for her. Once, my mother gave the two of them a ride to Goodwill so Jesse could buy clothes for Daisy. I went with them and asked my mother if we could pay. My mother had a kind heart.

"Jesse, let me take care of that," she said like it was her idea. And I felt proud for the ten dollars she spent.

We had a close call one day in late September. I was in English class and our teacher, Mrs. Gibson, was taking a break from her Nazi-like sentence diagramming to put together our ninth-grade play. She had enlisted the help of Mr. Lambert, the high school drama teacher, who had a calming effect on both Mrs. Gibson and the class. We were auditioning for parts and I assumed I would be a townsperson or perhaps the milkman. But when I spoke, Mr. Lambert looked up from the page and watched me.

"I think we have our George," he whispered to Mrs. Gibson, but I heard every word.

The school secretary, Mrs. Stewart, spoke over the loudspeaker in our room and called me into the office. I walked on air, having heard such encouraging words from a man who would become pivotal in my high school years.

"Matt, we have a situation with Jesse Woods and no way to contact her mother," Mrs. Stewart said gravely when I walked into the office. "She said your family might help."

"Sure. What's the problem?"

She searched my face. "I think it best if Jesse spoke with your mother, if that's okay."

"I can call her if you want."

"Why don't you go to the nurse's station and call from there? That's where Jesse is. But don't get too close."

I walked to a series of partitioned rooms at the back of the office. I didn't even know our school had a nurse. I found Jesse alone in a room, sitting on a plastic chair, her legs pulled up and her head down.

"What's wrong?" I said.

She looked up with red eyes. "Girl behind me in home ec said she saw something crawling in my hair. Teacher sent me down here and the nurse says I have lice. She won't let me go back to class and said I couldn't ride the bus. How am I supposed to get Daisy?"

Lice was the great stigma, the great leveler of haves and have-nots. If your family contracted it, everyone kept their distance. Anybody with a locker next to yours abandoned ship, just like people in the lunchroom.

"You probably caught it from somebody else," I said.

She gave me a look that I ignored and I picked up the phone. I dialed home but no one answered and I realized it was the day of the ladies' Bible study. I couldn't remember where the study was held, so I called the church office. It went unanswered as well.

"What happens if I can't reach them?"

"Guess I have to wait until you can," she said.

"I'll come back after English and call again," I said.

"How long you think it'd take me to walk?"

"Jesse, that has to be six or seven miles."

"If I start now, I can make it. They're not going to let me ride the bus. If your mom doesn't come, you need to get Daisy Grace. Just don't tell the lady who cares for her about this, you understand?"

My mind whirred with the responsibility. "It won't come to that. I'll get in touch with my mom and she'll come pick you up. You sit tight, okay?"

She shook her head. "If I got it, Daisy's got it. The nurse gave me this handout that says I have to stay home until it clears up."

"How do you treat it?"

She held out the sheet. "There's stuff you got to buy. I can't afford that."

I thought I might be able to find some information in the school library.

"My cousins had it once," Jesse said. "But I ain't asking them."

"I'll ask."

"Elden is the one who would know, but he's meaner than a snake."

I knew Elden Branch, Jesse's first cousin, from gym class. He would jog behind people as they ran laps around the baseball field and trip them. On the court, inside the gym, he would stand and bite his fingernails, staring at girls like they were pieces of meat on a smorgasbord. He looked like a series of bones held together with rubbery skin, but he had a wicked mouth.

I found Elden in the lunchroom after English and went through the line, weighing the best approach. I decided to play a part—the lunchroom would be my stage. I put on a confident look and walked past him, stopped as if I'd just recognized a long-lost friend, and spoke.

"There you are, Elden," I said, sitting across from him.

"You can't sit here, Plumley."

"I have a question. I'm new and there's a lot I don't know. And I heard you had experience."

"Experience with what?"

I leaned forward and lowered my voice. "Head lice."

He pulled his head back. "You got it?"

"No, but I have an English research paper to write. I was thinking about showing what people do to fix it."

He scowled. "You want information, you're going to have to pony up."

"Excuse me?"

"You going to eat that pizza?"

I looked at the tray. It held a square piece of pizza, a fruit cup, cut corn, a snack cake, and a small carton of whole milk.

"I'm not that hungry. Go ahead."

He grabbed it with a dirty hand and plopped it on his tray. "What about the cake?"

I pushed the whole tray to him.

Looking like he'd just won the lottery, he opened the cake and ate it in one bite, then talked around it. "Way we done it was my mama took us all outside and shaved our heads. Them nits hang on to the hair. It's better just to cut 'em off."

"What about your sisters?"

"She lined us all up. Didn't make no difference. Then we slept outside. Them things die in about a day. She washed the bedding in hot water and shook out the mattresses and we were good."

"You didn't use anything on your hair to kill them?"

He shook his head. "You can douse your hair in kerosene. That's what my grandma did. That'll kill the little buggers. But I heard about this kid who got too close to the stove."

I nodded, hoping he wouldn't provide any more details. It sounded like a story Dickie would tell.

He used his spoon once for the fruit cup, then tipped it back and slurped. "You live over near Jesse, don't you?"

"Yeah."

He grinned. "You get her yet?"

I understood what he meant but pretended I didn't.

He wiped his chin. "Last time she come over, we got her cornered at the corncrib. She put up a real fight."

I swallowed hard and stood. "Thanks for the information, Elden."

I went back to the office and heard Jesse talking with the nurse. I called my mother and father, but there was no answer. When the nurse left, I ducked inside and told Jesse what Elden had said about the lice. She got a far-off look. She had the prettiest hair I had ever seen. Soft and silky. For a country girl, she kept it clean.

"Okay," she said. "I got my daddy's clippers and it's not that cold at night. By Sunday we can move back in."

"You're going to sleep outside?"

"It's either that or the kerosene. But you got to get to Daisy if I don't make it in time."

"I'll get her. Don't worry."

"You'd better keep clear of us after today," Jesse said, opening a window. "I don't want them jumping on you."

"What are you doing?"

"Close this when I'm outside. And watch for me on the road when you go home. If I'm still walking when you pass, get Daisy."

I closed the window after she jumped down, feeling like I was watching Steve McQueen jumping the barbed wire in *The Great Escape*. I spent the entire ride home looking for her. We got to the Halfway Market and I hoped someone had given her a ride. Then I saw her, by the Buckner farm, swinging her arms and walking fast, her hair swirling in the exhaust and dust from the bus as we passed.

The bus driver did a double take, leaned out and looked in the side mirror, but kept driving. When we reached the stop by the gas station, I got off in a gaggle of kids so the driver wouldn't notice and headed to pick up Daisy.

The woman who cared for her lived in a small white house with a chain-link fence surrounding it, Jesse's bike propped against the fence. There were toys in the overgrown front yard and a swing set in back. A rusty tricycle lay on its side by the front door. I rang the bell. When no one answered, I knocked and the door opened.

"Matty!" Daisy Grace said from somewhere inside. The room was dark and there were gates up to block the kids from getting into the kitchen.

"Can I help you?" a woman said. She had a round face and a black tooth on the left side.

"Jesse Woods had to stay late at school and asked if I'd bring Daisy Grace home." I tried to sound authoritative.

"Well, I don't have the okay from her mother. I can't just let you take her."

I resisted the urge to ask if she'd ever seen Daisy's mother. "I understand. I'd feel the same way. I'm Matt Plumley. My father is the new pastor in town."

This news seemed to calm her somewhat.

"Jesse comes to my house to use the phone and we try to help her family out as much as we can."

"That's nice of you. If her mama had a phone, I'd call her, but she don't."

"Right. Well, I guess I could just wait here and make sure Jesse shows up."

The woman looked back at Daisy and seemed to have no big attachment. "If Jesse asked you to pick her up, I'm all right with it. You wait."

She got Daisy's things, which consisted of Daisy's coat and a metal lunch box with a picture of Charlie Brown raring back on the pitcher's mound.

"You tell her not to do this again. I need her mama to come in and set some things straight. And she needs to pay by the end of the week."

"Yes, ma'am."

I retrieved Jesse's bike while Daisy Grace stood on the porch and waited. I figured this was their routine.

"Where's Jesse?"

"She had to stay at school. She asked me to get you. Do you want to stop at the gas station and get a pop?"

The girl's eyes widened and I put my books in the front basket and we rode to the gas station. Daisy made the grape Nehi last a lot longer than I did. I'd returned the bottles and was trying to figure out what to do next when a car drove up and parked at one of the pumps. Jesse got out, thanked the woman driving, and ran to us.

"Matty got me a grape!" Daisy said.

"That's good," Jesse said. Then, to me, "So you got her all right?"

"The woman wasn't happy, but she let us go."

"You have a good day, Daisy Grace?" Jesse said, her face right next to her sister's.

"Yeah," Daisy said, scratching the top of her head.

"Come on, let's go home."

Jesse pushed the bike with Daisy in it and I walked beside them, asking what she was going to do.

"Today's Thursday. If we sleep outside tonight and tomorrow night, they should be dead by Saturday. Sunday at the latest."

"You're just going to wait 'em out?"

"I'll need to get our sheets and pillows to the Laundromat. That's what that woman was saying who picked me up. Wash everything in hot water."

"I'm surprised she didn't kick you out of her car."

"I told her it was my cousins. People are a lot more helpful when they're trying to solve other people's problems."

"You can sleep back on our hill," I said. "Dickie's tent's still up."

"He don't talk to you anymore, does he?"

I shook my head.

"I'm sorry about that. I was plumb put out with you."

"I know. I've got a couple of sleeping bags you can use."

She looked at me, realizing I had forgiven her without even saying it. "I wouldn't want you to have to delouse them."

We passed my grandmother's place, but I kept walking. Jesse seemed to like the company. When we arrived, Daisy jumped down and ran to Carl and hugged the dusty old dog.

"I thank you for what you done," Jesse said. "You didn't have to."

"I wish I could do more."

"Would you wait a minute?"

Jesse ran into the house and returned with a round blue tin and an extension cord she snaked out the front door. She rummaged through the tin and came up with hair clippers. The trimmer clacked and she banged it against her hand and adjusted something with what was left of her thumbnail.

"There. I can get most of it, but not the back. Would you do the honors?"

"I've never cut hair."

"First time for everything."

"Don't you want to put a thing on the end? You know, so you don't look like you just got drafted?"

"I need it as close as you can get it. Not taking chances. But don't let them jump on you."

I took the clippers and gingerly cut a two-inch section from the back of her hair.

"No, not like that," she said, grabbing the clippers. "Like this." She ran the shears through the front of her hair and took off a deep row all the way to the scalp. "Don't be bashful. Cut and let it fall."

Daisy came out and pointed, laughing at her sister.

"Don't you laugh. You're next."

"Why are you cuttin' it, Jesse?" Daisy said.

"So's I can go to the Dollar Store and get a bandanna. You can't wear a bandanna unless you have your hair short."

Jesse's hair fell in big clumps and I sidestepped it. Her hair was clean and soft. When I finished the back, she took the clippers and did the front and sides herself, then saluted me. "Private First Class Jesse Woods reporting for duty." She looked cute without hair, though it made her look even thinner. Jesse's hair was down her neck and I felt bad that she couldn't take a shower.

She struggled to get Daisy to sit still but finally cut her hair as well. Then she took a can of gas and poured it on the clumps and set it ablaze. The stink was awful, but Jesse said she just wanted to know those things were dead.

I wanted to help more, but she said they were off to the Laundromat.

"Let my mom drive you."

"If she drives us, there'll just be more questions. I got to do this myself. But if you could, get some kindling and firewood at the campsite. I'll be obliged."

"You're going to sleep there?"

"I think Daisy will do better in a tent than out in the open."

I had the fire going by dark and watched the two trudge up the hill. They had bought a loaf of bread and some ham from the grocery store and eaten half of it while they did laundry. The other half was for breakfast. Jesse had rinsed her and Daisy's hair out in the sink at the Laundromat. I found old covers in my grandmother's basement, and they used them for beds. Jesse brought their clean sheets and two pillows, which weren't much more than two lumps of cotton with covers on them.

"My mom made a pound cake yesterday," I said, holding out a paper bag with two pieces wrapped in wax paper. Daisy Grace squealed and ate hers quickly and licked her fingers.

I tended to the fire while Jesse got Daisy settled. The air was cool and made me think of football and the turning leaves. The grass was showing black on top. Jesse sat on a rock by the fire and wiped at her neck.

"I can get some marshmallows for tomorrow night," I said.

"Daisy will like that." She ran a hand through the stubble of her hair and yawned. "Matt, why are you doing all this?"

"I want to help."

"But why?"

"I'm like you. When I make a promise, I keep it. You remember your promise, right?"

She scowled. "You mean the one about not telling any-one about your brother?"

"No, the other one."

She put her head down. When she looked up, there were tears in her eyes. "I didn't know it was going to be this hard."

"You didn't know what was?"

"Everything." She wiped at her face and sniffed hard.

I tried to think of something to say but nothing came. Finally I smiled. "I can't wait to see the look on Dickie's face when he sees you."

She put her head in her hands and groaned. "Man, I bet I look awful."

"No," I said, swallowing hard. I had been thinking of a way to say something nice, to show her how I felt. But I kept holding it in. Now I let it go, not worrying how it sounded. "You could never look awful. You're beautiful, Jesse."

She stared at me a moment. "You need to get your eyes checked, PB."

I was glad I had finally said something, glad she knew what I felt, even if her response wasn't exactly warm. "Get some sleep," I said. "There are a couple potatoes in the fire for in the morning." I handed her another covered con-tainer. "And some salt and cow butter in here."

I took a long shower that night and felt itchy, but I told myself it was in my head. As I did my homework, I thought I felt something crawling but ignored it. I fell asleep reading *Great Expectations* for English and woke up too late to check on Jesse and Daisy.

In the morning, my father said there was a curious smoke smell in the air. I shrugged. "Maybe somebody's burning their plant bed."

"In September?" he said. He stopped me as I reached the door and folded his newspaper in front of him. "Did you hear about last night?"

I heard our bus rumble in the distance. "What?"

"Blass won his eighteenth. Pirates clinched against the Mets."

My mouth dropped. I'd been so involved with Jesse and Daisy I had missed it.

"Reds can clinch today against Houston if they win. Cincy and Pittsburgh for the National League crown."

"I can't wait for the Pirates to beat them and show you who's best."

My dad smiled. "Be careful what you wish for."

I ran down the driveway just in time to catch the bus. School dragged all day and I looked at my watch a million times, thinking of Jesse and what I had said. That afternoon I ran up the hill but they were gone. The fire had burned down to ashes and the potatoes weren't there.

I stayed at the house, excited for the weekend, and hurriedly ate dinner and told my parents I was heading for the hill. I grabbed my transistor radio and sneaked a bag of marshmallows.

"What are you doing back there, Matt?" my grandmother said. "Digging a hole to China?"

"He's excited about his favorite team," my mother said.

When I had enough wood for the fire, I sat by the tent.

Darkness came but no Jesse and Daisy. Then I saw a light coming up the hill. It turned out to be my father.

"Better come home," he said when he reached me, out of breath. "Storm's headed this way."

As the words left his mouth, the wind kicked up a gale and blew through the trees. The moon went behind a cloud and thunder clapped.

"You waiting on someone?"

I fiddled with the radio. "Just trying to pull in the Pirates game."

I left the marshmallows in the tent and returned with him, wondering about my friends.

The next morning I was up early. The first thing I noticed was the creek. It had risen with the torrent. My father read the morning paper with his coffee, my grandmother humming a Fanny Crosby hymn next to him.

"It's a gully washer," she said to me as I stared out the window.

My father joined me at the window and watched the water rolling through the bottomland.

"When are we moving into our own house?" I said, trying to keep my voice down.

"Your mother's asking the same question. Blackwood has things tied up. It shouldn't be much longer. That's my hope."

"Do you think it's because of the picture I took?" It was the first time either of us had brought up that day.

He put a hand on my shoulder. "There are some things

we don't control. And Basil Blackwood is one of them. I'm sure the picture didn't help, but you can't blame yourself."

I realized then, observing my father's peaceful acquiescence to the events of our lives, that I had kept my vow not to forgive him. I understood the pressure he was under at church and with my mother and why it was just easier to go along with Blackwood and not make waves. To keep the truth about Ben a secret. It all made sense because he always took things in stride, as if this were his spiritual gift. But it seemed to me that this wasn't the way to live. I wanted him to act, to do something, to stand up and be strong. But the more inaction he exhibited, the more tension there was in my grandmother's house and in the church. Things weren't working out the way people had hoped. We didn't have a big influx of visitors. The closest we had come to a baptism was a baby dedication. And my father's sermons weren't as forceful as Blackwood and some elders wanted.

"Life is never easy," my father said. "It may seem like it on the surface, but there's struggle to it all. When Jesus told the disciples to go across the Sea of Galilee, they got in the boat and obeyed. And that was when one of the biggest storms blew up. So obeying God's will can sometimes get you into trouble. But it's better to follow him into a storm than to stay on the shore alone."

This was one of the things my father liked to do— sermonize in the middle of life. I wondered if he was reminding himself of the truth as much as he was teaching me. I wanted to ask about Ben, but that was a subject best left to my parents' prayers. At the dinner table, my father would pray for "each and every one not at this table" and pause, a hint of regret in his voice. And then we would eat.

The rain ended in the afternoon and the creek stretched into the corn. I rode my bike to Jesse's and looked in the windows but the house was empty and so was the back-yard. A truck passed and slowed. Macel Blackwood, Basil's wife, usually spoke in grunts, but today she rolled down the passenger window and yelled, "If you know what's good for you, you'll keep your distance from that bunch, Plumley."

I waved and smiled.

Later, after walking the muddy path to the top of the hill, I found Jesse and Daisy. They shivered like wet animals in the tent. Daisy ate marshmallows by the handful.

"I've been looking all over," I said. "Where have you been?"

"Here and there," Jesse said. "Just waiting for the lice to die." She moved out of the tent and got me alone. "I'm scared, Matt. I think Blackwood wants me dead."

"You're paranoid. Why would you think that?"

"He's been poking around the property with a guy who has something he looks through. I think he's a surveyor. If they find out Mama's gone, he's liable to take it."

"He can't do that. Did your mother have a will?"

"I can't find it or the deed. I've looked everywhere."

"Well, he's not going to kill you. That's silly."

"You don't know him or his kin like I do."

Seeing her concern gave me an idea—I saw an opening here and pushed through. "Maybe it's time to get help."

"You stop saying that. We tell nobody."

"You just said that Blackwood wants you dead."

"I haven't found a will or the deed, but I did find my daddy's gun. And there was a box of ammunition in the closet. If Blackwood tries anything, I'm ready."

"Jesse, you can't threaten people with a gun."

"I ain't threatenin'. I'm just saying I'm ready for whatever comes down the pike. But I'm still scared."

It began raining hard and Jesse retreated to the tent. I ran down the hill through the mud and slept in a warm bed, thinking of her all night.

Chapter 22

The lights of Dogwood twinkled below and the air felt
as crisp as apple cider. Above were stars I couldn't see in
Chicago. The Milky Way stretched out toward infinity here
while in the city the light haze blocked my view. There's
something about looking into a night sky that makes you
feel small.

Mr. Lambert's words turned circles in my mind as I
made a fire. My concern for Dantrelle crept in and I smiled
at how quick-witted and funny he was. I couldn't imagine
a world without that little kid in it. I also couldn't imagine
a world where Jesse Woods walked an aisle and said yes to
Earl Turley. These concerns competed with each other as
I counted the stars.

As night deepened, the temperature fell and I thought

about returning to the house. Jesse had ignored my notes in high school. She'd treated me as if I were the one with head lice. The week I got my driver's license, I asked her to a movie. I asked her to prom two years in a row. There was always something in her refusal that sounded a little like regret. Call it intuition, call it denial—I sensed there was part of Jesse that wanted to say yes but held back. Though we never talked about it, I assumed it was because of what I did—or rather what I made her do. The promise I made her keep that kept us apart.

I put my hands behind my head and stared into the night, the crackle of the fire and the woodsmoke lulling me. Images of Dantrelle flashed through my mind and I felt torn between staying and just leaving. I must have fallen into a sleep so deep I was dreaming before my eyelids closed.

I still dream about being onstage and forgetting my lines. They call it "looking up." Or I dream everyone is dressed and I am naked and the audience laughs. The women laugh loudest. Sometimes my parents are in the audience, shaking their heads. Sometimes I see Dickie and his father. But when I see Jesse, she looks away.

This night, in this dream, I was transported. I saw bicycle tires in moonlight. I trembled at the sight of the house on the hill and the cemetery. A collage of images floated to the surface and I heard the flutter of massive wings and a man's raspy cough and a hand grabbed my throat and I gasped for air. Suddenly awake, sitting up straight, I saw a billion stars and, across from me, her face illumined by the flickering firelight, Jesse Woods.

Chapter 23

OCTOBER 1972

October 11 was cloudy, as if something evil was pressing down. I stood with an umbrella in the rain that morning and rode the bus knowing I had a piano lesson afterward. I had thrown hints at my mother and father, letting them know this was the most important day of my life. Game five of the National League play-offs. Gullet was pitching for the Reds and Steve Blass for the Pirates. The game would be played, ominously, at Riverfront Stadium in Cincinnati, after the conclusion of game five between Detroit and Oakland.

I knew the Pirates were going to their second consecutive World Series, and I told Jesse about it that morning. I had

watched every play-off game to that point. I had to be part
of it and couldn't understand why my parents wouldn't let
me skip my lesson for once. But they dug in their heels.

I stared at the clock in English, calculating the time the
American League game would start. It would be two or
three hours later that the Reds and Pirates began. I begged
God for a rain delay. I prayed there would be some shift in
the time continuum that would allow me to finish school
and my piano lesson and see the entire game before church
services began. Such are the prayers of a play-off–struck boy.

As Mr. Lambert discussed the subtle nuances of Grover's
Corners, New Hampshire, and the play we were attempt-
ing, I heard the voices of Curt Gowdy and Tony Kubek in
my mind. Everyone else seemed oblivious except for Gentry
Blackwood and Earl Turley, who wore their Reds hats.

After school I walked a few blocks to Mrs. McCormick's
house as I did each Wednesday. I sat on her front porch
listening for anyone with an open window who might be
watching the game, cursing myself for forgetting my transistor radio. I'd had it by the door that morning but walked
out without it.

Mrs. McCormick pulled into her driveway and parked
her Dodge Dart, moving with glacial speed as she opened
the door, stepped out, and closed it. Halfway up the walk
she turned and retrieved her massive purse from the passenger side. Several years later she reached the porch.

"And how are we today, Mr. Plumley?" she said with
a rattle in her throat. Her speech was singsong—she was
always guided by some inner melody.

"Fine, thank you," I said, champing at the bit to play the piece I hadn't practiced. My mother would arrive in an hour and I could at least hear the game on the radio—to the Reds side, of course, but I would endure that. I wanted Al Michaels and Joe Nuxhall to weep.

She opened the front door and I blew past her like Evel Knievel searching for a canyon, staring at the clock over her Zenith television. One flick of the knob and I would be in heaven, watching the game, helping my team. So close and yet so very far away.

I turned on the metronome and pulled out my Hanon Virtuoso Pianist exercises, left and right hands running up and down the scales, my wrists rocking. For once the metronome held me back. Mrs. McCormick finally sat and found the piece I was supposed to have worked on, flattening out the book. She glanced at me, then flattened it again.

At that very moment Steve Blass could be pitching a no-hitter. Willie Stargell could be swinging his Hillerich & Bradsby and connecting with a Gullet fastball. Roberto Clemente could be making an over-the-shoulder catch or throwing out a runner at home, preferably Rose or Morgan. I could hear the Pittsburgh faithful cheering somewhere near the Allegheny as my fingers picked out the right progression of Beethoven's *Moonlight Sonata*. I should have known from the menacing chord progression what the future held, but I gritted my teeth, tried to match the notes on the page with the keys under my fingers, and forged ahead.

Mrs. McCormick stopped the metronome. "Is something wrong, Matt? You seem preoccupied."

"I'm sorry." I sat up straighter and looked at the clock and put my hands over the ivories.

I tried the piece again, willing myself to get through the hour. If I could just concentrate hard enough on the notes and push through this, I could see the rest of the game.

The phrase stuck in my craw. I didn't want to see the *rest of the game*. I wanted to see *all of the game*. If I didn't, we might lose.

I hit a clunker and stared at my hands as if they had betrayed me for a few pieces of silver. Mrs. McCormick closed the book and turned to face me, her eyes enlarged by the magnification of her glasses. Her breath smelled stale with a slight hint of what I would later discover was Jack Daniel's.

"Young man, you will tell me what has you preoccupied or I'll chop your fingers off with the fallboard." Her words would have seemed biting and mean to most. To me, they were a welcome invitation to truth.

"I'm a Pirates fan," I said, choking. "Today is the fifth game of the championship. Whoever wins goes to the World Series."

She looked at me as if I were speaking Swahili.

"I listened to every game last year," I said, spilling my story. "I can name every player. I can imitate their swings. And when I watch or listen, it always turns out good. Except for the games I went to this summer. I'm afraid the game is going to be over before my mom picks me up."

She looked at me with disgust. Then she stood, hands on hips, and said, "Why didn't you say so? What channel's it on?"

My heart fluttered. "Three," I said.

She marched to the TV and flipped the knob, and there was the crowd and Curt and Tony calling the NBC telecast. The green Astroturf, the Pirates in their road uniforms and the Reds in white. Her picture was even better than the TV at my grandmother's house. It was hooked to an antenna on the building.

"You mean it?" I said, looking for the score. "We can turn the sound down and keep going."

"Nonsense," she said, pointing to the living room. "Sit in my chair. I'll make popcorn."

At that moment I wanted to become a piano teacher. I wanted to be this kind to someone else someday. I leaped into the chair, sitting forward to take in everything. The game had just begun and Curt and Tony were talking about Oakland's 2–1 win over Detroit. Reggie Jackson had gotten hurt on a play at the plate. We would face Oakland in the World Series when—and not if—we won.

"We won the first game against Gullet," I called to Mrs. McCormick. "Got to him early. I'm hoping we do the same today."

"Mmm-hmm," she said.

I couldn't hide my smile as I watched Gullet warm up in the top of the second. There was no score, but the Pirates were about to change that dramatically. We went up 2–0 thanks to Richie Hebner and Dave Cash. Just me tuning in had set things in motion.

The corn popped in a metal pot in the kitchen, and Mrs. McCormick brought a full Tupperware container with drizzled butter and an ice-cold can of Sprite. I didn't know what to say. I would have promised to name my firstborn after her or to master Mozart's compositions, but she didn't seem to need promises.

"What's the score?" she said as she kicked off her shoes and fell onto the couch.

"We're up by two. And that may be all Blass needs. He held them to one run in the first game."

Pete Rose doubled in a run in the bottom of the third, but in the top of the fourth we got the run back with another hit by Dave Cash. I jumped and pumped my fist. That was it. That was all we needed. I could already see the starting pitchers in game one of the World Series. If Blass got two starts, we were sure to win.

The time for my lesson was up, but my mom hadn't arrived. I was more than content to wait. In the bottom of the fifth, the most unlikely Reds player to hit a home run, César Gerónimo, did just that, cutting the score to 3–2.

The phone rang and Mrs. McCormick struggled to her feet and answered in the kitchen. She returned in the sixth and said my mother was going to be late. There were no other lessons after mine, so I could stay. I didn't think much about the fact that my mother wasn't there. I was so into the game I didn't care.

The seventh and eighth innings came and went and in the ninth the Pirates failed to score. We were ahead by one. Three outs stood between us and the World Series.

Three outs were all we needed.

Dave Giusti came in to pitch the bottom of the ninth.

He would face the most powerful back-to-back hitters for the Reds, Bench and Pérez. I found myself kneeling in front of the TV, clapping my hands and rubbing my palms on my pants, willing my team's defensive stand.

Bench hit a long drive to left field and my heart sank. But it was just a long strike, hitting to the left of the foul pole. I laughed. All those Reds fans jumping and waving thought it was a home run. How sad it would be on their drive home.

The count was 1–2 when Giusti wound up and threw an outside changeup that could have been strike three, had Bench not connected and gone to the opposite field. "Clemente," I said out loud. "Catch it, Roberto! Catch it!"

Curt Gowdy's voice tried to overwhelm the crowd. The camera switched to Clemente. I had seen him take home runs from players, jumping over fences to pick off the ball like a piece of low-hanging fruit. The numbers read 375 on the green wall. Clemente turned his back and I saw his familiar 21 and knew Bench had tied it. The crowd went wild. My shoulders slumped. Air went out of the room. I stared at Bench loping around the bases.

"What happened?" Mrs. McCormick said, walking in from the kitchen.

"Bench tied it."

"Oh, that's too bad."

"Looks like extra innings," I said. "When is my mom coming?"

"You can still watch."

Tony Pérez singled. A double play and a strikeout were

all we needed now. George Foster came in to pinch run and Denis Menke singled and moved him to second. Then Bob Moose, the starter in game two, came in to shut the door. He got a fly ball to right that advanced Foster to third, then a pop out. I gave a sigh of relief. One more out and we were into extra innings and the Pirates would throttle the Reds. I could feel it.

A car pulled up outside and my mother came to the door. Mrs. McCormick greeted her and they talked. I would listen in the car to the top of the tenth and watch the rest of the game at home.

Then I remembered it was Wednesday. Church.

Hal McRae stepped in. Moose fired a pitch in the dirt that Manny Sanguillen tried to backhand.

"No," I whispered.

The ball skipped to the backstop.

"No."

George Foster touched home plate and was mobbed, the Reds jumping like kids on a playground.

I sat on the floor staring at the TV. The empty feeling was indescribable. I was as hollow as a chocolate Easter bunny.

My mother walked inside. "Matt, it's time to go."

Like a robot, I stood and followed. Mrs. McCormick put a hand on my shoulder. "I'm sorry it didn't turn out the way you wanted, Matt."

All I could muster was "Thanks for the popcorn."

She smiled and I got in the car, the weight of what I had witnessed overwhelming me. It was like having a rug pulled out from under you while standing at the edge of the Grand Canyon, and the fall afterward was only half the pain. After 155 games in the regular season, all they needed were three outs. I imagined their locker room. How do you lose on a wild pitch? It was the stuff of Little League games.

Then came the most painful realization—I didn't have control or bearing on the outcome of the game. Pray, root, cheer, beg, and plead with God all I wanted and it didn't change the fact that the Reds were dancing and the Pirates were trudging to their lockers.

"You're probably wondering why I was late," my mother said, oblivious to the game. She drove the car with the front seat pulled as close to the steering wheel as possible and I angled my legs away from the glove compartment.

When I didn't answer, she said, "Matt, did you know that Jesse's mother died?"

I looked at her, horrified. "What?"

"Jesse's mother died some time ago. I thought it was strange she was taking care of her sister. The school called because she had given them our number. I went over to see if everything was all right."

"How do you know her mom's dead?"

"Jesse and Daisy weren't home. Your father and I talked with Basil Blackwood, and he said he hasn't seen Jesse's mother in weeks."

"No," I said. It was the same intensity that I'd felt regarding the Moose wild pitch.

"The sheriff came."

"*No.*"

"He found Jesse and it took a while, but she showed him her mother's grave. Did you know anything about this?"

"You can't do this," I said. The Pirates' loss already had me on the edge, but this was too much. "They'll take Daisy Grace. They'll give her to her cousins and they're mean."

"So you did know," she said, pulling to the side of the road.

"Where are they?" I said.

"Jesse and Daisy are fine. They're at our house waiting."

"Waiting for what?"

"Until the authorities decide what to do."

"The authorities? Mom, you can't let them do this. That was the deal. That's why she's been hiding the truth."

There was pain in her voice when she spoke. "Matt, why didn't you tell us? We could have helped."

I thought of my father and the photo. After that day in his office, I'd vowed I would never trust him again.

"I told her that. I said we would help but she wouldn't listen. She was scared they would give Daisy to the Branches. She had to keep it a secret."

My mother stared ahead. "Her mom died before your birthday."

I nodded. "That's why she had Daisy with her all the time."

I wanted to tell more, to say Jesse made me promise, but I put my head in the crook of my arm and swung at my emotion as if it were a hanging changeup on the outside corner. If only Guisti had thrown Bench a fastball inside.

It was a 1–2 count, for crying out loud. He could have wasted a pitch high. Bench never hit the high-and-tight fastballs. If only my mother hadn't become suspicious. If only we hadn't moved to Dogwood.

My grandmother was in a lawn chair fanning herself with the newspaper when we arrived. Daisy Grace played underneath the hickory nut tree. Jesse was nowhere in sight.

"Daisy doesn't know," I said. "Jesse told her that her mom went away."

My mother shook her head. "That's just cruel."

"No, she didn't mean it to be cruel. She did it to protect Daisy."

"Matt, they can't live there alone. You know that, right?"

"What's going to happen?"

"They'll get help. It'll be all right. But it won't be the way Jesse wants."

"The Branches will get Daisy and they'll treat her the same way they did Jesse!"

My mother stared at me like I wasn't her son. Then she softened and drew me in with an arm and we sat there for a minute in the dusk of a day I would never forget.

"I promise you, Matt. This will help. It's going to get better for them. You'll see."

I got out of the car and walked toward the house.

"Matty!" Daisy Grace yelled. She skipped over to me and stopped, her face in a pout. "Mama's dead. Policeman said Mama's not coming back."

"I know, Daisy," I said, patting her head. Her hair had

begun to grow back, but she still looked like a boy. "I'm sorry about your mom."

I noticed movement near the house as Jesse peeked around the corner. I walked toward her but she ran to the backyard like a scared cat. My father came outside. One look at him and I knew he didn't have the words I needed for either the Pirates or Jesse.

"I need to get to church," he said.

My mother glanced at the driveway as a sheriff's cruiser pulled up and parked beside our car, the window open and radio squawking.

"I think I should stay here, Calvin," she said.

He nodded. "You and Matt help Jesse and Daisy. We'll be praying."

"This is a real mess," my grandmother said, shaking her head. Who could disagree?

My father drove away and another car, a rusted Buick station wagon, pulled into the driveway and inched toward the house. Daisy instinctively stopped skipping and hid behind the tree. The Buick came to rest over a patch of peonies my mother had planted by the rock wall in the driveway. A man with hairy forearms and bibbed overalls opened the door and rocked himself several times to gain the momentum to stand. A large woman with a bulbous nose in a flowery dress wobbled toward the walk and my mother met them and spoke in hushed tones.

"We're awful sorry about this," the man said. "Hate to trouble you and your family."

"It's no trouble," my mother said.

The large woman smiled at Daisy and flung her arms wide. The girl shrank and dipped her head.

"Daisy, you get on over here and give me a hug," the woman said with a deep twang.

"Give your auntie a hug," Hairy Arms said, a command more than an invitation.

"Leave her alone!" Jesse shouted, running around the corner. "We ain't going with you."

The sheriff got out of his car.

"You'll do what we say, Jesse," Hairy Arms said.

Jesse looked straight at me. "I told you."

I wanted to tell her I hadn't revealed the secret. I wanted to say anything to comfort her or make things all right, but I had no words.

She gritted her teeth and grabbed Daisy Grace's hand and marched toward the barn. The adults tried to reason with her, following closely, but Jesse had a mind of her own. I stood by my mother when the screaming started. It was Daisy, yelling at the top of her lungs when Hairy Arms grabbed her. There was kicking and scratching and biting from Jesse. Soon, Daisy was in the back bench seat of the Buick and Jesse was yelling things not fit to print. A string of four-letter words flowed like water.

"Would you listen to the mouth on that girl," my grandmother said. "This is a mess and a half."

My mother tried to calm things, but Jesse was in a frenzy. Nothing my mother said could take the fight from her. The sheriff finally instructed everyone to move away. The man got down on a knee in front of Jesse and spoke softly.

"Anybody but the Branches," Jesse said. "You don't know what they done to me when I was young."

The sheriff held up a hand and talked lower. Jesse's breathing calmed, her chest not heaving as much. She finally nodded and walked toward the house. But she went crazy again when they put Daisy Grace in the back of the Buick. Jesse wouldn't get in. The officer spoke with Hairy Arms and the man got in and backed up, almost hitting the cruiser, then rolled toward the road. I'll never forget the sound of the gravel crunching under that man's balding tires.

The sight of Daisy being taken away alone must have triggered something. Jesse bolted down the driveway, banging on the Buick's back door. Brake lights flashed and Jesse flew into the car and hit her head on the windshield. She was stunned enough for Hairy Arms to grab her and get her in the backseat next to Daisy. Then they drove away.

Chapter 24

Jesse sat on a rock, staring at me, elbows on knees, as comfortable on the hill as a queen on a throne. She fit easy into the landscape or the crook of a tree or a teenager's handlebars. I rubbed my eyes and sat up.

"How you doin', PB?"

I smiled. "I'd offer you marshmallows if I had them. I already gave you all my daisies."

She grinned, showing her two front teeth that hadn't changed. "It took me a minute to figure out what was going on. I thought maybe Dexter Crowley was proposing."

"Thanks for coming."

"I figure you deserve it after all we went through." She picked up a stick and held it to the fire. "Remember when you first came here? You were a Butterball turkey."

"You didn't make fun of me, though. You and Dickie accepted me."

"And the pounds fell off as you rode that bike and climbed the hills."

"You guys sweated it off me." Memories of the three of us running the hills returned. "Do you think Blackwood ever figured out what happened to his horse?"

She shrugged. "I sure never told him."

"Do you ever see Gentry?"

She shook her head. "He's got a family now. Lives down in Ironton, from what I hear. I don't keep up with him."

The crickets sounded like a symphony. Small animals moved in the brush near the tree line. Something howled on the next ridge and Jesse stared at me. "What are you really doing here, PB?"

I winced. "I still have questions."

"I got a bushel basket full that have never been answered. Life is full of them. You ought to know that by now."

I looked at her hands, calloused and worn. She had nicks and scrapes from all the cutting and a couple of strategically placed Band-Aids. Hearing her voice was like listening to a song I had heard in my childhood and had never forgotten.

"If Earl catches you and me out here, things will get ugly."

"Isn't he having his bachelor party?"

"He's not into that kind of thing. The Lord really got hold of him."

"Then I don't need to worry. He'll turn the other cheek, right? Isn't that the Christian thing to do?"

"Maybe. But you might ought to worry about the other Turleys. They're not quite as sanctified."

"You think Shirley will come after me?"

She gave a hint of a smile. "She was sweet on you. I heard about it later. She must have given up on that dream because she's married and has two kids and another'n on the way."

"Are you serious?"

"Shirley turned into a really nice woman. Pretty, too. You missed a good one."

"I expect they'll say the same about you after you start having babies." I grabbed some grass and pulled it from the ground. "Which, as I hear, will be pretty soon."

Her mouth dropped open. "And where did you hear that?"

"The father of the baby told me."

She turned her head, a surprised smile on her face.

"Is it true?" I said. "It's none of my business. And I'm not judging you. But is that why you're getting married?"

She stood, hands on her hips, fire in her eyes. "Is that the question you want answered? You want to know if I'm pregnant?"

"Sit down," I pleaded.

She sat but didn't relax.

"Let me be honest. I'm not saying Earl is a bad guy. But it feels like you're settling for less than you're worth."

"And you're the knight on the white horse who's going to show me how much I'm worth?"

"I'm the guy who came back to see why you didn't keep the promise you made."

She rolled her eyes. "Oh, please."

"You said you'd marry me."

"Matt, we was kids. Besides, you didn't keep your side of the bargain."

"Yes, I did. I never said anything to anybody about your mother. And I did everything I could to keep Daisy safe."

Jesse walked in a circle around the fire, staring at the sky, and I remembered her barefoot days. She'd always felt more comfortable without shoes. She shook her head. "We was just kids."

"A promise is a promise. That's what you always said."

She looked at the lights below and muttered, "Some promises cancel others." Then she turned back to me and jutted her chin. "It was a youthful indiscretion. That's what you would have called it. You and your fancy words."

"You crossed your heart and hoped to die."

"I've hoped to die a lot of times between then and now, big shot."

I tossed the grass into the wind. "You told me once that people are the way they are and there's no changing them. You don't believe that about Earl."

"I think people are the way they are unless God gets hold of their heart. What do you think of that?"

"So Earl is what you want? He's going to make your dreams come true?"

"He's a good man. He's not like his daddy was."

"We're all like our daddies."

"Even you?" she said, and the silence cut like a knife. Then she said, "And what about me? Am I like my daddy?"

I didn't answer. My dream was still fresh. "You never told me what really happened that night."

"There wasn't nothing to tell."

The pain on her face was palpable and I decided not to press. "Okay, here's a question. After it happened, you cut me out. You ran away."

"I didn't run. We just grew apart."

"No."

"You got interested in drama and plays and—"

"I wrote you notes. I asked you out. You said no every time. Why?"

A big sigh. "I didn't do it to hurt you. I appreciated what you tried to do. But sometimes people just—"

"You hated my guts. You blamed me for what happened, didn't you? That's the only thing I can think of to explain it."

"Why in the world would I blame you?" she said.

"Because of what you promised your dad. Because of what you had to do."

She shrank a little, understanding what I meant. "Matt, I never blamed you. It had nothing to do with you. And you need to move on. There's got to be plenty of girls who use big words up there in Chicago."

I rubbed my forehead, thinking about Kristin. I shoved those feelings away and focused on Jesse. Maybe a story would soften her.

"I was at a party one night in college. The guys invited a girl . . . She must have been straight off the farm. They'd given her enough alcohol to kill a horse. And I got mad. They knew me as a mild-mannered drama guy, you know? But when I found her passed out, I went into a rage."

"Matt Plumley to the rescue," Jesse said.

"It was something you would've done. She probably never knew what happened. She probably went back to them. But she survived that night."

She sat and put her hands together, elbows on her knees, looking at the ground.

"Jesse, I don't know if anybody ever told you this, but you didn't deserve any of the bad stuff that happened to you. You believe that, don't you?"

She shrugged. "I reckon."

There was a long silence. Then I said, "I can move on. I just need to hear it from you."

She looked at me out of the corner of her eye like my grandmother used to look at me at her kitchen table. "Matt, if you and I had gotten together, one of two things would have happened. Either you would've had to convince me to leave this place and follow you, which is something I couldn't have done, or I would've had to convince you to stay here. And that would be like tying you up and making you fit into some box. My way of looking at it says neither one of those would have been right."

"And why are you the one who gets to decide?"

She cocked her head. "I've had people decide things for me all my life. It's part of the program. Get used to it."

"What if I moved back here? What if I taught? Or became a counselor?"

"I got no doubt you'd be a good teacher. But this place can't hold you. I knew that the first day."

"What do you mean?"

"You was scared out of your mind when you came to my house. That horse with the bloody leg and old Carl barking. My mama yelling from the window. And then me coming out, in all my beauty." She ran a hand through her hair and turned her head, making fun of herself. "Even though you looked like you were about to pee your pants, you cared more about that horse than you did your own fear. Right then I knew, *This is somebody who won't never be held back because he's scared.* That's what probably made me trust you when I couldn't trust nobody."

I watched her face as she spoke, her eyes twinkling in the firelight. It felt like she was walking me back to our childhood, just taking my hand and leading me to what we had shared.

"I fought for this place. I fought to stay here and keep what little my family could hand down. Others couldn't wait to leave, and I understand. But my roots are here."

"So you're saying there's no part of you that held out some kind of hope for the two of us? Never?"

"Hope is strange, ain't it? Hope in things that aren't real will make you do things that don't make sense.

I try to stay away from that kind of hope as much as
I can."

"It's easier to be afraid than to hope," I said.

"I ain't afraid."

I let our words settle, then said, "You can't control what
I feel for you, Jesse. And I can't control how often I think
about you or the fact that I love you. See, I said it. I've
always loved you. I probably always will."

She laughed. "Matt, you don't love me."

"Don't tell me that. You're not omniscient."

"There goes another big word."

"You don't know everything. You don't know who I love
and don't love. Or what's in my heart."

She closed her eyes and pulled her head back. "What
I mean is, you love who you think I am. You love who you
think I can be." She waved her fingers above her head. "You
have this magical concept of what you remember. The best
parts. You don't know the real me."

"The only reason I don't know you is because you ran.
And if that was because you couldn't stand me, I wouldn't
be here. But there's this sliver of *maybe* I've held on to.
I think you felt the same way for me and I want to know
if I'm right."

She turned away and put a hand to her face. I let the
crackle of the fire overtake us and listened for something,
her voice, her heart. Finally she spoke.

"I come to every one of your plays in high school."

"What?"

She nodded and her hair fell over her eyes. "I always sat

in the back in the dark. Brought Daisy a couple of times. But I saw every one. I even come to that one where you had the weird clothes and talked funny."

"*A Midsummer Night's Dream?*"

"I was so proud. It was like, when you were getting applause, somehow I was part of it."

"Why didn't you tell me?"

"Couldn't. You wouldn't understand the reasons and they're not important anymore."

"Yes, they are. Talk to me, Jesse."

She turned her back. I remembered the day I helped cut her hair. And the look of her bedroom. And her inner strength. And the love she had for her sister.

"Do you ever think of me, Jesse?"

She dipped her head. There was something breaking inside, and with Jesse you never knew where the breaking might lead.

"If you asked me right now to let you go, I would do it. If you asked me to let you marry Earl because this is who you love, this is the person you want to grow old with. Raise kids and sit on the porch in rocking chairs and drink sweet tea. I'll walk down this hill and never bother you."

"And why is that?"

"Because love wants what's best. If being with me is not the best, I'll be fine. I love you enough to let you go. But I need you to look at me and tell me that's what you want." I paused. "You can't say that, can you?"

"Yes, I can."

"Then turn around and—"

She turned quickly, her eyes filled with tears. "Let me go, Matt. Walk away. I love Earl. You got it?"

Her eyes betrayed her, tears running the length of both cheeks. She wore no makeup, no rouge smudged or eyeliner turned her face black. She was pure Jesse.

"I'm not buying the performance. If you meant it, there wouldn't be all those tears."

She gritted her teeth. "You said you would walk away if I told you that, and I just told you. I'm going to marry Earl."

Her words stung because they sounded true. I wanted to protest, to push back again, but there was something in her voice that made me believe her.

I moved past her, my back to her. "If you don't want me to turn around, you stay quiet. Don't say anything."

She didn't make a sound and I swallowed hard, looking into the darkness.

I took a few steps from the campfire, engulfed in darkness now. There was a fluttering of wings above and I scampered back up the hill.

"I thought you were going to walk away and not turn around."

"I heard something," I said, my heart beating wildly.

"Probably a crow. I swear, for somebody who wasn't afraid to come to my house or run to the Blackwoods, you sure are a scaredy-cat."

I caught my breath. "I never told you. That night. When I was at your house looking for you. Coming home through the woods, I saw him."

She rolled her eyes. "Sure you did."

"I'm serious. I didn't tell anybody, mainly because of what happened."

She ignored my revelation. "Matt, have you ever considered that maybe you didn't come back here to rescue me at all? Have you ever thought of that?"

Her words echoed something Mr. Lambert had said. But a noise below interrupted my thoughts. Lights flashed through the tops of the trees and Jesse stood and put a hand on my shoulder.

"You need to leave." Her voice got hard. "You need to run."

Chapter 25

OCTOBER 1972

Reds fans were giddy at school the next day. Those who knew I rooted for the Pirates rubbed it in. I couldn't blame them.

I looked for the bus that brought Jesse's cousins and watched it spill kids from their hollow, but Jesse wasn't among them. Later, I found Elden Branch at the food truck that came to school at lunch.

"Did Jesse and Daisy come to your house last night?"

He glanced my general direction as he shoved a pack of gum in his back pocket. "What's it to you?"

His teeth were short and green and I thought the stolen gum probably wouldn't help his oral hygiene. But I decided not to be his conscience.

"The sheriff was at my house last night. I just want to make sure they're okay."

"They're all right. Jesse didn't like being drug to our house, but she's got no say in it now that her mama's dead. You hear she buried her in their backyard? And was cashing her checks? You'd expect that from a Woods."

"Is she coming to school?"

Elden glanced at the guy taking money and shoved a Zero bar in another pocket. "She put up a fuss this morning. Lots of yelling and squalling and saying she wouldn't leave her sister. I reckon she'll come back to school directly."

"Tomorrow?"

He shrugged. "Why are you so all-fired interested? You sweet on her?" He cursed and laughed. "That's all she needs. Lead a preacher boy astray."

Later, I saw Dickie in the hallway. I was desperate for information, no matter the source. When he saw me, he turned and I ran after him. I gave him our usual greeting but he said nothing about a breakthrough.

"I know you don't want to talk to me, and I understand. But this is about Jesse."

"I heard what happened. You knew all along about her mama."

"Jesse didn't want anybody to know. I'm sorry for keeping it a secret. I'm sorry for everything."

Dickie shook his head and walked away.

The next day I watched the bus again and saw Jesse get off after her cousins went inside. As she exited, she turned away from the school and walked through the teacher parking lot, by the F-86 Sabre display, and back toward town along the main road.

"Jesse, wait up!" I called and ran across the street. A car's brakes squealed and I was nearly roadkill. The driver waved me across, shaking his head.

"Go back to school," Jesse yelled, walking faster.

"Where are you going?"

"They forced me to get on that bus, but they can't force me to stay."

I caught up with her, out of breath, hands on my knees. "Is Daisy okay?"

"So far, but I ain't waiting around for them to get a chance at her."

"What are you going to do?"

"What I have to do."

I heard the bell. "Jesse, wait."

She kept walking and didn't look back.

Rumors roiled the next couple days through the school and on the bus. Jesse was gone. Nobody knew where she was. Through one of her female cousins, I found out—by giving away another lunch—that Daisy Grace had been removed from the Branch home. She was gone before Jesse made it back from school.

"Who took her?" I said.

The girl shrugged. "They didn't tell me. Just said it was for her own good."

"That must have set Jesse off."

"She evidently cussed at them and run off. I don't know where she went."

"She's probably trying to find her sister."

The girl nodded. "I don't think she will, though."

"Why not?"

"I heard my parents saying they had to protect that little thing from her. Jesse's crazy."

"What? Jesse loves Daisy. She promised her mother she'd take care of her."

The girl scowled and took another bite of the corn dog that was previously my property. I tried to get more information but it was like trying to get blood from a turnip.

I couldn't bring myself to watch more than a few innings of the World Series. Just seeing Oakland with those mustaches against any team but the Pirates brought a sense of loss. Every time I saw the Reds in their bright, white uniforms, I saw what had been taken from me. In a small way, it felt like what Jesse must have felt—something dear ripped from her arms.

I clicked my CB every night to no avail and I rode past Jesse's house. I even went to the window to peek inside. Someone had taken Carl away and his chain lay tangled on the ground by the cinder block steps. I would have fed him scraps and filled his water bowl. Nobody had asked.

That Sunday my father began a series on the healings of Jesus. He had abandoned his verse-by-verse approach because of complaints that were no doubt encouraged by Basil Blackwood. We were in the tenth chapter of Mark where a blind man was begging at the side of the road when Jesus passed. The man cried out and people told him to be quiet, but Jesus said to bring him closer.

"This is one of the greatest questions in all of the Bible," my father said. "Jesus, the Creator of everything, the one who formed this blind man in the womb of his mother, says, 'What do you want me to do for you?'

"Now imagine that. God himself asks you what you want in life. And what does Bartimaeus say? He says, 'Rabbi, I want to see.'"

My father closed his Bible, which always gave me a sense of relief. Every time he closed his Bible, unless he held his finger there, it was only a few more minutes before he was done. And after a full morning of Sunday school and worship, I was ready to be unleashed.

"I submit to you that the question and the answer are exactly what we need today. I believe Jesus stands before us and asks us the same thing. If we say, 'Rabbi, I want a new house,' or 'I need a new spouse,' or anything less than 'I want to see,' we'll ultimately be disappointed.

"So what does it mean to *see*? For Bartimaeus it was physical. And when he opened his eyes and saw the world, the first thing he saw was his Lord. So that's one part of this miracle, of course. But there's also a deeper meaning to *seeing*. To really see means to look not just at the outside. To understand your life, you need God to illumine you and help you see.

"We sing, 'Open my eyes, that I may see glimpses of truth Thou hast for me.' But do we really mean it? Do we really want to see what God has for us? Do we really want to see the truth about ourselves, our motivations, or about others?

"I believe that to understand, you must enter like a blind man begging. And the past and present, when illumined by God, will help you move into the future."

My mother played "Open My Eyes, That I May See" and my father had us read the words as she played. Then we stood and sang the three stanzas, ending with the words, "Open my heart—illumine me, Spirit divine!"

I heard Basil Blackwood mutter something about "pop psychology" on our way out, but my father's words had brought more questions than answers. What was I not seeing about Jesse, about our family, my brother? What was I not seeing about my father?

After church that night, we drove home and I went to my room to change. I hung up my Sunday clothes and put on sweatpants and a T-shirt. From the closet I heard a strange noise. At first it sounded like an animal scratching, but when I moved toward my bed, I realized my CB was on and someone was clicking the mic.

"Wildflower, is that you?" I said, keying the mic.

A pause. Then her voice came over the channel in a whisper. "PB—whatever you do, don't come to my house. You hear?"

Her words didn't make sense. "Why not? What are you talking about?"

"I gotta go. Just stay away."

I tried to engage her again, but she didn't respond. I put on a jacket and headed outside.

"You want some hot apple pie and ice cream?" my mother said as I ran through the kitchen.

"Not right now," I said.

"You're not going out on your bike at this time of night, are you?" my grandmother said.

"I'll be back soon."

"You'll be hit quick as lightning," she said, shaking her head and digging into the pie. "People are driving lickety-split on that road."

My father poured his coffee and didn't look up.

I hit the screen door and jumped on the bike, speeding down the driveway. I took the corner too fast, my back tire slipping in the loose gravel, but regained my balance and stood on the pedals, pumping as fast as I could.

There was a light on in Jesse's house and I coasted past, trying to see. I turned around at Blackwood's gate and made the return trip, listening and looking. Why would Jesse tell me to avoid her house? Maybe she had found Daisy and didn't want to be bothered.

I leaned the bike against the mailbox, my curiosity high. Coming here after being warned not to was something Jesse would have done and that thought made me smile. I crept toward the house, hunched over and watching my footsteps, then peeked over the windowsill.

A man sat on the couch, staring at the television. NBC was airing their mystery movie, and *McMillan & Wife* was on. I thought Susan Saint James looked a little like Jesse.

The man got up at a commercial and wove his way into the kitchen and out of sight. There was something strange about the sleeve of his shirt—it hung to the side and flopped when he walked.

I looked for the CB in the living room, but it was gone. At the side of the house I saw the antenna's coax leading toward Jesse's bedroom window. Why had she moved the CB?

Moving back to the front window, I stood taller, trying to see into the kitchen. There was no one there, so I changed my angle a little but still didn't see anyone. Then I heard quick footsteps in the wet grass and someone grabbed my arm. His grip was viselike and bruising. He jerked me toward the house and I resisted, telling him to let me go with all the bravado I could muster. He pushed me toward the front door and said, "Get inside."

I opened it and fell on the linoleum. The man came in and slammed the door behind him. He twisted his head as if he wasn't able to focus. His eyes were a little too close together and he had a small mouth with two front teeth that jutted forward. There was stubble on his face and he appeared not to have bathed for a while.

"What are you doing here, boy?" the man said, leaning down. His breath smelled like tobacco and what I figured was stale alcohol of some kind.

"Looking for Jesse," I said, gritting my teeth. "Where is she?"

He pulled back and flipped his hand. "That's what I was about to ask you."

I stared at the empty sleeve, remembering Jesse's description of her father. "Are you her dad?"

"That's what some people say."

"Why didn't you come back when they needed you? Jesse's mom was sick."

The man kicked at me and pointed to the couch. I climbed backward onto it and he straddled a chair.

"I don't like your tone, boy."

"This house is not yours. It's Jesse's."

"Is that a fact? And she told you that?"

I didn't respond. He wasn't holding me down, but I felt glued to the couch. I looked down and saw a bloodstain and inched away from it.

He stared at me with a slack jaw. "Tell you what. You tell me where Jesse is and I'll let you go on your way."

He didn't know where Jesse was. That was good. I should have obeyed her warning, but concern sometimes trumps wisdom.

"I don't know where she is. But if you'd have come back and helped, you might know. She and her sister were all alone."

"What are you talking about?" he said, pulling a flask from his pocket. He placed it under one armpit and unscrewed it with his hand and took a long swig.

"Your wife's dead. Jesse was caring for Daisy Grace by herself."

The man took another pull of whatever he was drinking and drained the flask. "When did she die?"

"Back in July."

"What happened? Her lungs give out?"

"I don't know. But Jesse shouldn't have had to go through that alone."

He ran his tongue over his cracked lower lip, then snapped his fingers. "You just gave me a good idea, son."

Jesse's father dragged the chair across the linoleum into a bedroom. He grunted and strained and the metal chair creaked when he stepped up on it. I could have run but I was curious. Something moved in the ceiling and I heard a clanging. He brought a metal strongbox out that had a key in it, which he put on the chair and opened. He shuffled through some papers and held up a document.

"There she is." He laughed.

"What's that?"

"Life insurance policy. Paid it off back when she got sick the first time. Easy money."

"Jesse and Daisy deserve that."

"They didn't pay for this and they never put up with her jawin' like I did. Look right there. That's my name." He pointed to the page, drool spooling from one corner of his mouth. "Who are you? A Blackwood?"

I didn't answer.

He laughed and the sound was smoky and wet and crusty, like emphysema. He got down in my face and wiped at his mouth. "No, you ain't no Blackwood. You go to school with her?"

"She's the best friend I've ever had."

"Is that right? So after their mama died, where'd they go?"

"To their cousins."

"What cousins?"

"Go to the sheriff if you want to know."

The look on his face told me he didn't like the idea. "You don't know any more than I do. Get up and get out of here, tubby."

When I stood, Jesse's father grabbed my shirt. His hand had liver spots. "You say a word about me being here, and I'll hunt you down and kill you. Your whole family too. Understand?"

I nodded.

He let go of me and pulled a knife from his pocket and it opened with a click. "Maybe you need convincing. I could shave a little off those ears of yours, Dumbo."

I hit the door running but the man didn't follow. He was still laughing when I grabbed my bike, jumped on it, and rode home.

I grabbed a flashlight from the garage and turned it on as I walked past the barn. The batteries were low but I had enough juice to get past the tree line. Once I was to the meadow, I saw the faint glow of a small fire and ran to the top of the hill.

Jesse sat there, shivering. "How'd you know I was here?"

"I went to your house."

"What? Matt, what's the point of warning you if you don't listen?"

I told her what had happened, jumping to the life insurance policy her dad found.

She shook her head. "I looked all over for that

strongbox. Mama had the deed to the house in there and some savings bonds. Where was it?"

She cursed when I told her. "I never looked in the crawl space. He'll take that deed to the land and sell it. I know he will."

"Not if it has your name on it."

"He'll find a way. The only reason he ever came back was when he needed something. Money or . . ." She looked away. "You asked me about those scars on my stomach once. He's the one who give them to me. Cigarette burns. I'm glad you got away from there."

"Maybe that would be the best thing that could happen. If he sells the place, he'll leave."

"I promised Mama I'd care for Daisy and take care of the farm. And I aim to do that. I'm not going to let that old drunk steal our future."

I wasn't sure what kind of future Jesse was trying to hang on to. The land seemed worthless and the house was so ramshackle a strong wind could topple it. But people get attached to the familiar and I wasn't about to argue.

"Did he ask about me?"

I nodded. "And Daisy, too."

She sat up straighter. "What did he say?"

"He wanted to know where she was. I told him he ought to go to the sheriff if he really wanted to find you two."

She raised her eyebrows. "You said that to him?"

"Yeah."

"I never in a million years thought he'd come back." Her eyes darted like she was considering all her options.

"What are you going to do?"

"He wants whatever valuables he can find. So I got to wait him out. But I can't let him take that deed."

"Come to our place. You can sleep on the couch and in the morning—"

"No, your mama and daddy will go straight to the law. That's what got Daisy took from me in the first place."

I hung my head. "I didn't tell them anything about—"

"I ain't mad at you. I'm just . . . It was working, Matt. I could see it working out. I had it figured. I was keeping my promise to Mama. Daisy wasn't no trouble. And now she's gone. I keep hearing her crying in my head. Just squallin' and yellin'. She's got to be scared out of her mind."

"Any idea where she is?"

"I'm glad she's not with the Branches anymore, but she might be in some foster family. That could be worse."

"I talked with Elden's sister and she didn't know where she was."

She tapped her forehead. "I got to think. I got to get her back before something happens."

"It's going to get cold tonight."

"I got the fire. I'll be fine."

"Then I'm staying here with you."

"No, you go home. You're in enough trouble."

She was right. And if I stayed out, my dad would find us.

"I'm going to pray," I said, not knowing what else to say.

"Yeah, you do that. Pray hard, PB."

I felt guilty walking away. The light from the fire faded and I turned one more time when she called after me.

"Don't tell nobody you saw my daddy."

"I won't."

When I hit the path leading into the woods, I flicked the light on. There was a little juice in the batteries, but not much. I turned it on and off, making sure I didn't trip over a rock. When it rained, the trail turned to mud and the only way to navigate it was to step from boulder to boulder. The path had been cut into the hillside by a grader and one side led up while the other fell.

Something skittered in the brush near the path and I flicked on the light. I told myself it was just an opossum or a raccoon. Then I heard a whoop-whoop of wings and the creaking of a limb above. I stopped, my heart thumping.

"Hello?" I whispered.

I wanted to run but there was no light, no moon in the sky and my flashlight was useless. If only I had brought a burning stick from the fire.

Another thought encroached. What if Jesse's father had followed me? What if I had led him to his daughter? I couldn't shake the stale smell of his breath.

I took a few steps and flicked on the flashlight again. Nothing. I banged it against my hand. Still nothing. The wind whispered through the limbs and leaves. It was either that or someone above was talking, and I shivered.

I unscrewed the bottom of the flashlight, the C batteries loosened, and I screwed the bottom on again tightly. I could use it as a weapon if I had to.

A flapping above me, like a giant flag unfurled. I pointed the flashlight toward the sound and stared at the inky blackness. It was like looking into Satan's basement. I flicked the button and a quick burst of light shone into the trees. I'll never forget that image—a wingspread wider than the light could view and claws that grasped the limb like human hands. I raised the fading beam to see two red eyes. It stared, its head cocked to one side.

I dropped the light and ran.

Flapping again, above the treetops. I stumbled and tripped on a tree root, scrambling with hands and feet to find flat ground.

When I made it to the barn, the flapping stopped and I rushed down the hill and into the yard, running for the light in the house. I looked back once. The light from the lamp at the end of the walk showed enough of the barn for me to see the figure perched on top, looking into my soul.

I ran inside, kicked off my muddy shoes, and jumped in bed with my clothes on, covering my head with a pillow.

I knew this had been a warning. I knew something bad was going to happen. Someone was going to die. When I fell into bed, I didn't pray. It was up to me to do something. And I decided I wouldn't rest until Jesse and Daisy Grace were safe.

Chapter 26

Lights bounced up the hill and I wondered how any vehicle could make it up the narrow, rocky path. Jesse moved toward me and put a hand on my shoulder. "I mean it, you need to run. Get to the woods back that way."

"I've done nothing wrong."

"That's not what they're going to think. About both of us."

"If you're marrying someone who doesn't trust you, what's going to happen after you say, 'I do'?"

"My guess is, this isn't Earl. You can't judge a person by their family. You ought to know that better than anybody."

"What's that supposed to mean?"

She didn't answer.

The engine gunned and the vehicle moved past the tree line and over the limestone. The truck sat high and had huge tires and yellow running lights. The driver headed straight for the fire and Jesse pulled on my arm. "Matt, go. I'll fix this."

The lights shone in our eyes and I held up a hand to shield it. "A scared dog runs with his tail between his legs."

"A smart dog knows when he's licked."

"Maybe I'm not as smart as you think."

"It's your funeral."

The truck stopped a few feet from us and both doors opened. Verle Turley got out from behind the wheel and scowled at Jesse.

"Earl's been calling you." He slammed the door.

"I'm not his property."

I looked at her in shock. I thought she would defuse the situation but her words threw gas on the fire. I didn't recognize the other guy who crawled out of the passenger side, but he had that Turley look to him.

"Look," I said to Verle, my voice conciliatory, "I'm leaving in the morning, and I asked Jesse—"

"Shut up," Verle said. If I were his director in a play, I would have applauded his menace. He had the perfect inflection and venom. His voice gravelly, he told Jesse, "Go home and call Earl."

"I don't take orders from you."

I put up both hands. "I can explain this. Why don't you turn your truck off so we don't have to scream?"

Verle waved at the other guy. "Turn it off."

When the rumble died, I took a step forward, palms up, a puppy-dog look. It might have looked like fear.

"Verle, I asked Jesse to come here and answer some questions."

"You been hanging around all week. You was warned."

"And I'm leaving. There's an emergency in Chicago and I'm headed back."

"So tonight you were going to take what was Earl's, is that it?"

"He didn't take nothing," Jesse said.

"Would you shut up and get back to your house?" Verle said.

"Don't you never talk to me that way."

"Somebody needs to," the other man said. Something metal glinted when he shifted.

"Tommy, put that gun away before you shoot yourself in the foot," Jesse said. She glanced at me and frowned. "I told you to leave."

Now I had a good reason to raise my hands. "I told Jesse, if she wants to marry Earl, I won't stand in the way."

"You couldn't leave her alone, could you? I told Earl, I said, 'Plumley is going to try something.' And here you are with a fire and a bedroll."

"We was just talking," Jesse said.

"Yeah, right."

Tommy spoke to me. "Your daddy put you up to this?"

"My father agrees with you. He wanted me to leave Jesse alone."

"Sure he did."

"A friend told me Jesse was getting married. He knew how I felt about her."

"Who?" she said.

"Dickie."

Jesse stared into the night.

"Get in the truck," Verle said.

"I told you not to talk to me that way," Jesse said.

"Not you," Verle said. "Him." He took the gun from Tommy and lifted it toward me.

When I'd gone hunting growing up, there'd been one rule—you never pointed a gun at anything you didn't intend to shoot. That flashed through my mind as I stared at Verle.

Jesse stepped in front of me. "He just told you he's leaving in the morning."

"I'll leave tonight," I said. "I'll get in my car and get out of here now."

Verle lowered the gun and I relaxed but only a little. He looked at Tommy and nodded. Tommy lunged at Jesse, grabbing her arm, and jerked her to the ground. She yelped in pain or surprise, I couldn't tell which, and I grabbed at his untucked shirt. I heard a rip and Tommy cursed.

Something hit me in the back of the head and I saw stars. Disoriented, I put my hand back and someone grabbed me and dragged me toward the truck.

"Leave him alone!" Jesse yelled.

"Let her go, Tommy," Verle said. "Help me get him in."

They pulled me up and shoved me into the backseat.

Jesse was at the running board as soon as Verle closed the door. Tommy started the engine and the rumble was just as deafening inside as out.

She banged on the window. "Where are you taking him?"

"Get off the truck and go home," Verle yelled.

"Matt, are you okay?"

I put up a hand to the window. As soon as Jesse stepped off the running board, Tommy gunned the engine and drove through the fire, sparks flying. He raced down the hill and I had the same feeling I had on the roller coaster at Camden Park—a stomach-in-your-throat kind of tingly-leg weightlessness.

"Might want to buckle up," Tommy said, grinning.

I looked out the back window and saw Jesse silhouetted against the firelight. I thought that was the last I would ever see her.

The ride down the hill was as fast as the roller coaster and ten times as bumpy. My head hit the ceiling of the cab several times and instead of stars I saw galaxies. The earth beneath us smoothed out by the barn and soon we were in the driveway, rumbling to a stop.

"Where's the keys to your car?" Verle said.

"In my pocket."

He held out his hand. When I didn't respond, he said, "You want me to poke you in the head again?"

I dug into my pocket and gave him the keys. He handed them to Tommy. "Follow me."

Like a fisherman dropping his net, Tommy got out of

the truck. My headlights came on and the engine fired. Verle got behind the wheel and tapped the accelerator, spinning gravel into the yard.

"Where are you taking me?"

He pulled onto the road and gunned the engine. My headlights followed at a distance and then closed the gap.

"I have to get back to Chicago," I said.

"Shut up and relax." He turned on the radio to a country station. I didn't know which hurt my head more, the bang to my skull or the jumpy fiddle.

The winding road straightened and soon we were on the interstate. We drove an hour, then two, and finally crossed into Ohio and pulled into a gas station on a lonely stretch of road. Tommy pulled in behind us.

"Give me your wallet," Verle said.

I handed it to him and he gave it to Tommy, who pulled my car up to a pump and went inside the station.

Verle told me to get gas and I squinted at the fluorescent lights buzzing overhead, moths and bugs swarming. The pump came to life and the noise made me wince. Everything made me wince. I filled the tank, then replaced the nozzle and screwed on the cap. Tommy returned with my wallet and handed me a full bottle of Mountain Dew. He opened a packet of capsules he'd bought with my money.

"Those will help the headache," Verle said.

I took them and threw away the package and drank some of the soda. They watched me as if they were EMTs trying to determine if I was capable of driving.

"So you came back looking for answers. Is that your story, Plumley?"

"That's the truth."

"And are you satisfied?"

"Not exactly the word I'd use, but it'll do."

Verle laughed, then pointed toward the road. "Chicago is that way. As far as we're concerned, it's a one-way road. You understand?"

I nodded.

"We're going to follow you. If you try to turn around, you'll get more than a headache."

I opened the car door and fell inside. Verle came to the door. "This is it, Plumley. Don't come back before the wedding."

"Don't worry," I said.

He slammed the door and when I turned on the ignition, the radio was all the way up and Eddie Rabbitt sang "You Can't Run from Love." I turned it off and drove with his voice echoing in my soul, Verle's headlights blinding me in the rearview.

After a few miles, I settled into a rhythm and held the bottle of Mountain Dew to the back of my head. The capsules released and the pain lessened. The truck headlights receded until they became specks. And then they were gone.

I thought about Eddie Rabbitt's words and an old TV show came to mind—Chuck Connors getting his sword broken. *Wherever you go for the rest of your life you must prove you're a man.* That's how I felt about Jesse. I would always care. But some things simply can't be. And with that truth came a release, that I could let her go and move on. But alongside that thought came echoes of my father, the way he had lived and retreated from Blackwood. Was I free or imitating what I had seen?

It was a little past four and there was no light coming from the horizon. I pulled into a gas station off the interstate and found some loose change. If I kept driving, I would be home late morning and I could begin the search for Dantrelle. I didn't have a good feeling about him.

I found a pay phone and slipped the coins in and the phone rang once. Jesse picked up, her voice groggy.

"I thought I'd better let you know I'm okay," I said.

"I was hoping you'd call. What happened?"

"They made sure I was headed north."

"Where are you?"

"Cincinnati."

"Is your head okay?"

"I'm fine. Did you call Earl?"

"Yeah."

"You two okay?"

"I told him what happened and he said if it was him, he would have come back too."

"That's understanding. Maybe you're right, Jesse. Maybe he's different."

"He is, Matt," she said, her voice fading.

"You have to work today?"

"Yeah," she said. "But I get all next week off."

"Where are you going on the honeymoon?"

She didn't answer, and I could only imagine the exotic place Earl had picked. "So I guess this is good-bye," I said.

There was a rustling on the other end of the line. A truck pulling in behind me blasted its air brakes. I plugged my other ear and listened to Jesse.

"I did cut you out of my life, Matt. I know I hurt you. I think it was best for everybody, but I'm sorry."

I searched for something to say but nothing came.

"That was sweet of you to come back. I appreciate it. And I wish you all the best."

I swallowed hard and closed my eyes. "I wish you all the happiness in the world, Jesse. And I'm sorry if I made things harder."

She didn't speak for a moment and I thought maybe she'd fallen asleep. Then she said, "If it wasn't for you, Matt . . ."

"You wouldn't have been able to afford that bicycle."

"I got a long list of questions for God. Why some things happened and some didn't. I keep them on a sheet of paper in a keepsake box. Most people only keep the bad stuff you can't figure. But there's another I started. Things I'm grateful for. Good things I didn't see for a long time. You're at the top of the list. Thank you."

I said good-bye and meant it. When I hung up the phone, it was like putting a three-hundred-pound weight in a rack. And that's what it was. A surrender. A laying down of arms.

I walked to my car and sat near the air pump, letting the fatigue and pain coalesce. Fully awake now, I started the

car and headed toward Indianapolis. About fifty miles from
the city I stopped at a pancake restaurant and found a pay
phone near the restrooms. I knew I should call my parents.

"Hello?"

"Didn't wake you up, did I?"

"No, we're up early," my father said. There was a flurry
in the background. "Your mother has some news."

"Matt, I'm so glad you called. They found him! They
found Dantrelle!"

"What? Really?" I couldn't contain my joy.

"Kristin called a half hour ago."

"Where was he?"

"His mother was arrested and Dantrelle was put in foster care. He's fine, Matt."

My heart sank—I was glad Dantrelle was safe, but
the news of his mother was another hurdle. I thought of
Kristin finding him and how she must have felt. It made
the rest of the drive back feel less stressful.

"What time did you leave this morning?" my mother said.

"Early," I said, avoiding the details. "I'll be in Chicago
in a few hours."

My mother handed the phone back to my father.

"I'm proud of you, for coming to terms with all of this.
I'm relieved. I think it's best for everybody."

I thanked him and hung up with an unsettled feeling.
Was it something he had said? Jesse? Thinking it might be
my empty stomach, I sat at the counter and ordered pancakes. I thought of calling Kristin to find out more about
the situation, but I would be back in the city later.

As I poured syrup and took a bite, the smell and taste sparked something. It's funny how tastes can turn pages in the mind. I thought of Mr. Caldwell, retired from the sheriff's department. The sweet smell of pancakes and syrup brought up something he had said.

"When I pulled up, your daddy was talking to her."

I stared at my food. Another memory, ever so slight—a moment when Jesse had said something revealing. When I had brought up her promise, she had muttered something.

"Some promises cancel others."

Was she talking about her promise to marry Earl? Or was there some other promise she had made?

Then, Jesse's words—*"I think it was best for everybody."*

My father had said the same exact words to me.

"Is something wrong?" the waitress said.

I looked up, holding my fork halfway between the plate and my mouth. It was as if time had stopped. I could feel every heartbeat. Suddenly all the blurry things came into focus.

"Are you all right?" the woman said.

"Yeah, I think I am."

"Something wrong with the pancakes?"

"Not at all. I like them crisp on the edges. Like my grandmother used to make them."

"I'm glad to hear it," she said, wiping down the counter.

I looked at the clock and calculated how long it would take me to get back to Dogwood. And after I left a tip, I got change to make more phone calls.

Chapter 27

The day after I met Jesse's father, I found Dickie at school again. He saw me coming and walked the other way down the long hallway that smelled like WWII chewing gum. I caught up to him near the library.

"What do you want now?"

"I'm looking for a breakthrough," I said.

I hoped he would smile but he didn't. When he walked away, I grabbed his arm. "This is not about you and me or my brother or your dad. This is about Jesse. She needs our help."

"I'm done with you, Plumley."

"They took Daisy. We have to help Jesse find her."

"No. I don't have to help. But you need to let go of my arm."

I forged ahead. "If you could talk with her cousins, maybe they know something they're not telling me."

"I don't go near those people," Dickie said.

"You don't care what happens to Daisy?"

"Don't try the guilt trip. Let go." When I didn't, he clenched his teeth. "You want me to pretend everything is fine between us. It's not."

"I know that. I can't help what my brother did. I'm sorry about your dad. If I could do something about it, I would."

"You lied to me."

"I never lied."

"Every day you didn't tell me your brother ran to Canada, you lied."

"Dickie, he didn't want to get killed. What does that make him?"

"A coward."

"Okay, he's a coward. He should have gone to war. I wish he wasn't scared. But he's my brother. And I miss him, just like you miss your dad."

Kids passed us in the hall but unlike during a schoolyard brawl, no one congregated.

"You lied every day you didn't tell me about Jesse's mom."

"I promised her. Please, we need—"

Dickie pushed me to the wall. "Stop talking to me. I'm done."

It was like the end of some sad movie. Like shooting

Old Yeller and moving on. Watching Dickie walk away made me want to cry, but I knew I couldn't.

All through classes I tried to figure out a way to find Daisy. I could pretend to be somebody else and make a phone call. At lunch I tracked down every cousin of Jesse's I could find, but there was nothing new. On the bus ride home I looked in the windows of every house we passed, hoping Daisy would peek out by chance and I could tell Jesse where she was.

As the bus rumbled, more questions surfaced. What would Jesse do if she found Daisy? And what about her father? Jesse never wanted to see her dad, Dickie longed to have his father return, and I was ashamed of my father.

I looked at the hill behind my grandmother's house. That we were still living in that house felt crazy—we were supposed to be in the parsonage, but Blackwood was stringing us along, keeping my father under his thumb. I didn't see any smoke on the hilltop. Where was Jesse? Was her father still at their house?

I rode my bike to Jesse's but the house looked empty. A little further up the road I saw two figures standing by the gate at Blackwood's farm. I hid my bike in a grove of autumn olives by the road and crept through the woods until I got close enough to hear them.

"I got the deed back at the house," Jesse's father said with a crusty cough. "I just have to get it altered and we're good to go."

Blackwood looked at him like he was a stain. "What kind of change you talking about?"

"A technicality. It won't take long."

"What kind of technicality?" Blackwood said, spitting in the road.

"That wife of mine signed the deed over to my daughter. I just got to get her to sign it back to me." He held out a hand to shake. "So we're agreed on the price, right?"

"We're agreed," Blackwood said. "Get the deed situated and I'll get the lawyer to make sure everything is copacetic."

"I'll get it done."

"You have to find that daughter of yours first. Sheriff was by here this morning asking if I'd seen her."

"I'll find her. She's likely with my kin over on Gobbler's Knob—that's where they took the younger one. Spent all day finding a social worker who would tell me the truth."

"Well, you better get over there. Meet me tomorrow or the deal's off."

Jesse's father turned to leave, then stopped. "You don't reckon I could borrow your truck tonight?"

"I don't trust the likes of you with nothing of mine," Blackwood said.

Jesse's father smiled and waved his hand. "It don't matter. I'll get a ride."

I found Jesse on the hill trying to cook potatoes on a fire that wouldn't stay lit because of the rain. Dark clouds hung and creeks swelled.

I told Jesse what I'd heard and when I mentioned Gobbler's Knob, she perked up. "That's where Daisy is?"

"That's what he said."

"I can get there by riding past the haunted house."

"No, he's going there to look for you. You can't go."

"I'm not letting him near my sister. I'm going to bring her back."

"Jesse, that's like a dog chasing a car. What do you do after you catch it?"

She got up and wiped the seat of her jeans. "I promised my mama. I keep my promises."

I followed her down the hill, trying to talk sense into her, slipping and sliding. I told her it would be dark soon and that the roads would be muddy. She didn't listen.

She cut through the woods near our house and moved through the wet leaves to the road. I grabbed two flash-lights from the garage and hopped on my bike, reaching her house as she ran out.

"Where do you think you're going?" she said.

"I'm going with you."

"No, you ain't. Go back."

When she got on the bike, I saw a lump under her T-shirt in the back. A hundred yards past the Blackwood farm, she turned. I was keeping pace but just barely. Rain was steady now.

"You're not going with me, Matt."

"You need a flashlight. It's going to be late when you get there. And you'll probably need somebody to create a diversion."

"I don't need your help."

She stood on her pedals and rode hard to the base of the hill. Then she got off and pushed, glancing back. I clicked the flashlight twice and pulled up beside her. I couldn't believe how much stronger I had become since moving to Dogwood.

"If you go now, you'll be home for dinner," Jesse said. "Your parents are going to have a fit."

"They'll get over it."

She stopped at the top of the hill to catch her breath. "This is the last time I'm telling you. If I go alone, nobody knows. I get Daisy and slip away. Then you can help. But if you come along, there's going to be a posse."

"I stay on the hill till dark all the time."

"In the rain? Just hand me a flashlight."

I gave her one and watched her pull up the next incline. Over that ridge the road dipped, then flattened out until the next hill. I pointed my bike toward home, then looked back. Her legs pumped, muscles straining. She was nothing but muscle and bone and that long hair chopped short.

Water dripped from my hair and my shirt was wet and muddy from the back tire spray. Daylight faded and I looked at the treetops for red eyes or flapping wings.

People's lives turn on a dime, on some split decision they make to turn left or right. On some compulsion to be different from their fathers and act instead of passively looking on at life. Destinies are determined by such things. Mine was changed that night when I couldn't let Jesse ride alone. Call it hubris or fear that Jesse might be the one to die, but I put my feet on the pedals and pointed my bike toward the haunted house, the little cemetery, and the gate that would take us to Gobbler's Knob.

Every mud puddle, every fallen tree branch, was a step closer to Daisy. Jesse rode with purpose, pedaling hard. When she came to the end of the road and the gate, we couldn't get the lock off the chain. The rain fell in sheets. I suggested we turn back. She scowled and lifted her bike up and over the gate, letting it fall with a bang. She scampered over, hopped on, and rode away.

"Wait up!" I yelled.

"Go home!"

I picked up my bike and tried to do the same thing she had done, but when I crawled to the top of the gate, my pants got hung up and I put my hand on the rusty, sharp edge of the metal. I had a sudden fear of falling, of losing my balance and hitting my head and bleeding to death. I had visions of the Mothman. Maybe I was the one who would die. He had warned me.

"Give me your hand," Jesse yelled. She was standing in the muck with her face into the rain. Her shirt was soaked and I felt I should look away but couldn't. "Come on, we've burnt the daylight!"

Seeing my pants were caught, she reached up and yanked on them, ripping a hole. But I was free. I jumped down and hopped on my bike.

I kept the flashlight on as we rode, obsessed with the Mothman. We bounced along and hit a dense forest with trees spreading over us and blocking the water. The road was almost dry underneath and pedaling became easier. My light hit Jesse's rear and I saw the mud splatters up her wet shirt.

"How are you going to bring her back?" I said as I pulled up behind her.

"She'll ride in back like she always does."

"And what happens when the sheriff finds you and takes her away?"

"I ain't telling you nothing about the plan, PB. You help me get her. I'll take care of the rest."

Jesse stopped talking and slowed. When I caught up to her, she was wiping at her face.

"We'll get her," I said.

The road was impossibly long but Jesse seemed to have an innate sense, a magnet that drew her. We came to a fork with three choices. We could go right down a paved road, left to a dirt road, or straight up the hill.

"I remember this," she said. "I remember looking out the window and thinking we'd never make it in our car because it was bogging down. Come on, we're almost there."

I rode behind her as long as I could, then got off and pushed, running uphill. We came out at what looked like the edge of a field. I could only see as far as the flashlight beam but the land looked pretty and the trees were flecked with yellow and red and brown.

"Through here," she said, riding down a short driveway and jumping off. "Right there's the house on that knoll yonder."

I saw light through the trees but the rain picked up again and I put my head down and followed. We parked our bikes on the other side of an oak tree and Jesse started for the house.

"What about dogs?" I said.

"We've come too far to be scared of dogs," she said, running toward the house. She stopped by a small shed. "You stay here. I'll go look in the window."

I looked in the trees. "No, I'm coming with you."

"Suit yourself, but don't make a sound."

We crept toward the house. It had a covered front porch that reminded me of the Waltons' farmhouse. I kept the flashlight off and worried we would trip, but Jesse seemed to have cat vision. She rose up, peeking over the windowsill.

"That's the kitchen," she whispered.

"It's late. Daisy should be in bed by now, don't you think?"

"Let's hope so. It'll be easier if she's asleep."

We walked to the back, where there was a screened-in porch that held a white contraption with rollers on top. "What in the world is that?"

"An old-timey washing machine. See the crank handle? Mama used to have one of those but we got rid of it."

I heard someone talking inside. Jesse peeked, then ran to the other side of the house. Rain pitter-patted from the roof in pools beneath us. Jesse found another window, a dim light glowing inside.

"There she is!" she said in a whisper. She reached up to knock, then held back.

"What's she doing? Is she in bed?"

Jesse stared, then slid down, her hands still on the windowsill. "She's playing. She's got a doll in a stroller. Feeding it a bottle." She pulled herself back up, then slid down again. "I thought she'd be crying her head off."

"At least they're taking good care of her."

She scanned the room through the rain-drenched window. "There's a real bed in there, too. Not just a mattress on the floor. And a dresser with a mirror." Jesse looked at me, her chin puckering slightly. "She's wearing a new dress. And somebody's put a bow in her hair."

I shivered and thought of the return trip home. Daisy could catch pneumonia. The last thing Jesse needed was to lose another sister.

Jesse punched me in the shoulder. "Come on."

She moved to the front of the house under the porch, where we could get out of the rain. The temperature had dropped and I could see our breath. It wouldn't be long until winter was here.

"Are you having second thoughts?" I said.

"Mama always said no matter how bad things got, it was better to be with your family. People down in Kentucky offered to take me and Daisy until Mama got on her feet. But she knew we should stay together."

"But if Daisy is being cared for . . . ," I said, my voice trailing off.

"We used to have a Sears and Roebuck catalog. The big thick one. Daisy would flip to the toys and just stare at the dollhouses. She always talked about having a baby with a stroller and a bottle to feed it. No wonder she's not asleep."

She stared into the darkness. "I don't get it, Matt. If

God cares about sparrows and how many hairs you got, why does he let mean daddies come back?"

We had never talked about sparrows or hairs, and I wondered where Jesse had heard those concepts. Maybe from a radio preacher. It was the same conversation we'd had before, but my answers were changing.

"Maybe God lets us choose. Maybe he lets the good and bad happen so we can work it all out ourselves."

"Is that what you believe?"

"That's the way it's starting to appear to me."

The rain slowed and a little light peeked through the clouds from the moon, but only for a moment. I wondered what this secluded place looked like in the daylight.

"I wish everything could be like it was," Jesse said. "Mama sitting on the couch and Daisy bringing her flowers. We never had much, but we was happy."

"You'll be happy again, Jesse," I said, trying to deliver the line as believably as I could.

"Easy for you to say. You got two parents at home and the whole world spread out for you. What do I got?"

"You've got Daisy. And you've got me."

She glanced up at me but didn't say anything. Then she went back to Daisy's window and looked inside. I followed and knelt beside her.

"She's getting tired. When she rubs her eyes like that, she's ready to plop. I've seen her go to sleep standing up in the middle of the room and then she'll just fall over like a cut tree. It's the funniest thing you ever seen."

I put a hand on Jesse's back and she turned, the glow

from the bedroom on her face. I wanted to say how pretty
she was, how much I cared. When our eyes met, I didn't
know if she felt the same way about me or if she was turning some rock over in her mind to look for worms. She
leaned forward, water dripping from her face, and I met
her lips with mine. I'd always heard that you never forget
your first kiss. Whoever said that was right.

Jesse pulled back and brushed the water from her face.
"Come on, let's go," she said, turning. "I don't want to drag
Daisy out in this."

I smiled and followed. "Right."

The world felt like a better place. I could see Jesse coming to our house, maybe sleeping on the couch. I would
explain to my parents. They would help us. And if they
didn't, I'd work out some other plan. And I would steal
another kiss before morning. And when the sun came
up, everything would be all right. And Jesse could take
a shower and get warm.

As we reached our bikes, lights shone in the trees and
the rumble of an engine sounded.

We hid behind the oak and watched the truck pass,
pulling into the driveway. Jesse looked like she had seen
the Mothman. We had forgotten about her father.

"That was him."

"Who's the other man?"

"I don't know."

"We should get out of here before he sees you."

"I ain't letting him take Daisy."

Before I could protest, she ran toward the house, her

silhouette moving into the red of the truck's brake lights. When the truck stopped, she went to the right, out of sight.

The truck doors opened and both men got out and slammed the doors. I sat by the tree, frozen, unable to move. I closed my eyes and wished this were a bad dream. When I opened them, I was still there by our bikes and a bare lightbulb came on over top of the men on the front porch. The door opened slightly and Jesse's father pushed it wider.

When the door shut, I ran toward the house. There was yelling inside. The truck was still running, so the men didn't plan on staying long. I found Jesse at Daisy's window. She had the screen off and was trying to push on the glass but the window was stuck.

"I can't get it open," she said.

"Here," I said, falling in the mud on all fours. "Step up."

She hesitated, then put her muddy shoes on my back and it gave her enough height to reach the top of the window. A second later I heard a creak and voices inside like they were right next to us.

"You don't have no right to take her," a woman said. Her voice was sharp and husky.

"I got every right," Jesse's father said, a little louder than the woman, his words slurred. "She's my daughter."

"You turn around and get out of here, Wendell," another man said. "You ain't taking her in the shape you're in."

"You can't stop me."

"We'll call the law," the woman said.

I was so engrossed in the conversation I forgot about Jesse until the pressure left my back. I looked up to see her crawling into the room. I stood and peered in the window as Jesse closed the bedroom door and locked it. The argument escalated. Daisy looked at her sister as if in a daze, holding on to the stroller with one hand and the baby doll cradled in the crook of her arm.

Jesse tried to pick Daisy up, but the stroller and doll got in the way. Jesse grabbed the stroller and jerked it away, and Daisy let out a squeal that Jesse caught with one hand clamped over her sister's mouth.

"You want to go home, don't you?"

Daisy nodded, tears coming to her eyes.

"Then you need to leave these."

Daisy shook her head violently.

"We ain't got time for this," Jesse hissed. She grabbed the doll and tossed it on the bed.

Daisy reared back to yelp, but Jesse increased the pressure on her mouth.

"She can't breathe," I said from the window.

Jesse turned and gave me a look. Then she whispered something in Daisy's ear and the girl nodded. Jesse let go and grabbed the doll and stroller, handing them to me through the window.

"See, Matt's going to help us take your baby home. Aren't you, Matt?"

"Sure."

"Bottle!" Daisy said, pointing.

"Yeah, and your bottle too," Jesse said, handing it to me.

Jesse picked up Daisy and passed her through the window. I put the stroller and doll down and took the child, who wound her arms around my neck and held tightly.

"Go on," Jesse whispered as she climbed out the window.

I turned but heard a noise from the room that took my breath away. Somebody was jiggling the knob.

"Daisy? You in there?"

I ran past the porch with Daisy in one arm and the baby and stroller in the other. The bottle fell but I didn't stop. I heard a dull thud behind me, as if a body had fallen, then footsteps catching up.

"Get her to my bike," Jesse said, pain in her voice.

"What happened?"

"Just get her to the bike."

I heard a bang and then another, followed by a splintering sound coming from the house. We reached the bikes and Daisy whimpered. "My dress is getting wet!"

Jesse grabbed her and put her in the basket. "Hang on tight!"

She took off toward the road. I pushed my bike to the driveway and looked back as someone yelled, "Somebody's been in here, Wendell! There's mud all over. And the girl's gone."

I pulled the flashlight from my pocket and turned it on but it was little help because it bounced and jiggled wildly. I heard Daisy cry, begging for her stroller, which I had dropped behind the oak tree. Jesse told her to be quiet.

We were almost to the place in the road where it split in three directions when I heard the engine rumble.

"Here he comes, Jesse!"

"Faster, Matt!" she said, her bike rattling and jangling.

Lights in the tops of the trees above us.

Jesse flew past the road that went to the left and headed straight. I followed and the road quickly dipped as the headlights cast shadows on the hill. I slammed on my brakes and stayed with Jesse in the dip as we listened to the engine. If it came toward us, we were sunk. Instead, it barreled down the hill and out of sight.

"Yes!" Jesse said and clapped my back. "We did it, Matt!"

I reminded her we had a long way home, but it didn't take nearly as long to get to the gate and lift her bike over as it had riding there. I helped Daisy get through the fence and we continued past the haunted house. Daisy didn't sleep in the basket, but she didn't say much. She sucked on her thumb and kept her doll close.

"Where will you take her?"

"She's going to sleep in her own bed tonight. My daddy will be out hunting us till daybreak and maybe drinking. I could tell by the way he talked he was drunk."

"Who was the other guy?"

"Somebody from the Dew Drop, probably. I don't know. Maybe he promised a big payday for driving him over there."

"What will you do if he comes to the house?"

"That's why I brought this," she said, patting her rear.

I pointed the flashlight there and realized the thing under her shirt was a gun. "Where did you get that?"

"Found it in Mama's nightstand."

"Jesse, you're not going to use that—"

"I'll do what I have to."

We rode in silence down the series of hills and wound our way toward her house. When we got there, she took Daisy out of the basket and let the bike fall. Inside, she undressed Daisy, dried her hair with a towel, then got her in some dry clothes and put her to bed.

I looked for a clock but time wasn't a big deal in Jesse's world. She had a clock radio in her room, but that was it.

It wasn't until then that I began to wonder about my parents. They would no doubt be looking for me and concerned. I pictured my father up on the hill, trying to figure out where his flashlights went. My mother calling everyone in town, alerting the prayer chain.

Jesse closed the door. "She was asleep when she hit the pillow. It would take a crowbar to get that doll from her, so I left it."

"You sure you don't want to stay at our house?"

"No, you go on. Your parents are probably scared half to death."

There was no warning. No sound of a truck pulling up. The front door burst open and Jesse's father lumbered into the room with fire in his eyes. He was wet as a muskrat and he grabbed hold of the doorknob in order to keep himself upright.

"There you are," he said to Jesse, his speech still slurred.

"Go home, Matt," Jesse said. She nodded toward the back door.

The man pointed at me. "No, you stay right there."

"You get out!" Jesse yelled. "This ain't your house."

"I'll get out as soon as you sign that deed over to me."

"I ain't never doing that. Mama give this land to me and Daisy. It ain't yours."

Instead of lunging for Jesse, he came at me and with one hand grabbed me by the throat. I was so surprised at how quickly he moved. I couldn't dodge him—and his grip was tight on my windpipe.

"You agree to sign it or lover boy is gonna turn blue."

I was staring into his bloodshot eyes when the shot rang out. He let go quickly and looked down. There was a hole in the linoleum by his foot.

"You touch him again and I'll kill you," Jesse said, and I believed her.

Her father didn't listen. He grabbed me by the arm and pulled me in front of him. "You never was much of a shot, were you, Jesse?"

"All I got to do is hit you once," she said.

I expected Daisy to come out to see what the commotion was, but her door stayed shut.

"I know what you're doing," Jesse said. "You're going to sell the place out from under us to Blackwood. You never cared nothing about nobody but yourself."

Though his grip was strong, he only had one hand to hold me. I looked at Jesse, letting her know I was going to try something. I leaned back against the man, driving him into the wall, then spun to the floor. He let go, falling beside me. I was up and headed to the back door before he could grab me.

"Jesse, get Daisy and let's go," I said.

She held the gun on her father. "No. You go home. Call the sheriff. I expect he'll be able to deal with a drunk like this."

I felt bad leaving, but worse staying. I hopped on my bike and rode as fast as I could. The light was on at the end of the walk and I hit the door out of breath.

"What in the world?" I heard my grandmother say.

"Matt?" my mother said.

When I saw her, something broke inside. All it took was her voice to touch some place I was trying to protect. "Call the sheriff," I said, trying to hold back the tears. "Have him go to Jesse's."

Lights shone through the front windows and I saw my father's Impala. I broke free from my mother and ran to him.

"We've got to go to Jesse's," I said. "Her dad is there. He's going to hurt her."

"Are you all right?" he said. "Where have you been?"

"I'll explain on the way. Hurry up!"

"No, you get in the house," my father said. "I'll see what's going on."

I protested. I cried. I told him I had to go with him, but my mother held me back and he pulled away. I went inside and heard my mother on the phone with the sheriff's office.

"Everything's going to be all right," my mother said. "You'll see."

I got out of my wet clothes and my mother offered me food. But I couldn't eat. I was shaking and wondering what was happening. A few minutes later the sheriff's cruiser went past our house with its lights on, the siren off.

"Why don't you get in bed and rest," my mother said. "I'll wake you when we know anything."

I went to my room but couldn't think of sleeping. I wanted to crawl out the window and run to Jesse's. Instead I clicked the CB microphone, hoping she would respond. Fatigue eventually overtook me and I lay on my covers as visions of the red eyes mingled with Roberto Clemente turning to look up. Manny Sanguillen one-handed a wild pitch. Someone grabbed my throat.

I awoke as the front door opened, and I noticed sunlight coming through the window. I ran into the living room and saw my father taking off his hat and shaking water on the tile. He had a grim look on his face.

"What? Is it Jesse?"

He swallowed hard. "Son, Jesse's father is dead."

My mother gasped.

"I knew it would come to this," my grandmother said.

"How did it happen?" my mother said.

"Did Jesse shoot him?" I said.

He walked into the kitchen and sat and I followed, waiting to hear the news.

"He fell. He touched an electric wire and fell. There was nothing anyone could do."

My mind raced. There was no way it was an accident. Jesse had promised to kill her father and she had done it because of me. And only two living people knew the real truth.

"What about Jesse?" my mother said.

"They took her to the emergency room. To check her. The sheriff called family services to care for Daisy Grace."

"Those poor children," my mother said. "Losing a mother and now a father."

"What happened, Matt?" my father said. "Why did you go back there?"

"I was trying to help. We were trying to keep Daisy safe. She promised she would. Jesse always keeps her promises."

"I know, Son." He smiled, but there was something sad about it. "She's going to get the help she needs. Don't worry. Go back to sleep."

His voice comforted me. He seemed so sure. And I believed him. I believed everything he said because the son of a pastor should have no reason to doubt his father.

Chapter 28

For the second time in twelve years I walked into my father's office without knocking, water dripping from my hair on the hardwood. The smell of ozone was fresh and the earth felt like it was taking a long drink before it went to sleep for winter.

"Matt, what are you—?"

"We need to talk," I said.

He looked at me as if I were Lazarus being unwrapped from grave clothes. "You're supposed to be in Chicago by now."

"Something's come up."

He stood and grabbed a towel from his bathroom and

handed it to me to dry my hair. "Matt, you made your decision."

"I made a decision without knowing all the facts."

"What are you talking about?" He ran a hand through his hair.

"I went by Mr. Caldwell's house."

He searched my face but didn't understand.

"Jennings Caldwell. Retired from the sheriff's—"

"I know who he is."

"I saw him Tuesday. He said something that bothered me."

"Matt, you have to be exhausted."

"It didn't click until this morning. You know how driving helps you think. Stuff bubbles up. You ruminate like a cow chewing its cud."

He pursed his lips and patted my shoulder. "Let's get you home. It's clear this whole ordeal—"

"He was the first one on the scene that night. At Jesse's house. He said you were talking with her. You were on the roof with her."

My father squinted. "What are you talking about?"

"It didn't register at the time. From what you said, I thought you sat in your car and waited until the sheriff came. But he said you were up there with her when he arrived."

My father rubbed his face. I gave my words a moment to sink in, then took a step closer.

"Is it true?"

He put a hand to his forehead. "I'm sure Jennings is mistaken—confused after all these years."

"That's what I thought you'd say. So I asked him to get

the report from the station. It took quite a while." I put the photocopy in front of him. "The highlighted part is what you'll want to see. Right there. You were with Jesse when he arrived. On her roof."

He stared at the report, then looked up. "Matt, that was so long ago. You can't live looking in the rearview."

"But the whole point of life is seeing, isn't it, Dad? I never saw this before."

He pushed the page aside. "I don't have time—I have a lot to prepare for this weekend."

"Humor me. I've driven a long way."

"I don't know what you want." His eyes showed something close to fear.

"I want the truth."

"I've always been truthful with you."

"Really?"

"You may have had an impression about something I said—"

"No, don't blame me. You led us to believe something that wasn't true."

"I can't remember. I'd been out looking for you, praying you weren't lying dead in a ditch."

"What did you cover, Dad?"

"I was looking out for your own good."

I raised my eyebrows. "My own good or yours?"

Bewildered now, he cocked his head. "I don't know what you mean."

For a moment I felt sympathy for him. I thought he was genuinely confused. His tell was putting his hand to his temple and rubbing it. It was a crutch I had seen before, in prior conversations when he was caught in some small bend of the truth. He would do that to stall. It was then I realized where my acting DNA originated.

"Here's the question, Dad. Here's what I really want to know. Are you ready?"

His mouth became a tight line. "I have nothing to hide."

"What did you make Jesse promise?"

My words seemed to take the wind from him. His face showed palpable shock and guilt. Finally he pushed himself up from the chair and walked to the window, his one act of defiance against Blackwood. He'd spent his own money on a window. As he looked out, raindrops pelted the glass.

"When your father tells you something, you don't question it," I said. "Especially when your father is a pastor. I thought you had waited for the sheriff and then went to help Jesse. That's not the truth, is it?"

He clasped his hands behind him. "No, that's not the full picture."

"The full picture?"

"It's not the truth."

"Then tell me."

He stared at a discolored spot on the window where moisture was getting through and put a finger there. "I was looking for you," he said slowly. "Your mother was frantic. She didn't want to lose another son. I figured you'd come back. I drove around town and remembered Dickie. You two had been such good friends—I knew there was a rift after his father died.

"I knocked and his mother woke him. Dickie said you asked him to help find Daisy. He thought you might be trying to rescue her."

"Dickie figured it out," I mumbled.

"I was worried. I've known Wendell Woods since we were kids. I know he's capable of terrible things. When I learned you were looking for his daughter and that he was back in town . . ."

"How did you know that?"

"Basil Blackwood mentioned he had seen him."

"What did you do?"

"I drove to the Colwill home."

"Where?"

"The family caring for Daisy Grace. On Gobbler's Knob. Matt, we were more involved with Jesse's situation than you knew. We were in contact with family services after we learned of her mother's death. When you brought up the possible abuse by the cousins—the Branches—we asked that Daisy be moved from their home and suggested they not reveal where she was. It was our hope Jesse would be taken there as well. But she disappeared."

"You knew all that?"

"We tried to shield you."

I pushed the revelation away. "What about that night?"

"I came back from Dickie's before I drove to the Colwills'—it's a trek out there. As you know. And you were home. I drove to Jesse's, and their house . . . It was the strangest thing. The lights were on, but Jesse was sitting on the roof in the rain."

He took a breath. "I got out and called to her. Asked her what happened. She was shaking and crying. Shivering. She couldn't speak." He leaned against the pine paneling and it creaked.

"I went to the side of the house to help her down, and that's when I saw Wendell. He was on his back, his arm spread. His head twisted in a weird angle. I could tell he was dead from his eyes—I felt for a pulse and there was nothing.

"Jesse asked me to bring the ladder to the front of the house. I climbed up and sat with her. When she could speak, she said her father was going to hurt her. He had a gambling debt and needed money. She had a gun but she couldn't shoot him. She had taken the deed from him somehow, and he came after her. He said she could either sign it or he would kill her and he'd inherit the land."

He walked slowly to the other side of his desk and sat, moving his Bible. "She threw the gun into the field so he couldn't find it. Then she put the ladder against the roof, next to the electric wire. She hoped he'd follow and grab it in his drunken condition. And it was either that or the fall that killed him. She begged me not to tell anyone what she had done."

"What did you say to her?"

He swallowed hard. "I told her I wouldn't tell. And I said we would help her with Daisy Grace. The church has a benevolence fund. And there was a lawyer who could help her keep the farm, if that's what she wanted. If she wanted to sell, he would help her do that."

"What did she say?"

"She asked what she had to do in order to receive that care."

"And you said?"

He closed his eyes. "I said it was easy. All she had to do was give you up."

I turned to the window and stared at the water coming down. "And if she didn't give me up?"

"I would tell the sheriff all I knew. That she had planned her father's death. There would be a trial and Daisy would be sent away."

"You didn't."

He nodded. "I did."

"Why? It was self-defense. And she was a kid. She was just trying to save herself and her sister."

"It's all turned out for the best. Don't you see? Your mother was adamant that we steer you two away from each other. I went along with it. And to her credit, Jesse has never held it against me. She and Earl asked me to do the ceremony and I said an enthusiastic yes, partly because I wanted this to be the end. That's why I didn't tell you about the wedding."

I slid into the wooden chair beside his desk. Lightning flashed outside and a few seconds later thunder rumbled the windowpane.

"I always felt responsible for his death," I said. "I thought it was my fault."

"Why would you feel that way?"

"Because Jesse told her dad if he touched me again, she would kill him. And he grabbed me. So if I hadn't been there . . ."

"It was never your fault, Matt."

"What about Mom? Did she know this?"

He shook his head like a child caught in a lie. "I've never told her. And Jesse never talked, as far as I know." He looked up. "How did you put it together?"

"She said something last night. That some promises cancel others out. I always thought she shut me out after that night because I had made her kill her father."

"Why would you think that?"

"It's what I believed for so long. But she was really just keeping her promise to you. She was protecting Daisy."

"We helped her, Matt. The church came around her. Not perfectly, of course, but she's done so well."

"You kept Blackwood from taking her place."

He nodded. "Basil wanted the riffraff away. I think he wanted the memory of what Gentry did to Jesse to go away, too."

I stared at his desk and remembered the Polaroid he'd made me surrender.

"Now you have a choice, Matt. You've gotten what you wanted. You know the truth. If you expose this, it will come back on her. And me."

"But you can release her. She's trapped, Dad. She's like the horse we found."

He stared at me and I realized he had no idea what I was talking about.

Finally he said, "What good would releasing her do? She's marrying Earl."

"She deserves to make that decision free and clear. Release her from the promise she made."

"And if I do and she says she loves you, the Turleys will make her life a nightmare. And yours, too. Earl deserves better than this. He's an honorable man. No, the best thing is to move on. I think you know that."

"What about the best thing for me, Dad? What if I love her?"

"I'll never understand why you chose Jesse. Your mother would have been fine with any other girl in town, but you had to—"

"So this is about Mom? She pushed you into keeping us apart?"

"We both agreed Jesse wouldn't be right. With all we knew about the Woods family . . ."

"What right did you have to decide that?"

"We had every right. I'm your father. And I believe her choice of Earl means she wants to move on. The question is, will you let her? Will you do the hard thing and let her?"

I didn't answer.

"I've always tried to teach you that the Christian life is not about making the easiest choice. It's sometimes the harder way to live. I believe every person is called to do one difficult thing in life. And I think you have come to that place. This is your chance to sacrifice."

His voice was even and controlled. The gentle and reassuring sound usually calmed me, but not today. And as the rain fell and streaked the window, I didn't hold back.

"I could ask you to do the same thing."

Chapter 29

My mother did not understand why I was home. My father
spoke in hushed tones as I fell into bed, exhausted. I slept
like a dead man. I didn't think, didn't dream, didn't feel.

I woke to my alarm the next morning, my parents
gone. I showered and dressed in one of my father's suits,
the coat and shirt fitting nicely, the pants loose. I drove
to the church and parked behind it near the field and
picnic tables. Slipping in the back door, I was met by
Shirley Turley. Jesse was right—she had become a beautiful mother, and the kindness in her eyes surprised me.

"I didn't think you'd come to this," Shirley said, glancing at the front door.

"Don't let your brothers know I'm here," I said.

She gave a smile and I stole to my old spot on the bride's side and sat close to the wall. Everything in me wanted to scream this wasn't fair. But the revelation in my father's office made me believe I could make the hard choice. And it wasn't because I wanted to protect him, but to do the loving thing for Jesse.

A wedding is the beginning of two lives becoming one. It's a celebration of abundant life. For me, this day was a funeral for a long-held dream. And I knew I needed to stare at the casket to believe reality.

My father arrived with the groom and his party and ducked into his office. He exited and quickly approached when he noticed me.

"You shouldn't put yourself through this," he said, sitting by me.

"I need to."

"You're not going to disrupt—"

"It's nothing like that. It would be like stopping at the bottom of Golgotha, you know? I have to climb the whole way."

He smiled a little and put a hand on my shoulder. "I understand."

His touch felt somewhat like a kiss of betrayal, but that was something I would deal with later.

My mother walked down the aisle. Her gait was slowing. It was partly her age but also the toll of all she had been through with her life, her marriage, and her sons. She stopped and put her purse beside me, sheet music tucked under her arm.

"I thought you would still be sleeping."

"Like the suit?" I said.

She smiled, then moved toward the piano. The prelude consisted of hymns of the Savior's love and classical pieces that felt like sad longing and I closed my eyes. I had wanted the truth and I finally possessed it. But as I sat there, I wondered if the truth was what I *really* wanted. Was the truth enough?

I felt a presence beside me and looked up at Basil Blackwood in a dark suit, his hair slicked back with Brylcreem. He had not received the memo about using "a little dab." His face was grim, lines deeper than the Grand Canyon, and there was a skin anomaly on his left cheek that needed attention.

He leaned down, hands on his knees, head dipped so he looked at the floor. His voice was low and gravelly. "Do we have a problem here?"

I remembered the Polaroid he had destroyed and my father's betrayal. His thirty pieces of silver were this church.

"No, sir."

He edged closer and his breath smelled of stale tobacco. "Then I'd like you to leave. The bride and groom have requested it."

"Mr. Blackwood, I've waited a long time for this. A friend of mine is going to walk down that aisle and out of my life for good. I aim to see it."

"Verle will haul you out of here."

I caught his gaze. "You've been calling the shots a long

time. And you can remove me. But it'll be a fight. I don't think you want that."

He stood erect, looked at the door to the sanctuary, and shook his head. I turned and saw Verle, but I wasn't afraid. I hadn't come here to change the outcome of the service, just to witness it.

The door to my father's office opened again and he walked out leading Earl. The bridesmaids walked down the aisle in pretty, flowered dresses that might have been from a department store. When Shirley passed, she smiled at me. Then, something I hadn't prepared for, something wild and wonderful—Daisy Grace came down the aisle carrying a bouquet of daisies, pulling them one by one and letting them fall on her sister's path. She was beautiful and tall. The little girl in the backyard with the stubby-tooth smile was grown, and I had to wipe away the unanticipated emotion.

My mother's hands fell on the sacred chords of the song I knew as "Here Comes the Bride," and pews creaked as everyone stood. I rose out of duty and my stomach lurched. I took a couple of deep breaths to settle it.

And there she was.

Jesse Woods, as I had never seen her, but as I had always seen her, walked alone. She glanced at the daisies and I saw those front teeth and the view flooded my mind, the fishing trips and bike hikes and the little cemetery at the end of the road and her sister's gravestone. The voice of her mother and Carl's bark and all the dusty roads we shared. School bus rides and sorting out life by citizens band—and then the severing, cold silence.

As she passed, she glanced at me and the surprise on her face let me know Blackwood had lied about her requesting I leave.

I smiled and nodded, and she continued and took Earl's hands. My father skipped the part where he asked, "Who gives this woman?" There was no one to give Jesse away. And that was fitting. No one could have given her away but me. And that was exactly what I was doing.

The congregation sat as my father began his "Dearly beloved" message, and a strange sense of peace came over me. There are some things you do from duty and some that come from sheer love, but you don't realize the difference. Right then, in that pew where I had sat as a teenager, where I had heard the message of sacrifice and offering, things came into focus. I was letting go not because I was required to by any force on earth or principality or power in heaven. I was letting go because I wanted to *for Jesse*. That release, that surrender, felt like nails in my wrists, but at the same time like love from a bursting heart.

"Marriage is an honorable institution given by God," my father said. "Ordained by him and a picture of his bride, the church. What you see before you is the way God chose to describe the culmination of all of history. Jesus will return as the Bridegroom for his church."

"Amen," someone said behind me.

My mother slipped into the seat beside me and patted my hand. She unwrapped a peppermint and put it in her mouth, clearing her throat.

My father gazed over the congregation, then looked

straight at me. "If any of you has reason why these two should not be married, let him speak now or forever hold his peace."

I stared at my hands. Then my fingernails. The hush over the congregation was palpable. I looked at Basil Blackwood on the front row of the other side, his bald spot glistening red.

"Very well," my father said.

And with that, it was over. The ceremony would continue with rings exchanged and *I dos* and pronouncement of man and wife and "you may kiss the bride." It was a fait accompli. The reception downstairs would be an awkward affair, and I would pay my respects and give my blessing and slip out quietly. Or maybe I would just skip the reception and head toward Chicago.

It was the silence that unnerved me. I looked up and saw my father in a state of confusion. He paused and faltered as if he had forgotten the order of service. He pulled out a handkerchief and wiped his forehead, then brought a glass of water to his lips, his hand trembling. Then he touched his temple.

Jesse leaned forward and said, "Are you okay, Pastor Plumley?"

He looked at her, then closed his eyes tightly. "Oh, dear."

A murmur went through the congregation and my mother turned to me. "Something's not right. I think he's having a stroke."

I studied him carefully. "No, I think it's something else."

The longer my father waited, the more the congregation

murmured. Mrs. Talmage stood on the Blackwood side as if ready for an altar call. She was an emergency room nurse at St. Mary's.

"Do you need help?" she said forcefully.

Another touch of his temple. "I think I just need to catch my breath," he said, wiping his forehead. He found my mother and asked, "Please, could we sing the hymn we were going to sing after the ceremony?"

My mother rose quickly and went to the piano. The hymnal was open, everything prepared. She played the last line of "He Hideth My Soul," as an introduction and my father said, "Excuse me" and went to his study.

People stood and pulled out hymnals and whispered. Jesse said something to Earl and he shrugged. Dutifully, the congregation followed my mother's lead and sang the first verse as I took the long way around to the study.

Mrs. Talmage was inside, holding his wrist.

"I don't like this one bit," she said.

"Please, give me a moment," my father said. "Let me speak with my son."

She pointed a finger at him. "The sweating and the shortness of breath are classic signs of a heart attack."

"I assure you, I don't need a doctor."

Mrs. Talmage retreated. As she opened the door, Gerald Grassley entered. He was as close to a right-hand man as my father ever had.

"Calvin, are you all right?"

My father nodded. "I just need a moment alone with Matt. Thank you."

"What are you doing?" I said as Gerald closed the door again.

"Something I should have done long ago. Before today. Tell me it's not too late to find my backbone."

"It's not too late to get yourself killed."

"I asked you to do the hard thing. To sacrifice. You said you could ask me to do the same. And as I stood there today . . ."

The door opened and this time Basil Blackwood walked in with Earl close behind. "This better be good, Plumley," Blackwood said. "If you're sick, we can get somebody to step in."

"I'm not sick," my father said. "In fact, I feel surprisingly good considering what I'm about to say. And I do apologize. I take full responsibility. This is not fair to you, Earl, or to you, Basil, with all the trouble and expense you've gone to."

Blackwood pushed closer, a look on his face I had seen when he spat at me as a kid. "I want you out there before they finish this song. Is that understood?"

"I understand, but I can't marry Earl and Jesse today."

"And why in blue blazes not?"

The door opened once more and I heard the words "He hideth my life in the depths of his love." Jesse walked in, her veil still covering her face. Daisy pulled her train into the room and discreetly left. The small office was getting crowded.

"You all having a party without me?" Jesse said, deadpan.

I couldn't help smiling.

"Jesse, I was just apologizing," my father said. "I owe you one, too. I can't finish the service."

She took another step forward. "Are you sick?"

"No. It's because I violated my own rule."

"What rule is that?"

"Yeah, you never told us about no rules," Earl said.

"I have two policies I never break. One: I will not marry a Christian and an unbeliever." He held up a hand. "Now, I'm fully persuaded that both of you are sincere followers of Jesus. That's not the problem."

"This is crazy," Blackwood muttered.

"What's the other rule?" Earl said.

"Early on, I vowed I would never marry two people if I knew one of them loved someone else." He glanced at me. "I believe that to be the case here."

Blackwood charged my father. "You get out there and do what we paid you to do."

"No," my father said, shaking his head.

"Then you'll never preach in this church again."

"That may be true. Ever since I came here, you've reminded me how much control you have over every decision. I went along because I wanted the church to grow—I wanted to keep this position. Maybe I thought you'd change. That you'd listen to one of my sermons. But somewhere along the line I decided to just make you happy. And it's become a full-time job. I've wondered what it would take to make me stand up. I guess this is it."

Blackwood grabbed him by the shirt. "I'll sue for every penny you got!"

My father smiled. "Pennies is exactly what you'd get. I don't own anything, Basil, except the property my family handed down."

"Pastor Plumley, I don't get it," Earl said. "Are you saying I don't love Jesse?"

"No, I believe you do, Earl. That's the hardest part of this. Jesse is ready to marry you. But I have a hunch she's in love with someone else."

Earl looked at her. "Is that true?"

Jesse had been watching the proceedings with the interest of a hungry cat waiting to pounce on a scurrying mouse. She lifted her veil and glanced at me. I shrugged as if saying, *I didn't put him up to this.*

The song ended in the sanctuary and I heard the *whomp* of the congregation being seated.

Jesse squinted at my father. "Hang on a minute, Pastor. I've had people decide stuff for me all my life. I been sacrificing. Scratching and clawing every day. And I won't have you taking this away. I've dreamed of this since I was a little kid."

Blackwood raised a fist. "You heard her. Get your sorry behind back out there and finish this."

Before my father could answer, Earl spoke to Jesse, his shoulders slumped. "This is not about Pastor Plumley, though. I don't want you saying, 'I do' if you don't mean it."

Jesse swallowed hard and glanced at my father. Before she could speak, he said, "Jesse, I'm releasing you from any promise you made the night your father died. What I asked wasn't fair. Matt knows about it."

"What in the sam hill are you two talking about?" Blackwood said.

"You knew?" Jesse said to me.

"I stumbled onto it."

Jesse turned to my father and cocked her head. "So you got up there and were going to go through with this even though you thought I loved your son?"

I had never seen my father's face so pained. "I felt trapped. And then I saw Matt sitting there." He took off his glasses and raised a hand to his eyes. This was not an act, the emotion was real. "I asked him to sacrifice. To walk away. And I realized that wasn't fair. I'm the only one who can make things right."

Earl shook his head. "Well, you could have picked a better time, Pastor. I got our honeymoon tickets. I got the rings. There's people out there who drove all the way from Point Pleasant. This ain't right."

"Wait, wait, wait!" Jesse said, throwing down a fist. She turned from us, spinning something in her mind. "I promised my mama I would take care of my sister, and I done that. I'm proud of it. I made a promise to you, Pastor, and I kept it. I stayed away from your son. And I done sacrificed every dream I ever had to hang on to that land, though you've tried to rip it out from under me, Mr. Blackwood. And don't say it's not true because it is. So what I'm standing here wondering is, what do I get from all this promising? What happens to me and my dreams?" Her face was red.

Earl took her hand and gently held it in front of him. "Jesse, I love you. You're going to have my child. I want to raise that little one with you. And I don't want nobody taking my place."

My father and Blackwood looked stunned at the revelation. I also heard a stir from the congregation. Earl was standing close to my father and I realized his microphone was on. Why the man running sound hadn't cut it was a mystery, but it was probably the best theater in town since *Oklahoma!* ran on network television.

I got my father's attention and gave him the slicing neck sign. "I think they can hear us through your mic."

My father turned off the transmitter and there was a huge click in the speaker on the other side of the wall. Someone out there said something—it sounded like Mr. Grassley. The piano began again, my mother playing the introduction to "And Can It Be?"

Earl held on to Jesse's hand. "All right, tell me straight out. Tell me you don't love me. I got to hear it from your lips."

Jesse looked at me and I pictured her on that rooftop seeing her father on the ground and all the days and questions in between.

"Matt was my first love. It was sweet and innocent. And you was always saving somebody or something. So it makes sense you'd come back here to rescue me. But the way I figure it, you got to see that you can't rescue everybody. There's only one who can. And from what I can tell, you need to let somebody rescue you, PB."

The words felt like daggers at first, and then I heard the truth in them spoken from a heart of love.

"As for you, Earl, I done accepted your ring because you're the man I want to grow old with. I want to sit out on the front porch and drink sweet tea with you of a night and yell at the kids. You ain't perfect, and your family certainly ain't perfect, but neither am I. We've made mistakes already. But God has forgiven us and we're going to walk this road together. I'm choosing you." She looked at my father. "And if you don't want to do the service, we can go to the justice of the peace. It don't make no difference to me."

My father bit his lip and glanced at me. I gave him a thumbs-up.

"All right, then," Earl said. "Looks like we got us a wedding after all."

Jesse stepped toward me and reached out a hand, then held it in front of her mouth like she was going to spit in it. Then she smiled at me and shook my hand and ran toward the office door.

My father was the last out. He turned back to me. "You staying?"

"I think I've seen enough. Got a lot to think about on the drive."

"We both have a lot to think about."

He gave me a hug and I told him I'd call after I returned home. I sat in his chair listening to the vows. My father's voice sounded lighter, somehow, as if he weren't speaking from a script or onionskin, but from the heart. When I heard Jesse say, "I do," I took the stairs to the basement and exited the back door and left Dogwood.

Chapter 30

A week later I sat with Dantrelle in my kitchen as he wolfed down macaroni and cheese. We'd walked to Jewel for groceries and talked about the Chicago Bears and their season. He was excited to tell me about his new home and what he was learning in school. He commented on how different the view was from this side of the el tracks.

"Have you heard any more from your mom?"

He shook his head and grabbed a spoon to get the final bits of macaroni. "No. They say she's going to be in jail for a while."

I scraped the rest from the pan and he dug in with abandon.

"What I don't understand is why I can't live with you," he said. "I like my foster parents, but school would be a lot closer if I walked from here rather than driving to it every day."

"I wish I could offer that, Dantrelle. I can't right now. And I don't think it would be good for us. I think I need to keep being your mentor—your friend, rather than your parent."

A bell rang and I pressed the buzzer to let a visitor in the front door downstairs.

"Is somebody coming over?" Dantrelle said.

"A friend of mine is bringing dessert."

"You've got another friend besides me?"

"Don't look so surprised," I said, rumpling his hair.

I went to the door and opened it while Dantrelle watched from the table. The elevator stopped at the third floor and Kristin got off and walked into the apartment holding a plate of brownies.

"Miss Kristin!" Dantrelle said. He jumped up and hugged her, and I took the brownies and placed them on the table.

Dantrelle told her the same stories he'd been telling me all afternoon and she sat in rapt attention, listening and asking more questions. She leaned down to be on his level and got more information in ten minutes than I had in three hours.

We had dessert and Dantrelle said he wanted to swim again, but I told him his foster parents would arrive soon, so we took the elevator to the first floor and he ran around the atrium until they arrived.

He gave both of us a hug before he left, and I told him

I'd see him after school on Tuesday. He smiled and waved as he walked hand in hand with the two people who were trying to give him a fresh start.

"They seem nice," Kristin said. "He deserves someone who cares about him."

"He sure does."

"So you've recuperated from your trip?"

"I don't know if I'll ever fully recuperate, but yes. It was one of those eye-opening life events for me."

"Really?" she said. "That sounds ominous."

"Maybe I'll tell you about it someday."

She smiled.

"Listen, Kristin, there's something I want to say. About us. When you called it quits, I was upset. I didn't understand. But the more I've thought about it, the more I see you were right. We have a lot in common but we're not really on the same page spiritually. I couldn't see that. But the trip home opened my eyes."

"What did you see?"

"It's complicated. My dad was a pastor—*is* a pastor. So I picked up a lot of knowledge as a kid, but I think I confused being a Christian with being someone who rescues others. I've always felt that everything depends on me. It's hard to break out of that. To believe that God cares in spite of what you see and is really in control."

She was leaning forward with her chin in one hand, listening intently.

"What I'm saying is, I make a lousy savior. And I'm ready to leave that to God. To start over with him."

She nodded. "That's a great way to put it."

"I'm not saying this to get you to change your mind about us. I'm not trying to rescue our relationship. I wanted you to know that what you said made a difference."

She let me walk her down Wells Street, back to her dorm, telling me along the way about her classes and a difficult situation with a roommate. I thanked her for dessert and started to leave.

"Matt?" she said.

I turned.

"I can tell. There's been a change. I'm really glad for you. It feels like a breakthrough."

I smiled, then laughed, and then I put my hands over my face and couldn't stop the tears.

"Was it something I said?" she said.

"No, you made me remember something good. Something someone used to say."

She hugged me and I walked home with something burning in my chest, something white-hot and real.

Six months later, on the Cubs' opening day, the smell of spring in the air, I received a letter from my mother in her usual scrawl. She told me about the latest in the community, the deaths and events that felt distant. My relationship with my parents had opened a little and there was even talk of a family reunion that summer, with Ben returning with his wife and family.

Tucked into the envelope was a clipping from the *Herald-Dispatch*.

Jesse and Earl Turley, of Dogwood, announce the birth of their son, Matthew Richard Turley, at 8:15 a.m. April 2, 1985, at St. Mary's Hospital. He weighed 7 pounds, 8 ounces, and was 21 inches long.

I closed my eyes and brought back that summer again, tasting the watermelon and hearing the clicks on the CB and breathing the dust. Those days would always be part of me, and so would Jesse and Dickie and Daisy Grace. All the hurt and pain and longing and loss and joy began in the summer of 1972. And life had come from it. And I gave thanks to God for new seasons, new hope, and the promise of Jesse Woods.

Acknowledgments

IF I WERE TO ACKNOWLEDGE everyone who had a part in
this story, it would be a book in itself. I suppose I should
thank the 1972 Pirates and the 1984 Cubs to begin with.
Loss has a way of bringing good but painful stories.

I owe a debt to Grace, my maternal aunt I never met.
She was the inspiration for Daisy Grace and died during a
diphtheria epidemic in the early 1920s. She would toddle
into the field near my grandparents' house and pick daisies
for her mother, who always acted surprised when she
returned to the house. My mother still puts daisies on her
grave, though not as often as she would like.

Mrs. D. Wilson taught English at Milton Junior High
and provided my first summer reading list. Eighth grade,
as I recall. It was that summer I read *To Kill a Mockingbird.*
Life never returned to normal after that.

A relative who shall remain nameless uttered the
immortal line "Mommy made me all the whipped cream I
could eat." I've been waiting for just the right time to put it

in print. Also, it was my uncle John who asked how much
I weighed each time he saw me. I wish I could sit with him
again and hear that question or play a game of Rook with
him and Uncle Willy and my father. I miss their laughter
and wisdom.

My mother plays a special role in this book, as does
my father. He was never a pastor but he had the heart of
a good one. My mother taught me a love for words by
modeling a love for reading and classical music. They have
such broad shoulders on which to stand.

I will also thank my brothers for scaring the stuffing out
of me when I was younger with stories of the Mothman,
monsters, Area 51 Martians, flying saucers, and such. They
were model rocket aficionados and I learned to duck and
cover from them.

Thanks to Bud Voreland, Charles and Fran Bright,
Beth and Dave Calvert, and Brad and Jeanne DeVos for
their mentoring, modeling, and love. And to the congre-
gants at the First Evangelical Free Church in Hurricane,
West Virginia, who suffered through my song leading for
a season.

Sarah Rische, Karen Watson, Stephanie Broene, and
Shaina Turner at Tyndale made this a better book than I
could write. The best friend a writer ever had is a good edi-
tor, and I have a bushel basket full. As always, I am in your
debt.

My family puts up with a lot while I write. That's my
excuse for being distant and in some other world much
of the time. They are the best part of me and keep me

grounded. So to my children and my wife, Andrea, a wagonload of thanks for understanding even when you don't.

Finally, to the God from whom all blessings flow and his Son and the Spirit, I give thanks. May praise flow back to you for anything good that comes from this story and the truth and grace contained herein.

About the Author

CHRIS FABRY is a 1982 graduate of the W. Page Pitt School of Journalism at Marshall University and a native of West Virginia. He is heard on Moody Radio's *Chris Fabry Live*, *Love Worth Finding*, and *Building Relationships with Dr. Gary Chapman*. He and his wife, Andrea, are the parents of nine children. Chris has published more than seventy books for adults and children, including the recent bestselling novelization *War Room*. His novels *Dogwood*, *Almost Heaven*, and *Not in the Heart* won Christy Awards, and *Almost Heaven* won the ECPA Christian Book Award for fiction.

You can visit his website at www.chrisfabry.com.

Discussion Questions

1. Is there a particular year or season that was pivotal in your own life, as the summer of 1972 was for Matt? What was so important about that time?

2. When he calls with news of Jesse's engagement, Dickie says Matt owes it to Jesse to go back. Do you think he was right? Would you have counseled Matt to return to Dogwood? Why or why not?

3. Matt, Dickie, and Jesse bond partially because they are all outsiders in Dogwood society. How does being on the outside shape each of them? Can you think of a time when you didn't quite fit into a place or a group of people? How did it affect you?

4. Throughout the story, Matt highlights moments that he believes changed his future: He turned left his first day in Dogwood and saw the horse, eventually leading him to Jesse. He held on to his camera in the woods rather than dropping it. And on one fateful night,

he followed Jesse instead of staying behind. How do you think each event would've changed if he'd made a different decision? Was Matt right to think of these as turning points?

5. Describing his parents, Matt says, "I rarely saw them march together in my teenage years. Instead it was a push-pull, teeter-totter parenting method that left me disoriented, wondering which to trust and who was really on my side." Where in the story do you see Matt's parents demonstrate this dynamic? In the family you grew up in, what roles did your parents play? Did they "march together," as Matt wishes his parents would've?

6. Why did Matt's parents object so strongly to Jesse? What were they afraid of?

7. This story gives us several examples of the influence of fathers on their children—through Matt, Dickie, Jesse, Gentry Blackwood, even Earl Turley. What similarities do you see between each kid and his or her father? How have Matt's conflicted feelings about his father colored his view of God? Did you agree when he told Jesse, "We're all like our daddies"?

8. Mr. Lambert, one of Matt's teachers, saw and channeled Matt's talents when few others seemed to appreciate them, and even when Matt is an adult, his encouragement is "like water on a parched ground." Is there someone who has played a similar role in your own life, as a mentor and champion? What did that

person's encouragement mean to you—and if he or she is still in your life, what does it mean now?

9. Both as a teen and as an adult, Matt is frustrated by his dad's dealings with Basil Blackwood. He believes his dad should stand up to Blackwood, while his dad says, "I think trying to get along with him and keeping peace is one way to show I'm taking God's Word seriously." Whose perspective do you agree with? How might things have been different for Calvin Plumley and his family if he'd stood up to Blackwood from the beginning?

10. One important theme in this book is that human beings make lousy saviors. In what ways does Matt try to play this role? Has there ever been anyone in your life you wanted to "save"? What happened with that relationship?

11. How important is it to always keep your promises? Do you think it can be true that, as Jesse said, "some promises cancel others"? Or are there good reasons for breaking some promises? Can you think of any examples?

12. What did you think of the story's ending? Did all involved made the right decisions? What do you imagine the future holds for Matt?

also by
CHRIS FABRY

DOGWOOD

Small towns have long memories, and the people of Dogwood will never forgive Will Hatfield for what happened. So why is he coming back?

JUNE BUG

June Bug believed everything her daddy told her until she saw her picture on a missing children poster.

Christy Award finalist

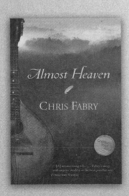

ALMOST HEAVEN

Some say Billy Allman has a heart of gold; others say he's odd. Sometimes the most surprising people change the world.

CP0682

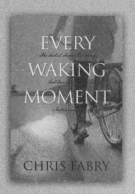

EVERY WAKING MOMENT

A struggling documentary film-maker stumbles onto the story of a lifetime while interviewing subjects at an Arizona retirement home.

NOT IN THE HEART

When time is running out, how far will a father go to save the life of his son?

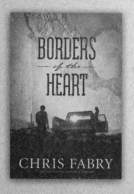

BORDERS OF THE HEART

When J. D. Jessup rescues a wounded woman, he unleashes a chain of events he never imagined.

Christy Award finalist

TYNDALE HOUSE PUBLISHERS IS CRAZY4FICTION!

Fiction that entertains and inspires

Get to know us! Become a member of the Crazy4Fiction community. Whether you read our blog, like us on Facebook, follow us on Twitter, or receive our e-newsletter, you're sure to get the latest news on the best in Christian fiction. You might even win something along the way!

JOIN IN THE FUN TODAY.

 www.crazy4fiction.com

 Crazy4Fiction

 @Crazy4Fiction

CP0021